THE PAPER CUTTER

Michael Bray

Michael Bray has been a training officer in the Australian Army, an international airline Captain on Boeing 747 and Airbus, and a commercial helicopter pilot.

He is now a successful businessman and property investor living on the Gold Coast of Australia.

This edition published 2010
Published by Michael John Bray
E-mail: mjbray555@internode.on.net
Copyright © Michael John Bray,2005
Cover design: Chameleon Print Design

The right of Michael John Bray to be identified as the Author of the Work has been asserted in accordance with the Copyright, Designs and Patents Act 1988.

Michael John Bray
The Paper Cutter
ISBN: 978-0-646-53335-3
pp 400

For Laurinda ...
The ecstasy and anguish behind the expression.

CHAPTER 1

Life is so fragile.

It was only three years ago that I almost lost her forever. We were up north on a skiing vacation and it was snowing heavily. By pure chance I had decided to take a different and seldom used trail back to our lodge. I heard a strange whimpering sound off to one side and decided to investigate. Stuck there, way down in a crevasse and helplessly upside down, was little six year old Casey. Why she had decided to play outside in those conditions, I'll never understand. She was half frozen, completely exhausted, and gradually becoming more covered by the steady snowfall. There's absolutely no doubt in my mind, that if I had taken my normal track, my daughter would have surely perished that day. Her tiny corpse would have remained buried in the snow until the next spring.

Anyway, Casey did survive that gateway in her life, and that day is past. Today is a brand new day and I'm excited, as you would be too. I'm about to have lunch with someone I cherish in one of New York's finest restaurants. It's Casey's ninth birthday and I'm happy because it's another milestone on her road towards adulthood. Unknown to me, today is going to be more than that. But for the grace of God, it may be the end of the road.

* * * * *

Midday spring showers have dampened the streets of Manhattan as my taxi rounds the last bend and approaches the grand marquee of the New York Icelandic Hotel.

'What the hell?' the shocked taxi driver curses unexpectedly as he violently swerves our taxi to avoid another vehicle. 'Goddamn maniac!' he shouts through the open window.

'Where'd you get your license? In a goddamn lottery?'

I'm forced from my relaxed position on the rear seat, into the side of the cab and grimace with pain as my hip collides with the door handle. A white commercial laundry van has galloped out of the hotel basement into the main stream of traffic, nearly collecting our taxi and almost ruining my day before it starts. I'm damned if I can understand why a laundry van should be driven so erratically and out of control.

'Nice work there, buddy. Thanks for the ride,' I say to the cab driver in appreciation.

'Yeah! Can you believe these jokers? Always in a hurry to go nowhere,' he replies as he pulls the vehicle to a smooth stop in front of the hotel.

I flick him an extra hundred bucks to make us both feel better, and step out under the awning. When I approach the entrance, I'm met by a surge of people all trying to get out of the hotel at the same time. In their haste, many are getting caught up in the revolving doors and tripping over one another.

I tentatively enter through the swinging glass entrance door of the hotel, wondering to myself why people always choose to get entangled in the time consuming and very heavy revolving doors. The swinging door is always immediately adjacent and is so much easier and efficient.

The hotel lobby activity is not what I had expected. What would normally be a scene of very civilized and well mannered ladies and gentlemen going about their business, is now a scene of distress. I stand still and need to take a deep breath as my eyes dart from side to side, trying to absorb the chaos before me. It seems that all hell has broken loose and people are milling everywhere, their expressions a combination of curiosity and awe. The shapes and colors of the people merge in my mind like images in a twisting kaleidoscope.

There's no doubt that something irregular has occurred. I can feel uncertainty and fear spreading throughout the area. Within seconds, the doors spin behind me and a couple of street cops come rushing through. Their senses are on full alert and their darting eyes are working overtime. I figure the best course of action is to stand out of the way and leave well enough alone. The madness is added to when there's a mingled wailing of police sirens outside as several squad cars arrive on the scene. The doors rotate again. Several more cops in uniform wade through the crowded entrance and spread throughout the area. I'm as curious as hell. Why is this crowd so disturbed? Exactly what's happened here?

'Stand well back now,' says one of the uniformed street cops to our small gathering of onlookers, who are already standing well back. 'You'll all have to stay where you are for the moment until we sort this out.'

The cop's face is beaded with sweat and the leathery lines of his expression tell me he's had some tough years of working the street. There's no doubt he's been through some rugged times during his long career and he looks like he should have retired ten years ago.

The stern resolve of those beat cop eyes is now clouded with emotion and his voice reveals a slight uncharacteristic tremble.

'Can't watch your loved ones too closely nowadays,' he mutters to the group as he shakes his head negatively. 'Ordinary everyday people just getting in the way.'

My whole body is incredibly heavy and it seems like I'm wearing lead boots. Maybe the force of gravity has suddenly doubled, but it's like I'm nailed to the floor and I'm stunned into paralysis. I stand planted in position at the front of the onlookers trying to make some sense of the cop's words. For some strange reason, I'm thinking he's directing his comments to only me. My pulse is quickening, my throat is dry, and my inquiring mind is searching for answers my vision can't provide.

'What's everyone looking at? What is it?' I nudge the guy behind me.

'I don't know. Something bad has happened here. Someone's gone crazy,' he whispers over my shoulder.

I'm stretching my ear towards him as his reply is almost drowned by the sounds of more sirens on the street outside. There are hotel staff members and uniformed cops in small groups around the lobby, but the focus of everyone's attention is the area leading to the elevator doors. One door is jammed open and the trouble seems to be inside that elevator. People are scurrying to and from that area and then mixing in small groups and conversing from one group to another. They all are trying to network and communicate like a confusion of industrial ants.

I'm wondering if all this communication will quickly lead to some common sense. Maybe they'll all soon group together and exit the lobby as ants would, marching in line through the revolving doors to form a new nest in the next hotel.

'Stand aside! Make way! Stand to the side please!'

The shouting is now behind me and the revolving doors are spinning once again. I'm being pushed to the side quite vigorously as two more street cops enter the lobby to clear the way. Two paramedics in starched white uniforms now burst through the entrance and hurry towards the elevator. They carry small steel suitcases, and their faces express a tireless dedication to duty.

I regroup with the other onlookers and we're all being held in position by the three or four uniformed cops. My feet are still heavy and I'm happy to be standing still. There must be seventy or eighty people within the confines of the lobby area. My ex-wife Audrey and daughter Casey mustn't have arrived here as yet. I can't see them anywhere, or maybe they're outside the hotel now and being prevented from entering by the cops. I'm relieved that they're not part of this mayhem, but I want to find them just the same.

'I have to get outside,' I'm yelling at the leather face cop.

'Just stay back,' he responds without even looking at me.

I realize that others are trying to leave as well and they're also being restrained.

'No one can leave,' another cop yells at us. 'The hotel's sealed off and you'll all be questioned.'

'I have to meet my daughter and her mother. Please! They're outside.'

'Just stay where you are for now. We have to sort this out as quickly as we can,' says the leather face.

My feet are glued to the tiles and my spirit dampens. I can see my own reflection in the mirrored column before me and I think to myself how insignificant and unimportant is my person at this moment. I'm an ant in a frenzy of ants. I'm no more important than the ant to my left or the ant to my right, also wanting to leave the hotel lobby, also having their ant like protests fall on deaf ears. I take the moment to reflect on my temporary helplessness and realize that it's not often that I have no control over my environment. I'm the so-called business tycoon, leader of men, respected and praised by everyone, or almost everyone. I usually call the shots around me.

Thinking that I may as well relinquish my dignity for the time being, I'm now beginning to surrender to the situation. I'm entering a semi-trance. I think it's actually a human self-defense mechanism that's taking control of my senses. It's the kind of mental numbness that takes place when you shrink from hideous reality, the state of denial one enters when confronted with appalling possibilities. By entering my medieval hypnotic dream, I don't have to face up to my worst fears. I'm protected from the unthinkable.

The arena of activity before me is starting to resemble a Shakespearean stage.

'My kingdom for a horse!' I shout above the commotion, and then feel embarrassed, realizing what I had yelled out.

I had even sounded theatrical. Leather face stares at me for a second then shakes his head in disbelief. He must think I'm a weirdo. Feeling quite helpless, I look straight through him and return to my pensive imaginations. I take a couple of minutes to appreciate the Shakespearean similarity and my eyes are riveted to the dramatic presentation.

It's a swarming chaotic scene set amidst spatial grandness of the first order. The stage is indeed impressive with outstanding quality. This is a beautiful lobby of rich polished maple woods, colorful granites and luxurious marble. Everywhere is the essence of royalty. Delicate lace cornices surround amber walls and majestic mirrored arches grace European paintings. Polished surfaces and etched glass mirrors reflect the large Persian Tabriz carpet of blue and gold spread centrally over the marbled floor. The strategic positioning of antique furniture items enhances the scene. Display cabinets of fine jewelry and costumed figurines overlook Elizabethan bureaus and small porcelain writing tables. Cherry leather Chesterfields are arranged in twos and threes to create convenient discussion centers and absolutely everything is dominated by an all embracing crystal chandelier of huge proportions, illuminating the whole area in an interplay of light.

To the left, a sweeping ornate staircase ascends to a mezzanine restaurant, an architectural heaven of subdued lighting accenting classic European design. I can now imagine Audrey, Casey and myself ascending that staircase hand in hand for our birthday lunch. I can't wait to meet them.

I see my own portrait in several of the mirrored columns. Here in front of me is Joseph Egan, a relatively youthful looking forty nine year old, brown hair, now graying at the sides, green eyes, now creasing at the sides and healthy fit body, now slightly bulging at the sides. I'm thinking that I'm not too bad looking in my cashmere beige jacket, wool blended slacks, black patent leather shoes, crisp white shirt, and silk Parisian tie. At least Audrey would always tell me that I'm good looking.

Dear Audrey. She really knew how to make me feel good about myself and the best part is that she really did believe it.

Audrey's voice is drifting through my head. 'Joe, you're my handsome husband. Joe, you're the only man for me. Come to bed now Joe. I'm waiting for you.'

What had happened to our marriage? How could two people so worthy of each other make such a mess of their relationship? It's not as though Audrey didn't know what she was getting into. She knew what I was like when she agreed to marry me. She was well aware of the lifestyle she was entering. I was desperately in love, yes! However, nothing in this world could change the forces that were driving my life forward. They were instilled in the very core of my being from a very young age. People are so different aren't they? I just can't help the way I am. Even as a child, I knew I would be successful. Not because I was intelligent or clever at school. I wasn't. It was simply because I was greedy, very, very greedy.

The talent I had for making money wasn't sophisticated. It was developed from the depths of dire poverty. My quest for achievement and wealth was carved from the squalor of the New York slum districts. The dampness and hunger of my earliest years had created a demon inside me that constantly needed to be fed. I can still feel the demon growling. How do I continue to feed it? It seems this starving demon inside me can never be satisfied. The more I give it, the more it demands.

I quickly discovered that my way to success and recognition was the way of the dollar. Yes I had to become wealthy, and then wealthier, and still wealthier, not for the material things that money can buy, but only to feed the demon of greed. The sensual allure of wealth and its trappings can stave off the hunger but not satisfy the man. Paper money no longer interests Joe Egan. He's more motivated by the challenge of the deal and the recognition of his peers. Paper money is just paper.

Poor Audrey! She loved me dearly but she couldn't be married to us both. That demon finally forced her out of the marriage and she tried so hard. Nine years of peace and love turned into war and conflict. The sad part is that we're still in love, but now from a divorced distance. Two years of trial separation didn't work either, trying everything to restore our marriage not only for our sake but to rekindle a family life for little Casey. Even the skiing vacation we would try together had ended in failure when I left hastily to attend to a business opportunity. Audrey couldn't cope with that. Not many women can.

So I guess Audrey's not to blame at all. I fell in love with her and I made her love me. She really didn't know what to expect and I knew all along. I guess I just thought I would succeed at marriage the same way I have succeeded at everything. What I didn't know, was that marriage is not a business of gaining the advantage and closing the deal. It's a connection of love, of giving and understanding, of wanting more for the other party than you do for yourself. I know that now. I just wish I could convince the demon. However, I still have my daughter's love. I know Casey will grow to understand what happened between her parents.

Beautiful sweet Casey! All my prayers and dreams were answered when I had held that little baby in my arms, baby Casey Egan.

'Just a quick hold now of your daughter,' said the nurse and she couldn't help but smile.

'She's my little princess,' I said as my eyes filled with tears of joy.

'We'll look after them for you now. Your wife needs to rest. You'll be with your wife and baby soon.'

I noticed the tears of happiness in the nurse's eyes and I'm sure she noticed mine. Before I handed her back to the nurse, I looked down at the baby in my arms and felt the warmth of fatherhood. I recognized myself in that little glowing face. It's hard to believe that she's nine years old today and already displaying her mother's daunting beauty with the same tangled blonde locks and eyes of blue. I'm so happy that our family can be reunited for a birthday lunch. I'm thinking now how delighted she'll be when I present those diamond earrings in that small velvet box. That's what my princess likes, little shiny things in little velvet boxes. I'm smiling to myself now as I imagine the look on her face and I feel for the velvet box inside my jacket. I'm satisfied that it's secure in place. I just know there'll be some happy tears in those beautiful blue eyes as she tries them to her perfect ears and I can watch her blonde golden tangles fall around them.

Audrey won't approve. I know that. I can already guess her reaction when she sees diamonds.

'She's too young for real diamonds. You always try to spoil her with expensive gifts. What she really needs is a father who can spend time with her.'

I won't listen. I never have, and that's the shame of it. I just know Casey is destined for greatness, and greatness deserves diamonds. I'm filled with warmth when I'm thinking of Casey, so beautiful, both on the outside and the inside. I can't wait to see her.

The magic bubble of my trance is suddenly burst with the sharp tone of a cop's voice. It's old leather face and he's yelling directly at me.

'Get back I'm telling you! Clear the way and move aside!'

I stumble and trip as my feet become unstuck from the floor, and I fall backward into the people behind me. Hands reach out from each side and support my armpits, preventing me from falling any further. I look to the side and smile in confused gratitude at the onlookers who had saved my fall, and my eyeballs widen as I'm once again facing the reality of the situation.

This time, it's two plain clothed detectives who spin the revolving doors and enter the performance. There's no mistaken identity here. Detectives usually seem to be all from the same clan and you can identify them so obviously by their clothes. The senior detective fits the mold perfectly with his rumpled tweed coat, creased pants, white shirt with dog-eared collar, and cheap nondescript tie loosened at the neck. He's so evidently a cop, but he shows his shield anyway as he walks to the elevator. The street cops in blue nod their acknowledgement. The other young detective looks like he is acting undercover from being a cop. He's the trendy type with a slick black ponytail hair-do and black T-shirt tucked into black denim jeans. Around his shoulders, he wears a long black trench coat with the belt dangling at his knees. He always has to display his badge at any crime scene he visits because he really looks more like a Mafia hit man than he does a member of the NYPD.

The older of the two detectives recognizes the leather face and they shake hands in passing.

'You still beating the street, Ollie? You must be close now?' asks the detective.

Leather face smiles and they eye each other in mutual respect. 'Frank Berne, well what'd'ya know? Only thing I'll be beating next year is a golf ball.'

I watch the detectives march by, and feel sure that these two professionals will know exactly what to do. Law and order will be forthcoming. The older one, Frank, must be about my age, late forties, and a little too overweight to chase felons. He even looks more overweight with his short gray crewcut and rounded face. The frown lines of his expression suggest that he carries the burden of New York's crime statistics squarely on his shoulders. I catch a glimpse of the Browning .38 stuck into his belt holster. The sidekick, Jimmy, is a good physical specimen. He's at the other end of the spectrum, firm well-muscled body of an athlete, and looks like he could outrun a delinquent racehorse if he had to.

'Give it to me from the top. What have you got?' says the older dick to another blue uniformed cop near the elevator alley.

'Detective Frank Berne. Your reputation precedes you. Well, we've got an assault victim, pretty beaten up, face smashed in, these guys are having trouble keeping her going,' says the uniform.

'Why don't you pull out your notebook Jimmy?' says Frank to his sidekick as he rubs his hand back through his closely cropped hair.

'Sure Frank, sure. I know the routine.'

As Jimmy feels for his inside pocket, the Glock semiautomatic flashes a chandelier reflection from a tan shoulder holster. Both men are then quickly engulfed in a sea of hotel staff and blue uniformed cops who are all trying to talk at the same time. They hastily take control of the group and then proceed into the elevator.

Several more minutes pass and the whole lobby is now buzzing with police activity. I'm starting to get extremely mentally agitated and very physically tensed. I'm now really beginning to worry about Audrey and Casey. Where in blazes are they? Why hadn't I thought of it before? I must be losing my senses with so much confusion around me. Audrey usually carries her cell phone and I could simply give her a call.

'Audrey, everything is all right. I'm stuck inside the lobby with all this madness going on. Can't imagine what's happened. Just be patient and we can still make the lunch reservation.' I'm actually rehearsing the conversation inside my head as I'm finding the tiny cell phone in my pocket.

I speed dial her number in anxious anticipation of finding them safe and well outside on the sidewalk. I don't wait for her to answer.

'Hello Audrey. Where are you? Are you both all right?'

I'm suddenly very confused and I'm desperately trying to rationalize the voice I hear replying on the line.

'Lieutenant Frank Berne here. Who am I talking to please?'

My throat is no longer capable of producing sound and I can't respond to the question. I drop the phone. The ramifications of what I had just heard are slowly beginning to focus and I have to steady myself against the mirrored pillar. My heart is pounding so hard I think that it's about to burst. I'm feeling dizzy as my brain struggles with swirling thoughts of significance and consequence. The kaleidoscope stops turning. The final image is crystal clear and painfully obvious.

'What in hell is that detective doing answering Audrey's phone? Isn't he in that elevator over there?' I'm trying to speak to anyone, but my dry throat is raspy and nothing comes out.

'Face smashed in, having trouble keeping her going.' My brain is resonating with the words I had just heard.

My mind is racing with images of Audrey and Casey and my sense of balance is reeling. I can feel the blood rush from my brain and the center of my chest freezes over. I'm now crashing towards the floor, sinking down in a lead bomb of shock and horror. The ceiling of the lobby rotates above me and the huge chandelier spins out of phase.

My head hits the floor with a thud.

CHAPTER 2

Lieutenant Frank Berne was well accustomed to the likes of what was going on in the elevator. For him, it was almost a daily occurrence. In fact, he breathed a sigh of relief as he decided that relatively speaking, it really wasn't all that horrible. He'd seen unconscious people by the thousands and plenty of dead bodies as well, in all different states of mutilation and dismemberment. If you're a New York homicide detective, you're going to get the lot, and he'd seen his share.

Frank was an old hand and he'd come up the hard way, cutting his teeth on the street beat and then working undercover in the Bronx. The bars, brothels, and crack houses of New York had been his stomping ground, and old Frank had developed his own way of doing things, his own method of evening the score.

Time after time, Frank would orchestrate the downfall of back alley dope peddlers, rapists and child sex offenders. The criminals themselves were as unaware as the police were, that Frank's machination was in operation. He would set one scumbag against another scumbag with anonymous innuendo of treachery and double cross. Usually they would blow each other's brains out in back alleys, thereby saving the cops any further aggravation.

Frank's idiosyncrasies were frowned upon, yet tolerated by his superiors. They couldn't agree with them, but would usually turn a blind eye anyway. Oh yes! So very effective were the methods of Frank Berne.

It seemed to Frank that he'd been called to this job a little too prematurely. This was no homicide, or at least, not yet. This woman wasn't dead. At this stage, what he was looking at, was an assault and battering, although a vicious assault at that.

The paramedics were still frantically trying to stabilize the victim and Frank bent over to get a quick look at her face. What with the oxygen mask and the severe bruising, there wasn't much of her face left to see.

He could make out that her blank and unresponsive features were now caked with a blend of makeup and dried blood. Underneath, her expression was hollow and vacant. The paramedics had inserted leads and surgical dressings everywhere and they had told Frank that they didn't think she would make it.

'We're giving it the best go we can,' said the worried looking medic. 'By the look of her face, you'd think she just did three rounds with the heavyweight champ.'

Frank reasoned that the most likely cause of her injuries was two or three forceful punches to the face, one of which had splintered her nose cartilage and probably forced the upper nasal bone directly into her brain.

Frank initially thought that the pungent fumes that filled his nasal passages were rising from the medications being administered to the victim by the paramedics. He recognized the smell as being similar to the stench of a city morgue autopsy, maybe that which emanates from the use of chloroform or ether. He noticed that the medics were also wheezing from the odor and as his eyes scanned the surroundings he saw that there were several pieces of broken glass on the floor.

'You boys using chloroform or something?' he questioned loudly and one of them answered without turning from his work.

'Not ours. Looks like someone's tried to use ether on her then resorted to this!'

Frank was surprised to see her handbag was still unopened and he methodically retrieved it. His eyes swept over the woman's body and it seemed apparent that she was not only a person of elegance and beauty. She was also a woman of substance.

'Classy dame,' he muttered to himself.

She was dressed in a light blue Chanel suit with black and silver stilettos, now off her feet and arranged in the corner of the elevator. He gathered up the shoes and noticed that the right shoe was damaged at the tip. He was surprised to see that she still had her jewelry. And beautiful jewelry it was. Diamond earrings, a delicate gold necklace with a ruby pendant, and what must have been at least a five-carat diamond engagement ring. He looked for the matching wedding band but couldn't see one. Then he noticed the watch. Frank was sure he'd once seen a similar watch in a magazine article and it was on the wrist of Princess Diana. Yes. Oh yes! It was the same looking solid gold Cartier Panther wristwatch. These items had been carefully removed by the paramedics and were arranged in a row in the far corner of the elevator.

Frank collected the watch and jewelry items and systematically placed them in a small plastic bag he extracted from his pocket. He then opened the designer handbag and cautiously checked the contents. He retrieved the cell phone, checked the call register, and carefully placed it in another plastic bag. The remaining items were the usual lipstick, cosmetics, keys, notebook, gold pen, and a small wallet containing several hundred, and a few twenty-dollar bills, business cards and a driver's license.

A quick look at the license revealed that it belonged to an Audrey Egan with a Staten Island address. Frank studied the face in the photograph and he was nauseated at the transformation it had undergone during the brutal attack. He then placed all of these contents into a third plastic bag.

He took another long lingering look at the pathetic woman. She was in her mid thirties with a perfect figure that most women would envy. They wouldn't envy her now! When the medics checked her pupil dilation, Frank could make out that she had blue eyes that had now become still and glazed over. Her hair was a tangled mass of blood-ied blonde. Her clothing seemed to be reasonably in place and there were no pockets to examine.

Frank's experienced eyes had recorded every detail of the crime scene and it was now time for him to stand slightly back and do some serious thinking. A more concen-trated analysis of the elevator interior and some finger print dusting could be carried out once the woman was stabilized sufficiently and taken to hospital.

Frank rubbed his chin and thought about how this crime presented. There were several mysterious factors to this as-sault, the main one being a lack of obvious motive. This woman had not been robbed. Her jewelry and handbag were still in her possession. There didn't seem to be any evidence of sexual assault. Her clothing was in place and undis-turbed. The Staten Island address and the nature of her be-longings indicated a person of some social standing and education. Surely, she wouldn't have been impolite or abu-sive so as to provoke the kind of beating she had received. There was no apparent reason for this to be an aggravated assault. Yet the rights of this petite attractive woman had been violated in the most brutal way.

Frank figured that the category of the injuries indicated very forceful blows, more than likely delivered by a mature male. Could this be seen as one of those cowardly senseless assaults for which there is no motive? He had seen plenty of those during his years. Or, could it be the act of some wacko crazy dope-head acting by impulse rather than rea-son? There are plenty of creeps like that in New York, but not usually in classy hotels like the Icelandic. Then again, Frank thought to himself, maybe it could be construed that the victim had some company known to her and they were arguing. Maybe the asshole had simply lost it there and then, and belted her. Yeah, this assault had some missing link that could be the answer to a lot of questions and that link was yet to be found.

It was unmistakable. This was an assault, not a murder, and the case would be given to another cop to handle. He could then get on with the many homicides occurring around New York each and every day.

Frank was listing in his mind the course of investigation that would be recommended to the officer put in charge. There were several things that should now be done. Check the woman's identity, check to see if she was a guest of the hotel, if not, then why was she in the elevator? Study the notebook for clues and try the memory bank of her cell phone. What about the last number called and received? Surely a woman like this would have a vibrant social calendar. Let's find out what her friends and relatives know about her presence in the hotel and question the hotel staff about what they saw and heard. The people being retained in the lobby area may know something. In fact, the offender may even be amongst them and, like many of the sick individuals who inflict injury on others for personal pleasure, he could be sticking around to survey the results. Last but not least, any hotel security cameras may have recorded information of the people involved. Hotels of this category would normally have at least a front desk camera, if not elevator cameras.

'Hey! Check the mask! Mouth tube now! What's this? She's slipping! Syringe quickly!'

Frank's train of thought was interrupted by the exclamations and sudden accelerated actions of the two paramedics. He fearfully watched them as they sprang into a well-rehearsed co-operation of CPR procedure.

They were losing the woman in their care and Frank could sense the immediate urgency as they frantically tried to reverse the situation. The woman was not responding. Seconds seemed like lifetimes. The situation had turned really critical. Her pulse and respiration were at first erratic and then ceased. A last attempt to revive the woman was made by an injection of pure adrenaline directly into the heart muscle. This resulted in the woman's chest cavity heaving a few inches off the elevator floor then subsiding in a huge sigh similar to the final puff of a tired steam engine.

Her death was dramatic and irreversible. Frank winced and his legs felt unsteady. The shoulders of both paramedics slumped simultaneously, and despite their mutual disappointment at the outcome, they acknowledged each other's efforts with a clasp of hands. Frank had great respect for these competent men. He knew they were responsible for saving life every day and he didn't envy them one bit.

Frank's heart sank to new depths as he gazed at the sallow face of Audrey Egan. The glow of life drained from the victim's features as he peered into her graying eyes, and he became furious. It was so goddamn senseless and unnecessary. This was the result of a sick and twisted mind at work. There was no need for this to have happened. It was another terrible waste of human life and it was another lurid and devastating murder image that Frank would never be able to get out of his memory. Now, there was one thing for sure. The victim would no longer be able to identify her assailant. He wanted to get his hands on the scumbag responsible for this atrocity and he wanted to get his hands on him now.

This was no longer just a ghastly assault. In the eyes of the law, it was a vicious and cowardly murder, a tragic conclusion to a young woman's life. Frank Berne knew that he now had a homicide investigation to deal with, and justice had to be done. Anomalies had to be reconciled. He didn't have to wait very long for the investigation to offer him some valuable insight. Was this to be the missing link he needed?

From inside one of the plastic bags he held in his hand, Frank could feel the vibrations and then the ring tone of the deceased lady's cell phone. He quickly retrieved the phone with his fingertips and made efforts to minimize any mess-ing of fingerprints. Frank was anxious to speak to whoever was calling the pitiful corpse. He didn't have time to answer the phone as a shaky voice was already coming down the line.

'Hello Audrey. Where are you? Are you both all right?'

'Lieutenant Frank Berne here. Who am I speaking to please?'

Frank questioned the caller but all he could hear was background noise. At the same time he could hear the scuffles and commotion going on near the lobby entrance. It took him only a moment to sense that it was the same background noise he was hearing on the cell phone. He was making a mental note of the fact that the caller had used the word 'both', presuming there were two people present.

'Frankie! You'd better get out here. There's someone you're gonna want to meet.' Jimmy the sidekick was summoning over Frank's shoulder.

'Oh yeah, who would that be? Tell me the whacko is out there in that crowd.' Frank swung around as he spoke.

'I'm telling you that he just might be, Frank.'

'Jimmy, you get onto the family and find someone who knows this woman well enough to give us a positive identification. Maybe a classy broad like this has a driver outside?' Frank was steamed up.

'Right onto it Frank,' answered Jimmy buoyantly.

Frank continued briefing Jimmy. 'Also, get this elevator sealed off with tape for the Coroner's investigation boys. No one gets in. And make sure they check her nails for gouged residue. You got it? Oh, and yes! Don't forget to pull any security cameras in the hotel.'

Frank didn't have to repeat himself. He knew Jimmy well enough and he was confident the crime-scene technicians would come up with some useful results.

After handing the plastic bags and the woman's shoes to Jimmy, Frank made his way through the crowd to where the lobby merged into the elevated entrance area. Near the lobby entrance doors, he could see Ollie and some other boys in blue attending to this joker, who might even be identified as the wacko offender. This suspicious character had made the phone call to Audrey Egan's cell phone. He then passed out on the floor and it could probably be from the burden of all that guilt. Frank straddled over him and gazed at his face. He couldn't help being impressed at the way this guy was dressed. He must have been wearing a few grand's worth of clothes at least, and Frank was stunned by the glitter of gold when he noticed the Rolex wristwatch.

One of the spectators nearby suddenly leaned in close, and then piped up.

'Hey, isn't that Joe Egan? Yeah. Joe Egan from Egan Enterprises. You know? The tycoon guy. The billionaire!'

CHAPTER 3

Strong hands have a firm hold on both my upper arms as I'm tumbling out onto the corner of Lexington and East 66th Street. It's the kind of firmness that tells me that I'm not under arrest, but equally, that I'll be going where I'm told to go. I'm still reeling from the shock of finding out that it was Audrey who was involved in some kind of bashing, and that no one had the faintest idea about Casey's whereabouts. Suddenly, I'm the person who's the subject of everyone's attention.

I'm flanked tightly by the two plain clothed detectives as they carve our way through the sidewalk crowd. They've extracted me from the sheer chaos of that hotel lobby, and I'm certain they're well intentioned, simply protecting me for my own good. It's just as well I have them holding me up because my sense of balance is off and I'm quite unsteady on my feet.

This time of year there's usually lots of rain and it's just beginning to sprinkle now. The patrol cars are flashing red and white lights along the curb and there's already a media awareness of what's happened. A few inquiring press reporters are shooting questions I can't answer, and several photographers lean in, clicking cameras with their incessant flashbulbs. Curious bystanders are wondering what all the fuss is about, and I swing my head from side to side, looking for any familiar face. Some people recognize me as I'm bustled past and many stare in at me with cynical eyes.

'My daughter was with her. I have to find my daughter. You have to listen to me!' I'm yelling at the fat right hand side cop known as Frank.

'We'll be able to talk about it soon and do something about finding your daughter. It's in your best interests to come with us down to the station and give us as much information as you can.' His tone is polite, yet affirmative.

A couple of news media vans have parked outside the Icelandic and one of them is blocking the way of the police vehicle. The younger detective is telling them to clear the way as my head is pushed down and I'm guided into the rear seat.

I feel strangely comfortable when the door of the cop car finally closes and I'm left in an eerie solitude. It's like an escape from a nightmare getting into that car and I sag back breathing a sigh of relief. I'm now left in relative quietness, although I have to turn my head away when another camera flashes from the sidewalk. The cops talk for a while with the media and then gruffly climb in. I can't help noticing an expression of achievement spread across their faces. It's as though they've done the community a service and they've finally got their man. I'm fearful that they think that man is actually myself. Finally we pull away and head south down Lexington Avenue, apparently for the NYPD 17th Precinct station on 51st Street.

As we settle into a driving rhythm, I sit quietly and ponder the worst possible outcome for Audrey and the whereabouts of Casey. The wipers slowly whack across the screen to clear the raindrops as the young guy is driving and the older detective is busy on the radio. He seems to be intermittently talking into the microphone and then jotting things into a notebook. After a while he shakes his head and nudges young Jimmy to pull over. The car swerves to the curb and jerks to a halt. Frank is now hanging over his seatback, staring at me and obviously struggling with what he has to say.

'Mr. Egan, I think you should know that it definitely was Audrey Egan who was the victim of the assault back in that hotel. We've just now received information through the radio. Her chauffeur has positively identified her body and she is Audrey Egan. I'm terribly sorry to inform you that your wife is dead.'

I sit silently transfixed on his face. It's like a knife being thrust into my heart and then twisted. My stomach feels hollowed out, as though a missile has passed through it. In spite of this, my eyes are vacant and my expression is blank. In the back seat of this squad car, I had strangely prepared myself for her death, and was almost expecting to hear what he now said. Maybe, the full impact of my grief would manifest itself later in some other way, but at the moment, my brain is in a state of numbness. He looks at me in search of a telltale reaction to the heartbreaking news, a sign of extreme grief, shock or anger. There's nothing. Frank Berne gazes at me in astonishment.

'Did you hear me? Do you understand me? I'm telling you she didn't make it!' Frank's not happy with my reaction.

'What about my daughter? What has happened to Casey?' I respond in a soft drawl.

The younger detective turns to face me. 'Hey, you're so worried about your daughter? Why haven't you tried calling home or your girl's school on that cell phone of yours? She's probably there.' His voice has a sarcastic resonance that really grates on me.

'Steady Jimmy,' says Frank softly. 'Wait till we get down to the station.'

The car pulls out again and slowly continues southward towards the Lower East Side. Jimmy shakes his head and curses. I can feel my temperature rising.

'You've no right to talk to me like that. I'm not the criminal here. You're being most inconsiderate.' I'm staring at the back of their heads and I'm ready to hit someone.

'We'll talk about it soon Mr. Egan, but in the meantime we have to inform you that you are also a suspect at this stage. There are some questions to answer.' Frank speaks in a slow and deliberate tone.

'Regardless of what you think detective, I expect to be spoken to in a proper and civil fashion.' I put on an important voice for him.

I can't believe their scary attitude. What in blazes are they talking about? How can I be a suspect in this? Maybe I should make a call to my lawyer Wyatt Prendergast right now and get him to meet me at the precinct house.

I'm dialing my cell phone but the first call is to Audrey's home on Staten Island. There's a chance that for some reason, Casey didn't go with Audrey after all. Maybe she's just relaxing at home watching the television or listening to music. I know she's not at school because her private college has already started vacation.

'Yes hello. Mrs. Egan's residence. Can I help you?' It's Mary-Lou, the housemaid, who has answered and already her voice sounds shaky.

'Hello Mary-Lou. This is Joe Egan. Have you heard from Casey?'

'Oh Mr. Egan Sir,' Mary-Lou is now beginning to sob. 'Poor Mrs. Egan! Have you spoken to the police? Have you heard the news? Oh dear!'

'Mary-Lou, listen to me. This is very important. Have you seen or heard from Casey?' Mary-Lou's sobbing is infectious and I'm also crying through my words.

'No sir. She went with Mrs. Egan to meet you in Manhattan. I haven't heard from them since.'

'Mary-Lou, if you hear anything at all, make sure you call me immediately.'

My next call is to the personal cell phone of Wyatt Prendergast. I'm fortunate that he answers on the second ring.

'Prendergast!' It's a stern impersonal answer.

'Wyatt. It's Joe Egan here. I need your help urgently.'

'Joe. Just a second.' There's silence on the line and after a few seconds, his voice continues. 'What's the problem? How can I help?'

'Well, I'm in the rear seat of a police squad car and I'm being taken down to the 17th Precinct station.'

'Christ Joe! What happened?'

'Audrey's been murdered, and…and…Casey was with her.' My words are breaking down with the emotion and shock I'm feeling.

'My God Joe! That's terrible. Are you sure she's dead?' He knew Audrey well and I can't believe his coldhearted response.

'Yes. They've told me she's dead.'

'Jesus Christ! Are you okay?' Now he sounds shocked.

'No I'm not. They say I'm a suspect,' I state back to him.

'Wait. Wait a minute. Who says?'

'The police say. That's who. They're taking me in. I need you to get down to the 17th Precinct,' I plead with him.

'Now listen to me Joe. Are you under arrest? Have they read you your rights?' Wyatt takes on a professional tone and I know I'm going to get some good legal advice.

'No. No. They say I'm to come with them. That's all. They want to question me. They say it's for a good purpose.'

'Okay. If you're not under arrest, you don't have to go anywhere. If you are under arrest, you have the right to remain silent. Joe, quite frankly, that's what you should do.'

'But Wyatt, I'm worried about Casey. Don't you see? I have to get Casey back. If I don't help the police, what hope is there?'

'Joe. My advice to you is not to say anything until I get down there. I'm on my way.'

Wyatt Prendergast has given me the only advice a lawyer can offer under the circumstances. However, I'm well aware that it's not his family we're talking about. If I don't co-operate with the cops, it could well be the wrong course of action. It could jeopardize Casey's situation. I turn my attention to the front seat and shout out loud.

'Lieutenant. You have to listen to me. My daughter Casey was with Audrey. They were both there. They were there together. Do you understand?'

'Okay Mr. Egan. We hear you,' says the sidekick from the corner of his mouth.

My sense of urgency does not seem to transmit to these imbecile cops. They seem to think it's of little importance. All in a day's work for them I suppose. But this is me! These are matters affecting my very heart and soul. Why are they so indifferent, so clinical? This is the time for panic stations. Poor little Casey may be suffering right now. I need to get some action out of these two idiots and I need to get some action now.

'Now listen here you two!' I'm yelling once again. 'Can't you see what's happening here? This is my daughter we're talking about…or SHOULD be talking about!'

'Just calm yourself please.' Frank now talks from the side of his mouth. 'There's no sense in getting all excited. That won't help anything.'

'Well someone has to get excited around here. You guys just don't seem to want to listen to me. Do you know what you're doing? Why aren't you trying to locate my daughter? She could be dead. I want to speak to the Police Chief. I've called my lawyer and he's on his way. Do you know who I am?' I can feel the mercury level going up.

I'm losing my temper well and truly, and now it's me doing the gripping, with both hands on the detective's shoulders. The police vehicle pulls to the side once again and big Frank whips around and removes my hands in one swipe. I sit back despondently waiting for his lecture.

'Mr. Egan, I'm telling you only once. Sit quietly and enjoy the ride. Just settle yourself down and we'll discuss this at the station. I assure you that if your daughter is missing, we'll do all we can to locate her. I also want to stress to you that you are not under arrest at this stage. However, believe me when I tell you, that it's in your very best interests, and those of your daughter, for you to co-operate with us and accompany us to the station to answer some questions. Understand? Enough said!'

These cops think I'm involved somehow and I can't believe their incompetence. Although it's infuriating, I realize that I don't have too many options for the moment. I manage to calm my body, but not my mind. What could have happened to Casey? Maybe she was able to escape the assault and hide somewhere. Was she still hiding in the hotel in some hallway closet or in a service area? Could she have made a getaway to be now hiding in the car park down below? Maybe she ran outside through those revolving doors and into Central Park. What dangers lurk there after sunset? The light is starting to dim and I hate to think about it. My mind is racing now and my stomach is bilious with gastric upset. Why am I wasting time in this cop car when I could be out looking for her? Everyone should be out looking for her.

My forehead is resting against the side window and I gaze at the streets now spattered with raindrops. Rain won't help much if she's out in the park, but I'm hoping it will only be a short spring shower. I can't help but search for Casey as we drive along. Every time I see a small girl amongst the sidewalk pedestrians I strain my eyes to see if it's her. Wait a minute. Look under that umbrella. Isn't that Casey holding the hand of that man there? I'm stretching my neck around and squinting my eyes as we pass. Blonde hair, nice little yellow suit, black strapped buckle shoes.

'Stop! Stop! Pull over!' I'm screaming this out as her face comes into view. Oh no! It's somebody else. It's not my Casey.

'What the hell?' Jimmy yells and the car lurches and stops.

'What are you yelling about?' says Frank Berne. He is red in the face.

'I thought. Well, I thought....' I feel so disappointed and I can't get my sentence out.

'Just let us do the thinking you basket case.' Jimmy has to have his few words and I'm geared up to punch his lights out.

Then again, maybe I should give these policemen a chance. Better to have them on my side and get them working for me rather than against me. I better do as they say for Casey's sake. Surely once they get their act together, we'll all be out there trying to find her. I decide that I really can't do much more than co-operate at this stage and see what materializes from it.

I continue to gaze at the afternoon sidewalk activity as we drive down the East Side district of lower Manhattan. Spring is usually my favorite season, but right now it's raining steadily and looking very dark and lonely out there. The flashing lights of the city are multiplying in reflections on the wet pavements and asphalt streets of New York. People everywhere are scurrying for shelter. At least they're together in their little family units and are able to go home together. Tonight they'll be holding each other as loving families do in their warm and comfortable apartments. I'm really feeling melancholy now and I desperately want to hold little Casey once again in my arms. It's unbearable to think that I may not hug her again. She's all I have left. She's my heart.

I slouch down into the spongy curves of the vinyl seat and rest my head back. My temples are still throbbing with a moderate ache. I close my eyes and try relaxing my facial muscles to relieve the tension. It's impossible to clear my mind and the images of Casey come flooding back.

I'm drifting back to our most memorable experience together, a most precious time for father and daughter, when love, honor and respect are concreted in place and set in time.

'I know what we should do Casey. Your Mum's going to be busy with her charity meetings and you have ten days before school recommences.' I'm cupping her face in both of my hands and staring into her baby blue eyes. 'You and me princess. Los Angeles here we come. I always said we'd do Disneyland together, and now we shall.'

'Daddy, can we really? Is it true daddy?' Casey's eyes are dancing with excitement and her smile is a mile wide.

'Is it true? Just watch me.' I'm grinning as I reach for the phone. 'Please get me the number for United Reservations.'

My thoughts are flowing freely now and there's a subconscious smile across my face. The tension headache slowly dissipates and has been replaced by fleeting images of happiness. For seven days Casey never left my side. It was simply two for the road, father and daughter bonding.

She was six years old at the time and just the perfect age for Disneyland. We sat together and giggled uncontrollably throughout the flight. The days at Disneyland and Universal Studios were filled with happiness and togetherness and the evenings in the hotel were spent reading stories, talking and singing. At night I'd tuck my little girl into her single bed with a bedtime story and in the morning I'd inevitably awake with her sleeping on my back or at my side. The flight back to New York was a time to reflect on our week together and flick through the many photographs we had to show Audrey. The way Casey hugged me in the taxi made it all worthwhile when she whispered into my ear.

'Thank you for taking me Daddy. I love you so much.'

My eyes snap open as reality bites.

'Just sit tight Mr. Egan and we'll open your door and get you out,' says Frank Berne as the cop car pulls to a stop outside the precinct house.

The two cops hold my arms and press down on my head as they get me out of the vehicle. If I'm not under arrest, they're certainly putting on a good act. I'm being escorted once again in that certain authoritative manner up the concrete steps and into the precinct station. I'm hustled and bustled past a variety of interesting characters. I've never personally experienced the inner sanctum of a New York cop station but I can't help comparing it to the many television series depicting cop shops like this. I'm looking at the same stale discolored hallways and staircases and also the same drab looking cops and criminals as well. I look around at the many prostitutes, transvestites and dope peddlers in all stages of the detainment process, and then at the blue uniformed street cops and the plain clothed detectives yelling, either at their subject criminals, or at the processing staff who line the long timber counters. Many are dressed in crumpled suits and some are dressed in jeans and T-shirts. I try to compare what I'm seeing to the lobby of the Icelandic Hotel, and I decide that it's just another Shakespearean stage play in the middle of Act Three.

'In here please Mr. Egan,' says detective Frank Berne.

They're pulling and pushing me into a small office of frosted glass wall panes framed with scratched timbers badly in need of a polish. The office looks like a junkyard with piles of papers, large yellow envelopes, and scattered items of stationary equipment everywhere. Pictures and photographs of wanted criminals are pinned and stuck in every available piece of wall space. Stupidly, I study them to see if my own face is among them.

For some strange reason, this small office fascinates me and I'm thinking how sharply it contrasts with the huge immaculately designed office I myself occupy on the top floor of Egan Center. But why do I feel rather privileged to be allowed in this dingy little room? My feeling of privilege is soon turned to a feeling of abuse when Jimmy the sidekick pins me forcefully down into a stiff wooden chair.

Frank Berne sits at the other side of the desk and now opens his mouth to speak.

'Now Mr. Egan, it's time to answer a few questions for us. What were you doing at the Icelandic Hotel?'

I really don't feel like answering a bunch of stupid questions asked by these suspicious cops but I remember the promise of co-operation I had made to myself in the squad car. I dig deep for some tolerance.

'Well Lieutenant Berne, I had an arrangement to meet my ex-wife and daughter. We were to celebrate Casey's ninth birthday over lunch and I was going to give her a gift.'

With that, I feel for the little packet inside my jacket and produce the opened box for both detectives to see. They lean forward, nod in acknowledgement, and resume their staunch posturing.

'Are we to understand that you are divorced from Audrey Egan?' asks Frank.

'That's correct.' I'm reasonably calm.

'Why at the Icelandic Hotel? Is that where the big shots meet? What's so special about there? Why meet there?' asks the ponytail sidekick using his best interrogative tone of voice.

'Why the hell not?' I don't like his smart-ass manners and he knows it. I prefer Frank Berne to be asking the questions. 'It's a nice place to meet, and the mezzanine restaurant is one of our favorite places to dine.'

'If we check with the restaurant, will we find a reservation in your name?' asks Frank.

'You surely will. Please check!' I feel as though I'm wasting my time here and I'm getting agitated once again. 'Listen, can't you see these questions are stupid? Why do you doubt me? We should be trying to track down my daughter instead of wasting time with stupid questions. She's out there somewhere and we're spending precious time in here!' I throw my hands out in frustration and shake my head in despair.

Frank Berne's eyes widen as he speaks. 'Now once again Mr. Egan, I would ask you to co-operate with us. We have to doubt everyone at this stage and you're no exception. So I'm asking you to sit back and answer our questions carefully.'

Frank's voice seems to have the required affect and I sit back. He hands me a glass of water and I drink it down thirstily. He takes the empty glass and places it carefully on the shelf to his rear. I can't help but think that the collection of my fingerprints on the glass is his objective, rather than a concern for my fluid intake.

'Who else knew you would be meeting your ex-wife there?' asks Frank.

'Oh, I suppose her housemaid Mary-Lou, her driver Benedict, and I guess the staff at my office. It's been planned for a while now as a special occasion. I guess many people knew. There is the staff at the restaurant, the doorman Leslie, anyone who Audrey talked to and Casey's friends for that matter. It's also possible that they may have been followed.'

'Why do you think they were in the elevator? Weren't you supposed to meet in the lobby?' Frank is asking the questions and jotting things into his notebook.

'Maybe the assailant wanted some privacy so he invited them into the elevator for a private assault. I don't know! You should be telling me. You're the detectives!' I'm trying to remain calm without much success.

'Do you know of anyone who might want to hurt your ex-wife or your daughter?'

'No. I can't think of anyone. Everyone loves them, including me.'

'Oh, you were on good terms?' Frank looks surprised.

'Yes. Very good terms, of course!' I stare him straight in the eye.

'Do you yourself have any enemies who might want to hurt you?' asks Frank.

'It's possible. In the business world, everyone competes. They're all potential enemies. Who knows?' I'm really thinking about this question. Could this be a key?

'Why do you think she was attacked?' Jimmy is once again getting in on the act and I don't answer his stupid question.

'It must be unpleasant losing custody of your daughter. Was it a bitter pill to swallow? asks Frank softly as he shakes his head at Jimmy.

The sidekick's storming about the office and not paying attention. He stops, turns, stares directly at me and raises his voice. He's blurting out once again.

'Some kind of big shot aren't you? Always had everything your own way but then you couldn't hang on to your own wife. Maybe, you just made sure no one else could have her either?' Obnoxious Jimmy is smirking through his words.

I can feel the fervor boiling in my veins at his incredibly insipid remark. He begins to laugh but I don't. I want to caution him again but I can feel the volcano erupting. The tensed coil in my gut, which tightens every time he opens his smart-ass mouth, decides to uncoil itself there and then. In one involuntary motion, my hands disappear under the desk in front of me and lift it, with some kind of alien energy, into the air. The desk flies up and back with my hands forcing it. Frank Berne is caught by surprise and tumbles back and over like a fallen statue. The desk lands on top of him.

Jimmy the sidekick is also caught off guard but reacts with lightning like speed, instinctively reaching for his shoulder holster and the Glock Special. He manages to get it half drawn as the desk collides with his shoulder and my hand collides with his neck. He's now on the floor and I've got him well pinned with one hand around his throat and my other hand holding his gun to the floorboards. I'm amazed at my own strength and at what I have accomplished. I then suddenly become confused with what should come next in my offensive and I loosen my grip on his neck. He starts to sputter and spit as his eyeballs return to their sockets and his blue face returns to a more natural pink color.

I'm back in control of myself and am beginning to realize what I have done, when the room fills with people around me. I feel the grip of hands dragging me up and off. They're the strong hands of Frank Berne and I'm now firmly being repositioned bodily into the wooden chair.

'Everyone out! You too Jimmy! Get the hell out of here!' Frank is furious at the sidekick idiot. Jimmy, and the few other cops who have come to the rescue, don't have to be told twice. They quickly leave the office.

Frank tries to lift the desk, and I quickly move to help him uttering a false apology for my actions. We restore the desk roughly to its former position and Frank motions for me to resume my seat in the wooden chair.

'You, Mr. Egan, better learn to control that temper of yours. Get a grip or you'll find yourself rotting in the lockup. I won't warn you again.'

I'm beginning to like this fat Irish cop and I compose myself again.

Frank looks at me compassionately and hesitates.

'You're not under arrest Egan and I'm sorry about Jimmy. He gets a bit excited sometimes but he's a good cop. We shall ask you to give us a full description of your daughter and a good photograph would help as well. Understand? You can rest assured we'll be looking to find her. You look like you need some rest Egan.'

Frank is working hard to gain back some ground after the damage done by Jimmy. He's staring me straight in the face and it's like he's playing some kind of game or something.

'Listen Egan. I'm going to ask you a question and I want you to consider it carefully before you answer. You hear me Egan? Answer it carefully and you'll be free to go.' I stare blankly at him and nod in approval.

'Joe Egan. Do you have any knowledge of the whereabouts of your daughter, Casey Egan?'

I can't believe my ears. Just when I was beginning to have some faith in this man, and he's asking me this? I take a few seconds to swallow another rising outburst and transform it into something more controlled.

'Listen Berne, I have NO knowledge of the whereabouts of my daughter. Now that's the last damn question I'll be answering today. You place me under arrest, read me my rights, or get the hell out of my way. I'll be walking out of this lunatic asylum now, and thanks for nothing!'

I get up and push him aside. He doesn't try to stop me and I'm marching through the confusion of cop shop characters towards the exit. I hear him call after me, and it sounds like the dialogue of a western movie.

'Don't you be leaving town Egan. We're not finished with you.'

* * * * *

The street outside is damp, gloomy and unfriendly. Even though the temperature is a comfortable seventy-two degrees, I feel left out in the cold with no clues to guide me. I'm devastated that there's no help forthcoming from the police and I'm furious that Wyatt Prendergast never bothered to show up. I turn northbound and splash in the sidewalk puddles as steady rain spatters my cashmere jacket and patent leather shoes. I reach for my cell phone and dial the number for Prendergast.

'Prendergast!' The same impersonal reply comes back as before.

'Where the hell are you? I've just spent an hour inside the cop station.'

'Joe. Sorry. I was held up. I'm on my way. Did you tell them anything?'

'Look. It's too late. I'm on my way home now. I'll call you back later.' I make my disappointment quite obvious with the tone of my voice. I end the call and decide to talk to him when I have the patience, if I have the patience. Wyatt's always been there for me in the past and I can't understand his lack of performance. I can only think that he himself was close to Audrey and it must be a great shock for him as well.

Wiping the water from my Rolex reveals the time at 4.05 p.m. There's much to do. I should check the office and my own home message machine. Maybe there's news of Casey. The area around the Icelandic needs to be checked and also, the nooks and crannies of the hotel interior require a thorough search. Matters of a business nature will have to wait and I'm confident that Sharyn Cooper, my young and efficient secretary, and Andrew Barton, my very capable office executive, will both have matters of business well under control. I hail the first yellow taxi that comes along and I'm quickly in the rear seat and out of the rain.

'Take me to Lexington and East 66th. I want to cruise the streets in that area. I'm looking for my daughter. She's nine years old and she's missing.'

'This kind of thing ain't so unusual in New York City,' he utters to me and stamps the cab into motion as the windshield wipers slap time.

The taxi ride provides another brief session of relative tranquility as I peer through the trembling raindrops on my side window. As they hesitate and then fall one by one to form little branched highways on the glass, I'm reminded of my own life. Every occasion is another junction in the highway of life at which to hesitate and choose. There's no back

back peddling. Each chosen direction determines what comes next and denies what might have been.

I'm thinking of the past, the happy years with Audrey and baby Casey, when my cell phone suddenly vibrates me back to the present. I reach for it quickly, as always, trying subconsciously to beat the ring tone.

'Yes hello, Joe Egan here.'

'Joe. Oh dear Joe. It's Sharyn. I'm so sorry to hear about Audrey. It's all over the news. Joe, are you all right?' Sharyn's voice is soft and caring.

'Thank you so much Sharyn. I know. Oh...dear... dear..... Audrey...... She.. she.. deserved.. deserved..' I'm struggling to find the words.

'I know Joe. It's tragic. Where are you now?' Sharyn interrupts me and her voice is now more businesslike.

'I'm in a taxi on the East Side. Did the media mention Casey?' Although the last thing I need is sensationalized news coverage, I'm desperate for any information of my daughter.

'No, there was no mention of Casey. Do you have her with you?' Sharyn hangs on her question and I can sense that she has more to tell me.

'No I don't, and I'm very worried about her. Have you heard anything at all?'

'Joe, come to the office straight away. It may be about Casey. Someone's delivered a mysterious looking envelope and it says on the front to be opened by Joseph Egan only. And Joe, the words are pasted from newspaper cuttings.'

CHAPTER 4

Sharyn Cooper stood in front of the long mirror in the entrance hall of her office. She fingered her throat gingerly and repositioned the black pearl necklace around her slender neck. Joe was on his way and she wanted her appearance to please him.

She lingered for a while studying her full length with a critical eye. Although her role was that of a businesswoman, she liked to retain her femininity as much as the position would allow. If she would exceed the limits of Joe's expectations, he would usually let her know with a comical hint or gesture. It would generally take the form of a compliment, but Sharyn knew what it really meant, that he wanted her to dress more conservatively.

'You look very beautiful today Sharyn,' Joe might say. 'Much too pretty to be inside an office.' Sharyn knew the true meaning.

Today could very well be one of those days. Sharyn just loved to dress in pretty clothes and she was slightly anxious that Joe's compliments might be coming her way. Caressing her magnificent figure and ample bust, was a simple, though lovely, cotton dress with fitted bodice and sleeves, and a neckline which revealed the smooth skin upon her neck and over her delicate collarbone. Her white shoes were conservative with single strap and stiletto heels. A single charcoal pearl pendant earring hung delicately from each tiny earlobe and her neck was graced with a matching string necklace. Sharyn's make up was subtle and sophisticated. She was a born beauty with a natural pastel complexion and little make up was required. Her rich long auburn hair was worn up and back with the occasional glossy strand tangling down beside her hazel eyes to frame a portrait face of serene loveliness.

Yes, Sharyn was indeed a beauty and Joe was well aware of it. He had always managed to keep his distance from her in personal matters. She was far too valuable to him in a business sense, and his own business sense told him not to ever compromise their relationship. Today, Sharyn was afraid she had gone too far. Joe was not intended to make an appearance at the office and she had no business engagements to be concerned with. She had dressed herself up to freely express her femininity and to feel her womanhood openly.

Sharyn Cooper was no ordinary secretary. Better to describe her as 'the woman behind the man'. She was a loyal personal assistant and Joe Egan was the subject of her loyalty. Four years employment with Egan Enterprises had reaped huge financial rewards, and Sharyn had Joe to thank for the very healthy state of her own accounts.

The more money Joe Egan made, the more incentive bonuses would be paid. With only herself and Andrew Barton as permanent staff, these bonuses had dwarfed their normal salary and Sharyn was now a very wealthy girl indeed. At the wonderful prime age of thirty-seven, she had more than four million dollars in her name, enough to last her for a lifetime.

However, it was not financial matters at the root of her devotion to Joe. She was in love with him. Love was felt in her heart at the initial interview when she first looked into his liquid green eyes, and love had blossomed ever since. It was a love that Sharyn had kept a secret from the man who was twelve years her senior. Every part of her existence wanted him to know of her feelings and it was no easy task to keep them a secret. She had always been terrified that the level headed Joe would not return her affection, and she had to be sure of his interest if she was to take the plunge.

Sharyn made a final adjustment of her clothing, running both hands down the sides of her slender body. She then moved away from the mirror, more satisfied now that she may pass the testing eye of Joe Egan. She made her way into the main office area where Andrew was busy at one of the many computer terminals. His was a world deep within the academic journals of calculations and equations and he seldom came up for air. Sharyn was always impressed at his dedicated work ethic.

'Joe's on his way Andrew,' she said softly so as not to break his train of thought.

Andrew made a soft murmur to acknowledge her without looking up and continued tapping at the keyboard.

There were other reasons for Andrew Barton's exemplary performance at Egan Enterprises. He was a business machine in action and a perfectionist by nature. Not only were Andrew's thought processes in synchronized mechanical harmony, his body was as well. Standing six feet tall and weighing one hundred and eighty-five pounds, he was in supreme physical condition. Forty minutes on the rowing machine every evening assured him of that. These orderly qualities were a blessing for the benefit of the office administration.

Andrew needed the picture on the wall to be exactly level, the office equipment to be of clockwork precision, and the balance sheet to be a work of art. Nothing but detailed perfection would satisfy Andrew and he worked tirelessly at it each and every day of his life. These peculiar traits had worked to the great benefit of Egan Enterprises and Joe could always be assured that the accounts were accurate to the last digit. The combination of Sharyn's flexible efficiency and of Andrew's obsessive compulsive behavior enabled Joe to freely exercise his entrepreneurial skills and make more money.

It was unknown to Sharyn and Joe, that behind Andrew's tremendous discipline and hard work, his personal affairs had not faired so well. His quest for exactness, although an advantage for office management, was a huge obstacle for creativity in his own life. To build on one's wealth requires a flexible attitude rather than an obsession with accurate figures. Instead of taking the calculated risk required for a windfall profit, poor Andrew would, time and time again, concentrate only on the numbers, not seeing the wood for the trees.

Put him at a card table and Andrew the mathematician could count the cards and calculate the odds. Where he had trouble, was in the art of bluff. The bets were appropriate and correctly placed. His cards were always perfectly arranged and called for. Andrew Barton just didn't know when to hold them and when to fold them. The other players could read him like a book, and that was always his downfall.

Andrew's life was that of an eccentric, or maybe it could be better described as that of a nerd. His somber existence wasn't to be envied. He was so set in his ways and married to his computer, that it was difficult to imagine him ever living with a wife and a household of children. No woman could tolerate his peculiarities. Consequently, Andrew was destined to a life of disconsolate loneliness. Usually, he would work back at the office late into the night and on other occasions he would be ringing the door buzzer at his favorite illegal gaming club. The card table was where Andrew would often find himself into the early hours of the morning. He would play for long sessions, dark brown hair slicked into place, horn-rimmed spectacles, cream pants with floral suspenders, and matching floral bow tie in perfect horizontal alignment.

The other players were always impressed with the way Andrew was so neatly dressed and groomed. His playing chips were always aligned in tidy little stacks. He never varied his appearance and he never varied his exactness. To the delight of the other hardened gamblers, he also never varied his playing strategy. Overall, it was sobering and depressing. It was an endless cycle of Andrew, failing at the card table by night, and then striving to redeem himself with business excellence the following day.

Sharyn stood behind Andrew for a few moments and admired the progress being made on his latest computer spreadsheet. Andrew and Sharyn, when working together, would often produce amazing results. Their contrasting abilities, when combined, became a formidable force driving the company into greater profits. During the marketing frenzy of Egan Center and the subsequent consolidation of Joe's enterprises, the office required many people. There were secretaries and receptionists, clerical teams dealing with specialized projects, and accountants and lawyers constantly at work. The office was a hive of activity as the empire grew. Now that the business was largely self-perpetuating and stabilized, only a few staff were required. The few temporary office workers, who were occasionally employed, seldom lasted more than a few days, as direct control saved time and prevented mistakes.

Although both Andrew and Sharyn shared an equal level of responsibility at Egan Enterprises, Sharyn considered herself slightly superior to Andrew and much closer to Joe. It was Sharyn who, more often than not, linked Andrew and Joe together in business dealings and kept the harmonious and exponential growth of the company on track.

Sharyn gazed through the huge picture window at the impressive row of Manhattan skyscrapers. The atmosphere was an orchestra of hazy sunset rain showers, gradually dissipating and allowing intermittent yellow light beams to break through covering New York's West Side. Sharyn experienced a flush of goose bumps and felt the power and the glory of seeing it from the top of Egan Center.

Sharyn Cooper was in awe of Joe Egan and admired his many achievements. She stood before that picture window and reflected on the many stories Joe had told her during

47

the previous four years. He had openly discussed his rise to fortune and fame and she listened for every last morsel of information, every detail about the life of the man she loved.

As the only child to an Irish immigrant mother and Hungarian Jewish father, Joe was encouraged from his earliest childhood to save money and invest wisely. With the help of fatherly advice, he had developed an extraordinary gift of looking at problems in an incredible alternative way. Yes, Joseph Egan had certainly seen the wood through the trees when he embarked upon the continued development of his huge business empire. From its humble beginnings, to the success story it had now become, Egan Enterprises was an instrument of Joe's uncanny way of getting things done.

* * * * *

Joe Egan's move into property development provided him with a depth of wealth he never could have envisaged. His father, who had paid rent to his dying day, had often lectured Joe to become a landlord himself as soon as possible.

'Don't spend your whole life making the landlords wealthy Joey.'

'Make the nickels and dimes, but invest the dollars into houses.'

'Everyone needs a roof over their head Joey. Remember that!'

Joe took his father's advice. His first nickel and dime business venture was the breeding of small parakeets on the rooftop of their old tenement building. Joe would put them, one by one, into small gilded cages and sell them around the neighborhood. His enterprise was an immediate success and 'the parakeet-boy' as he became known as, recorded a handsome profit in his very first business year.

As soon as his bank account balance was sufficient, Joey was granted his first mortgage loan and he purchased the tiniest least expensive flat available. This was the start of his real estate pyramid. The rent from one flat would help pay for the next and he, slowly but surely, climbed the ladder of wealth. Joe always remembered the words of his father.

'It's too late for me, but you my son, have all the time in the world. The rental income always goes up and the mortgage payments always go down. Think about it Joey.'

Joe did think about it and he still does. Feelings, instincts, and experiences from the past were handed down from father to son. Although he inherited no money from his parents, Joe inherited the knowledge of their mistakes and a determination to do better. Much, much better! He would make his parents proud and create new respect for the Egan name.

Joe's huge rental income deposits were soon pouring into the accounts of Egan Enterprises. He couldn't ignore what was happening on Wall Street, and he quickly recognized the vast potential of the Internet phenomenon. With a new opportunity staring him in the face, he redirected the income stream into the Silicon Valley stocks of the technology boom. Yes. The compounding of great wealth was under way. Joe was in the big league. His investment in a small technology company called 'Silicon Resolutions' provided Joe with a fast small fortune. Once again his father's advice echoed in his thoughts.

'A profit is not a profit Joey, until the cash is in the bank.'

Joe knew that he could push his luck only so far, and his instincts told him that these companies that defied gravity were heading for a fall. For him, it just became too scary and unsettling. He shocked everyone when he liquidated his sizable investment in 'Silicon Resolutions' and then sold out of the market altogether. The gurus on Wall Street didn't agree. They thought it was just plain stubbornness. They were wrong. The stock markets of the world nose-dived and the financial world shuddered. Wall Street plunged and pulled anyone who dared to hang on, down with it.

Joe's timely switch from his vast holdings in the boom-ing dot-com shares to the safety net of bank deposits had provided him with a huge advantage. Cash! It was this cash reserve combined with his brilliant insight that led him to Egan Enterprise's most lucrative investment idea to date. Then, it was the performance skills of Sharyn and Andrew that helped him implement that idea and turn it into a vast empire.

It had occurred to Joe that the new Wall Street tycoons and the young dot-com millionaires and billionaires all wanted to live in the same place, and they all wanted to live in luxury. However, that place didn't readily exist. That is, not until Joe Egan got in on the act. Joe had identified the need and then he had set about to provide the solution. That's how money is made. The desired location was Park Avenue on Manhattan's Upper East Side and the ultimate solution was Egan Center.

The incredibly wealthy tycoons of Wall Street had made phenomenal fortunes from intangible investments and they now demanded the best. Egan Center was built around that demand. Absolutely nothing was wanting and the occupants would forever feel spoilt in the lap of luxury.

Because Egan Center was unsurpassed in size, quality and location, the apartments were snapped up in a feeding frenzy of competition. Purchasers had money overflowing in investment accounts, and prestige became the issue of importance rather than price. Everyone competed for a bet-ter combination of elevation and view than his or her coun-terparts. They would pay what was required to achieve their desires, and Joe literally cleaned up in the process.

* * * * *

Rising thirty-eight stories above Park Avenue and encompassing the area of what had previously been six buildings, Egan Center was cleverly orientated so that most of the gracious residences offered overwhelming views, either of the City, Central Park, or the East River with its dramatic bridges and beyond. The conservatory and atrium blended with the private outdoor gardens making the residents feel as if they'd escaped the city.

The 282 residences were constructed in three towers of differing heights being 18, 28, and 38 stories. The lower levels of each tower contained four apartments per floor and the upper six floors had only two apartments per floor. The very top two levels of each tower consisted of one massive penthouse residence. The apartments differed in design and decoration but each one was a miniature palace in its own right. The interiors resembled the classic Park Avenue apartment layouts of the 1930's, with separate wings of entertaining and sleeping.

Blending classic design with modern amenities, Egan Center captured the grace and grandeur that is Park Avenue.

In the race for the very highest floor in the center, there was ever only going to be one winner, and that winner was Joe. Yes, he had kept the very top penthouse apartment in the highest tower as his own home and the floor immediately below it was to house the offices of Egan Enterprises. Above Joe's penthouse, on the rooftop level, he had opted for a personal helicopter landing pad to be constructed rather than the expected swimming pool, terraces and gardens. Although his busy lifestyle temporarily precluded him from getting his helicopter license, Joe intended one day to fly his own chopper to and from that rooftop.

'You want the best that New York has to offer? Then, you reside at Egan Center.' The advertising motto quickly became the trendy thing to say in every business discussion.

Booming Wall Street was soon focused in and Egan Enterprises was catapulted into mega millions. Prices of apartments ranged from $8.75 million to $64.75 million. As they were sold, the money rolled in and was quickly reinvested into solid secure high yielding bonds.

The sudden demise of Wall Street's share market had been catastrophic for the Wall Street bulls. It had little consequence for Joe Egan. He had cashed in, re-deployed, and continued his climb to the summit of wealth and power.

* * * * *

Sharyn moved away from the wide picture window and wandered into Joe's office. She went to his desk and sensed that her presence was where Joe often worked alone. It was her way of being around him and she briefly sat down in the leather swivel chair to enjoy the experience. She studied the suspicious long white envelope that had been delivered with the office mail and wondered about its significance. The front of the envelope displayed a very simple and concise instruction.

TO BE OPENED ONLY BY JOSEPH EGAN

The lettering, although cut from different items of newspaper text, was neatly arranged and easy to read. She knew that it must be carefully examined prior to opening to conform to security procedures and she waited patiently for Joe to arrive. The foyer security intercom hummed a mellow tone, followed by the voice of the entrance security guard.

'Mr. Egan has arrived and he's on his way up. Thank you.'

The phone on Joe's desk began to ring and Sharyn felt she had time to answer it.

'Yes, Egan Enterprises.'

'Hello. It's Wyatt Prendergast here. Who am I speaking to?'

'Wyatt. Hello! This is Sharyn Cooper.'

'Oh, Sharyn. Is Joe there yet? I just want to make sure he's all right, that's all.' Wyatt's voice sounded quite gruff.

'He's all right Wyatt. He's on his way up now.'

'Okay. I see. Just tell him to call me if he needs me.' He ended the call abruptly without giving her time to speak.

Sharyn didn't like Wyatt Prendergast. He had been Joe's lawyer from the original conception of Egan Center and had never once let Joe down. She just didn't like the man. Sharyn saw Prendergast as a slick business lawyer without a heart. In her opinion, he was just a little too slick. What both Joe and Sharyn didn't know, was that Wyatt Prendergast had some serious personal problems. Although he had raked in a personal fortune from the legal account of Egan Enterprises, Prendergast had invested almost all of it into the high flying and very promising NASDAQ Company, 'Silicon Resolutions'. Unfortunately, Silicon Resolutions came crashing down with the rest of Wall Street, and Prendergast was left with a long string of heavy debts. They were debts that could take him the rest of his life to pay off. Despite this, Prendergast would always exude the appearance of wealth and success. He was always dressed in the finest black wool suits with the most exclusive mirror black patent leather shoes. Yes. He looked the part of a wealthy Upper East Side lawyer, even if he wasn't.

Sharyn hurried to the office reception area and she was aware of her pulse quickening and a strange tingling sensation in her tummy. Seeing Joe always had that affect on her and she readied herself for his presence. She would once again conform to propriety, hide her affection, and feign indifference.

The elevator doors parted and Joe stumbled into the reception area. Sharyn was startled at the appearance of the man who now stood before her, not the Joe Egan she knew, but a shaken, disheveled, highly agitated and chronically fatigued version. The man appeared so lonely in his desolate troubled world that her heart immediately went out to him. She wanted desperately to rush into his arms and comfort him with soothing words of compassion. The bond that existed between them seemed so obvious to her, and she wanted so desperately to convey her feelings to Joe, but she rationally denied herself once again. It was not the right time and place. She knew that he wanted to read what was written within that envelope, and he wanted it to lead him to Casey, alive and well.

CHAPTER 5

The steady rain has now finished cleansing the streets and sidewalks of Manhattan and the atmosphere is a blend of misty sunlight and rising steam. As the yellow taxicab eases through the enormous wrought iron gates of Egan Center and pulls around the circular tiled driveway, I'm aware of the toll this ordeal is now taking on my mind and body. Each time I raise my forearm to check the time, I notice the ever-so-slight trembling at my fingertips. My body is devoid of its usual sparkling energy that has now been replaced by a numb sinking sensation.

A glance into the rear vision mirror reveals my sallow expression and red tearful eyes. I look away and try to perk myself up knowing that the best chance for me to help my daughter is for me to stay alert. I try to be optimistic when I think of little Casey. Every time a gloomy vision of death attempts to intrude, I switch my thoughts to a happier more positive outcome. Despite this, my head is heavy with a dull ache and I look forward to any opportunity to swallow some aspirin.

The vehicle slides into the carriage area beneath the Roman ceiling of gold frescos and comes to a halt within the quadrant of tall supporting marble columns. The passenger door clicks open and Leslie the doorman is there to greet me. Leslie has dutifully attended the main entrance to Egan Center since the inaugural opening. With no family of his own, he's always there, morning and evening, opening and closing doors for the rich and famous in his pin-striped pants and black coat of tails. I usually take some time to be polite towards him and exchange some friendly words whenever I pass by. I'm well aware that his routine existence is in sharp contrast to my own and I've always sensed that there may be a slight bitterness on his part as he watches me come and go. There are some people who admire success and good fortune and there are others who are simply resentful.

'Mr. Egan. Good afternoon Sir. Miss Casey not with you today?'

'Well no, she's not today Leslie, but thank you.'

When the taxi driver hears my name 'Egan', he spins his head around with a look of dismay on his face and then fixes his gaze on my gold Rolex.

'M...Mr..Mr. Egan himself?' he stammers.

'Thanks for looking after me driver.' I hand him a one hundred dollar bill and step out of the cab.

'Keep the change,' I say, looking back at him with a weary grin.

The pressed bronze entrance doors automatically swing to the side with one click of Leslie's remote and I breathe a sigh of relief to be within the familiar territory of Egan Center. One of the two elevators reserved for floors thirty-one up to thirty-eight is waiting in position and I wave my hand at the security desk as I enter. A six number code into the small selection panel is all that's required, initiating the fifteen-second ride. The elevator comes to life and with a gush of compressed air, blasts smoothly upward to the thirty-seventh level.

The doors soon slide open and I stumble forward into the reception area of my offices. I'm delighted that Sharyn is standing there to greet me. There's a compassionate look in her eyes, and I'm aware that she's someone who really cares. She's a vision of beauty standing before me and I feel so good to be in her presence. I'm conscious that Sharyn now means more to me in a personal way than she ever has, and I want to be closer to her. I want to hold her. For a fleeting moment, I instinctively feel like telling her how I feel. However, discretion prevails and I know that this is not the right time. I'm speechless and I gaze past her looking for Andrew.

'Joe, the envelope's on your desk. We've done nothing and called no one. Andrew and I thought it best to call you straight away.'

'Sharyn, you did the right thing. Let's go into my office and we'll see what it's all about.'

Andrew rises from his chair and strides down the corridor in my direction to greet me.

'Are you all right Mr. Egan?' Andrew still enjoys the protocol of using my surname. It fits in with his sense of correctness and he feels uncomfortable calling me Joe.

'Well, I'm not really having a good day Andrew. Anyway, how are you? Is everything here on track?'

'The business is fine as usual Sir.' I see by his manner that he's anxious to get back to whatever project he's working on.

'That's good Andrew. I know I can always rely on you. Sharyn and I will be in my office if you need us. I'll let you get back to whatever you're doing.' I watch as Andrew walks back to the main office and diligently resumes his keyboard typing.

Sharyn and I continue into my office. The style is very different to the rest of the center. For good reasons, I've created my own personal space to be sparsely furnished and ultra modern. Although I adore the beauty that comes with classical decoration, this area is to remain free from distractions.

My mind is a treasure chest of ideas when I'm inside this room of azure blue velvet and polished chrome. The flooring is pale washed timber and the concealed lighting subdued yellow. In the center of the vast floor area stands a semi-spherical silver and black desk enclosing a rotating black stitched leather armchair. The entire wall to the rear of the desk consists of a tropical aquarium with glowing corals of every color and swaying seaweed. Hypnotic fish of many species drift aimlessly in passive motion through crystal clear water. The opposite wall, being the main subject of my vision as I sit at my desk, has wide tinted glass doors encasing a panoramic and breathtaking view of the city skyline over an expansive terrace. Off to the side, there's a comfortable lounge set with welded pewter and turquoise leather for occasions of a less formal nature.

Sharyn leans forward as I sit at my desk and I take the envelope in my fingertips to examine its sinister features.

'Do you think we should contact the police?' Sharyn is hesitant.

'No, not at this stage. I have to think. What we do from here on is absolutely crucial for Casey's survival. Hopefully, this is a ransom note of some kind, and that means that Casey is still alive.'

I gently put it down on the desk and consider opening it there and then.

Sharyn wants to slow things down and she's now showing great wisdom. 'We should have it x-rayed and security checked if you're not going to report it.'

'It's almost certainly a ransom letter Sharyn. I don't feel like waiting for procedural things. Casey's life may be at stake.'

I pick up the envelope once again and caress its outer layer to try to feel for hard objects. Apart from a slightly lumpy area to one side, I satisfy myself that the contents are not of the letter bomb variety. I'm very much aware that this is a turning-point decision in my life, and Casey's life. If I am to call the police, I should do it now and allow them to handle the opening of the envelope. But, surely it's reasonable to open it myself. It may not even be a ransom note and I should discover its contents first and foremost.

I decide to open it without further reluctance. I find a slim silver paper knife in the top desk drawer and decide that it's a suitable implement to slice open one side. My thumb pushes the thin glistening blade from its casing and I use the sharp tip to perforate the envelope's edge. It comes apart quite easily and I instinctively close the blade and put the paper knife in my trouser side-pocket. Maybe it's the sense of danger I'm experiencing or the rage that's building inside me, but this simple little paper knife in my side pocket makes me feel more secure.

With a little tug of my forefinger and thumb, the contents of the envelope slide out onto the desk pad and I'm now carefully unfolding what seems to be a foolscap page of pasted newsprint.

'Looks like you may be right Joe. Casey has been kidnapped.' Sharyn is moving around to my side of the desk to get a closer look and I feel the warmth of her body beside mine.

Without reading the text of the letter, my eyes immediately focus on two small objects in two different areas of the page. Both have been carefully stuck down with cellophane tape.

'Oh dear God! Dear God! This is Casey's hair.' My stomach churns and heaves as I reel backwards in a state of delirium.

Tumbling out from under the tape, I'm shocked and horrified to see some blonde tangled curls snipped from the head of my little girl. My trembling fingers touch and twirl the soft locks of my daughter's beautiful hair, and I'm overcome with the notion that this may be the only tangible remembrance of her body for me to forever hold on to.

'Bastards! Mongrel bastards! What have they done to her?' I fall back into my leather chair and I'm now looking at my two trembling clenched fists as I shake them into the air.

'Easy Joe. Easy.' Sharyn's hand is massaging my right shoulder and I can feel extreme tension across the nape of my neck. It's as though I'm carrying a subcutaneous torsion bar across my shoulders and my neck is being hideously twisted.

Sharyn's rhythmic kneading is working its magic and I regain my composure to go back to the letter. There's another object beneath some clear tape and it appears to be a microchip of some kind? Yes. It looks like a cell phone card. I hesitate for a moment and decide to leave both the card and hair in place without further disturbance. I hope that forensic examination or DNA testing is not my subconscious reasoning.

Hastily, I read the main text and then restart at the top to study the detailed meaning. It looks like a set of instructions, all in newsprint and all meticulously pasted in little rows.

WE HAVE YOUR DAUGHTER UNLESS YOU MEET
OUR DEMANDS SHE WILL BE KILLED
IF YOU CO OPERATE SHE WILL BE RETURNED TO
YOU ALIVE
IF YOU GO TO THE POLICE YOU WILL RECEIVE A
PACKAGE CONTAINING HER SEVERED FINGER
YOU MUST FOLLOW OUR INSTRUCTIONS
PRECISELY
FOR EACH MISTAKE YOU MAKE ANOTHER
SEVERED FINGER WILL BE SENT TO YOUR OFFICE
PUT THIS CARD INTO A CELL PHONE AND WAIT
FOR OUR CALL

I read it again and then again. My pulse is racing and my palms are wet with perspiration. I can think of no immediate course of action other than to follow the instructions. Going to the police would be insane, especially after the treatment they dealt out to me previously. For God's sake, they wanted to lock me up. No! No! No! Surely, police involvement would only result in the worst possible outcome, Casey's dead body in a casket. These people are desperate and ruthless. Look what happened to dear Audrey when she tried to resist. The best chance for Casey is for me to meet their demands and hope she will survive. They've warned me not to make any mistakes and I must not. I'll be more accurate in my actions than ever before in my life.

Sharyn is aware of my level of anxiety and she's considerate not to interrupt my thought process. Her hand still rubs my shoulder.

'Sharyn, will you please get me some aspirin and water?'

She releases her grasp of my shoulder and, without a word, leaves the room. I swing my chair around for some quiet reprieve, and become tranquilized by the tropical marine paradise filling my field of vision.

I fix my sight on a gently oscillating yellow and orange rainbow fish, swaying insensibly with no fixed direction or course of action an

d I liken it to my own situation. What to do now? How to handle this critical situation? How is Casey possibly coping with her captivity? It's one thing for the authorities to have a policy for kidnappers. Don't give in to their demands? Don't negotiate? Will they want more and more? That's all fine when the victim is not related. It's a different matter altogether when it's your own flesh and blood at stake, when it's your own daughter! I'll do anything they ask in order to get Casey back.

'Oh dear God! What will I do? What can I do?' I call out in anguish.

The rainbow fish turns to face me as though he's now listening to my words and his little mouth opens and closes as if to offer some whispers of consolatory advice. I'm mesmerized by his beautiful features and try intensely to tune my mind to his, in order to gain some wisdom from his aquamarine world. Is this a sign from the heavens above? My mind changes gear and I'm aware of my attitude strengthening, becoming more determined and resourceful.

'I must be prepared. I must be vigilant. I must have Casey returned safely to me. I must not be defeated by these people.'

My instructions are self-directed and I blurt out these words with volume and confidence. The rainbow fish releases an air bubble of approval from his puckered lips and turns to swim away.

Sharyn re-enters the office and Andrew is beside her. They've heard me yelling and Sharyn's eyes are moist with tears. Andrew is holding a glass of water brimming with effervescent soluble aspirin. He has an uncharacteristic concerned expression across his normally precise features.

'Mr. Egan. Is there any possible way that I can be of assistance to you in your troubled times?' Andrew hands me the glass without looking at the letter on the desk.

'Thank you Andrew. What you can do, is keep the ship afloat and on charted course. I may be away from the helm for a while.' I guzzle down the aspirin and instantly feel more refreshed.

'I'll be needing Sharyn to come with me, so you'll be on your own.'

'You can leave the office up to me. Don't worry about a thing.' Andrew sounds sympathetic.

'Actually, there is something else you can do. Although we've always been fair in our dealings, there are many of our clients who have been badly smitten by the stock market meltdown. Many of them have declared insolvency. Some are very resentful at least. Do you know what I'm saying Andrew?'

'Are you saying that the people responsible for Mrs. Egan's death are our own business associates?' Andrew seems surprised at my revelation.

'I'm saying that it's a possibility. In fact, it's quite possible that we have vindictive enemies residing here in Egan Center. There would be several purchasers of apartments who now regret their impetuosity. These are also residents who see me entering and leaving all the time and this, in itself, would ferment their dissatisfaction. Therefore, I want you to compile a list of our clients who fit that category, clients who have gone bust and may be desperate. I know there may be hundreds, so I want you to condense it down to a short list of ten residents. I mean the ten clients who, in your learned opinion, would be most likely to be bitter and twisted towards me.'

'I understand perfectly Mr. Egan. I'll commence immediately.'

I decide to keep the details of the kidnapping and the threatening letter strictly between Sharyn and myself for the time being. Andrew obliges me by slowly dropping his head. He takes two paces to the rear, swings around as if on a parade ground, and walks out of my office.

Sharyn takes the empty glass from my hand and holds it to her breast as though it's a new found valuable possession. I smile at her and her eyes twinkle in reply.

'Are you taking this whole thing to the police? Joe, you know they know how to handle these things. It's too dangerous to go it alone.'

'I know Sharyn. I know. But it's more complicated than that. You can see what they've written. They say they'll kill Casey. I can't risk not doing exactly what they say. Don't you see?'

'I can see that Joe, but they might kill her anyway and then kill you as well?' Sharyn draws back realizing that her negativity is not helping my mood.

'All I want out of this is to get Casey back alive. I don't care about the cops winning or losing and I don't care about the monetary costs. I just want my daughter back.'

Sharyn's eyes are wet with emotion and I can see that she's trying to hold back. I remember that Casey and Sharyn are so very close themselves and that she loves my little girl as much as I do. This must be very difficult for her and she really is putting on a brave face to help me.

'Joe, I'm so worried for you. Please, don't do anything rash.' She's fighting back the tears.

I rise to comfort her and she falls into my arms. It feels so good and so right and I hold her close. With one hand around her tiny waist, I use the other to nestle her head into the curve of my shoulder. I'm caressing her soft hair, the slow movement of my fingertips now massaging the muffled sobs away. She turns her face upwards and our lips are touching ever so lightly. Sharyn sighs, pulls back slightly to rub her nose across my nose, and then brings her lips close to mine. I find myself wanting to succumb to the passion of our embrace and my knees are trembling as my hand continues to guide the back of her head. My fingers become lost in her hair as I pull her closer and then, hesitantly and ever so slowly, I release from our engagement. I regain control of the situation and slowly separate our bodies. I collapse back into my chair and she sits on the corner of my desk with her legs crossed and a far away look in her eyes. No words are spoken for an agonizing minute and the magical encounter is lost and gone.

'My dear Sharyn,' I whisper softly. 'I'm so sorry.'

Sharyn looks at me and she's somewhat embarrassed but happy at the same time.

'Oh Joe. What happened?'

'I don't know, but I like it,' I quietly joke and she's pleased with my response.

'I tell you what Sharyn. I'm going to put this letter away in the drawer here. There's nothing I can do until I hear from them and I'm damn sure I'm not going to let the cops mess this up for me.'

I open the top drawer and deposit the letter and envelope. I also retrieve another standby cell phone from the second drawer and carefully set about inserting the card as instructed. As I'm doing so, Sharyn gently rubs my shoulder again and I feel at home in her company.

'I'm taking this phone up to my apartment. I need a drink and I need to get some rest to handle this effectively.' I'm trying to be logical.

'Well you definitely need some rest Joe, but I need the drink.' She's trying to lighten me up and it's working.

'Joe, you know where you can find me if you need me, and you know how much Casey means to me. Don't leave me out of this. Call me the minute you find out more.'

Sharyn leaves and I know that our relationship has entered a wonderful new phase.

CHAPTER 6

Blue Featherman sat slumped in the darkest corner of Pelma's Bar and Grill. If you wanted to find a sleazier, grimier, and more flea ridden establishment, you'd have to look far and wide. The bar was situated in the ugliest most crime infected area of The Bronx and was inhabited by men only. Most were old graying alcoholics who had nothing to go home to and many were cheap petty criminals and ex-cons generally having no other way to spend their time.

The stale air was alive with swirling illuminated yellow smoke and the flooring was thrown together with old dusty raw timber boards. Apart from a couple of crooked neon advertisements for Kentucky Bourbon and some graffiti covered posters for Custom Chopper Motorcycles, the walls were bare rustic wood planks. What could hardly be called music vibrated through some shaky ceiling speakers in a dull base beat, relentless in its pulsating monotony.

The barman, himself an ex-inmate along with many of his customers, looked as though he would slit your throat as soon as look at you. So much so, that any newcomer to Pelma's would often approach the bar to order a drink, and then feel so intimidated they would retrace their steps and make a hasty exit onto the pavement.

* * * * *

Blue Featherman, or 'Feathers', as he was more commonly known, rented a room directly above Pelma's. He would, more often than not, spend the evening drinking cheap smelly rum and sucking earnestly on self-rolled cigarettes before crawling upstairs to collapse fully clothed onto a lumpy striped mattress.

Feathers' previously red hair was stringy and loosely tied into a tail at the back. It was now prematurely gray, dirty, and stained with tobacco. A greasy goatee beard was similarly stained. The remainder of his chin and cheeks was covered with heavy stubble, which helped conceal a dark oily complexion and deep acne scars from long ago. No one would believe his age to be less than fifty-five because his forty three years of existence had been spent in self-abuse and premature aging. A life of alcoholism, chain smoking, junk food and drug abuse had taken its toll.

Feathers was always dressed in exactly the same way, white undershirt with yellow stains, black jeans, western boots with silver toecaps and imitation silver spurs. Around his waist was the only belt he possessed, black leather with rows upon rows of rusty silver colored studs. In the colder months he would be seen wearing a chaffed black leather jacket with a strap dangling at the side. Because of the offensive odors that always originated from his favorite corner of the bar, many of the other usual customers wondered if these were the only clothes that Feathers owned and if he seldom bothered to wash them. They were generally correct.

Feathers looked very well suited to his dingy bar environment. He was well used to confined areas and his stale little corner was a good reminder of the rank prison cell in which he had spent a good deal of his life. He often stewed over the circumstances that led to his lifetime of crime. The prison psychiatrists had usually come up with the same old diagnosis. He was self-gratifying, attention seeking and manipulative due to a dysfunctional family background. His mother left home when he was an infant and his father subjected him to a childhood of abuse and cruelty. This was the origin of his fantasy world and this was the root of his evil ways. Feathers agreed with the analysts and subsequently considered himself not responsible for his own actions.

He had a sexual appetite that needed to be satisfied and young children were his prey. It was an endless continuing burden he was to carry through life. He wanted to be around children. He wanted to gain their confidence and befriend them. He wanted to fondle and caress them. He wanted to have sex with them and, God forbid, he wanted to inflict pain and injury to them. Yes, Blue Featherman really liked children. Most of all he liked the taste of their flesh.

Feathers sat there waiting and pondering. He was feeling aroused after thinking of the many children he had been obsessed with throughout his life. His mind drifted to the circumstances of his arrest and conviction. Why was he to blame? His own upbringing was responsible. He was just following orders from a distant voice inside his brain. It wasn't easy to find an unsuspecting child in New York. People held onto their children very closely. They were so worried about the likes of pedophiles that vulnerable children were never left unattended. The shopping centers were his best chance and Feathers had used them as his hunting ground.

He had singled out the delectable little girl who had strayed from her mother in the department store and his eyes were glazed with excitement and anticipation. She was a perfect choice with her long blond hair that curled down to her small immature breasts. Feathers only had to look at her and he knew she was ripe for the picking. He had an instant desire for this girl and he grinned like a mad Cheshire cat. The pitiless child was so relieved to be found by the shop policeman. He had put her mind at ease when he promised to take her home to her mommy. All she had to do was hold his hand and follow him out of the store. She stopped her crying and clung to the hand of her good Samaritan, Mr. Feathers. The little girl was rescued and she now had renewed faith that people were good.

Feathers sucked back on his cigarette, coughed and spat another phlegm ball into the corner. He thought about the man who had put him in prison. The detective known as Frank Berne had hunted him down like a dog. It was like a personal vendetta for that cop. He just wouldn't let up. Feathers was bitter that he had been held wholly to blame. What about the inner voices that led him to that shopping center. He had not been in control of himself when that lost girl came along. Sure! There had been other evil foreign forces working through Feathers when the little child was later found in the thick woods, staggering, lost, and crying for her mommy. The difference this time was that she was now bruised and beaten with savage bite marks inflicted to every part of her tiny body. Her most precious parts had been ripped apart and were bleeding profusely from being repeatedly raped.

Feathers knew that he wasn't to blame. He couldn't be. These were surely not the actions of a human being. Some other species must be responsible and he considered himself innocent of any wrongdoing.

Frank Berne didn't quite see it that way. Although it was not a homicide, when Frank heard of the circumstances, he immediately put himself in charge of the investigation. The little girl was finally released from the hospital, but would never be released from the memories and scars. Her nights would forever be filled with haunting nightmares of her attacker and her life would, for always, be a labyrinth of fear and trepidation. How was she to ever trust any man? How was she to ever experience a normal relationship?

Due to her condition, Frank was unable to question the victim and was made to wait for several days by the hospital medical authorities. At long last he was given permission to sit in attendance as the psychiatrist in charge would tentatively show to the frightened little girl, pictures of farmyard animals, cartoon figures, and comic book characters.

Intermingled with these pictures was the occasional photograph of men, woman and children partaking in family activities. Also randomly included were the mug shots of known pedophiles and sex offenders.

Frank's eyes were filled with tears as he watched the reaction of the little girl when the photograph of Blue Featherman was displayed before her terrified eyes. Her blood pressure doubled and her pulse escalated violently when she stared at the face of her attacker and relived the horror of those events. Her mouth was opening but her throat was gagged in silent screams for help. Her body started to gyrate in a spasmodic fit of terror and she began to lash out furiously with her hands and feet. Frank was saddened at what he was witnessing and well understood why he was made to wait so long to be able to see the girl.

Sexual crimes against children were Frank's pet hate and the beastly nature of this offence turned him into a trembling volcano ready to erupt at any time. That time came about one dark and windy night in the alley behind

Pelma's Bar and Grill when Frank finally caught up with Blue Featherman. Frank had grabbed him from behind and had thrown him to the ground. This was no copy book police technique. Frank came down heavily on the back of Feathers and pinned him face down. One hand held a vice-like grip on Feathers' left arm, twisting it almost to breaking point. His right knee nailed Feathers' right arm to the ground and his right hand gripped a handful of that dirty sticky hair. Feathers' head was yanked back with the back of his head almost touching his shoulder blade. The Adam's apple of his throat threatened to burst through the skin as Feathers' eyes stared back and up into the steely glare of Frank Berne.

When Feathers related the details of the abduction and rape but blamed some kind of inner voice, Frank was tempted to avenge the little girl's ordeal there and then. With no one else around as witness, Frank could put a slug between this monster's eyes and save the taxpayers the expenses of a trial. Frank released his grasp of Feathers' head and allowed it to bash down onto the asphalt. His right hand then went back to draw his Browning .38 from its holster. The volcano was now at its crescendo and Frank was being driven by his own need for personal justice. His finger vibrated and hesitated on the trigger as the eruption subsided. Silver handcuffs occupied his reappearing hand and they were forcefully applied with a ratcheting click. The children of New York would now be a little bit safer.

* * * * *

Feathers now sat in Pelma's Bar and resentfully contemplated over his eight long years in a prison cell. He thought that, one day, he would get even with Frank

Berne. Maybe Berne would have a young son or a daughter and Feathers would pay the child a little visit.

'Yes,' he thought, as he sat where he always sat. 'One day I'll get even and make up for that lost time.'

His last cigarette had barely been snuffed out and Feathers was already sticking another paper to his saliva-moistened lower lip as he methodically rubbed the raw tobacco in both palms. His mind was racing with thoughts about his newfound opportunity to make a fast buck. It wasn't every day a fancy pants dude with money to throw around would come his way and Feathers was going to make the most of this sucker.

He flipped the lid of his flint lighter and lit up the rolled cigarette with a more than adequate yellow flame. Leaning back to inhale the burning fumes into his already decaying lungs, he closed his eyes and sniffed back heavily to clear his mucous filled nasal passages. This was followed by a heaving wet cough and a projectile ball of filthy phlegm, which he spat into the corner at his feet. He watched the sucker dude return apprehensively from the lavatory and resume his stool immediately opposite. Feathers eyed him up and down and speculated as to how much he was worth.

'Know anyone who'd be interested in an easy dollar?' he had whispered cautiously into Blue Featherman's ear when he first entered the bar.

'Why, you're looking at him mister. But we all know that most easy dollar chickens eventually come home to roost, don't we?'

Feathers was proud of his clever reply. This dude now knew he wasn't talking to any half-wit.

The fancy pants dude had been told he would find a suitable candidate going by the name of 'Feathers' in that bar, and the information was correct. He had chosen the worst looking bad ass low life scumbag he could see when he approached Blue Featherman. He had a very good reason to do so. The job he needed to be performed required a person of extremely low moral virtue, a man of dubious character who might do most anything for money, someone who had little to live for and therefore little to lose.

Feathers appeared through the smoky dim light to be exactly that kind of loser. His particularly horrible nature fitted the bill precisely.

'Well, you wait right here my friend, and I'll be back in a minute to enlighten you with an idea to make a lot of money.' The dude seemed excited.

'I ain't going anywhere pal. I'll be right here where I always am.' Feathers had no intention of leaving. He wanted to fleece this slicker for all he was worth.

The unlikely duo now sat face to face, sizing each other up in their readiness to negotiate in dealings of a contemptible nature. At first, Feathers was skeptical. Was this dude a plant of some kind, meant to lead him back to prison? Could it be pure coincidence that he was talking about grabbing some child? The more this dude opened his mouth, the more Feathers was convinced he was genuine. The cops just wouldn't come up with such a smart plan. He had to be for real. When Feathers listened to the elaborate plot, he became quite excited. This wasn't a difficult task he was being asked to perform. For him, it was quite a natural thing to do.

The job entailed dressing up like a laundry guy, driving a white van into the basement car park of some classy downtown hotel, and then riding the elevator up and down for a while. He was to familiarize himself with the photograph of a little girl. When that girl entered the elevator he was to grab her and get her out to the country somewhere to an abandoned farmhouse. It all sounded too easy and he couldn't wait to get started.

Feathers tried to act nonchalant when payment for his duties was announced. This guy was offering him one hundred thousand dollars for something he would gladly do for nothing, abduct a little girl and get away with it. One hundred grand would get him out of this life and into some real action. Maybe he could go down to Florida where all those respectable folk retire and he could start a new life. Sure! This was exactly what he needed.

'And also,' Feathers was now thinking fervently, 'all those retired folk will have their grandchildren coming to visit.'

Feathers gritted his teeth and slowly shook his head. 'I ain't doing this for no lousy hundred grand. Two hundred, and maybe we got a deal.' He held his breath in anticipation.

To his amazement the bluff paid off and the dude agreed to the higher payment. The deal was struck and the plans were worked out during the next two nights. Feathers was as happy as a pig in mud.

This job had been thought about in fine detail. Nothing could possibly go wrong. It would be as easy as taking candy from a baby. Knock off a van from a nearby commercial laundry, drive the van in and under the hotel, and take the laundry cart into the elevator. The dude would make a phone call to the concierge requesting a message to be delivered to the girl's mother in the lobby. The message would supposedly be from the girl's father asking them to take the elevator to the mezzanine level restaurant.

Feathers would be waiting in the elevator with some ether, a liquid used as an anesthetic. He would disable the girl and her mother with the ether. He would place the girl into the laundry cart and take the elevator down to the car park, leaving the girl's mother down there in the trash area. He would then load the girl into the van, make a slow steady exit so as to not attract attention, and drive leisurely out of New York. His only stop along the way was to be at a pre-arranged gas station to meet up with the dude and cut off a piece of the girl's hair. No problem! Then, onto a little known country intersection called Tuxedo Junction.

From there, it was simply a matter of waiting in a deserted ramshackle farmhouse with a cell phone and the girl, waiting for the dude to come and give him his two hundred grand. Feathers wondered about how he might relieve the boredom if he was made to wait too long.

* * * * *

When the morning of the big day finally arrived, Feathers sat on the edge of his single iron bed and looked out of his window at the alleyway below. These boarding rooms had been home to him for a good part of his life. He was absent for his eight year prison term and had come straight back to them thereafter. It was time for a change and two hundred thousand dollars would certainly enable him to get out of there once and for all.

Feathers looked down at the alleyway and thought of his arrest by Frank Berne, right there on the pavement below. He determined that he had some homework to do. He had to take every possible precaution to make sure that this job was a success. This time he won't be caught. No way! No mess-ups. No more sitting in a stinking rotten prison cell thinking about the good life outside. This was his big chance and he was going to take it.

As soon as the shops opened their doors, Feathers was out there full of nervous energy. The shop assistants were frightened by his appearance when he wandered about the cosmetic counters studying the make-up and hair products. One of them contacted the store security guard who stood at a distance just waiting for Feathers to do something wrong.

'You can't arrest someone for the way they look,' the guard had responded to the counter assistant.

Feathers didn't do anything wrong. He simply purchased some cheap make-up, blush and eyeliner, then a five-minute dark brown hair dye. He then went to the pharmaceutical department for the ether, latex gloves, and trimming scissors. To finish, he made a quick visit to the clothing section for the white shirt and pants, and his shopping spree was at an end.

He sat back in his smelly room and looked into the cracked wall mirror in front of him. He had meticulously dyed his hair in the communal bathroom up the corridor and felt so embarrassed when another boarder had walked in on him. There was Feathers, standing completely naked with plastic gloves on his hands and brown dye everywhere. The old man had quickly apologized to Feathers for intruding and retraced his steps out of there. Like a fool, Feathers had painstakingly dyed his hair and beard and now he had to cut most of it off.

He studied his facial features and wondered how he was going to transform his craggy threatening appearance into that of a gentle respectable laundry employee. He reached for the scissors and started on his hair. By the time he had cut it back to a shorter length, the full beard hanging below made him look ridiculous. The more he cut off his beard, the more he had to cut off his head, until inevitably, he was gazing at a short back and sides with virtually a stubble at his chin. Next, he went to work with the make-up dabbing his pocked cheeks with the blush and touching his yellow eyebrows and lashes with the eyeliner. He then fitted comfortably into the white clothes and stepped before the mirror to review the end result. There looking back at him was a cross between Harpo Marx and a vaudeville Charlie Chaplin. In any case, it was certainly one hell of a difference to the Blue Featherman of old, and he did look fifteen years younger. Overall, he thought, not a bad transformation.

* * * * *

Feathers was a little more nervous about the proceedings than he had expected. Stealing the laundry van was the easy part. It even had an appropriate trolley cart in the back. He felt very self-conscious all dressed up in that laundry man's uniform and he was having trouble steering the stupid laundry cart along a straight course. His disguise was hardly convincing, as he looked more like a mortician, with the white uniform clinging with sweat and latex gloves on his hands.

The soaked cloth he had prepared kept drying out and his ether bottle was already half-empty. As he entered the elevator, he found himself trembling with irritability and dripping with perspiration. His state of anxiety only worsened as he waited in the elevator. Up and down it went, the doors opening and closing. Every time people would enter, they would grimace at the smell of ether, thinking that it was a dry-cleaning fluid, and show surprise that the laundry cart wasn't in the service elevator instead. Each time, Feathers would just hang his head and mumble an excuse.

'The service elevator ain't working.'

He was becoming increasingly anxious and afraid of being found out. One of the hotel guests had looked down at Featherman's feet and screwed up her nose when she saw the silver scrawled toecaps of his cowboy boots sticking out from the cuffs of his new white pants. Feathers tried to smile at her and talked with a Texas drawl.

'Howdy ma'am. You have a fine day now ma'am.'

The image of the two hundred grand and his new life in Florida helped him to persevere with his predicament. He was getting fidgety, even more nervous and impatient. Finally, when Feathers was at his wit's end, the elevator doors opened on the ground level. In stepped Casey Egan and her mother hand in hand. They both smiled apprehensively at Feathers as the doors closed and the elevator started upward.

Feathers knew that time was of the essence and he sprung into action. In a flash he had pushed a dismayed little Casey into the corner. With one hand, he smothered an ether cloth to the face of Audrey Egan and he held the ether bottle ready in his other hand to replenish the dose if need be. Everything was going to plan until Audrey's right foot swung back and then forward again to deal a forceful blow to the shinbone of her attacker. Feathers grimaced with excruciating pain as the ether bottle slipped from his hand and the cloth fell from Audrey's face. The bottle smashed on the floor below and the elevator filled with the sickening heady fumes.

Feathers himself was becoming affected and his brain was swimming.

The moment had turned to confusion as Audrey began to kick and scream and Casey wriggled from his grip. Knowing that the elevator would reach the mezzanine level at any instant, Feathers acted on impulse. He was swift and strong. His right fist delivered two full force punches to Audrey's face and she fell to the floor in an unconscious heap. He grabbed the ether cloth and smothered Casey's face as the doors parted to an empty passage. With the little girl still writhing in his hold, Feathers pushed the button for the car park level and the doors slid closed again. The girl was quickly unconscious and in the laundry cart by the time the basement had been reached. Feathers had no time for intricate details. He left the woman where she had collapsed and then bundled the girl, cart and all, into the van. With a heart pounding with excessive stimulation, he sped out and up into the busy lunchtime traffic, almost colliding with a yellow taxi at the top of the ramp.

'Goddamn maniac!' he heard the taxi driver shout. 'Where'd you get your license? In a Goddamn lottery?'

It wasn't a pretty job, but he had pulled it off. Blue Featherman thought of Florida and grinned like a madman as he drove away from The Icelandic Hotel and headed out of Manhattan in the direction of Tuxedo Junction.

CHAPTER 7

This is going to be one hell of a night. I have trouble sleeping at the best of times, even when I have little cause to worry. Tonight won't be any exception. My heart is still racing like a wind-up toy and I'm too tired and too worked up to sleep. I've just parted with Sharyn after a knee trembling embrace and there's a segment of my mind that wants her with me tonight. I know it seems inconsistent with the trauma of Audrey's death and Casey's abduction, but some things just feel right. In any case, my tortured mind won't permit the added complexity of passion and desire to intrude, and it will probably have to wait until my daughter is safe and sound.

I'm doomed to this state of uncertainty about Casey's return, and it's driving me crazy. I feel so completely helpless, and it's a situation I'm not accustomed to. God damn the mongrel bastards for violating my family like this. I don't even know if Casey's alive. If they've hurt my princess, I'll send them to hell with my own hands. I can only hope and pray for some divine intervention to keep her protected from harm. I do know that most kidnappers keep their subject in one piece, so as to prove life for ransom. This seems little comfort however, when I think about the letter and the threat to chop off Casey's precious little fingers.

This is the first time I've had to deal with the death of someone close since my parents passed away, and I'm really not coping with it. Although we were separated and then divorced three years ago now, Audrey is still very much in my heart. Our times together were so happy and memorable and, after all, she is Casey's mother. I haven't yet been able to make any sense of it, and my whole abdominal diaphragm senses a strange void. It feels like a torpedo has passed straight through my midsection and left a huge gaping hole.

When I try to rationalize what's happened, it all seems so surreal and unfair. It's more a matter of feeling so very, very sorry for Audrey. It's a complete waste of her beautiful young life just when she had everything to live for. She's going to miss out on so much and it seems so very unjust.

My apartment, normally a comforting sanctuary from the hustle and bustle of business life, now seems cold and uninviting as I enter its portal alone and dejected. My mindset is not helped when everywhere there are photographs of the people dearest to me. There's my wedding photo with Audrey. I've kept it there mainly for Casey's benefit. Then, there's the family snapshot with Audrey, Casey and myself. Also, I look to the side bureau at my daughter's school portrait and my heart feels completely wrung out.

I fix my gaze on a painted oil portrait of Audrey and Casey, framed in gold leaf and hanging ominously at the end of the entrance hall. Audrey rests, elegantly poised amidst a beautiful flowerbed of yellow roses. At her side sits Casey, draped in lilac fabric with her buttercup hair cascading down around her shoulders. To the rear of the garden, there's a row of Roman columns intertwined with green and white jasmine vines. Audrey's wearing a lovely white summer dress and her long blonde curls are adorned with a tiara band of yellow daisies. Her calm expression and placid smile exemplify the pure innocence of an angel.

I stare in awe, transfixed on the portrait of mother and daughter. Rays of sunlight are streaming down and bathing them both in a golden hue. The whole scene indicates a period of peace and contentment. I'm angry that present circumstances are so very different, and I think of how one's fortunes can change in an instant. Audrey has had her beautiful life snuffed out by one evil action, and what mental and physical abuse Casey is undergoing, only God knows.

I resurrect my sensibility and I'm gradually aware of another strange and overwhelming sensation. Why is it that today, I feel like a foreigner in my own home? This apartment always welcomes me as I make my way into its huge expanse. Nine thousand square feet of my own making, decorated in my favorite style, and furnished with my own handpicked enumerated bits and pieces. Although I choose to live in Manhattan, I've been able to recreate a little bit of Sedona Arizona right here in New York City.

Around me now in this grand entrance hallway, are rustic timber beams against yellow ocher stucco. The furniture is handmade in the style of old Mexico and several decaying steer horns overhang beige terracotta flooring. The theme continues with subtle variation as I move from room to room until I reach the three thousand square feet of master living area. Visitors invariably gasp in disbelief when they enter the slightly sunken lounge area. Surrounding them on three sides is an impressive gallery of proud buffalo heads separated by Native American Indian headdress. The other wall has a bulky centrally positioned stone fireplace with books shelved on both sides. Above the fireplace, in splendid color and detail, hangs a gigantic oil painting on canvas depicting 'Custer's Last Stand'.

It's not the décor everyone would like, but it's what pleases me and makes me feel comfortable. I can usually breathe a sigh of relief when I come home to my familiar surroundings. Why is it that I'm feeling so uncomfortable right now? Is it just because of the trauma of today's events or is it simply my imagination? Goddamn it, I do have a sixth sense and it's telling me now, that somebody else has been in this apartment. Maybe they're still here.

I painstakingly move from one room to another and I can tell there's been an intruder. The hairs on the back of my neck are now standing on end and my heartbeat is quickening with every step. As I pass through the library, my hand instinctively goes inside my pocket and retrieves the forgotten paper knife. My thumb slides the blade forward and I continue into the master bedroom. I can see that the housemaid has completed her daily cleaning routine and everything is positioned correctly. I'm used to the housemaid coming in each day and that's not what I'm sensing now. It's not a scent in the air. It's not a sound I'm hearing. My eyes are satisfied that things are in place and as they should be. My mind however, is telling me another story. Someone has paid me a visit and they're hiding in this apartment.

I know I'm tired and exhausted but I'm not going crazy. I've searched every room now and I'm the only person here. I think! I've ended up back in the lounge area and I slide the silver paper knife shut and put it back into my pocket. I slump down into the comfortable folds of a leather sofa with the glazed eyes of ten buffalo watching over me. Sometimes, I imagine that an eye blinks or an ear twitches. It must be my mind playing tricks because they're all winking and twitching now.

Even the huge timber beams that divide the ceiling seem to be creaking and groaning. I really need some shuteye, but more than that, I need a stiff drink or maybe two.

I sit forward now to remove my jacket and kick off my shoes. Yes, that feels better. The two cell phones are digging into my sides so I dislodge them and place them next to me on the side table, making sure that they're still on and fully charged. The crystal decanter tinkles as the golden liquid of Glenfiddich Special Old Reserve pure malt whiskey flows generously into a cut crystal glass. 'My God, that's Heaven on Earth.' I whisper to the nearest buffalo after savoring my first taste.

The fireplace leaps into action when I press the appropriate button on the side panel and I can now relax to the crackling of burning embers. A serious scotch drinker will drink it neat, at room temperature with no ice, and I'm a serious scotch drinker. The hypnotic tranquilizing effect of the Glenfiddich scotch is almost immediate and after sipping a second drink down, the buffalo are becoming more animated and agitated. The flames in the fireplace appear as dancing ballerinas in orange and crimson costumes, and George Custer is lashing out with his saber as the battle rages at Little Bighorn.

I'm on my third scotch and deciding it had better be my last. My body is heavy and uncoordinated as I drag myself to my feet. After taking one final gulp, I stagger towards the master bedroom and the disapproving buffalo heads shake in violent protest. They seem to be warning me that my sixth sense is correct and I'm not alone in this apartment. I hope that the buffalo are mistaken because I'm in no shape to defend myself now. I'm lucky to be able to get myself to bed, but get to bed I shall.

One of the most difficult tasks a man has to perform is to get satisfactorily out of his clothes and under the sheets when he's completely exhausted of any energy and intoxicated with pure malt whiskey. I grit my teeth, and with one struggling determined effort, manage to finally fling away my last item of clothing and collapse into bed. I'm asleep as my head hits the pillow.

* * * * *

Insomniacs complain of a strange phenomenon, that of being so tired that their body is crying out for rest, of being physically incapable of keeping their eyes open, and of being literally asleep on their feet. In this extreme condition of debilitation, they are only able to remain asleep for one or two hours before they once again are awake to the curse of insomnia. I don't usually have trouble staying asleep for a while after downing three glasses of Glenfiddich premium malt, so I'm somewhat surprised when my eyelids stretch wide open and I stare at the ceiling of my dimly lit bedroom. I must have been asleep for a couple of hours because I'm feeling more sober and relatively alert.

'Did I hear that sound or not?'

My hands explore my body under the covers and I realize that I'm completely undressed. A cold shiver shoots down my spine and my whole body is covered with an outbreak of goose bumps. I should have heeded the buffalos' warning and now it's too late. Have the murdering kidnappers come to take their revenge? Have they come to kill me? I feel so vulnerable in my nakedness that I want to hide my head under the bedclothes like a frightened child. Several options flood my mind in an instant. Grab the side lamp as a weapon? Roll out of bed and into the corner? Get under the bed? What am I thinking?

There's another swishing sound from the opposite side of the bedroom and the open doors slightly sway with an eerie groan. I sit bolt upright in bed with my whole body now trembling in a state of terror.

'Who's there? What do you want?' My eyes are staring at the open doorway and I try to sound authoritative and confident.

There's a stream of dim yellow light coming in from the lounge area and I see a figure moving around the leather sofa where my jacket and shoes had been left. The pale figure now moves to one side and disappears from my view. I hear another swishing sound and a shudder goes through my soul. I want to react in some clever way to defend myself from harm but my mind is in neutral and my body is in a state of paralysis. I can only sit with my sight transfixed on the open illuminated doorway and wait for my fate to be determined.

In one flowing movement, the intruder reappears and enters my bedroom. The figure stands before me now, the darkened face indistinguishable and silhouetted by the yellow light of the lounge room and framed by the dark surrounds of the open doorway. I'm astonished that my fear is suspended because the outline before me has a peculiar familiarity. My brain is desperately grasping for some kind of resolution. Who is this person? Why is there a sense of recognition?

'Who are you?' I whisper.

The figure takes one steady step backwards and the silhouette is no more. The light shines down in front and the identity is revealed. I can now understand why there were swishing noises and the figure seemed pale and white.

The lady standing before me is wearing a long white funeral shroud and around her blonde tangled hair I can clearly see a tiara of yellow daisies, the same tiara of daisies I often gaze at in the portrait painting at the end of the entrance hall. Her face is youthful and beautiful with the same lovely calm expression and serene smile. Rays of golden hue bath her features. My eyes follow the length of her slender figure downwards and I notice that her feet are not touching the floor. She's positioned in the space around her and she's hanging in graceful suspension.

'Is that you Audrey?' I ask softly.

'Joe, he means to kill our little girl.' Her voice is as soft as velvet to my ears.

'Who does? Audrey? Who wants to kill her?' My body is now completely at ease and I perceive a wonderful inner peace in Audrey's spiritual presence.

'Don't believe him Joe. Don't trust him.' Her voice is so soft.

'Who? Audrey? Who is it?'

'Joe, you must find Casey and help her. He intends to kill her no matter what you give him.'

'I will help her Audrey. I will save her. Who wants to kill her? Please Audrey! Tell me who wants to kill her.'

Audrey's image becomes transparent and begins to flicker. The shower of light from above her figure grows dim. I can see she's smiling at me once again and then she completely vanishes from my sight.

'Who is it? Please Audrey! Who is it?' I'm still asking her and I can hear her fading words.

'Joe. It's him. The man in black.'

Audrey's voice is nothing but a whisper as she answers. The bedroom doors slowly close and then there's absolute tranquility with nothing to be seen or heard. She's gone and the room is in complete darkness. I'm trying to focus on what she had just told me and I rehearse the words over and over in my mind.

'The man in black. The man in black. The man in black.'

The words have a hypnotic effect and I slump back into the soft downy pillows. I shut my eyes again and start to feel drowsy. Audrey's words of warning are fading from my mind as I drift away into a deep sleep.

* * * * *

I have the sensation that time has passed and that I've been actively dreaming through troubled sleep. My mind is aware that I'm once again awake but I have to keep my eyes closed. They're quite heavy and there's a slight ache at the base of their sockets. I stare into the back of my eyelids, and the dark void has turned to a morning glow. I need to just lay here in these comfortable satin sheets and think about what I've experienced. My God! Have I witnessed a miracle? Was I hallucinating? If it was a dream, it was so real and clear that my whole life may just as well be a dream. I know this kind of thing does happen.

People often talk about strange occurrences after the death of somebody very close and personal. Sometimes, it's an apparition of the spirit or a vision of some meaningful supernatural phenomena. Usually, it's an unexplained drop of water on the forehead or a familiar voice in the night offering a word of cautionary advice.

I gradually open my eyes and re-enter the reality of my earthly existence. I realize that my Rolex is still around my wrist and that it's the only attachment to my naked body. Audrey's words are ringing in my ears. 'The man in black. The man in black.'

I'm haunted by the dream of Audrey's spirit and confused by the heavenly message it conveyed. The man in black could be anyone at all. Almost everyone wears black at some time or another, and the New York business yuppies often do. I don't see how that advice can possibly be of help. It only serves to confuse me more. Was it just a dream floating down from the heavens, or did it really and truly happen? I decide that there is no resolution. I should accept the fact that miracles are performed by the hand of God and therefore no answers are required.

'The cell phones! Where are the cell phones?' I glance at my wristwatch to realize that I've been asleep for at least ten hours. My mind switches to a fully awakened state. I have to help Casey. With a leap, I'm up out of bed and running into the lounge room. There I find my two cell phones, right where I had left them, next to the leather sofa. I grab the standby kidnapper's cell phone to inspect its screen.

1 MISSED CALL

Goddamn it! That vitally important call. The call register declares an unknown origin, probably a public phone in the city. My heart is heavy with despair and I sit down into the sofa to think about the situation.

The very first and simplest task I was to perform was to await their call and receive further instructions. I can't believe that I've failed already. The thought of Casey suffering because of my negligence is too much to bear and I promise myself that the cell phone will stay on my person at all times, an extension of my body. I have no option but to wait and hope that their horrible threat is not carried out, and that Casey will have another chance. I insert the charging lead to restore the battery to full life and then settle down to wait for another call.

It's not long before a piercing ring tone sends a cold chill down my spine and I'm fumbling to pick up and answer without dropping the cell phone in the process.

'Hello,.. Joseph Egan here.' I'm answering into the wrong dormant cell phone and it's my normal phone that continues to ring. Disappointed and relieved at the same time, I change phones to respond.

'Yes, Joe here.'

'Good morning Mr. Egan. It's Andrew. I'm at the office. Are you all right?' Andrew's voice sounds slightly distressed.

'Good morning Andrew. Yes I'm fine. Is everything on track down there?'

'Yes sir. All the accounts are fine and I'm expecting Sharyn to arrive any second. But Mr. Egan, I had to call you immediately. Another letter similar to the first in appearance has been delivered.'

'Andrew? Is it… Is it flat? No wait. Don't! Don't handle it. Just wait for me to get down there.'

'That's fine sir. It's on your desk and we'll wait for you.'

Before I do anything I decide that I have to be fresh and alert. A good shower and shave, some new clothes, and I can make a clean start to the challenge confronting me. With a fully charged cell phone in each jacket side-pocket and my paper knife securely in my pants pocket, I'm as rested and prepared as I'm going to be, and I make my way to the door.

I spend an emotional moment in the entrance hall staring at the portrait of Audrey and Casey. Casey's eyes appear to have a certain sadness about them now and I find myself counting her fingers. With a cold chill down my spine, I change my gaze to Audrey's features. The smile is still there but her expression seems less tranquil and serene, as though she's once again trying to warn me of impending danger. I realize that my hand has a tight hold around the paper knife and my resolve is reaffirmed to do whatever it takes to avenge her death and save our daughter.

CHAPTER 8

Sharyn was surprised that another envelope had been delivered because she was only really expecting any further communication to be by way of the cell phone in Joe's possession. She stood at Joe's desk and studied the new envelope. The outward appearance didn't indicate anything other than folded paper to be enclosed, and the text was once again cut and pasted from newsprint. She heeded Andrew's advice and made sure not to disturb it in any way, as she anxiously waited for Joe to arrive.

It wasn't long before Joe entered and she heard him greet Andrew in the main administration area, before striding towards his own office. When he appeared in the doorway, she walked towards him and smiled generously. She was so very pleased to see the man she loved, and she immediately noticed that he did indeed look fresh and alert. It was obvious that he had regained his vitality and readiness.

'Good morning Sharyn. It's so good to see your lovely face.' The words could have been set to music as far as Sharyn was concerned.

She beamed a full smile back to him and he gave her a brief hug with one arm as he passed.

'Good morning Mr. Egan,' Sharyn joked and then she quickly regained her composure.

'Have you received any phone calls from the kidnappers, Joe?'

'Well, I'm sorry to say that I haven't spoken to them and I hope that's not bad for Casey.' Joe's voice had changed and it was shaky with emotion.

He sat down in his chair and Sharyn resumed her now familiar position at his desk, seated on one corner with one shapely leg drawn up and crossed over the other. Joe studied the envelope carefully and with trembling hands, picked it up to feel for its contents. The outer inscription looked the same as before. Joe retrieved the other envelope from his drawer to compare the two. They were almost identical with the same words.

TO BE OPENED ONLY BY JOSEPH EGAN

Joe still could not relax even though no sinister lumps were present and he now thought he would be spared the horror of finding human flesh inside.

'Was this envelope delivered with the office mail as before?' Joe looked at Sharyn nervously.

'The doorman, Leslie, called up and said it had been delivered to him. He couldn't remember who or when.' Sharyn thought about the significance, if any, of this information.

The cogs in Joe's head were turning slowly and systematically and he wondered again if he should call Frank Berne to help him get out of this mess. So far, his own handling of the situation had not been very impressive. However, he guessed that Frank Berne would react in an unsympathetic way if Joe rang him now. By not informing the police initially, Joe had burnt some of his bridges, and he now felt he was almost committed to go it alone. He decided that it was the better course of action.

From the inside of his pocket, he withdrew the paper knife, flashed the blade, and meticulously trimmed open the edge of the envelope. With his fingertips he withdrew a single folded foolscap page, which he carefully straightened by using the small blade. The newsprint was evenly pasted in the center of the page.

ONE MISTAKE EQUALS ONE FINGER
MAKE SURE YOU ANSWER THE NEXT CALL

These few words were all that was needed to return Joe to his previous state of agitation. His hand tightened around the paper knife.

'What the hell do they mean by that, Sharyn? Does that mean they've cut off one finger?' He was furious at the double meaning and his inability to question them about it.

'Well no, Joe, it doesn't say that and I'd suggest that Casey still has all of her fingers. Otherwise we'd be looking at one of them now, my dear, dear Joe.' Sharyn was trying to sound reassuring.

'It's not going to help if we presume the worst, Joe. We have to think positively and our hope will keep her alive and safe.'

'Yes Sharyn. Thank you. You're right of course.' He squeezed her hand within his hand, and with the other, replaced the paper knife into his pocket.

Joe knew that it would take more than hope to keep Casey alive and he felt with his fingertips for the two cell phones in the side pockets of his jacket.

'Enough of this. We should get out of this office. There's really nothing we can do except wait for the phone call and then I have to be in good shape. Let's get some fresh air, if such a thing exists in Manhattan. Some food wouldn't go astray now. We have to keep our blood sugar levels up, you know.' Joe was trying to perk himself up, but he was also famished.

'How does some brunch sound to you Sharyn?'

Sharyn smiled at him and nodded eagerly.

'All right then. Brunch it is. I know just the right place.' Joe was happy and comfortable to be with Sharyn and it was apparent.

Leslie glared at them as they crossed the foyer towards the exit.

'Good morning Mr. Egan Sir. Miss Cooper. When do we get to see Miss Casey?' His words were happy and convincing.

'Leslie. Good morning. We'll see her soon now. Leslie, can you recall who delivered that envelope to you this morning? The suspicious one?' Joe looked straight into Leslie's eyes for any clue of deceitfulness.

'No recollection whatsoever Sir. I've already informed Miss Cooper.' With that he opened the door and stood to one side.

'Walking today Sir?' Leslie was talking more like a robot with every passing day.

'Yes Leslie. Lovely spring weather. We shouldn't waste it.'

* * * * *

The morning was bright and clear as the couple stepped out onto the pavement of Park Avenue. Sharyn's arm instinctively curled around Joe's arm and their pace quickened. It was obvious at that moment that there was no where else they would rather be.

The glow of sunlight was a welcome reprive from intermittent showers, and Joe and Sharyn were so glad to be outside in the fresh spring atmosphere. They felt a warmth and invigoration to be in each other's company. Sharyn knew it and understood her own feelings completely. Joe was well aware that it felt so right and so good, but he was yet to fully comprehend where it was leading. No words were spoken. At that moment, things were better left unsaid. As they walked arm in arm, they were conscious of the secure physical and mental attachment that means happiness, and that's all that mattered.

You could say that Joe and Sharyn were the perfect couple. They just looked good together and that was that. Joe was the pinnacle of style and taste in black wool and cotton-blend slacks. His accessories were well chosen, black fine leather shoes and belt from 'Ferrand', his favorite shoe store adjacent to the Trevi Fountain in Rome, pure white linen shirt by 'Daniel Corot' of Paris, and a blue silk necktie embossed with a pattern of spun gold link. He was wearing the jacket he chose for himself from the parade catwalk whilst attending the Paris fashion awards last year, a simple but elegant 'Pierre Cardin' silk and wool double breasted in silver and black thread.

Sharyn had followed her heart rather than her head and once again was dressed to be the feminine lady. Her delicate figure looked as smooth as fine bone china in a pale blue nomadic chic skirt with a white chiffon blouse and white satin jacket. Her appearance was well worthy of the location as she stepped along Park Avenue in her dark blue crystal-encrusted strappy heels by 'Louis Vuitton'.

The handsome couple headed westward and stepped across Madison Avenue toward Central Park. They were enjoying the experience so much that they extended their walk by turning south to pass the elegant stores of Fifth Avenue. Sharyn was so happy to simply follow Joe's lead. She just adored his maturity and strength of character and she couldn't imagine feeling as safe and comfortable with any other man.

Joe thought his mind was playing tricks on him when he found himself pulling Sharyn across to the display window of the prestigious 'Emmanuel Fifth Avenue Jewelers'. He also noticed that she wasn't resisting and that her hold of his arm was slightly firmer.

'What are you doing Joe?' Sharyn asked innocently.

Joe really didn't know what he was doing. He had acted on impulse and he blushed with embarrassment. In his confusion, he was aware of his powerful desire to please Sharyn and to shower her with gifts. He also knew that his life was so very packed with Casey's dilemma, that his powers of reasoning were being scrambled. He even thought of proposing to Sharyn there and then, and had to grit his teeth in restraint.

'You know Sharyn, I just love jewelry. I admire the workmanship. Look at these diamonds. Do you like diamonds?'

'You're asking a lady if she likes diamonds?' asked Sharyn with a laugh. 'I thought you were hungry?'

Joe was feeling a different kind of hunger right now. It had been some time since he had been so close to a woman and his body was telling him that it had been long enough. He was now aware of a very strong physical attraction to the lady in his company, a force that was overwhelming him, and it was a feeling that could not be denied. He had liked Sharyn since the day he met her, liked her as a person, and admired her intelligence and talent. Now he was entering a new dimension. He was beginning to fall in love with her. He wondered if she was meant to be, whether she was put on this Earth for him, and him only. Was it their destiny to fall in love? Was she in love with him? The passion of their embrace certainly seemed like a recipe for love. One thing was now clear to him. He wanted more of her, and soon!

They stood hand in hand like two children looking into a sweet shop window. Prominently on display, was one of the finest galleries of exquisite jewelry in the country. Bracelets, earrings and pendants in gold and platinum were adorned with every type of brilliant gemstone imaginable. Glistening rays of colored light beamed from the many rubies, emeralds and sapphires lining the crystal glass shelves.

Sharyn's eyes were dancing with fascination at the dazzling exquisite diamond necklaces draped from the back row of Egyptian busts. Her hand squeezed Joe's in her excitement. Joe, being the ultimate businessman, was mesmerized by the loose diamonds. Each one was perched on an ultra thin glass needle tower especially blown for the purpose. As though protruding forward into space, before his eyes were stones finely finished in Belgium by the world's master diamond cutters, diamonds that were cut to exacting mathematical proportions to show maximum brilliance.

Joe liked jewelry. Oh yes. However, his passion was diamonds. In diamonds he recognized the true investment value of a precious commodity. Here before him, was a wonderful example of the finest diamonds available, and also the most expensive. He liked their versatility, such great value represented in tiny objects, compact and easily taken from one place to another, saleable anywhere in the world, and the object of every woman's desire.

Although Joe had always fancied the white brilliant cut stones from the African mines, he couldn't take his eyes of a huge pink diamond of about four carats that was centered in the display. It would have originated from the

Australian Argyle mines, now becoming famous for the production of pink stones.

Joe glanced down at his Rolex, itself circled with small brilliant diamonds at every hour mark, and saw the time was almost 10.30 a.m. He started to think of his little girl and wondered how he could be looking at diamonds at a time like this. Audrey was dead, Casey was in peril and he had been thinking of material things. Was he mad?

Joe knew too well that human relationships, family and love were of supreme importance. A new Cadillac doesn't create ultimate happiness. In fact some of the happiest people Joe had known were moderately poor. Look at his parents and his own childhood. A life of struggling poverty had also been a world of inner happiness. Yet some of the wealthiest people he had known were also the saddest. Many of their lives were plagued with dreary depression and introspection. They accumulate material assets in their quest for happiness and shy away from human contact. Although incredibly wealthy in his own right, Joe knew in his heart that the real source of happiness could only be found in the love of friends and relatives.

Joe was ready to sacrifice every material object in his possession if it meant saving Casey from harm. He had been enjoying his morning with Sharyn, yet his soul wept for Casey. He had been feeling good, and now he felt guilty for feeling good. Maybe the human heart has many facets just like a brilliant cut diamond. Maybe it can feel joy, sorrow, love and pain all at the same time, and still beat on in wondrous perplexity.

'We should be going, or brunch will turn into lunch,' he whispered.

'Yes Joe, why don't we continue?' Sharyn was aware of a slight shift in Joe's mood and she knew he was thinking of Casey.

Together they continued to stroll and turned north as they took in the sights and sounds of Fifth Avenue. They could smell the apple blossoms as they crossed to the large iron gates of Central Park. Through the park they walked as perfumed garden beds filled their senses with rows of yellow tulips in full spring bloom. Apart from the happy birds twittering in the overhanging trees, the park was peaceful and quiet. Sharyn and Joe paced in step, past a reflecting pool filled with water lilies and lingering goldfish. Sharyn delighted in the solitude, and knew she had found her Shangri-La with the man she held so close to her side.

As they approached their destination, Joe retrieved the cell phones from his jacket and inspected the screens for network coverage and serviceability. Satisfied that they were in order, he replaced them both and inadvertently felt the razor sharp paper knife in his pants side-pocket.

'A little bit of heaven right here in New York City.' His right hand now moved from his pocket and squeezed Sharyn's arm. 'Look there!'

Of all the restaurants he had visited, 'The Tavern on the Green' was the prettiest and most romantic establishment in Manhattan. Joe could think of no better venue for dinner than its elegant Crystal Room. It was a celebration of light and reflection with the shimmering crystal chandeliers and a fabulous semi-circular vista of the park gardens. For a fine brunch however, Joe knew that an intimate affair such as this required the sumptuous Park Room. There, they could dine a-la-carte beneath antique

Baccarat chandeliers in a private garden surrounding a period fountain.

Joe was recognized immediately by the headwaiter and the service began, not too intrusive, not disrupting, but there. They had absolute privacy, yet their glasses were replenished and the table silently rearranged as need be. The food was light and nourishing with Scandinavian smoked salmon and avocado sandwiches complimented with two glasses of Moet et Chandon champagne. Small crystal goblets of lemon sorbet with chocolate wafer were then served to cleanse the palate and the aroma of steaming African blend coffee stimulated the senses. 'The Tavern on the Green' was a magical experience and Sharyn's eyes sparkled as she reveled in the luxury.

'What do you have planned Joe, when they call? Do you have any ideas what to suggest?' She forced a little smile, which then turned into a look of concern.

'No idea at all. I can only plan to be as mentally alert as possible to make an assessment of any instructions and respond in the most optimum way. It's then that I'll have to think on my feet, be flexible in my handling of these people, and most of all, remain focused on my temperament. I must keep a lid on my temper.' Joe was shaking his head.

Sharyn made herself ask, 'Do you think you will have to give them a ransom of some kind?'

'I guess that will eventuate, but I wouldn't be surprised if the kidnappers don't even know what they want themselves. They're probably making it up as they go.' Joe was now thinking of the dream.

'Sharyn. In my drunken slumber last night, I dreamt that Audrey came to see me. I wasn't going to tell you about it, but it was so real and so weird, I have to tell someone.' Joe was straining with emotion and he went on.

'It was powerful, dramatic and haunting, but at the same time it was calming and serene. She came to me as such a vivid image. Have you ever had a dream so stark in reality, you were unsure whether or not it really happened?'

'I think everyone has dreams like that Joe, especially after the loss of a loved one. Your mind is so active, it's a wonder you can sleep at all.'

'I remember every detail by heart. In the dream, she told me to beware of a man in black. I know it sounds crazy. Surely it's meaningless. Everyone wears black. Look at the waiters in this restaurant. They're all wearing black.'

'Time will tell us the answers. Dreams are an extension of our subconscious. Maybe the man in black represents your subconscious fear of the unknown. You poor darling!' Sharyn felt pity for Joe and rubbed his hand as she spoke.

'Well, that could account for it. But, I'll never forget any of it until the day I die. What happened to me was astonishing, and I wanted to tell you about it. There's really nobody else for me to talk to about something like that.'

'I'm glad that you've decided to share with me Joe. You know, Audrey's only been gone for a day. It's natural for you to be grieving. You were together for a long time.'

'That's true, but we've also been apart for a long time. Still, a portion of my heart belongs to her and it always will.' Joe looked at Sharyn for approval.

'I understand that. You wouldn't be the man you are if you didn't feel something. That's why I love you.'

The minute the words slipped from her mouth, Sharyn bit her lip and gently bowed her head toward her lap.

Joe could see her lingering embarrassment, and saved the moment by taking both of her hands in his and whispering softly.

'Thank you Sharyn. I love you too.'

They sat there in silence breathing faintly with her hands cupped in his and two hearts pounding steadily. Neither of them knew what to say next and seconds seemed like minutes. The beauty of the moment had overwhelmed them both. They were mesmerized by their own feelings and they barely noticed anything else around them.

Joe's heart jumped in his chest when the simultaneous vibrations and alarming ring tone of the kidnapper's cell phone suddenly shattered the tranquility.

'What the hell!' he exclaimed loudly as his position shifted.

Sharyn knew that she must not make a sound as Joe reached into his jacket pocket and then raised the tiny phone to speak.

'Yes, Joseph Egan here.'

The voice was barely distinguishable, as it was low in volume and monotone in pitch. It sounded as though it was synthetically produced and electronically altered. Joe placed his finger in his opposite ear and strained to listen. His right index finger felt for the volume button on the side of the phone and the clarity improved.

'You are to follow these instructions precisely if you wish to see your daughter again. We will exchange the girl for an amount of ten million dollars packed into soft sports equipment bags.'

'But the weight........' Joe's answer was cut short.

The synthetic machine filtered voice continued over his. He quickly concluded that he was listening to a taped recording and he stopped speaking immediately as the voice continued.

'If you inform the police or try to deceive us in any way, your daughter will be harmed. Remember one mistake equals one finger. Be sure to have the money ready by nine o'clock tonight. Remember, unmarked one hundred dollar bills packed into soft sports equipment bags. Await our further instructions on this phone and once again, NO COPS! ....If you wish to leave a message, speak after the tone.'

Joe was amazed at what he was hearing. He had to think quickly and get some kind of message through to these kidnappers. The tone sounded and he spoke affirmatively.

'Do you know how much ten million dollars weighs? It would take five bags. I need more time. More time! Please! Please! Don't touch my daughter. She's only nine years old. She's a baby. I'll meet your demands, but if you harm her I'll.........I'll.....' Joe was saved from saying the wrong thing as the voice machine on the other end of the line clicked off and the line was dead.

Joe desperately tried to retrieve the number on the cell phone register. The call was once again of unknown origin. These clever people had meticulously arranged for themselves to be untraceable. Yes, they were intelligent and evil at the same time. Joe was dealing with the worst kind of criminals. It appeared that there was more than one involved. It was possibly a gang of professionals. Then again, a lone kidnapper would also use the plural sense 'us' in his threats. This would intimidate the relatives and strengthen his position. Maybe a single shrewd individual was responsible for all this chaos and terror.

Joe looked at Sharyn as he placed the cell phone back into his jacket pocket. He could see the tears welling in her beautiful eyes and he wanted to kiss them away. Sharyn was afraid to speak and waited for Joe to absorb what he had heard.

'Sharyn, they want ten million dollars packed in soft sports equipment bags. It's impracticable. It was a re-cording. I couldn't even speak to them.'

'That's GOOD news! It means she's still alive.'

'We hope she's still alive Sharyn. In the dream, Au-drey warned me that they intend to kill Casey, in spite of any ransom payoff.' Joe looked beaten.

'Come on Joe. This is not over yet. Stay positive. You always tell me that winners never quit and quitters never win.'

Sharyn knew that the best way she could help Joe was to inspire him with new hope and resolve, always the woman behind the man. Joe firmed his resolve.

'Well we don't have much time. Ten million dollars in all those bags is a challenge in itself. I'll have to find gigantic bags and then we'll need a forklift to carry them. Surely they would be better off if the money was packed into a vehicle and the vehicle was delivered to them.' Joe was actually planning a better way for the criminals to succeed. He was astonished. Whose side was he on? He quickly determined that he was on the side of Casey, and a successful execution of the ransom delivery was in her best interests. He should inform the kidnappers of his im-provement to their plan, but how? Maybe when they next called he would have the opportunity to leave another message. He must be prepared in advance and have the message written down. It should be concise and to the point, as the time interval allowed for a response was barely sufficient. His message had to also convey confidence and co-operation to give the kidnappers a sense of well being and achievement. To upset them would be to endanger Casey. If their plot failed, they would probably kill her. He concluded that he must do everything in his power to help them succeed.

Joe gestured to the waiter that they had completed the meal and he promptly came forward to attend to Sharyn's chair. The young man's eyes sparkled when he noticed the one hundred dollar bill that Joe had left for a tip.

'Thank you so much sir. Do you require transport?' the headwaiter asked as he escorted them towards the exit.

'No thank you. We'd prefer to walk today. The meal was delicious.'

'Very well Mr. Egan. And, thank you Ma'am. Have a pleasant afternoon.' Sharyn couldn't help but speculate that the man talking to them was dressed entirely in black.

* * * * *

Joe and Sharyn stepped out onto the cobblestone driveway leading away from the restaurant and Joe's mind was humming with activity. He had tasks to perform and plans to prepare. Most urgently he had to make arrangements for the money. This was an enormous sum to deliver in paper. Amounts of tens of millions of dollars were always transferred electronically and they usually appeared as typed figures on ledgers and balance sheets. Seldom was the actual paper money required.

What would his bank manager think of this? Joe thought. He concluded that it didn't matter what the bank thought. It was Joe's money, and he could do with it as he wished. He decided that time was of the essence and that he should hail the first available taxicab to expedite their journey to the bank.

'Stuyvesant Chase Bank on First and Fifteenth please driver.' Joe was feeling for his own cell phone as the taxi leapt forward.

He dialed the offices of Egan Enterprises and was pleased to hear Andrew's voice on the line.

'Is there anything to report Andrew? Both Sharyn and I will be away from the office, probably all day.'

'No Mr. Egan. Everything's running smoothly, as you would prefer. You can rely on me sir.'

Joe was pleased that he needn't be concerned with the business affairs. Andrew attended to every detail with a rare dedication to duty.

'Andrew. I need to accumulate ten million dollars in one hundred dollar bills. The money has to be carried by me in several sports equipment bags, but I'm telling you Andrew, I don't know how we can accomplish it. Don't ask me why or how. I just have to do it. The bags would have to be very large and I don't have time to have them custom made.'

'I understand. I'll get onto it immediately. You say several sports bags?' Andrew seemed diligent as always.

'Yes Andrew. That's correct. I'll attend to the sports bags. I want you to adjust the accounts. I don't know how you're going to do it, but the money has to disappear from our balance sheet and not be subject to any future federal inquiry. Do you understand what I mean?' Joe knew that if anyone could achieve such a miracle of accounting, it would be Andrew.

'I know precisely what you mean sir. Leave it to me.'

'Okay. I'm on my way to the bank now. Can you call them and have the money arranged in advance?' Joe was now thinking at fever pitch.

'I'll do that immediately sir. The amount should come from our number four account.'

'Thank you Andrew.' With that Joe ended the call and began to speculate what the driver was making of all this. Taxi drivers were generally good people but he had to wonder how many criminal plots originated from overheard conversations from the rear seats of taxicabs.

Joe sat back and rubbed shoulders with Sharyn to do some plotting of his own. He contemplated various options. If he had the money vacuum packed into wrapped plastic and used the largest parachute type sports bags fitted with custom made roller wheels, he may just be able to comply with a ransom delivery on his own. Otherwise, he could convince them that a delivery vehicle was needed. Maybe it would be best to stall for more time and have the bags custom made.

No mention had been made of the method of delivery, and without this information Joe was unsure of the best option. In any case, he needed to establish the exact dimensions of ten million dollars stacked in one hundred dollar bills, and he thought that the bank should be able to provide that measurement.

The kidnapper's cell phone erupted again and Joe grappled for the handset to hopefully have an opportunity to ask for information. This time, when Joe pressed the phone to his ear, the electronic voice he heard was an improvement over the previous recording in both volume and clarity. Sharyn cuddled closer to Joe's shoulder and moved her ear close to his. She regretted her action when Joe shook his head and fidgeted away from her. He wanted to concentrate one hundred percent on the phone call, and some personal space was required. He listened intently.

'There is a change to our instructions. For the return of your daughter, our demand is for ten million dollars equivalent value in cut precious diamonds. The diamonds are to be a selection of loose brilliant cut stones between one carat to five carats in size. They must be of high quality and color and made available for delivery in a silver colored aluminum attaché case. The diamonds will be graded and valued by us prior to the release of the girl. Have the diamonds available by nine o'clock tonight and wait for our call.'

Joe waited for the voice to continue. It was obvious his previous message had hit home and he wanted to leave them another one. This time there was no such opportunity. The recording ended abruptly and the line was silent.

Sharyn sat on her side of the taxi quietly awaiting Joe's response. He said nothing as he sat deep in thought staring into the cell phone display. Finally, after two or three minutes, he realized that he had inadvertently isolated himself from Sharyn and amends had to be made. He placed the phone back into his jacket pocket, reached for her hand, and edged over to her side. She wanted him to speak first.

'They want to collect the ransom in diamonds now.' His mind was active as he spoke.

'Is that better or worse?' Sharyn hesitantly asked.

'Well I suppose it's better. At least it's achievable. Well, I think it is.' He was trying to decide for himself.

'Joe, you mean we have to deliver ten million dollars worth of diamonds? How do we? How can we?' Sharyn was still puzzled.

'Believe me, it's a better way. You know how valuable a tiny diamond can be. It eliminates the problem of bulk, and transportation, and cash counting, and, yes it's much better, sure, but by 9 p.m. tonight?' Joe was formulating a plan in his mind as he spoke.

'Driver, change of plan. Please head down to West 47th and 5th Avenue.' As he delivered his instruction to the perplexed driver, he reached for his own cell phone to dial the office of Egan Enterprises.

'Andrew, Joe here. Have you been onto the bank yet?'

'Yes Mr. Egan, I'm waiting for them to call me back. They don't have that amount of cash on hand and tell me that it has to be ordered in advance. When the manager realized that it was for yourself, he said that he would handle it personally, and I'm now waiting for his return call.'

'All right Andrew. Things have changed. I still need the money to be available but it probably doesn't need to be in cash.'

'I'm not quite sure what you mean sir.'

'Just have the amount ready for deduction from that account and standby for me to give you verification. There's still a slight possibility that I will need the hard cash to do this deal, but I won't know until later this afternoon. I'll call you back, all right?'

'Yes sir. Leave it to me. I'll have things prepared and I'll await your call.' He seemed happier.

Andrew had supported Joe through many larger deals than this one and he didn't need to ask questions. He wasn't interested in the art of the deal. His expertise was in the mechanics behind it.

Sharyn's support was of a more personal nature. She was so pleased to be able to share this very dramatic period with Joe and wanted to make his personal trauma easier to bear. For her, it was a delicate balance of supporting him in his time of need, and not getting in the way of his unique style of getting things done alone. As always, she knew she could enhance his performance and bring out the best in him by saying the right things at the right time. She knew it, and so did he.

'Joe, surely there's something I can do to help you with this. I'm feeling a bit useless here. What can I do?'

'Just being with me is enough Sharyn. It helps me to have you around and I do value your opinion. You said you like diamonds, didn't you? And, all women like shopping. So, that's how you can help me now.'

'Good. What do you want me to do?' Sharyn was hanging on Joe's reply.

'Let's go diamond shopping to the tune of ten million dollars.'

CHAPTER 9

The taxi ride to the 47th Street diamond district seems long and frustrating as we stop and start through the Manhattan traffic lights. Sharyn seems to be calm and comfortable at my side, but I'm becoming more and more worried about meeting the deadline of nine o'clock. There's so much to accomplish before close of normal business hours.

'What do you have in mind Joe? How many diamonds do you think we need to give us ten million dollars worth?' Sharyn is now cuddled in closer than normal.

'Hey! You're reading my thoughts now. That's exactly what I was wondering. I really don't know the answer, but I know a man who can help us. He's a difficult man to get to see at any time. Although I don't really keep up with my father's side of the family all that much, I think there's enough Jewish blood in my veins for him to grant me an audience.' I'm dialing for assistance as I speak.

'I'd like to call Zinkow Diamond Merchants on 47th Street please.'

'How do you spell that sir?' the woman's voice promptly replies.

'Zinkow, Z I N K O W.'

'One moment please. Would you like to be through connected?'

'Yes please. Thank you.'

My ears are now subjected to a recorded message in a heavy Jewish accent detailing the history of Zinkow Diamond Merchants. How fifty three years of traditional family business has resulted in one of the largest importers and cutters of the finest stones, also being of the utmost integrity, etc, etc. 'Your call is valuable to us. Please wait to be attended to at the first opportunity.' Then some classical music followed once again by; 'Your call is valuable, etc, etc.' Then, 'Please listen to learn more about 47th Street.'

I'm thinking to myself and find that I'm speaking out loud. 'How good were the days when you could make a phone call and actually speak to the person you were calling.' I'm shaking my head but Sharyn nods in agreement.

Long gone were those days now and I'm frustrated by it. But, my mission is to get an interview with my distant relative Jacob Zinkow. Our last contact was for the purchase of Audrey's engagement diamond and I know that Jacob is probably the highest rung in the diamond ladder available to me. He's my best chance and I have no choice but to wait and listen to the tedious recorded story as it unfolds.

'Zinkow Diamond Merchants Company is situated in New York's 47th Street Diamond District. This is the world's largest consumer market for diamonds. Over ninety percent of the diamonds that come into this country go through New York City and most of them go through the diamond district. The diamond district is centered on West 47th Street between 5th Avenue and 6th Avenue, one block south of Rockefeller Center, three blocks south of Radio City Music Hall along the Avenue of the Americas, or three blocks south of Saint Patrick's Cathedral, along 5th Avenue. Zinkow Merchants, being an approved site holder for De Beers, are in the wholesale business of supplying high quality diamonds as loose unset stones to the jewelry trade. Our reputation is built on a tradition of providing precious goods together with precious knowledge.'

Thankfully, the thick discourse is now interrupted by the pleasant female tones of a receptionist.

'Sorry for keeping you waiting. Can I help you please?'

'Yes. It's Joseph Egan here. I'd like to speak to Mr. Jacob Zinkow.'

'I'm sorry sir. Mr. Zinkow is in a meeting right now. Would you like to leave a message?'

'I'd like to wait and speak to him personally. It's very, very important. I assure you that he will want to speak to me. It involves a large purchase of stones and the matter is urgent.'

'One moment please Mr. Egan.'

I've been to see Jacob at Zinkow Diamonds once before and I almost know what to expect. The impression one gets through the telephone is that they have a huge impressive office with sparkling showcases and uniformed staff to impress the customers. I remember well my last visit to see Jacob, and I have a rather different image of the office surroundings at the other end of the conversation.

'Mr. Zinkow is grading. He will see you at two thirty. Is that satisfactory?'

'That's fine thanks. We'll be there at two thirty. My assistant, Miss Sharyn Cooper, will also be with me.'

I'm happy with the result. I glance at my watch and see that the time now is just after one o'clock so we have ample time to find a silver attaché case. We should be able to conclude the diamond purchase with enough time to arrange transfer of funds before close of business. If not, I'll have to stall for more time or maybe just pretend I have the ransom available. It may still lead me to Casey.

Sharyn senses my elevated state of anxiety as my mind juggles with the schedule leading up to the nine o'clock ransom deadline.

'How are you coping Joe? There are so many things to accomplish in so little time.' I feel the pressure of her hand in mine.

'We should be able to do what they've requested. Although, I'm still hoping for some kind of breakthrough, anything that might lead us on another pathway to Casey. We need to gain an advantage and we need for those bastards to make a mistake. I swear to you Sharyn, if they do, and if I get my hands on them, they'll have hell to pay!'

'Easy Joe. You'll have your chance. I know you will.' Sharyn can feel the sweat in my palm and she wants to calm me.

I relax a little and stare through the cab window at the shoppers on 5th Avenue. I'm thinking back to my father's words to me, and I remember them well. I was only a small child trying to sell parakeets around our neighborhood to earn pocket money. Well, things weren't going as well as I would wish. Demand for my business was growing and I was having trouble constructing the cages and getting my school homework done at the same time. I broke down in front of my father and cried my eyes out when another order was cancelled due to the delay.

'I can't make the cages in time. There's too much to do. There's my schoolwork and my chores and…' I was sitting on his lap now and weeping openly.

My father was not going to help me build those cages. He knew that wasn't the solution. Doing the job for me, would only postpone the problem. What he gave me that afternoon were great words of encouragement, words of wisdom that still ring true today.

'Joey. Dry those tears. Things aren't as bad as you think. I know it seems like such a difficult task. I know you think you can't cope with it because the mountain before you is so very steep and high. But Joey, I want you to try something for me. Instead of seeing the whole problem in its enormity, I want you to break it down into little pieces. Try to negotiate your task in bits and pieces. One step at a time, Joey. Work it into tiny stages and concentrate on jumping only one little hurdle. Once you've done that, put it behind you and only think of the next little hurdle. One obstacle at a time Joey. Don't try to jump them all at once.'

My persuasive father helped me a great deal that day. Needless to say, I was able to handle the birdcage situation then, and better able to handle adversity ever since.

'One step at a time, Sharyn. One step at a time.' I find myself talking to Sharyn as though she's been listening to my thoughts. She snuggles in closer and responds as though she really has been.

'Yes, I know Joe. That's right. One step at a time.'

'That's how I can cope with all of this Sharyn, by breaking it down. My immediate obstacle is to have the diamonds available in the silver case and to be ready and able for tonight's delivery. Also, we must look for a crack in their shell, a weakness that we can use to our advantage.'

'Are you sure this man Jacob Zinkow can supply us with so many diamonds? How well do you know him?' Sharyn asks suspiciously.

'My mother came from the Falls Road area of Belfast. She was pure Irish. My father, even though he didn't eventually choose to be orthodox himself, had a conservatively Jewish father. So, I guess you can say that I'm one quarter Jewish. There's the connection.'

'Joe, I thought you were either all Jewish or not Jewish at all.' Sharyn looks puzzled.

'Well, either you practice Judaism or you don't. That's true. My father didn't, and I don't. In any case, my grandfather was an orthodox Jew and I have quite a few relatives in the community.'

'I hope you've been nice to those relatives Joe. Looks like we really need their help today.'

'I have to tell you, there does exist a little bit of animosity, not so much towards me, but more a carry over from my father's days. You see, the fact that he didn't attend synagogue and follow the faith, was a great disappointment, not only to his own father, but also to the many family relatives. At the time, he was shunned by that side of the family, and I don't think they ever forgave him for it.'

'Do you think they might still resent you because you are his son and you're now so successful?' Sharyn whispers.

'My relatives have always been polite and friendly to me, and Jacob Zinkow is no exception. I'm not sure what they really say and think. The Jewish business network is so sensitive to traditional values and my empire has been built without its help, so who knows?'

'How are you related to this Jacob Zinkow?'

'Oh, didn't I mention that? He's my cousin. And, he is an orthodox Jew.'

'He's your cousin? And you hardly ever see him?'

'Our worlds are so far apart and, as I said, even though relations are congenial, there is some underlying animosity there.'

The taxi swings into the jewelry district and Sharyn's eyes light up at the sight of so many gem retail establishments gathered into one small area. Immediately, it's easy to see who's in control of the diamond industry of New York. Every second person on the sidewalk seems to be of the Jewish faith. I ask the driver to pull the cab over, and we alight into the hustle and bustle of 47th Street.

Sharyn doesn't waste any time before she's mesmerized with the sparkles and spangles of the first display window and I'm again standing at her side looking at the loose diamonds. The stones are indeed beautiful. The main difference with these diamonds is the price. There's one peculiar trait of a valuable precious diamond. Once it leaves the shelves of the retail store, it strangely becomes less valuable. Yes, that's right! If you purchase a diamond at the retail price, then turn around, re-enter the same store and try to sell it back, you'd be lucky to be offered one third of what you paid. That's why it's so important to deal as high up in the chain of supply as possible. For me, that means dealing with Jacob Zinkow.

I figure there's about half an hour up my sleeve to purchase an attaché case and I'm trying to do some mental arithmetic as to the size and weight of so many diamonds. I can recall Audrey's diamond is about five carats and that cost about one hundred and twenty thousand dollars. If I work on ten million dollars worth, that makes about one hundred and ten larger diamonds. Therefore, if I double that mass to allow for the smaller ones, or even triple it to be sure, I still get three to four hundred diamonds. Fine then, there's surely no problem with dimensions. The weight should come in at between half a pound and one pound, or as they refer to diamonds, two hundred and fifty grams and half a kilo. A normal size briefcase should be sufficient to carry the ransom.

'All right, Sharyn. We want to purchase a hard aluminum silver colored attaché case with a damn good secure latch on it. Let's go. There should be something suitable in one of these jewelry shops.'

The second shop we enter has a small exhibit of jewelry boxes, merchant briefcases and watch trays at the rear of the store. The little hurdle of finding a suitable case is quickly behind us as we leave the store with the perfect silver colored attaché for the job. I can now focus my attention on getting the best diamond deal in town. With the case in one hand and Sharyn's grip on the other, I'm crossing the busy street with the old brick façade of the Intercontinental Building in my sights.

'Where do we find Zinkow Diamond Merchants? Do you have the address?' Sharyn breaks into a slight jog as she hurries by my side.

'I think I can find it. There, in front of us. That building! I remember it's on the eighth floor.'

The Intercontinental Building must be the smallest and oldest building on the block and I can see that the outer structure is badly in need of some restoration. With so much sidewalk activity in front of so many retail shops, it's not immediately obvious where to enter. After some weaving in and out of the wrong arcades we eventually find our way into the lobby and head towards the elevator.

* * * * *

The lobby looks like it should belong to the old Paris bourgeoisie. There's a stained glass chandelier hanging from the ceiling and red velvet upholstery lining the wooden benches on either side. The caged elevator must be from the last century and Sharyn is reading the framed maintenance authority to check the validity before we ascend.

I pull the rickety cage door closed, press the stained porcelain button for the eighth floor, and the whole apparatus rattles its way skyward.

'I thought you said this was as high up the diamond chain as you could get?' Sharyn is looking at me as though we may be in the wrong building.

'It's a weird industry Sharyn. When it comes to the larger wholesale suppliers, there's not much glitzy glamour at all. They leave all of the alluring enchantment to the retail outlets on the street. Most of these upper floors are filled with the trading rooms where mere mortals such as us must never tread. That's where a connection is needed to gain entry, a connection such as Jacob.'

The cage shakes to a stop and we step off into a long narrow corridor with several wooden signed doors, almost all with Jewish sounding names boarded on the outside. Half way down on the right is a heavy oak and brass door with the name of Zinkow etched in gold. To Sharyn's amazement, there's no bell or buzzer and the unlocked door opens easily to permit our entry.

She understands why, when the door opens into another vestibule and we're staring into an arrangement of three separate security cameras overhanging a huge door of iron bars. This is a door that Al Capone would need a bulldozer to break through. Apart from the intercom button, which I promptly press, there's no other furniture or decoration whatsoever.

'Come on through Joseph.' Jacobs's deep voice bellows through the speaker as the lock clicks open and the iron door simultaneously shifts slightly on its hinges.

As heavy as it appears, the door of iron bars swings easily as I pull it and we walk through into another similarly uninteresting room of slightly larger proportions. This time, there's only one camera peering down at us over a second door of iron bars. The first door clicks shut behind us and for a moment we feel trapped in what is actually a prison cell. Sharyn's tightening clasp on my arm is signaling me to do something about our claustrophobic entrapment, but the door in front now clicks open and we are able to enter the sacred office of the diamond dealer.

The secretary sitting in the tiny cubicle as we enter the room has barely sufficient time to utter a greeting when Jacob's huge torso comes bounding through from his own office and his loud voice causes Sharyn to recoil in terror.

'Welcome! I bid you welcome Joseph.' He shakes my hand and before I can speak he carries on. 'And, may I introduce myself to your assistant? Young lady, it's so nice to meet you. I'm Jacob Zinkow and you are…?'

Poor Sharyn is rather overwhelmed by Jacobs's huge frame and loud voice and she holds my hand as she opens her mouth to answer. Before she can get a word out, Jacob's thundering roar interrupts again.

'Sharyn Cooper isn't it? Yes, my secretary has informed me already. Very nice to meet you Miss Sharyn Cooper.' With that, Jacob extends his large fatty hand to Sharyn and holds it with a tender touch as he turns his head towards me.

'Joseph. I am so sorry to hear of Audrey's tragic passing yesterday. I offer my sincere condolences to you. My prayers have been with you since I heard.'

Jacob hangs his head momentarily and then comes to life once again. 'By the way, have you met my very capable secretary? May I introduce you to Desdemona?' Jacob bows at the waist and extends one arm out wide towards his secretary. 'She is responsible for the management and processing of millions of dollars each and every day. And, may I say that she does so with great efficiency and expertise.'

Desdemona is a slightly built girl of plain appearance and she smiles sheepishly as Jacob continues loudly.

'Come through! Come through! Have they found the person responsible for all this evil? How is your daughter managing?' I try to respond but Jacob speaks on without taking a breath.

'It's been too long Joseph. Please sit down. Sit down. Here, take this chair and this one for Miss Cooper. Feel free.'

Jacob and Sharyn break into a light one-sided conversation with Jacob doing most of the questioning and answering. I'm trying to remember all of Jacob's questions, as I still haven't had a chance to open my mouth to speak. He seems to ask a question then speak right over the top of it before I can answer. He is so boisterous and his greeting is so overextended, I have to wonder about his sincerity when his manner is so exaggerated like this. I sit back to survey the surroundings.

It's been many years since I was last sitting in this office and not much has changed. Although the building is old, the structure itself is extremely heavy with concrete walls several feet thick. The architecture is classically Victorian creating an atmosphere of warmth and solidarity. To my left is a beautiful window case, spoilt by the inclusion of thick steel bars through which several roosting pigeons are leering in at us.

On the rear wall is a striking advertising poster of a burglar cat-woman character. She's wearing a black latex skin suit and she seems to be precariously poised on the edge of a Paris rooftop. The full moon is illuminating her streaming blonde hair and she has green cat's eyes with long black eyelashes. Her arched back suggests a feline prowling position with claws extended and red luscious lips curled back in a snarl. Clenched between her ivory white teeth, is a huge sparkling ten-carat diamond on full display.

The remainder of Jacob's office is an absolute mess. There are documents piled high in every corner and a layer of dust coats the many cabinets and bookcases. Below the window stands an old steel safe with ornate brass patterns welded to the exterior. Strangely, the safe door is hanging open, revealing the many small drawers and trays of merchandise within. Resting against the adjacent wall, the double-barreled twelve-gauge shotgun is more for show than for practical use.

In sharp contrast to the rest of his office, Jacob's desk is relatively clean and tidy. A huge writing pad has ink doodle sketches everywhere, and a silver penholder contains more pencils than pens. There are monitors beside the desk displaying several stagnant images of the two entry vestibules through which we had previously entered. A modern high-tech set of electronic jewelry weighing scales is positioned on a small cabinet to Jacob's left.

I can see by the hint of desperation in Sharyn's eyes that her powers of listening are almost exhausted and that she needs for me to save her from the burden of Jacob's attention.

'Jacob. How is your wife Sophia? And, your family, how are they?' I open my mouth for the first time to interrupt him.

'Well my cousin, they are all well, quite well.' Jacob's expression changes to an even more serious tone and he continues.

'But you Joseph, how are you coping? And of course, your daughter must be so devastated and distraught with the loss of her mother. Are the police having any success in their investigation?'

'Well, it's difficult. It's sheer hell. It's a very traumatic and sad time for everyone and the police say they are doing all they can. But so far they haven't come up with any leads.'

'Well, let us all hope and pray that the criminal is brought to justice.' Jacob sits back in his chair and strokes his long black beard.

Apart from the few gray hairs and extra pounds of weight that seem to be added to his girth every time I see him, Jacob looks almost the same. Along with the many other traditional Jewish gentlemen walking the pavement of the Diamond District, Jacob is also dressed in black. A black yarmulke with Star of David border covers his curly black hair and a black tzitzis with strings dangling from the four corners drapes over a black silk vest and woolen pants.

As he speaks, his bulky fingers twiddle the old string of beads handed down from father to son before him, as though they might hold the key to solving life's many problems.

'You say you are in need of help. How can I help?'

'I want to purchase ten million dollars worth of diamonds and carry them out of here at the end of this meeting.' With that, I reach down and swing the silver attaché up onto my lap. 'In this attaché case.'

Jacob roars with laughter and rolls his chair back with his hands in the air.

'Only you Joseph! Only you could surprise me like this.'

My heart sinks. Jacob notices my reaction and quickly continues.

'Don't worry my friend. It is no problem. No problem. With this I can help. Yes. But there are so many different ways to achieve this. You know with diamonds Joseph, there are so many variables. Is it for investment?'

'The purpose is confidential Jacob, but I must have them today.'

'As I say, it is no problem. We can do this. Do you mean ten million dollars in retail value or wholesale? What size and shape?' Jacob's bead fiddling is speeding up as he is now talking about his favorite subject. His brown eyes begin to flicker with excitement.

'I need ten million dollars worth in wholesale value. They must be high quality diamonds of between one to five carats. For demonstration purposes, I also require some cubic zirconia of about the same quantity and weight, so the two parcels are similar in appearance. With the choosing of the diamonds, you will have to help me of course.'

'Cubic zirconia, Joseph? These are virtually worthless. They have a token use for costume jewelry and we find them suitable as a marketing tool. But otherwise, they have no value.'

I pause for a moment wondering how much information Jacob needs to know.

'I know, but it gives me the option of demonstrating the parcel characteristics without using the real diamonds. I ask you to leave it at that. I really cannot tell you more.'

'Sure! It's all right. Your business is your business. However, I warn you not to get the cubics mixed up in any way with the real diamonds. I want to be very explicit. To the untrained eye, it is very difficult to distinguish between them. However, let us firstly attend to the genuine product.'

Jacob's eyes flash to the ceiling and his red leather chair shoots back and to the side on squeaky roller wheels. The beads disappear into his vest side pocket and his hands begin to tap the different trays and drawers within the old ornate safe.

'You are a real mensch, my cousin. You should come to visit, not only for business you know.' Jacob's deep voice is now resonating from within the chambers of his safe as he decides on the appropriate tray to withdraw.

His body now swoops around and upright into sitting position, and the red leather chair wheels back to the desk. In his grasp, is a narrow shoebox containing hundreds of folded white paper parcels, which he firmly plants to the side of his desk pad. He sucks in his huge stomach, opens the drawer to his right and takes out a black velvet scroll, which he now rolls open across the entire center of the desk.

As the white halogen ceiling lights beam down from above, I can feel Sharyn's hand slide into mine and clasp tight in anticipation of what is about to happen. Jacob skillfully fingers through the white papers one by one as he mumbles a Yiddish psalm through the dense coils of his beard. He decides on one particular envelope and spreads open its inner blue wax paper folds. Our eyes are treated to a fire dance of fine white sparkling diamonds as he scatters them across the black velvet in a single motion.

'Here, in front of you my cousin, is about one half of a million dollars. But, as I said, there are many variables, as you know, with diamonds. A slight improvement with the color or the clarity can multiply the value. Remember that we have different shapes and sizes, colors and imperfections to deal with. It depends upon what the customer is looking for. We deal in illusion to give people pleasure. This is our business.' I can see that Jacob is in his element and doing what he does best.

'I know Jacob. I've always had an avid interest, but I am really in your hands. The diamonds are to be an assortment of sizes between one to five carats in size and of high quality. Oh! And yes, they are to be brilliant cut. The other qualities I am leaving for you to choose.' I am hoping that Jacob will take over now and handle the finer details.

'Yes. Yes. I will choose for you. No problem. Let me see.'

Jacob's right hand returns to fingering through the envelopes as he studies the penciled codes written on each paper fold. Without looking, he retrieves a pair of fine long tweezers from the drawer and places it on the black velvet with his left hand.

'Yes. Yes. Yes. Let me see. Not to potchkeh around now. I have some work to do.' Jacob is talking to himself.

As he loses himself in the many little parcels, I sit back to observe the diamond grader in action. He scatters the black velvet with more and more diamonds from which he chooses and arranges the most suitable into little rows.

'Here is a nice stone. Yes. This one presents well.' He continues his jabbering.

'You know Joseph, the market assigns value to a diamond on the basis of its carat weight, its cut, color, and its clarity. Because the bigger stones are harder to find, they have more value per carat than a smaller stone. The brilliant cut to which you refer Joseph, is the traditional round cut stone which maximizes the light that is returned to your eye from the diamond, or the brilliance.'

Jacob's large fingers now resemble the members of a well-practiced orchestra with the man himself conducting the symphony. Like Swiss clockwork, the papers are opened and the diamonds sorted and graded. With expert precision, Jacob's tweezers capture each diamond for weighing on the electronic silver scales. One by one, the tiny unique universe within each stone is scrutinized through his small optical loop. He hums and talks as he works.

'The color Joseph! The color is a major determinant of value. Most diamonds have naturally occurring color but the finest and rarest appear colorless. We should be looking for preferably a 'D' color but surely nothing less than 'E' or 'F' stones. And last but not least, we must determine the clarity. We are talking about the naturally occurring inclusions in the stone. Yes Joseph, each stone has a story to tell, a character all of its own to make it an individual creation of Mother Nature. We are looking for your stones to be internally clear, or only very, very slightly included. The stones we are wanting here are flawless or internally flawless, but at the very least VVS1 diamonds.'

Poor Sharyn. She is sitting quietly by my side without uttering a word, and I can sense that she's finally becoming overwhelmed by the wonderful sight before her eyes. Diamonds are a girl's best friend at any time, but this many shiny precious stones are enough to rattle the nerves of the strongest of the female sex. I can feel her slender hand beginning to tremble in my grasp.

It takes about one hour and forty minutes for Jacob to finally complete his task and the required diamonds are now spread across the black velvet scroll before us.

'Here we are Joseph. We have your diamonds.' Jacob sits back to admire the treasure, and he instinctively reaches for the beads from his vest pocket.

'As you requested, there is greater than ten million dollars in wholesale value. The stones are an assortment of round brilliants between one to five carats and they can all be considered to be of fine color and clarity. The least expensive is this one-carat diamond VVS1 and F color, about eleven thousand dollars, and the most expensive is this beautiful example here. Look! A magnificent diamond of five carats weight and internally flawless in clarity. Also, this stone is slightly pink in color making it the rarest and most valuable in the collection. Its wholesale value is in the order of one million one hundred thousand dollars. All in all, we have one hundred and seventy six diamonds totaling four hundred and thirty one carats. Is this to your satisfaction my friend?'

'Yes. That is completely to my satisfaction. It's difficult to comprehend how ten million dollars can be compressed into such a small mass.'

'Ah! To the uninitiated, this is true. But, this is the nature of these wonderful precious objects and why everyone wants to possess them. People have adorned themselves with jewelry of one form or another since the beginning of mankind and they will continue to do so. Besides being an expression of your own taste, diamonds are a connection with a long romantic tradition and a mystical past. They are the hardest natural substance known to science and this, my cousin, has made them the stuff of legends. You can see, the way that Miss Cooper is looking at these little beauties. She is a woman, and Yes! You can see. She is under the spell.'

Of all the diamonds arranged before us now, there is one, and only one, shining star. One soul lifting diamond that mesmerizes, hypnotizes and enchants any person who would dare to gaze into its depths. The diamond is, of course, the exquisitely flawless five-carat pink stone, which captivates us all. There it is, standing out amongst its peers with a glistening sparkle that can only be matched by the gleam in Sharyn's eyes as she stares in amazement at its magnificence.

It is now quite apparent that my concern about the size and weight of the ransom parcel and whether it would fit into the attaché case was completely unfounded. The diamonds scattered before me would easily be contained in a small tobacco tin and readily carried in my pocket. It makes me wonder if the kidnappers are expecting the attaché case to be overflowing with the treasure and I hope their possible disappointment won't manifest into Casey's further misfortune.

Using the edge of the tweezers, Jacob slides the diamonds onto a small silver scoop and funnels them onto the scales. He jots something down on the desk pad and then empties the stones into a small green velvet pouch. He pulls the drawstring tight, wraps it twice around the top and plops it back onto the weighing scales.

'The total weight is eighty six point two grams.' Jacob sits back leaving the parcel where it is on the scales.

'Thank you Jacob. But, there is some other related business we have to discuss.'

'Yes of course. Of course! We must arrange the payment,' Jacob says as he takes up a silver pen and begins another doodle on his desk pad.

'Yes Jacob. There are two matters to resolve. Firstly, how to pay you ten million dollars. You see, I would insist that no records be kept of this transaction. It must be completely off the books, and the details of these proceedings must go no further than this room. Is that possible?'

'We have no books and records before us. Do you see books and records? If I have the cash and you have the diamonds, who needs books and records?' Jacob's desk pad doodle is forming into a marquise diamond of perfect shape, proportion and cut.

'Thank you Jacob. The cash. I need to take the diamonds with me today so we must arrange the money quickly.'

I glance at my Rolex and see the time is already 4.40 p.m. This doesn't leave much time. I have to call Andrew quickly.

'Can you bring the cash to this office? It is the best way,' says Jacob.

Jacob's doodle is complete and he draws a large dollar sign next to the marquise diamond sketch.

'Yes. But it will take several trips to complete and I won't have time before the end of banking hours.' My brow is beaded with perspiration as I look down once again at my wristwatch.

Jacob pauses and gazes at me. He seems to be silently enjoying watching me sweat in this, his moment of supremacy. I hate him and I love him. The wheels are turning in his head and he finally bellows profusely.

'Time! Time! Time is your enemy and time is your friend. Joseph, we are family and we have known each other for a lifetime. Today, time will be your friend. You will pay me when you will pay me.'

With those words, Jacob grabs the pouch from the scales and tosses it across the desk in my direction. Sharyn's hand instinctively goes out to catch it but mine is somewhat quicker. I am now able to massage the diamonds through the green velvet as I open the attaché case on my lap.

'Now you require a similar package of cubic zirconia?' Jacob rolls his eyes as if he's disgusted in having to handle these worthless copies.

'Yes. If you don't mind, it would help me enormously with the deal I have in mind. So, yes please.'

Jacob once again dives into the drawer of his desk and surfaces with a small metal biscuit tin, which he opens to display a mass of glittering cubics. Without hesitation, he empties a quantity of assorted cubics into another green velvet pouch, weighs them, adds a few more, and then hands them to me.

'Now that will be ten million dollars for the diamonds and an additional seventeen dollars and sixty cents for the cubics.' Jacob smirks and hesitates. 'I'm joking of course, my friend.' He now laughs with a thunderous roar at his own comedy.

'Thank you Jacob. I'll make sure not to get these two pouches mixed up.'

I take out my pen and scribble a small inkblot on the green cubic pouch before placing it in my pocket next to the paper knife.

'My office manager, Andrew Barton will be in contact with you to organize the cash. Now there is the second matter. Although this may puzzle you, I ask that you just accept what I have to say in good faith. You see Jacob, I may not require these diamonds after all. It is possible, although highly improbable, that I may wish to return them to you for a refund and I want some guarantee that I can do so. Of course, I would reimburse you for your inconvenience.'

'There is no inconvenience. You have the diamonds, I have the cash. I have the diamonds, and you have the cash. Whichever way, the scales are balanced and we understand one another. Don't worry yourself over these things. This is the diamond business and today our business is complete. Take the diamonds? Bring back the diamonds? We are in agreement.'

Jacob's arms go out in a friendly gesture as his large frame rises from the red leather chair and he circles his desk towards us. The attaché case seems so very large to carry the small parcel of diamonds, that I'm conscious of them shifting around inside. I swing the case to my side and stand up bringing Sharyn to her feet beside me.

With the same boisterous enthusiasm that we were greeted with, Sharyn and I are now escorted to the door whereupon we are subjected to the same sequence of iron bars locking and unlocking for our exit. With a final handshake and pat on the shoulder, Jacob then talks us through the vestibules and once again his thunderous voice gives us little opportunity to get a word in edgeways.

'Tread cautiously my friends. Beware of the mystical properties of the diamonds. Will they bring you luck and good fortune or will they reap havoc and anguish? Remember Joseph. Which will it be? The sparkle and felicity of the British Crown Jewels or the dreaded curse of the Hope Diamond. I wish you well. I wish you both well. Shalom.'

Jacob's voice fades behind the closing door and Sharyn breathes a huge sigh of relief.

'Phew! Sharyn. Now you've met Jacob Zinkow. He's one man you will never forget. Now you can see why I seldom visit him. He's so hospitable. But, oh how he can wear you down.' I take Sharyn's hand as we make our way along the corridor.

'Joe, he's so loud. My ears are ringing. How does his wife put up with it?' Sharyn is dazed by the whole episode.

'I don't know how, but she does. Sophia simply adores him. But, I do recall my childhood. I remember that Jacob was banned from our house when the other children came to play. My mother just couldn't tolerate his loud voice and his boisterous manners. Now I can see why. He was always the odd one out. Actually, after all the family bitterness since then, I'm surprised he's so very friendly towards me now.'

* * * * *

It's not long before the two of us have the comforting reprieve of another taxi ride. This time, we're heading back to Egan Center to await the next stage of this unfolding drama. We've accomplished much in a short time and I'm now ready and prepared to receive the delivery instructions. I have the demanded ransom ready in the required metal attaché case. As an option, to fool the kidnappers if the opportunity arises, I have an identical pouch of cubic replicas in my pocket. Also, as a viable alternative, I've negotiated the return of the stones to Jacob with a refund of the cash.

It seems that one more hurdle has been negotiated which means that there is one less hurdle to overcome. The time is now only 5.25 p.m. and I have some three and a half hours up my sleeve. I feel that I'm one significant step closer to finding Casey, and I need only to await the next call on the kidnapper's phone. That feeling of relief is short-lived however, because the taxi has now paused in traffic and the driver swings his head in my direction.

'Mister, I know I'm not paid to tell you this, but I'm pretty damn sure you're being tailed.' He talks like he's an expert at these things.

'What do you mean, I'm being tailed?' I whip my head around peering through the rear window as I speak.

'Well,' he continues, 'there was a guy watching you from the alleyway when you hailed me over and he grabbed the taxi behind us. I think he's a couple of cars back and still following us.'

I strain my eyes to try to see through the vehicles to the rear but I can't distinguish much through the distortion.

Sharyn looks back also as the taxi resumes its forward motion.

'Do you think it's him Joe? Has he been watching us and calling us on that phone at the same time?' Sharyn shudders as she asks.

'It's possible. It's something I haven't considered.' I answer Sharyn and then direct my question straight back to the driver.

'Are you sure driver? You may be mistaken.'

'Man, that's up to you to decide. I've told you what I've seen, and what I've seen is someone taking more interest in you guys than what they should, okay?' He shrugs his shoulders and eyes me wryly in the rear view mirror.

'Yes. Thank you for telling us. You've done a good thing. Thank you. By the way, what did this person look like?' I'm hoping that his next sentence will be a description of the murderer and kidnapper.

'Couldn't see much of him at all. Not much to go on. He was dressed all in black with dark sunglasses. Acting real suspicious like.'

The taxi pauses again and I'm thinking fast. I notice my fists are clenched and the rage is building in my chest. Sharyn senses what I'm thinking and clutches my arm as she speaks.

'No Joe. It's too dangerous. Stay here and let him follow,' she pleads.

One part of me wants to exit the taxi and run back to the vehicle in question. I'd be able to rip the door open and have that kidnapper in my grip. I'd throttle the life out of him if he didn't tell me where Casey was. The other more commonsense part is telling me to stay put. I can't jeopardize Casey's life any further. I have to wait for her to be saved. Let him play out his little game. Let him think we don't know he's there and let him follow us around. I'll wait for the right time, my time, and then I'll pounce.

'You're right Sharyn. We'll let him follow and we can wait for the right moment. Don't look back. We'll pretend we don't know he's there.'

I'm so uneasy thinking this criminal will be watching my moves that I reach to feel the paper knife in my pocket and my forefinger momentarily caresses the razor sharp blade. My own cell phone suddenly bursts into life, and I'm grappling to silence it.

'Joe Egan,' I sputter into the mouthpiece.

'Mr. Egan. It's Andrew. Are you returning to the office?'

'Yes, we're heading back that way now. Why?'

'Well sir, there's a Lieutenant Frank Berne here to see you and he says he's prepared to wait as long as it takes. What shall I tell him?'

I'm thinking fast. As much as I'm tempted to do so, I mustn't tell the police about the sinister person on our trail. That would open up a 'Pandora's Box' and be the end of the game. I'm wondering what Berne wants me for. If he was there to arrest me, it would ruin the schedule for the ransom delivery. It may in fact be the difference between life and death for Casey. I would have to steer clear of him completely. On the other hand, if he has some vital information about the investigation, it could serve to help me in my dealings with the kidnappers. It may even be the key to her survival.

'Andrew, has he intimated at all what he is there for?'

'Well no sir. He just seems adamant that he will wait.'

I hesitate, and then decide. 'I don't want to talk to Frank Berne on the phone. I'll hear what he has to say in person when I arrive there.'

CHAPTER 10

Blue Featherman was a bad driver at the best of times. Driving at close to seventy miles an hour certainly wasn't improving his chances of staying on the road. His license had expired years ago and he had neither the reason nor the ability to renew it. As he struggled to steer along the undulating gravel road, his mind was occupied by something other than safe driving. He was thinking about the young female that he held captive in the rear of the van.

Feathers was thinking fast and furiously and he couldn't believe his good fortune. He had pulled off the biggest job of his life and it was a turning point. His reward would be a huge load of fast cash and better still, his opportunity to ravish a cute innocent child. He had adhered to the plan well and he now stopped the van on the side of the road.

The girl was still unconscious in the laundry cart and Feathers licked his foul smelling lips as he cut a lock of blonde hair from her head. He then decided that he should leave her inside the cart and return to complete his mission. Before he did so however, he paused, and felt a surge of exquisite ecstasy when his eyes ran down her luscious body. He had to exercise all of his self-control to resist the urge. Feathers desperately wanted to take one voracious bite of her baby pink flesh. Instead, his bacteria laden furry tongue started to whip around his lips. He licked her neck, her cheeks, and her eyelids, and he planted a full devouring kiss to her unaware mouth. It was only the stench of the ether that caused him to stop. He reluctantly jumped back into the cabin to continue the drive.

As Feathers turned into the quiet suburban gas station, he could see a black Chevy Silverado pickup parked off to the side. He pulled up behind it and waited for the dude to come to him. He couldn't help but notice the red bumper sticker that depicted a chrome V8 engine extruding flames and underneath, the words:

UNLEASHED FURY

After a while the driver's door swung open and out stepped the dude. He looked in every direction and then slowly walked up to the van window. He had to squint his eyes to recognize Feathers through the disguise and then he was more relaxed.

'What the hell happened? Any hitches? All go to plan?'

'Sure! Everything's done. The little bitch is in the back asleep. Had some trouble with the mother, but got through it.'

'Oh! What kind of trouble? What do you mean?'

'I told you it's done. Everything's done. No problem!' Feathers spat a ball of filth at the dude's feet making him take one step back.

'Had trouble with the mother? What happened to the mother?' asked the dude.

'Had to smack the bitch. She was going to wreck everything. It was all coming apart.'

'Are you sure you weren't followed?' The dude looked back along the road as he asked.

'Nah! No-one even had the chance to watch me leave. We're safe.' Feathers scowled. 'And, here's your bit of hair. When do I get my money?'

The dude stuffed the hair into his pocket and looked around once again. From his other pocket, he produced a hand drawn map of the area around Tuxedo Junction and handed it to Feathers.

'You'll get your money when this is finished, and it's far from being finished yet. Just get the girl to the house and wait. Don't do anything stupid. Just stay low and stay quiet. And, make sure you keep your hands off her. For now we have to keep her alive and healthy and we may have to prove it to them before any money is paid. If you mark her in any way, it could mean you don't get a cent.'

'She's all right. She's healthy. Looks cute in that dress though!' Feathers licked his lips and grinned.

'Just keep your hands off her until this is all finished. Understand? When we're through this and have the money, I don't care what you do. Just don't touch her now,' the dude growled.

'Are you going to hand her back?' Feathers worried.

'Not likely! She's seen you and it's too dangerous. When I say it's time, you'll have to get rid of her. Just don't tell me anything about it. I don't want to know. Understand? Just make sure you bury her where she'll never be found. Never!'

These words gave Feathers renewed hope that he would have his sick party and he felt a surge of excitement in his loins.

The dude backed off and returned to his Chevy pickup. With a roar of that unleashed fury and a screech of the wheels, the red bumper sticker faded into the distance.

Feathers started the van's engine and pulled out onto the road. His personal quest was going just fine. The only thorn in his side was that slick fancy pants dude. It was his attitude that upset Feathers. Firstly, he was acting all superior like he was from some superior race or something, and secondly, he was getting all worried about the kid being touched. He had told Feathers to lay off, God-damn it! Feathers thought that he himself had done most of the work, and he suspected that the dude was going to get a lot more than two hundred grand. He decided that if the chance came up, he would grab as much of the ransom as he could and snuff the life out of that dude. See who would be the superior race then?

* * * * *

Nine years old is a confusing age for a young girl. She still has the mental maturity of a child but her body is racing towards adolescence. It's also an interesting and rewarding time of life, when family members answer innocent questions of impending puberty in a loving and tender way.

The minds of some young girls progress quickly towards womanhood at the age of nine, but for some, it is a slow awkward process, with the mind being continually perplexed by adult themes and issues. It's almost like a race between mind and body, and the heart is caught in the middle trying to cope with the resulting mayhem.

Casey Egan was of the latter kind. Although she was quickly forming the physical characteristics of a pretty young lady with small developing breasts and a slight feminine curve to her waist, Casey was still very much a little child in her soul. She was still clinging to her fluffy stuffed doll as if it was her own child and she would suck her thumb while sleeping. When most of the other girls in her school class were already infatuated with the older boys, Casey was more interested in climbing trees, dressing up as a princess, and looking like Pollyanna. There was one pudgy fat boy, about her own age and who she thought she was beginning to like, but she really didn't know why. She just thought that he looked like a stuffed toy, something that Pollyanna might like to own.

Yes indeed, for Joe Egan's little girl, the age of nine was an age of naiveté. So you can imagine how her sweet innocence was suddenly shattered into a million fragments when this poor little girl was subjected to the horrible spectacle of Audrey Egan's face being distorted and crushed before her very eyes.

The sight of Blue Featherman, the hotel laundry man, burying his large clenched fist into the trusting face of her own mother and the subsequent splattering of blood around the elevator, was almost beyond her powers of comprehension. The trauma of witnessing that atrocity nearly caused her tender, delicate and loving heart to stop beating altogether. The state of insensibility forced upon her by the ether cloth was actually a blessing in disguise. Without its anesthetizing affect, she probably would have died from the tremendous shock of such a violent experience.

When little Casey's eyes slowly began to blink, her brain was still somewhat doped by the evaporating ether fumes of the rag draped loosely below her jaw. Drifting through the ether smell, she was immediately aware of a pungent taste in her mouth. The odor reminded her of grandpa who always had bad breath when it came time for her to kiss him goodbye. It was an old man taste and she tried in vane to spit it away.

Her eyes finally opened wide to the linen interior of the laundry cart and her mind began the heart wrenching reconstruction of what she had been through. She was panic stricken when her powers of reasoning were unable to cope with the ensuing struggle to make sense of what was so very senseless. Her world had entered a state of madness. These terrible things just couldn't be happening to her. Surely, she would soon be aroused from sleep by her mother, comforted back to rest, and the nasty dream would be ended.

The jolting roughness of the pot-holed road below caused her to tumble back and forth from side to side inside the linen cart, and the stale ether laden air was making her vomit into the cloth rag at her face. Was this the hell she had been told of in scripture class? Was this her punishment for being naughty? How long would it last? When would it be finished? She sobbed with tears welling in her eyes as she dragged the cloth from her mouth and began her desperate cry for help.

Blue Featherman's erratic driving didn't make it easy for Casey to extract herself from the laundry cart, but she was finally able to gather her strength, get to her feet, and peer tentatively over the edge to view her surroundings. When she realized that she was imprisoned in a traveling container, and everything was completely foreign to her, she had second thoughts and wondered if she should just stay where she was in the cart. Maybe she was safer there? Maybe no-one even knew she was there. Her young mind was now grasping for answers and ideas.

Suddenly her escapist instinct prevailed over reason, and she wriggled up and out of the smelly cart. The interior of the van was very dimly lit, light coming only from a small circular air vent in the ceiling and also from a small rectangular window on the front wall. The floor, ceiling and sides were all constructed of metal plate and the twin rear doors were locked fast. Casey had trouble keeping on her feet as the van rounded another bend and she was flung from one side to the other, ending up on her hands and knees once again. She managed to reach the rear doors and she banged her tiny closed fists and yelled in despair.

'Help me please! Let me out! Oh please help me! Mommy?' she cried through her tears.

Once again she was down on her hands and knees and making her way to the front wall. The loose laundry cart tumbled towards her and bashed into her side as she dragged herself up to look through the small window. What she could see only served to heighten her shock and horror and she recoiled in terror falling once again to the floor below.

The window had given her a good view into the front cabin of the van, and there sitting at the wheel was a strangely familiar person. The images and events of the hotel elevator came rushing back to her mind. This man was the devil himself disguised as a laundry man. He was everything bad and evil. He meant nothing but fear and terror and pain. He meant death!

Casey's hands covered her eyes as she sobbed and whimpered. Her mind could gather no useful ideas and she feared that she would surely be killed when the journey came to an end. Yes. She was going to die. This beast of a person would open the doors, grab her with one hand and with his other hand closed in a fist, smash her face until she was dead. This was her fate and there seemed nothing that she could do. She looked down through the dim light at her pretty clothes and cried. Her half-heeled strapped shoes were scuffed and damaged, the new nylon stockings she had been allowed to wear were now torn and soiled, and her pale yellow birthday dress was splattered with blood from her own mother's face.

'Oh! Mommy! Please help mommy. Help me daddy.'

Casey started to think of her daddy. Surely, he would find her and save her life. He was amazing. He could do anything at all. Yes. He was going to help her just as he always does. Why, he would probably be there when the van came to a stop and he would take her into his arms when the doors are opened. That's what will happen. Yes. Casey was predicting the scene of her dad swooping her up into his arms with the same loving tender fatherly affection he always shows.

'Come on my princess. You're with me now. Dry those tears now.'

Was this how the nightmare would end? This was how she wanted it to end. And, this is how she would previously rely on all bad dreams to end. But, something had changed in her way of thinking. She was growing up and maturing. She was learning to face up to reality rather than close her eyes and pretend. This wasn't a Disney house of horrors. These terrible events were really happening, and she better get herself together to do something about it.

Casey so admired her father. She had listened to his words of wisdom and learnt from them since as long as she could remember. She recalled the many times she had cried with frustration when her playtime had ended in failure, or her school project was seemingly too difficult for her. Daddy was there to give her advice.

'Come on. Dry those eyes. One step at a time princess! Remember what I've always told you. One little hurdle, then look at the next.'

Casey thought back to recall as many words of wisdom as she could. She wanted to be grown up enough to do something clever. She wanted to help herself. In what possible way, she didn't know, but things change. Opportunities arise, and when they do, you have to be ready. Yes. Daddy had told her that. And yes. She now could remember his words to her when she was so frustrated at not being a fast runner. The school sports carnival was on and Casey knew she couldn't run as fast as the other girls of her age. She was so afraid of coming last. It would be so embarrassing in front of her parents and friends, and especially her dad. He was an achiever. He would be expecting her to win. She wanted to avoid the race and daddy could see something was wrong. He had taken her aside and hugged her.

'Casey, listen to me. I know you don't want to compete. Some people are born fast runners and some people are born naturally slow. There's nothing we can do about it. Achievements are made in different areas and we all must accept the natural talents God gave us. Look at what a good swimmer you are. I don't care in what position you finish. What's important to me is that you try. If you give it your best shot, then that's all I expect. Whether you come first or last is not what matters. What counts is that you try your hardest. In my eyes princess, that makes you the winner.'

Joe Egan's words were resonating in Casey's head and she decided there and then to grow up. This was her chance to do so. This was her time to wait for an opportunity and to try her best. She would succeed out of this ordeal and make it her father's proudest moment.

* * * * *

By using a normal commercial road map, Feathers had successfully managed to navigate his way to Tuxedo Junction. He slowed the van to familiarize himself with the surroundings and it didn't take very long.

The junction was merely a dirt track that crossed the more prominent road at right angles and disappeared on both sides into a thick forest of tall pine trees. Off to one side was an old general store in urgent need of new siding and repainting. Two rusty gas pumps that had seen better days, had adopted a precarious lean to one side. An old green rocking chair with a tasseled cushion was poised on the porch, and around onto the sidewall of the store, the local pay phone booth was attached. Apart from a rickety old Ford pickup and a blue Toyota sedan that were parked side by side, that was all there was to the place.

Feathers parked the van further down the road and jumped out. He banged his fist a few times on the side of the van to shut up the girl's whimpering and headed in the direction of the general store.

* * * * *

The young lady behind the counter was disgusted and a little bit afraid at the appearance of her new customer. Louise Shackleton knew every one of the local inhabitants of Tuxedo Junction, and this fellow definitely wasn't one of them. He looked her up and down and then glared into her eyes as he burst through the insect barrier ribbons. It sent a freezing shiver down her backbone and she didn't like it. Louise also didn't like the manner in which Feathers then looked at her little six year old asthmatic daughter, Nancy. Feathers, on the other hand, liked very much what he saw.

'Hello little girl. What's your name darling?' Feathers smiled and showed his rotten teeth.

Little Nancy cringed at his image, slid down below her play table, and hid in fear. She started to wheeze softly and reached back up to the table to grab her asthma puffer. Feathers turned back to Louise and displayed his teeth once again as he laughed with a throaty rasp. His laughter was interrupted by a ringing sound that filled the room.

On the wall panel behind Louise was a small brass bell hanging on a string. The string was jerking up and down and the bell was shaking and tingling. Louise knew that this was her signal to rush upstairs and attend to the sick old man. She looked across at little Nancy and then glanced at Feathers, and she felt quite sick in the stomach. The irritating bell was ringing and ringing and Feathers was wondering what it meant.

'What's that noise all about lady?'

Louise grabbed a pair of scissors from the counter, spun around and cut the string. The bell fell to the floor and all was quiet.

'Oh nothing! Just a sick man upstairs is calling me.' Louise blushed.

'Well why don't you go then and help the man?' Feathers licked his foul lips.

'I will. I will. But, I have to serve my customers first. Now, what is it that you want?' She managed a smile.

'I want some supplies lady. Beans, bread and coffee will do, and give me those cigarettes and a bottle of rum. And, give me that chocolate there.'

Louise complied with his order without looking at his face or speaking a word. She was well aware that this unusual man didn't belong in these parts and she wanted him out of the store with the minimum of fuss. Her wish was granted when Feathers paid her the money and left. He would have liked to stay longer and then he'd be able to get to know that mother and daughter so much better. His first priority was to get the Egan girl to their destination and he knew that he should go. Maybe, he thought, he could come back to the general store again and the little girl would be playing outside.

Feathers tossed the supplies onto the passenger seat and jumped into the van. He grabbed the hand drawn map from the seat beside him and turned it around in every direction until it seemed to make sense with the road crossing. He grimaced with annoyance as he turned the van to the right, onto the muddy track and into the forest.

The final stage of the van's journey to the farmhouse was intolerable. The wet conditions and fading light had caused Feathers to lose control at one stage when his heavy foot had locked onto the brake pedal at the wrong time. The van slipped and skidded down the hillside until it shunted to a stop before a trickling rocky creek bed.

Feathers opened the driver's door and exited the van by tripping and falling onto the ground. Light rain had once again started to fall and the splashing mud around his hands and knees worsened his mood and made him swear vehemently. Feathers looked through the mist to a small clearing on the other side of the creek bed and he could see the remains of an old ramshackle cabin. This was no farmhouse of any description. His room above Pelma's Bar and Grill was like the Plaza Hotel compared to this rubble of timbers. He heaved in discontent and spat a ball of mucus into the creek bed as he scrambled to his feet.

The cabin consisted of a square box of maybe one or two rooms and obviously constructed from the pine trees of the clearing. There was a porch on the front side with a set of timber steps and handrail. A half rusted out metal chimney protruded from the shingled roof and much of the exterior siding of clapboards was damaged or missing. Feathers wondered how long his stay might be.

Unsatisfied with the prospect of carrying the girl across the creek and through the rain to the cabin, Feathers jumped back into the van and started the engine. He was confident that the initial momentum of the van going down the shallow bank would be enough to carry it onwards, across the stony creek bed and up the other side. From there, it would only be a short slide through the pine cones and he would be at the shack.

Feathers shoved the van into drive but before he could start the windscreen wipers, the muddy sole of his cowboy boot slid from the brake pedal onto the accelerator. The van lurched and stomped forward like a bucking mule over the rocky bed. One front wheel lodged itself in between the rocks and the van began to tip and roll. Feathers froze behind the wheel. He locked himself in position to helplessly watch the outside world turn upside down, then onto one side, teetering slightly. He winced with pain and was initially stunned. When he saw the dense gray smoke spiraling up from the engine, he tried earnestly to dislodge himself.

As the van rolled, terrified Casey was bounced heavily from one side to the other in the rear compartment, not knowing where she was or what was happening. Her young powers of reasoning could make little sense of why the van was tumbling. She knew she was in the wilderness and that it was raining. That much she had seen, through the small front window when she looked past the driver at the road ahead. She was aware that the van had then stopped and she had listened to the front door opening and closing. The initial thought that crossed her mind was that the evil driver had now pushed the van over a cliff and she was falling to her death.

When the van came to rest on its passenger side, Casey at first felt as if she wanted to retch. It was her basic instinct, rather than powers of reasoning, that came into play. She took a deep breath and looked up to see that the rear doors had twisted in the crash and the lock had burst open. With a burst of energy that would have propelled her to the lead in any school running race, Casey kicked both feet at the cracked doors and they were immediately flung outwards. She scrambled out onto the stones and then up and out of the creek bed, stumbling, almost falling as she ran. Her initial reaction was to head towards the cabin she now had in her sights. As she looked around, it was the only sign of civilization to be seen and she thought that there, help may be sought.

Casey cried out for help and repeatedly slipped and fell in the mud as she headed for the cabin. As she came closer and closer, she was increasingly aware of two disheartening reasons for her to change her plan and head for the forest. Firstly, the cabin now looked as though it was probably uninhabited and unlikely to offer any possibility of assistance as a safe haven. Secondly, she was aware of Feathers' shadowy figure hot on her footsteps. With his eyes blazing red, he was bounding through the damp ground and coming up behind her at an alarming rate.

Casey swung her body to the right and headed in the direction of the creek. The forest floor sloped downwards and she thought she was able to run faster than before. Her father's words were playing in her pounding brain as she pushed her legs as fast as she could.

'I don't care in what position you finish. What's important to me is that you try. If you give it you're best shot, then that's all I expect. Whether you come first or last is not what matters. What counts is that you try your hardest.'

Even her father could be wrong on occasions, and this was one of them. Where Casey finished in this race, was of the utmost importance. This time it was a matter of life or death. One thing was for sure. Casey was going to give it her best shot and she was definitely going to try as hard as she could.

She willed herself down the slope faster and faster. Her party shoes were now floundering and flapping by their straps. Her ankles were cut and bruised from the hundreds of pinecones and twisted sticks that made up the forest floor. The yellow birthday dress was torn and shredded from brushing against the pine bark on either side as she ran.

She continued parallel to the creek bed down through the pine trees until her tired little frame could hardly endure any more. Her energy was expended and her scratched feet were bleeding and sore. She could almost feel the stale breath of the ugly monster on the back of her neck as he closed in behind her. She could hear his muttering and swearing and she was terrified of what may occur if she didn't keep running. As she brushed a stinging bush of pine nettles from her face, she cast her vision through the raindrops onto an expansive lake of uninterrupted water.

Casey knew that God never bestowed her with a gift of running fast. She also knew that when it came to swimming, few of the other girls could even come close. Feathers made a desperate attempt to grab the girl's clothing by diving at her as she entered the shallow bank. His hand was able to clasp the strap of one shoe as it snapped from her ankle. He was left lying in the mud to watch her splash into the lake and swim away.

The fresh cold water helped to revitalize a tiny exhausted body and Casey was initially able to swim with new energy. She was so relieved to leave the monster behind that she began to smile and laugh between her breaths in a state of delirium. Normally, she would be able to swim the expanse of that lake with no trouble at all. She had achieved longer distances at the school swimming carnival and had succeeded over all the other girls.

This time, however, her mind was up to the occasion but her body was just too weak. The tumbling bruising ride in the laundry van and the race with the devil through the pine forest had taken their toll. Her nine year old figure was devoid of sufficient energy. That she had not eaten anything since having a slice of toast for break-fast, meant that her little engine was now simply out of fuel.

Casey's swimming came to a stop about one third of the way across the lake and she looked back through the last glow of daylight at the shoreline near the cabin. Feathers was nowhere to be seen and she wasn't sure if this made her feel more, or less, secure. She certainly felt less secure about being out in this lake with no energy to carry on. Surely, her fight to survive wasn't going to end like this. She didn't want to drown in this lake, but then again she thought it surely would be preferable to ending up in the hands of that monster.

There was no way she was going to make it to the other side and she doubted whether she had the energy to make it anywhere but down. She fixed her eyes on the closest shore, other than that near the cabin, and decided it was to her left. With a defying squeal, she managed to tear herself out of the yellow dress and be rid of her one dangling shoe. Left only in her underwear, she was able to slowly swim for the left bank taking three or four strokes with rests in between. It was a weak and semi-naked little girl who finally dragged herself up onto the soggy mud to collapse face down in complete exhaustion.

The light of day was almost totally gone and the rain had settled into a steady downpour when Casey's semiconscious body was suddenly flipped over. With her last ounce of strength, she rolled and twisted and kicked out, but it was no use. A heavy bulk was straddling over her and pinning her down. She gasped and choked, with her mouth wide open in a silent scream. Her bulging blue eyes were crying through the rain as they locked onto the steely gaze of the mud spattered horror mask that was Blue Featherman's ugly face.

CHAPTER 11

The prospect of having a murderer secretly watching your movements is enough to send shivers down your spine, and Sharyn is definitely feeling the strain. The taxi ride to Egan Center has been a process of increasing tension for her and now that we are pulling into the driveway, I am doubtful that her nerves are up to any more of these cloak and dagger games. Quite naturally, her grasp of my arm has been tightening by the minute, and it's now making me feel more and more uncomfortable. Her eyes have been flickering from side to side as other vehicles pass by, and she constantly looks into the taxi mirrors for a glimpse of the man in black.

Frank Berne had assured me that I wasn't to be arrested, at least not at this stage, and he is waiting to ask me some important questions vital to the investigation. I'm not looking forward to seeing him again as I'm in too deep with my own activities to tell him anything at all. It's preferable that I really stay clear until this is all finished, as the more I speak to the police, the more I have to deceive them.

As we jump out of the taxi at the entrance to Egan Center, I find myself tentatively looking into every possible piece of reflective glass. I want to get a look at this character following us, but I don't want him to catch on. There are so many people getting in and out of the taxis outside, that my imagination is running riot. Most of them are now appearing sinister and criminal looking. I feel nervous and vulnerable standing outside the vehicle. It's immediately obvious that Leslie is not there to help us and guide us in as he usually does. The security guard substituting for him opens the doors for us to enter.

'Thank you. Where's Leslie today? Not well?' I ask.

'No Mr. Egan. Leslie has gone away for his vacation. One week it is I believe sir,' the security guard utters as he escorts us through to the elevator.

'Well then, I want you to keep your eyes open for anyone acting suspiciously. I know that's a stupid thing to tell a security guard, but we have reason to believe that we may have been followed here.'

'Very well Mr. Egan. I'll keep my eyes peeled.'

I think to myself that maybe I should not have mentioned anything. If the security guard tries to apprehend someone, it's only another possible thing to go wrong.

'Thank you. However, if you do sight a shady character, don't try to approach him. I simply want you to get a good look at him so as you can give an accurate description later. Do you understand?' I'm now regretting that I brought this to his attention in the first place.

'That's fine sir. I get the picture. You just need to get his description.'

We're quickly in the elevator and shooting for the top. If my follower tailed me to the building, his journey has now come to an end. There's definitely no way he can get past the lobby with the sophisticated level of security in place. The thought also crosses my mind that this character may be unassociated with the kidnapping altogether. Maybe he's just a petty criminal who noticed us coming out of the building and concluded that the attaché case would contain valuables? Maybe he just wants to roll us and get the case? Who knows?

I'm really thinking now that I have to lose this person before the ransom delivery, just in case he intends to mug me. I don't want to be mugged at any time, and certainly not while carrying ten million dollars worth of diamonds.

* * * * *

The time is now 6.10 p.m. and most of the lights of New York are at full strength as we enter the offices of Egan Enterprises.

'Sharyn. I'd like you to check with Andrew and tell him to finish for the day. I might need him fresh and energized tomorrow. I'm going straight through into my office to prepare for Frank Berne's questions. Can you wait five minutes and then show him in?'

'All right Joe. Five minutes.' Sharyn's in her secretary mode.

I walk into my office and I'm happy as always to be there. I quickly greet the tropical fish and then sit down to gaze through the giant glass doors at the evening lights of downtown Manhattan. The attaché case seems safe enough positioned at my feet. I place the cell phones on the desk and study them.

After pausing to think, I pickup my own cell phone and dial the number for Vision Helicopters and my friend Scooty Menzies. He was dubbed 'Scooty' during his time in the Army Aviation Branch and he now specializes in transporting high profile executives and celebrities around the vicinity of New York.

If you were going to entrust a helicopter pilot with your own life, you wouldn't go past Scooty. After receiving his initial training in the military, Scooty went on to hone his skills in the jungles of South East Asia. When it comes to flying helicopters, old Scooty's done it all, from lifting machinery to and from the typhoon swept oil rigs around Borneo, to the low level transportation of guerrilla militiamen through the crocodile infested river beds of Irian Jaya.

Scooty's return to home soil was followed by a short stint in the Police Air Wing flying surveillance, and when his rebellious personality had him in constant conflict with those of superior rank, good old Scooty just resigned and went out to start up his own outfit. With all that experience behind him, you know you're as safe as you're ever going to be. I guess my number is stored into his phone because he answers with my name.

'Joey Egan. Long time no hear from. What is it? You don't like flying in helicopters anymore?'

'Scooty, you know I do. You also know how busy I am. Soon Scooty! We need to get together and have some fun soon.' I'm grinning from ear to ear.

One thing does occur to me. As increasing age seems to channel me into a more mature way of acting and thinking, I'm still a child at heart. Deep inside of me, is that same little boy who would scale the rooftops of the West Side tenements, playing with the pigeons and dreaming of the future. Sure, I often use Scooty to transport me for business engagements and sometimes to and from 'Mayfair Lodge', my countryside estate. However, every now and again, I like to let the kid in me escape for a while and just have some fun. Scooty's 'Eurocopter Twin Squirrel' is the perfect fun machine.

'Joey, can you get away for a couple of hours tomorrow? I have to drop a sky diving team from fourteen thousand feet over La Guardia. The seat next to me is vacant if you want to do the flying? What about it buddy?' Scooty is cheerfully effervescent as he always is.

'Scooty, you know I'd just love to be in on that. But, no can do! Too much happening. Maybe next time I'll take you up on your offer.' I'm feeling about twenty years old.

'Sure Joey, sure! But I've got to get you out from behind that desk of yours man. It's time for you to get your license buddy. There's fun to be had and a lot of living to do. You're alive man! This isn't a dress rehearsal.' For Scooty, life is a bundle of fun and he lives it.

'Sure Scooty! In a couple of weeks we'll do some stuff. Not now! I'm calling you for a job tonight. You fine with that?' I'm changing to a more somber mood and I'm back to my real age.

'Tonight? Yeah! Just name it,' Scooty enthusiastically replies.

'Well, I want to charter the Squirrel to standby for me between 8.45 p.m. and 10.45 p.m. I have to deliver a package tonight and I don't trust the people involved. I can't tell you too much, but I want you to cover me from the air in case I need to be lifted out.'

'Hey! That sounds cool. Love it! Right up my alley.' Scooty's excited. 'No bookings tonight. You're on Joey.'

'All right then. The pad upstairs is clear, so get here about 8.45 p.m. and I'll tell you more. Better still, make it 8.30 p.m. ETA. Oh! And make sure the night vision recorder is serviceable. I want you to track me by GPS and film what happens.'

'Right! Got it! Wilco buddy, over and out!' Scooty shouts and whoops, and then hangs up.

My hand goes down to open the second drawer and I'm able to peruse the elaborate panel of buttons and controls within. I choose the appropriate section for communications and select the office monitor to its record position. Whatever Berne has to say to me, is going on tape.

If they try to crucify me, I'll fight every inch of the way. For all I know, Berne himself is wired to the hilt and intends to record my conversation. I now select the intercom button.

'Sharyn, will you show Detective Berne into my office please?'

Sharyn enters my office with Frank Berne and they both cross the room towards me. She hands me a yellow folder as I rise to shake Berne's hand.

'Hello Detective. Come and take a seat. I'm not sure that it's a pleasure to see you, but we'll see.' I shake his hand as his head swivels around in astonishment.

Sharyn bends forward and whispers to me in a matter of fact way. 'This is the list that you asked Andrew to compile.'

I put the folder down in front of me and watch Sharyn's feminine sway as she crosses the floor and leaves. I now focus my attention back to Berne. He looks exactly the same as last time. I'd wager a thousand dollars that he's wearing the same craggy clothes as before, except maybe this time the dog-eared shirt collar is buttoned down.

'I knew you were a big name Egan. But, I have to tell you, this is impressive.' He's staring past me now at the aquarium with his mouth gaping and his eyes wide open.

'Thanks Lieutenant. I like it too. Care for a drink?'

'No thanks. I don't. Not on the job.' He wrinkles his brow and stares at the folder on my desk as he sits.

'Where's that partner of yours? What's his name? Jimmy?' I ask as I take my seat.

'Oh! He's on an assignment. Maybe better to talk to you alone this time eh?' He smiles then continues.

'I'm here because there's been a new development in the case of Mrs. Egan's murder and I'm hoping you can give us some information.'

He fidgets and looks uncomfortable talking to me from across the desk. I want to find out what he knows, but at the same time, I don't want this meeting to last any longer than it has to. If the kidnapper's cell phone goes off, the last thing I need is Frank Berne sitting there while I'm trying to communicate with the kidnappers.

I stand up and point to the turquoise leather lounge suite as I speak. 'Fine. All right then. Why don't we move to the lounge? It may be more comfortable for us both.'

We sit down face to face and he gets straight to the point.

'Have you ever had any contact or had dealings with a man named Blue Featherman?' He eyes me suspiciously. 'He's also sometimes known as 'Feathers'.'

'No. I don't think so. No one of that name comes to mind. But I'd have to check our record of clients. Wait just a minute Lieutenant.'

I walk back to my desk, open the yellow folder, and run my finger down the ten itemized surnames. I can see that Andrew has written a concise description under each name, and an account of why each of them may have reason to be vindictive. Although a couple of the entries seem vaguely familiar, the name Blue Featherman is not amongst them. I look back at Berne and shake my head.

'Well Detective, as I said, I don't think so. But, I shall get my secretary to double check our client database for his name.' I move back to the lounge and resume my seat.

'I doubt that you'd find his name in your client list,' Berne shuffles in his seat and repositions himself as he casts me a sarcastic smile. 'The man's a degenerate scumbag and he wouldn't be affording the likes of this.'

'For heaven's sake Berne! If that's the case, what makes you think that I might know him?' I'm remembering that the conversation is being recorded.

'Because he's a prime suspect in the murder of Audrey Egan.' He adopts a smug expression and continues. 'Is it possible, you may have met him in some other way? Maybe in some of your other dealings which I'm sure you'd rather not tell me about?' He looks away as he speaks and runs his hand through his short brush cut hair.

'Listen Berne! Here we go again. I'm not interested in your innuendo. If you have something to accuse me of, come out and say it. Otherwise, keep your snide remarks to yourself.' If he was sitting above a secret trapdoor, I'd now push the button to be rid of him.

'Yeah sure, sure! Well, tell me then. Have you heard from your daughter?'

'No I haven't as yet. Do you have any information regarding her?' I can sense the frustration.

He looks at me with a more compassionate expression and gives me the disturbing news.

'This character Blue Featherman has been linked to the murder scene, and if he's grabbed your daughter, I'm afraid she's in grave danger.' He shakes his head and frowns.

'What do you mean Lieutenant? What do you know about him that makes you think he's involved?' I sit back to listen, feeling rather sick in the stomach.

'Featherman's a low life creep of the worst kind. The best place for him is in hell itself, and why he was out on parole, I'll never understand. We risk our damn necks to get these assholes behind bars where they belong and what happens, eh?'

Berne shakes his fist into the air in a state of rage and continues.

'Anyway, he's out, and this is what happens.'

'What happens? What do you know? Tell me what you know.' I'm starting to construct an image of this Featherman in my mind and I don't like what I see.

Berne continues, 'The lab boys pieced together the label from a broken bottle in the elevator and they were then able to trace it back to the department store where it was purchased. It seems that old Feathers was in there buying up supplies for some kind of disguise and made himself famous with all of the security cameras. We also dusted a fingerprint fragment from a piece of the broken bottle which subsequently matched his, and on and on from there.'

'What's a bottle got to do with it? What do you mean on and on from there?' I ask feeling even more sick.

'Well, when we checked the hotel security cameras, all we got that was out of the ordinary was a white laundry van arriving into the basement car park prior to the murder, and then leaving in a hell of a hurry afterwards. Just so happens, however, that the van was stolen the same morning, probably by our friend, Mr. Featherman, I'd say.'

I simply can't believe my ears. My face is frozen into a fixture of shock and disbelief as I cast my mind back. That would be the same laundry van that almost collected our yellow taxi outside the Icelandic Hotel. I now wish to God that we had collided full on, and I would have Casey with me right now. I even tipped the cab driver a hundred dollars for skillfully avoiding the very scoundrel who murdered Audrey and who now holds my daughter for ransom. I keep my thoughts to myself and look Berne in the eye.

'It seems like he's our man then. Let's hunt the bastard down and get my daughter back.' I turn my expression of shock into one of rage.

'I'm almost afraid to ask Lieutenant. What was he in jail for last time? And also, what's that bottle in the elevator all about?' I try to catch his eye but he pulls his gaze away.

Frank Berne's lip begins to quiver slightly, revealing the pain he feels deep inside as he answers my question.

'Blue Featherman is a monster of the worst kind, an obsessively cruel psychopath. He has a history of preying on small children. He's a known pedophile and he should be behind bars. The bottle was filled with ether fluid to render his victim unconscious.'

It's hard to imagine worse news. The vision I had constructed of him was far too kind. It now transforms into something much worse. My mind embarks on a frenzied slideshow of gut wrenching images of my little Casey being devoured by a horrible monster in black robes. She's naked, and lashed by her hands and feet to the four corners of a rickety iron bed. The ugly monster is probing and prodding at the most innocent and delicate parts of her young body, and his yellow bloodstained fangs are dripping with saliva. The hysterical little girl is confused and terrified as she thrashes about in distress and agony. The vision fades, but the sickness in my stomach intensifies.

My moist eyes begin to blink as they become blurred with tears. The fluids in my belly are now swirling and rumbling as I lean over the edge of the turquoise lounge. My head is thumping, my legs are weak, and my whole body begins to tremble. I heave uncontrollably, vomiting the contents of my stomach onto the office floor at the feet of Frank Berne.

He jumps to help me and places one hand around my shoulder.

'My God man! Are you all right? You better have some water. Hey! Take it easy. Come on now. We'll find her. We'll get her back.'

I'd say that right then and there, my name was permanently struck from Frank Berne's list of prime suspects.

'I'll live. I'll be all right.' I catch my breath and stumble to my feet. 'If there's nothing else Detective, I'd like to be left alone for a while.'

Frank Berne stands, nods, and shakes his shoulders in an attempt to rearrange his crumpled clothes. I'm still recovering from my vomiting episode, and Berne walks himself to the door and closes it behind him. I can hear Sharyn talking to him in the outer office as she escorts him to the elevator.

I grab a hand towel from the cocktail cabinet and get down to the unpleasant task of cleaning up the mess, which itself causes me to feel more shaky and weak in the knees.

It seems that I have finished my meeting with Detective Berne just in the nick of time because the kidnapper's cell phone now starts a tremulous dance across my desk top. I stumble over the floor and quickly sit down at my desk, taking a pen in one hand and the phone in the other. The now familiar electronically modified voice commences to prescribe the terms of tonight's ransom delivery.

'You must follow these instructions carefully to see your daughter again. You are to bring the diamonds in the metal briefcase to the Subway station at 68th Street and Hunter College. Come alone. Inform no one. Be there at

9.30 p.m. sharp. Wait for further instructions on this phone.'

I jot the details down on a notepad and shove the piece of paper into my pocket. The subway station they're talking about is a mere three blocks from Egan Center and only a five-minute walk at most. I had thought about flying off the pad with Scooty to avoid my shadowy follower down below, but three blocks away? Maybe that's an unnecessary precaution. If he was a thug, there to rob me, it's doubtful he would still be waiting around after so much time. If on the other hand, he was one of the kidnappers, he would surely be only monitoring my movements to see if I was complying with their orders, and, maybe decide that I'm not. I conclude that I'll leave on foot with the diamonds and have Scooty in his helicopter, watching me from above.

Sharyn knocks and opens the door to enter. Frank must have told her of my sickness attack because she's not surprised at all when she sees the state I'm in.

'Are you all right Joe?'

'Well, yes and no. When I heard about the creep who's probably behind all of this, it made me sick to my stomach. He's not only a murderous bastard who's got Casey, he's a fucking pedophile. I swear to you Sharyn, I'll make him regret that he's…...'

'Yes Joe. We'll get our hands on him and he'll pay. Now you need to relax a bit. Get some fresh clothes on and put your feet up for a while.' She takes up her usual position, with her long legs crossed over the edge of my desk.

I try to turn my anguish into a smile as I speak.

'Well, yes. You're right of course. Let's go up to my apartment. And by the way, I have some news for you. I received another call while you were outside and they've given me some instructions to follow. I'll tell you about it later. Now we have to get up top. There's a helicopter coming onto the pad soon and I better get there to check it's clear.'

I stand up and grab the folder on my desk as I continue. 'You need to rest as well and I'd like you to be in my apartment tonight when I'm out handing over the ransom.'

'Fine Joe. I'll fix you some food while you're having a shower and we can get ready.' She swings her legs around and stands up next to me.

'By the way Sharyn, do any of these names mean something to you?' I open Andrew's folder as we cross the floor.

Sharyn shakes her head and takes my arm as I continue to study the ten surnames in large print. I'm stopped in my tracks when I focus my vision on the detailed information written in small print under the second entry. My shoes are riveted to the floor and my head goes into a spin. Although the surname stirs nothing in my memory, the other information immediately identifies the person we're talking about. I gasp with complete surprise.

'Good God! Sharyn. Have you read this? Have a look here. Look at this here!'

Sharyn concentrates on the page I now hold out before her, but I decide to read the information out loud.

Name:.....MURCHISON. L.T.
Age:.......43 years
Details:...Mr. Murchison was the principal executive of 'Silicon Resolutions', a top ten performer on the New York NASDAQ. Listed by Forbes as having a personal net worth of approximately three hundred and twenty million dollars, his dealings with Egan Enterprises in-

cluded the intended purchase of the top-level penthouse in Tower Two of Egan Center. The penthouse had been reserved by Murchison from the initial marketing stage of the venture and a substantial deposit had been paid. When Mr. Joseph Egan, the main individual shareholder of Silicon Resolutions, apart from Murchison himself, suddenly liquidated all of his held stocks, the company was substantially downgraded by two of the major Wall Street rating agencies. This, together with the subsequent technology crash, pushed Silicon Resolutions into a Chapter Eleven and rendered Mr. Murchison penniless. As a result of the bankruptcy process, the assignment of the Egan Center penthouse was consequently cancelled, and his six million dollar deposit was forfeited. Mr. Leslie Murchison is presently employed as the security doorman of Egan Center Tower One.

CHAPTER 12

Many of the high flying companies of the Technology Boom were, quite simply, elaborately decorated hot air balloons defying the laws of gravity. 'Silicon Resolutions' was a prime example of such a balloon. The outer skin was impressive and convincing but the real guts of the company was exactly that. A lot of hot air!

With the new found convenience of Internet communications fueling the nation's sense of economic well being, the investment industry was full of hype. It seemed that all a company had to do was include the words 'dotcom', 'tech', or 'silicon' in their company name, and everyone wanted in. People were more afraid of losing their ride on the bandwagon than they were of losing their money, so they all wanted to jump on.

The process of carefully researching a company's fundamentals for growth potential had given way to irrational impulsiveness. Who cared what the production figures were or what profits would be generated? What mattered was the way the shares performed. If the share price was going up then that was the profit.

Leslie Murchison was five foot eleven inches of plainness. He was the kind of guy you could meet for the tenth time and still not recognize him. He was medium build, dark brown hair, brown eyes and bland face. I guess you could refer to him as 'average looking'. He was a quiet, unassuming, very boring, and also, a completely brilliant person. Lonely and single, he had nothing better to do with his time than to devote it all to his work and his computer.

During the mid-nineties, Leslie would often wonder how he would be able to escape from the rut he was in. As an independent financial adviser, he would spend the days talking about the financial woes of his customers. At night and throughout the weekends, he would sit at home at his computer, formulating financial blueprints for them to follow. More often than not, the problems involved minimizing and delaying tax responsibilities to achieve the unimpeded exponential growth of funds.

Leslie knew that one very clever way to delay the burden of taxation was to channel money offshore. By funneling funds into independent offshore companies situated in tax-free havens, investments could temporarily be isolated from the jaws of internal revenue, and thereby remain free to multiply at a faster rate. For the money to become once again available to the investor, tax would surely have to be paid eventually. But not during the off-shore growth of the capital. And that was the key issue.

From this popular tax minimization scheme, Leslie stumbled across the basis of a new enterprise. Both simple and brilliant in principal, the core business of Silicon Resolutions was an Internet web-site. By way of this user-friendly investment club, investors could enter their personal details and online bank account facilities. The chosen monetary deposits would then flow from their respective home accounts into the offshore accounts of tax-free companies.

The funds would be paid to Silicon Resolutions which would in turn, redirect them into international mutual funds in the tax havens of Vanuatu or Andorra. Along the way of course, Silicon Resolutions would deduct two lots of commission. Firstly, from the investors themselves and secondly, from the investment companies into which the money was deposited.

His business was definitely up and running. Silicon Resolutions had been floated on the NASDAQ and investors were scrambling to jump on board. In actual fact, the business of online offshore investment was doing very well and the company did have reasonable fundamentals for continued growth. This positive news was, however, blown out of all proportion because the probable break-even point was still some two or three years down the track.

Even though the fledgling company was yet to declare a dividend, the word 'Silicon' implied that the share price would surely rise, and rise, it did. From its initial public offering of fifty cents per share the price attained the dizzy heights of sixty-two dollars in the short time span of eleven months.

It wasn't the commissions that swelled the coffers of Leslie Murchison. They were barely sufficient to pay the lease on his new Wall Street office. Leslie's accounts flooded with a new kind of spending power. Credit! As the share price of Silicon Resolutions skyrocketed into the stratosphere, Leslie's personal net worth was propelled along with it. His wealth was contained in the huge holding of shares he had allocated himself from the inception and his net worth was reflected in the price of those shares. As his net worth grew, so too did his credit rating. Leslie Murchison could buy whatever he wanted and whenever he wanted it. All on credit!

Well it didn't take Leslie long before he could start enjoying the benefits of being a successful business owner. He had discovered an exciting new way to spend his time and he was never going to be bored again. Leslie was going to spend money. He knew that he could never spend it all, no matter how he tried. His wealth had gone from zero to three hundred million dollars in less than one year and he had concluded that he would never have to worry about money again.

It's strange how so many financial advisers and accountants fail to listen to their own advice. They spend hours and hours meticulously organizing the accounts of other people. Yet, at the same time, their own personal affairs can be in a state of complete shambles. So many times had Leslie advised his clients to take some profit out and lock it away.

'Yes. Take some out along the way.' He would give his advice to the successful company executive who was riding high on a crest of company profits. 'Make some hay while the sun shines,' he often would say.

Why was it, that all of these basic principals went flying out of the window when he himself joined the ranks of his own clients and started to ride the wave of success? Maybe it all happened too fast for him to comprehend the enormity of it all. He should have known that the tide of his good fortune could turn in an instant. He should have known not to have all of his eggs in one basket. And, he should have known that no one ever went broke taking a profit. Yes. He should have known and he should have heeded his own advice. But he was too busy having fun.

Along with his new financial freedom, came a whole new way of thinking. Leslie's old ideas of caution had now become ideas of flippancy. His words of self-advice were simply, 'I'll take it!' and, 'I'll take that as well!'

'I'll take it!' Leslie had said to the showroom representative from the driver's seat of the new red Ferrari.

'I'll take it!' he had said to the salesman from the bridge of the luxury ninety-foot ocean cruiser.

'I'll take it!' he had said to Scooty Menzies from the passenger seat of the Bell 206 Jetranger helicopter.

Scooty controlled the cyclic with his right hand and ran his left hand through his wavy gray hair as his blue eyes gleamed. His mouth had dropped wide open when Leslie had accepted his offer to sell. He had only mentioned the idea as a joke and he couldn't believe his good fortune when Leslie had jumped in to buy the helicopter.

'Right on Leslie! Right on.' Scooty nodded his head in a diagonal motion and whooped.

Scooty Menzies was ever so pleased to meet Leslie Murchison. Leslie had quickly become one of Scooty's main sources of revenue and the main contributing factor in the rising success of Vision Helicopters.

With gold and platinum credit cards spilling from his wallet, Leslie had wanted himself, and all of his staff, to travel everywhere by helicopter. It was almost a daily event and Scooty's small one-man operation was booming. He was able to upgrade from his aging Bell 206 to the latest Twin Squirrel Eurocopter when Leslie accepted to buy his old machine for double what it was worth.

This was typical of Leslie's mode of operation. He was so wealthy on paper that he had become reckless with money. Instead of investing in appreciating assets, he was pouring the value of his shares into the purchase of depreciating liabilities, and he was borrowing more and more money to do so.

'How long can it last? How long before the bubble will burst?' These were the words written in almost every financial column and were also the thoughts on Joe Egan's mind as the share price of Silicon Resolutions soared higher and higher.

Leslie Murchison was too busy having fun to be reading financial columns. He was in a state of euphoria as he went from being ferried around in his helicopter to red-lining the mighty engine of his F40 Ferrari. Leslie was in Porto Fino on the Italian Riviera and sun baking on the stern deck of his ocean cruiser when the message came through.

'Sir. A message has been received for you to contact your office in New York as soon as possible.' The Italian ship's waiter retrieved Leslie's cocktail glass as he spoke.

Joe Egan had decided that enough was enough when he sold off his share portfolio. One of the first to go was the volatile Silicon Resolutions which Joe suspected had run its course and was overdue for a severe correction. The first parcel of shares to be sold achieved a staggering sixty-two dollars per share representing a profit on his investment of some twelve thousand per cent. As his program of selling continued, the share price fell accordingly until the final parcel was liquidated at forty-eight dollars per share.

The news of the sell-off came as a shock to Leslie Murchison as he looked around at the magnificent interior of the cruiser's stateroom. He couldn't understand why anyone would want to dump the stocks in his company and undermine the share price. The market was healthy and rising steadily. Surely this phenomenon was to be short lived and the price would recover to achieve even greater levels in the near future. He decided not to panic.

Even at the new share price, his fortune still tallied a gigantic two hundred and forty million dollars and it would increase from there. He could look forward to soon becoming a billionaire. Leslie decided that there was sufficient margin in the share price of his company to withstand a fifty percent drop in the share price and still leave him little cause to worry about financial matters. He re-

176

laxed and returned to the sundeck for another cocktail and to listen to more of the classical Italian arias he had developed such a liking for.

The financial editorial that lay open on Joe Egan's desk the following morning had nothing good to say about Silicon Resolutions. Joe's sell off had sparked a renewed interest in the stock by New York's business critics. They continued to investigate the true merit of the company's underlying business and labeled the objective of tax avoidance as being unpatriotic and un-American. One columnist actually called for a Federal investigation into the activities of Silicon Resolutions dubbing it 'Wall Street's Runt'.

The news of the agency down rating and price collapse gradually spread around the investment community and the damage to the reputation of Silicon Resolutions was irreparable. Although a slight rebound did occur at the opening bell of the next day's trading, the spike was short-lived and the stock commenced a slow but steady downwards spiral from which it was never to recover. Within three days, the changing mood on the trading screens of New York's NASDAQ had become painfully apparent and the falling market was gathering momentum.

All good things come to an end and the tragic end was near for many dot-com companies including Silicon Resolutions. The share price finally stabilized at a feeble twenty-two cents. Leslie Murchison's net worth in the company was now one million and sixty four thousand, five hundred and sixteen dollars. When the dust finally settled and the banks had deducted the liabilities of the year's flamboyant extravaganza, he was left with a net worth of minus thirty one million, three hundred and ninety two thousand dollars. Leslie Murchison was bankrupt.

Strangely, Leslie wasn't devastated. He had enjoyed a wonderful experience of unheard of wealth and in a way, he was glad it was ended. He took it on the chin when the Italian shipping company sent their representatives to escort Leslie from the futuristic vessel. He smiled in amusement when his Ferrari was repossessed, and he looked back sentimentally as he walked from his helicopter for the last time. The man who had made it and lost it in record time, now adopted an 'easy come, easy go' attitude about the whole thing.

He was subconsciously aware that it had to end sooner or later. The life he was living wasn't real and he knew it. Some people know how to handle vast fortunes and some people simply don't. Leslie was much better at advising people how to handle vast fortunes rather than actually owning one. He now concluded that if he had stayed on the road from rags to riches, he probably would have died. Maybe killed in a helicopter crash or smashed to pieces in the tangled wreck of his Ferrari. All things have a reason and a purpose, and his purpose now, was to come back down to Earth.

During the ensuing weeks and months, Leslie was to develop another additional purpose to complete his re-entry from orbit. He resolved that he wanted to remain in the company of rich and famous people, and the person he had heard more of than anybody else was a business tycoon by the name of Joseph Egan. Yes. Leslie decided that he wanted to get as close as possible to this man to satisfy his interest. Maybe, he could even gain some kind of employment in the very company that precipitated his own downfall? He wasn't a sore loser. He'd had his fun, and that was that.

Was it infatuation or was it curiosity? Was he being influenced by something buried in his subconscious mind? Leslie wasn't sure. He just wanted to be in Joe Egan's close proximity and he wanted to rub shoulders with the man. He just didn't understand why.

CHAPTER 13

As a person infatuated by helicopters since graduating into long britches, there's nothing that stirs the fervor in my veins more, than watching a helicopter in motion as it descends right before me.

I'm definitely stirred up now as I listen intently to the familiar distant sound. The thick cool air of the Manhattan evening still carries enough moisture to make the blades SLAP, SLAP, SLAP, as the Twin Squirrel appears at a steep angle above Central Park. As Scooty makes his approach, he keys his transmitter in the required sequence to light up the rooftop pad for the landing, and soon thereafter, the helicopter's landing lights flash a blinding glare in my eyes.

The blue and gold giant bird grows larger and larger and the slapping of the blades changes to a deafening WHOP, WHOP, WHOP, as my heart races with excitement. Blade tip spray illuminates in neon radiating splashes and the down forced compressed air clears the pad of anything not tied down or hanging on. I grip the metal railing behind my back with both hands as the huge machine completes an intrusive dynamic touchdown and the chaos of it all subsides to a rhythmic idle.

I can't help but feel a great sense of satisfaction at seeing the impressive looking machine sitting right there on my own rooftop. It's not a money or power phenomenon. I've always wanted to fly one of these beauties, and one day, I know it will be me behind those controls. It's one more goal to achieve and one more ambition, but for now, it's Scooty's domain.

The right hand side pilot's door swings open and there's Scooty, with a serious expression, methodically gliding his fingers over the buttons and knobs to shut down the engine. With that complete, the engine dies and the blades gradually wind down. Scooty can't help himself and his expression turns to a wide grin as he steps towards me dressed in a khaki flight suit with an assortment of badges down the sleeves. His tall figure stoops instinctively as he approaches, with the blades still swishing above his head. He then stretches to his full height and carries himself with his usual confidence as he strides closer. His thin, lanky, six foot six figure is a sweet vision for sore eyes and I'm pleased to see him.

'Joey, my man! How're ya doin'?'

'Hi buddy. Good to see you,' I reply with high spirits.

We shake hands and he nearly knocks me off balance as he slaps my back and then grabs my shoulder as though I'm his kid.

'What's going down, Joey?'

'Come inside Scooty and I'll tell you all about it.' I lead the way.

We leave the helicopter slowly sweeping the cold air and we step down through a doorway to the security door. A few more steps to descend and we're soon entering the upper vestibule of my penthouse where Sharyn is anxiously waiting.

'Hello Scooty.' She smiles bashfully.

'Hello Sharyn. You're still as beautiful as ever.' Although always the ladies man, Scooty means every word of his compliment.

Scooty kisses Sharyn on the cheek and we move through to the living area where we can sit down beneath the jury of buffalo heads to talk. I look across at my old friend as he tries to relax in the leather sofa and I study his craggy likeable appearance.

For a man of only thirty-seven, the stresses and strains of his flying career have left him a man beyond his years. Although his body is fit and taut from regular exercise, his wavy hair is prematurely gray and his face is creased with the worry lines of a fast exciting existence. Despite this, the effervescent sparkle of his blue eyes and his smiling white teeth comes shining through. There's no mistaking Scooty. He's definitely one of a kind. When he was created, they threw away the mold.

'Scooty, you're like a brother to me and I always know I can rely on you in times of trouble. I'm in trouble and you haven't heard the half of it.' I pause for breath.

'Well, tell me all about it.' He looks anxious.

'You know what happened to Audrey yesterday. She was brutally murdered while waiting to meet me for lunch.'

'I'm so sorry, man. It wasn't only you who loved Audrey, Joe. Many people loved her.' Scooty hangs his head as he mumbles.

'Scooty, in my opinion, the police are mishandling the whole thing. They even suspect me as the murderer.' I can feel my words quicken as I speak and my voice is starting to tremble.

'Hey Joey, I still have some connections in the force. Maybe I can get some action for you.' He sits forward and pounds his knee with his fist.

'What you need to know is that Casey was with Audrey yesterday. Whoever killed Audrey, then also kidnapped Casey, and they've contacted me with a ransom demand. The meet is tonight.'

'I wouldn't be handing over any ransom unless you see Casey safe and sound at the same time. Hey man! You need the cops in on this.'

'No cops!' I wave my hand in despair as I reply.

'They know how to handle these things Joe.' Scooty shakes his head in disagreement.

'Scooty, listen to me. No cops!' I'm boiling over and Scooty shrinks back as I raise my voice.

'Cops have fucked this thing up from the start and I'm doing this my way. I don't trust them on this. All I want is to deliver the ransom and get my daughter back. These guys aren't negotiating. They don't even give me a chance to talk to them. It's all one sided.' I'm ranting emotionally.

'Jesus man, they sound ruthless,' says Scooty.

'They ARE fucking ruthless. We're Casey's only chance. You got it? With Casey safe and sound, I'll spend the rest of my life hunting these bastards and making them pay for what they're putting me through. But, first, I have to get her back.'

'Sure! Sure! You're the man Joey. Tell me. Have the cops come up with anything at all?'

'They think they know the guy who killed Audrey and took Casey. He's a known criminal and child molester, a real low-life freak.' I'm shaking my fist in the air.

'Hell man! I'm with you on this. I'm with you till we get Casey back.' Scooty frowns and tightens his jaw as I continue.

'There must be someone else behind it though, because this scumbag guy just isn't smart enough to contrive an elaborate plot and devise such a clever means of communication.' I check my watch as I speak and see that it's 8.45 p.m.

'Any ideas yourself who could be involved? You must have turned a few people offside with the construction of this place,' Scooty queries.

'Well, there's one joker who's starting to look a bit malignant. He's part of our security team and has also worked as the doorman of Tower One. Seems he may have just cause to be resentful, but we have no proof.'

Sharyn hasn't said a word and she's just sitting and taking it all in.

'Leslie Murchison? Joe, do you really think he's implicated?' She interjects, and then regrets doing so when Joe creases his brow and glares at her.

Scooty can't believe his ears when the name sinks into his memory.

'You ARE fucking JOKING! I knew a Leslie Murchison.' He bangs the palm of his hand on his forehead as he shouts. Both Sharyn and I are completely stunned with surprise.

'What do you know Scooty? Maybe he's someone else you're thinking of?' I ask.

'Well this guy used to charter my Jetranger all the time. He was a big money man with his own high-flying finance company. Sometimes it was just for himself and sometimes it was for his friends and staff to joyride around. Man, he was raking it in, just like you Joe.'

'Scooty, I think we are talking about the same person.'

'Sure Joe. But this Murchison I was flying around was nothing like a murderer or child molester. He was a cool guy enjoying his success.'

Scooty seems so pleased to be able to contribute and he's getting more excited as he continues.

'Man, he even bought my Jetranger from me and he was talking about moving into one of your penthouses.

Then, he just faded away like it was all a dream and I never heard or saw of him again.' Scooty searches my eyes for a response.

'Well, I think that I, inadvertently, was the reason his dream bubble was shattered. Maybe he's bitter and twisted, and maybe he's not the so called cool guy he used to be.' I sicken at the thought that I may be the reason why Murchison hates me, why Audrey was killed, and why my own daughter's life is on the line.

'Right Joey! We'll do this together. I'm your puppet. Just tell me what to do and how I can help. Anything man!'

I can see that Scooty would risk his life to help me and I grab his arm to express my appreciation.

'All I want you to do is be there in the air. I have to take the ransom alone. That was specified in their demands. Stay high enough so as not to arouse suspicion, and keep the infra-red rolling. If we can get a clue with the video, we'll be able to feed it to the police afterwards. I'll be in contact with you via my hands free mobile, and I'll tell you of my location at all times. Can you do that?' I nervously look at my timepiece again.

'Sure. That's easy, but what if it all goes to shit man? What then?'

'Then Scooty, you may need to get me some help. Just do whatever you think is best. Dust me off out of there or call the cops. Play it as you see it. Understand?'

'All right Joey. You got it. Just tell me you're taking a gun with you.'

'No. I don't own a gun.' My hand feels for the silver paper knife in my pocket as though it's some kind of suitable substitute.

'Your lucky day man. I've got a .38 caliber in the chopper. .., always carry it right there. ..., Figure if I'm

186

on fire and I'm going to go down in a fireball, I may as well put a bullet in my own head and save myself the agony.' Scooty grins.

My mind is pounding at a thousand miles an hour and I spring to my feet and start to pace the floor with buffalo eyes watching my every move.

'All right. Here's the deal. It's now ten to nine and they want me at 68th Street and Hunter College subway at nine thirty. Scooty, go and get me that gun and any rounds you can find. I'll change into some jeans and a sweatshirt. I'm not going down any subway without an attitude happening. Sharyn, I want you to just stay here and wait for us to call in. You may need to help us if we fly back in with Casey.'

I briskly walk into my wardrobe area and choose items of appropriate clothing. I pull a black polyester baseball sweat over my head and drag a pair of black denim jeans up and belt them at the waist. A black ballpark cap and black sneakers finish the attitude look, and I stand back to survey the results in a full-length mirror.

My God! Without realizing what I was doing, I'm now looking at the man in black. It makes me wonder if I'm going completely crazy. Maybe I'm my own worst enemy? Maybe I should have called Frank Berne and told him everything. Too late for maybe. Too late for regret. No time for hesitation.

I transfer the paper knife and the bag of cubic zirconia to my jeans pocket and put on a blue denim waist jacket as I leave the wardrobe. Scooty and Sharyn are in deep conversation as I reappear. On the coffee table before them gleams a silver .38 Smith and Wesson Bodyguard revolver with a single cardboard box of rounds.

'You ever used one of these Joey? Just aim at the chest and squeeze the trigger.'

'Thanks Scooty. I'll remember those instructions old friend.'

I reach down and nervously pick up the revolver. It feels icy and hard in my hand and I'm surprised that it feels heavier than expected. My God, the closest thing to a .38 Smith and Wesson I've experienced is the childhood cap gun that my father gave me, and that's going back a few years. I snap open the gun and carefully count five bullets waiting precariously in little chambers to perform their flights of death.

After spinning the mechanism and feeling more comfortable with the feel of it in my grip, I put the gun in my right side jacket-pocket and the box of rounds in my left. I take the kidnapper's cell phone and shove it in my jeans and my own cell phone goes onto my belt with the lead pushed up inside my shirt to the earpiece.

'Okay, Scooty let's get wired up.' He reaches for his cell phone as I speed dial his number.

Scooty answers and we're hot wired and able to talk to each other constantly. I pick up the silver attaché and feel the small bag of diamonds shift inside. My Rolex tells me it's just past nine o'clock and I know it's now or never. Sharyn comes to my side with tears in her eyes, and she clings to my neck with a long kiss. I can feel that both of our lips are trembling.

'Joe. Don't get yourself killed doing this. You have to stay alive if you're going to save Casey. Keep safe for her and also, for me Joe.'

Sharyn releases her arms from around my neck, and her moist pleading eyes are looking deep into my soul.

'I don't have any choice here Sharyn. I have to do what it takes to get my daughter back. If she's still alive, I know she'll be waiting for me to get her out. She'll be depending on me and hanging on, waiting for ME!' My

188

anxiety is turning to rage once again and regard for my own safety is the furthest thing from my mind.

* * * * *

It seems that my life consists of a series of extremely stressful gateways, gateways of trauma intervened by long periods of calm in between. These gateways are usually hazardous and have to be negotiated. There's no choice and no way around them, only right through the middle to the relative tranquility on the other side.

The first such gateway was when I was only four years old. I had left my mother's side and run out onto the street to chase some pigeons. With a happy gleeful smile of delight across my face, I had run straight in front of a black Buick sedan. I still wonder to this day, not only how I survived it with mere cuts and abrasions, but also how fate could have put my own Uncle Jack behind the wheel.

This was followed several years later when I was struck down with Glandular Fever. Seven days in a coma and ten weeks in a hospital ward, was followed by a miraculous full recovery. Even the doctors had feared the worst for me and had expressed their grave concerns to my relatives.

Another gateway of trauma was my parent's death nine years later. It was almost impossible to bear. My mother was the first to pass away and my father died three months later with a broken heart.

Now, here I stand. This is another goddamn gateway with Audrey's murder and Casey's kidnapping, and I'm as sure as hell going to charge at it with every ounce of energy I can muster. It may be too late to save Audrey, but for Casey and I, there's sure to be greener pastures on the other side.

'Scooty, get airborne. I'm out of here guys. I'm going to get my princess.'

CHAPTER 14

Sharyn and Scooty watched as Joe, resembling a vigilante commando and as determined as a dog with a bone, marched quickly out of the room in the direction of the elevator foyer. They knew he was a man on a mission of personal justice. They knew they shouldn't follow him.

'Scooty, what are we going to do?' Sharyn whimpered.

'I don't know Sharyn. He's going it alone with this. May God help him, because he won't have anyone else around.' Scooty spoke quietly and gravely.

Scooty was himself determined to do his part as best he could and, if it came to the crunch, he knew he would fly his chopper right into Times Square to get Joey out of trouble. Sharyn walked behind him as they climbed the last rack of steps back up to the heli-pad. Scooty jogged across to the dormant Squirrel, gave Sharyn a wink and a wide flashing grin as he opened the pilot's door, and hauled himself up onto the pilot's seat.

His hands momentarily took their customary position on the controls, his left hand checking the collective lever was in the fully down position with the locks released, and his right grip smoothly caressing the cyclic handle and its associated triggers and buttons. He didn't have to think about what he was doing. It just happened automatically. The minute he sat in any helicopter, his hands and feet would act in unison as though synchronized through a central intelligence, independent of his own brain.

Scooty was just born to fly choppers and that was the long and short of it. In his bedside drawer, he still kept the few letters and photographs his father had sent home from the Vietnam War. Still a small toddler at the time, Scooty could hardly comprehend the context of each letter as his mother would read them out loud. He couldn't understand the big words, and he also couldn't understand why his mother would burst into fits of uncontrollable sobbing when she was barely halfway through each letter.

Scooty had always liked the photographs of his dad in a military flight suit, especially the picture of him standing with his crew of three in front of the green Iroquois UH-1 troop carrier helicopter. Scooty cherished that photograph. It was his best material link to the father he never knew, the father who was still missing in action. There was one thing he did know. Aviation blood was flowing through his veins and flying helicopters was his destiny.

When he slipped the headset over his ears and clicked the intercom button to integrate his mobile phone, all Scooty could hear was the background static from Joe's cell phone.

'Joey. It's Scooty here, checking in. Can you read me?'

There was still nothing but background hash and Scooty figured Joe was still inside the building. His fingers continued to glide across the cockpit panel instruments like the maestro conducting an orchestra and the Squirrel jet turbines whirred into life, first one, and then the other. Hydraulics checked, radios, anti-collision light on. Soon the whole apparatus was purring and vibrating like a sleeping giant awakened to a new dawn, and Scooty was once again at home.

With the huge blades now cutting through the cool moist air, Scooty wound the engine RPM and torque up to the required range and the chopper was like a cat poised to leap into the air with the slightest provocation. Scooty wasn't just sitting in that helicopter; he was part of it. Although his eyes instinctively scanned every instrument, he could fly blindfolded if he had to. His pilot senses were so well honed that his body and mind could feel how the engine was performing and what the helicopter was doing. In this configuration, the pilot and machine were one. Scooty was the helicopter.

After twisting his head around to check the skies were clear, Scooty gave a final 'thumbs up' to Sharyn as she stood out in front. With such great power at his fingertips, he smoothly raised the collective and the blast of air became hurricane force. He noticed that Sharyn was now having trouble holding onto her delicate skirt and at one stage it whipped up around her face, revealing her beautiful slender legs and lace panties. He winked at her and with a broad grin on his face, pulled the blue and gold chopper smoothly up and around in one synchronized flowing action. Sharyn just stood there watching the marvelous machine diminish upward. She was overwhelmed by the incredible energy of what she had witnessed.

Scooty raised the Squirrel quickly up to two thousand feet and positioned himself over the front of Egan Center in a suspended hover. He activated the night vision camera recorder and zoomed it down to Park Avenue until the sidewalk pedestrians were clearly visible on his cockpit screen.

'Scooty, can you hear me? I'm on the sidewalk head-ing north on Park Avenue and 66th Street.' Joey's voice was now coming clearly through his headset.

'All right Joey, I'm zooming down now and I'll try to lock on with the infra-red. I'll be looking for you to turn east on 67th Street.'

Scooty managed to lock the camera onto Joe's figure as he approached the intersection and he checked again that the recorder was rolling. His heart went out to Joe Egan and he really wanted to be down on that sidewalk, side by side with the man he admired. There was Joe, a solitary man on a mission, a lone gladiator, meeting his foe head on, to save the daughter he loved so much.

Scooty unzipped the leg pocket of his flight suit and retrieved some spearmint gum, which he pushed into the side of his mouth and started to chew furiously. He moni-tored the screen with the flashing magenta brackets around Joe's image and allowed his mind to recollect. He thought of his first meeting with Joe and how they had subsequently become friends.

* * * * *

Scooty had been trying to establish himself in the skies of New York as a charter helicopter pilot, but he always had trouble working for a boss. He wanted to own his own business but lack of money was always an obsta-cle and he just couldn't get the break he needed. To solve the problem, Scooty started a helicopter business without a helicopter. He paid to have business cards printed and went banging on doors to introduce himself. Customers simply presumed that the Bell 206 Jetranger depicted on his card actually belonged to Scooty. They gradually be-gan requesting his services and his business was off the ground. Clients didn't need to know that Scooty would charter the Jetranger every time a job came in. He would simply add on his margin and the clients were none the wiser.

One of those clients was Joe Egan. Joe wanted Scooty to do an aerial survey up and down Park Avenue and take numerous photographs of the area around 65th and Park. The job required angle shots from every direction and perspective possible, including low-level shots to simulate the views obtainable from various floor elevations. Scooty assumed the shots were for the planning stage of a new building. He didn't ask too many questions. He just did what he was hired to do. During the whole process, it was Joe who would ask most of the questions. He wanted to know everything about helicopters and how they were flown, and his appetite for information was insatiable.

'Tell me Scooty, how'd you get started flying helicopters?'

'Hey Scooty! What's a machine like this worth?'

'Scooty, how'd you make it spin on its axis like that?'

Joe and Scooty were like chalk and cheese. They didn't have very many similarities at all, and their lives, personalities and lifestyles were worlds apart. However, it soon became apparent to both of them, as they sat side by side in that helicopter, that they shared one wonderful infatuation. Helicopters!

Whilst hovering above the future location of Egan Center, Joe had continually asked about the Jetranger and its running expenses. Scooty just wasn't capable of deceit.

'Well Joe, the truth is that I don't own this beauty, but MAN, how I'd like to.' Scooty was slightly embarrassed at his confession.

'It's achievable Scooty, if you want it bad enough.'

'No way! Believe me, I've tried. I've trudged the city from top to bottom trying to get the finance, and what chance have I got? Always the same story. Our bank can't offer you the money, Mr. Menzies. We're not in the business of financing depreciating assets.' Scooty looked across at Joe and tried to save face with a wide smile then continued.

'What they were trying to tell me was that they wouldn't finance a jungle mercenary chopper jockey with no credit rating. That's what they were trying to say.'

'Scooty, listen to me.' Joe spoke firmly into his boom microphone. 'It's achievable, like I said. You didn't get the finance because you didn't offer them anything in re-turn. Believe me, I've been in deals of one kind or an-other all my life, and I can tell you the way it is and al-ways has been.'

'What do you mean Joe?' Scooty was all ears, and he was in no doubt that Joe had a rare wisdom and experi-ence in business.

'Well Scooty, every deal has an east and west, a left and right. You know what I mean? Two sides. A deal must be a perfectly balanced instrument, and then, it is a successful deal. A perfect deal has no losers, only win-ners. Everyone has to be a winner, and then your deal will go through. The trouble with your deal was that it wasn't a two-way deal. The banks saw themselves as po-tential losers. There wasn't enough in it for them, so they weren't prepared to enter into a losing situation.'

'But Joe, it is a winner. My business is successful. I just don't own the helicopter, and helicopters don't de-preciate. They go up in value.'

'I know that, but the banks weren't offered a big enough carrot. They weren't offered a perfectly balanced two-way deal.' Joe liked Scooty, and he seemed to feel a brotherly affection for him from the start.

'I'll show you what I mean Scooty. Here's a balanced deal where both parties win.' Scooty turned up the volume on his headset to get every morsel of information, and Joe continued.

'I'll have a talk to my bank manager and put in a good word for you. He'll more than likely set you up with the finance you need to buy this Jetranger. That's what's in it for you. Now in return, you have to promise to teach me to fly a helicopter one day. Just you Scooty! No one else will do. That's what's in it for me. Now do we have a perfectly well balanced two-way deal that has every chance of success? What do you say Scooty?'

'I say that we've got one hell of a deal, Joe,' he replied cheerfully in high sprits. 'One hell of a deal!'

Scooty put on his familiar grin from ear to ear and the two friends shook hands in mid air. The deal was done and the friendship was forged in steel.

CHAPTER 15

I can already feel the adrenaline pumping through my body as I descend in the elevator to the lobby of Tower One. To say that I'm a fish about to leave the water is an understatement indeed, something immediately recognized by the lobby security guard when the doors open.

'Is that you Mr. Egan? Interesting attire sir! Going out on foot?' He has a look of astonishment on his face and he stares down at the silver attaché.

'Yes. That's right.' I mutter. 'Anything suspicious to report?' I feel somewhat embarrassed being dressed like a street kid.

'Nothing at all sir. Enjoy your stroll and take care.'

The cool damp air hits my face as I step out onto the sidewalk and quickly pace north in the direction of Hunter College. The sounds and sirens of uptown Manhattan are pouring into my right ear. I distinctly segregate the blade chopping background noise of the Twin Squirrel coming through my cell phone earpiece which is fitted snugly into my left ear. I'm unable to see the helicopter as I scan the misty night sky above, but I feel a little safer knowing that Scooty's infra-red camera is casting a watchful eye over me.

'Scooty, can you hear me? I'm on the sidewalk heading north on Park Avenue and 66th Street.' I pause for a second but decide not to look up.

'Okay Joey, I'm zooming down now and I'll try to lock on with the infra-red. I'll be looking for you to turn east on 67th Street,' he announces energetically.

'Scooty, I think someone is following me. He's back about a quarter block and he stopped when I did and waited for me to start walking again. I think he's carrying what looks like a closed umbrella.'

I can feel the tension building in my bones and guess that it's probably the same shady character who was tailing us before.

'Wait a minute Joe. I'm filming the area behind you.' Scooty's voice is muffled and now slightly distorted.

The helicopter background noise is now becoming more dominant. I turn east onto 67th Street and notice that the shady figure dressed in black makes the turn as well. I'm now convinced he's following me. I can make him out a little more clearly now and he seems to be dressed in a black trench coat, and, yes, he is tapping a green umbrella on the sidewalk as he moves.

The beads of sweat are forming on my brow, and the armpits of my sweatshirt are now wet and sticky. I think it's the thought of the handgun. It's the apprehension I have of using it to actually shoot someone that's giving me the shakes. I'm wondering not only if I'm capable of aiming and shooting at another human being, but also whether I could live with the guilt thereafter.

I've always rationalized that I'd be capable of killing for only three reasons: to defend my own life, to fight for my country, or to protect my family. It certainly seems easier said than done, now when I'm walking around New York at night with a paper knife in one pocket, a gun in the other, and realizing that I've watched too many action movies. I feel for the .38 in my pocket and wrap my hand around the grip, remembering Scooty's instructions.

'Just aim at the chest and squeeze,' I rehearse under my breath.

'Okay Scooty, I'm just coming up to 68th Street subway now and it's almost 9.30 p.m.'

'I'm hovering overhead at two thousand feet, and locked on,' Scooty shouts through the confusion of noises in the cockpit.

I stand at the subway entrance and look back down Lexington Avenue. My follower with the green umbrella has disappeared, and apart from the occasional person entering and exiting the stairway, I'm on my own. My left hand has a firm hold of the silver attaché and my right is still clutching the handgun in my pocket when the kidnapper's cell phone vibrates to life in my jeans. I jump with fright, and my hand precariously tenses around the gun. I decide that in future, I'll keep my finger well away from the trigger unless intending to fire. When I answer the call, the now familiar electronic monotone voice feeds my faculties.

'If you're at the subway station, and you're listening to this message, you're one step closer to seeing your daughter. Bring the diamonds in the metal briefcase and come alone. Take the 9.40 train south to 14th Street at Union Square and wait on the platform. Don't miss it!'

There's no time to lose. I almost drop the phone as I spring into action, descending in leaps and bounds down the stairway. There are only a few precious minutes until 9.40 p.m. I have to inform Scooty.

'Scooty! They've got me catching a train to Union Square. You got it?'

'Got it! Got it!' I hear him scream. 'I'll be overhead at Union Square.'

201

I jump the turnstiles and stumble onto the gritty platform as the train pulls in. There are now several people waiting in small gatherings against the yellow tiled walls and I move towards the third carriage. As the doors slide open, I can look back along the train. I'm sure I catch a glimpse of a green umbrella dangling amongst the figures as they enter one of the rear carriages. I nervously stand inside near the doorway as the train lurches forward and rattles into the darkened tunnel.

'Scooty, I'm in the train!' I yell out, and the other passengers wonder what the hell I'm yelling for. I'm thinking that they're probably just as suspicious of me as I am of them.

There's no response from my cell phone, and all I get is an ear full of static. I end the call and relieve myself of the irritating noise. The carriage is both smelly and chilled as I look around at the other occupants. It's not a place I'm accustomed to and I feel insecure and lonely now that contact with Scooty is lost. Interrupted lines of spray-can graffiti give a personal touch to what would otherwise resemble the inside of a refrigerator. The few other people scattered around the carriage look uncomfortable and pathetic as they stare solemnly into space. Not one person converses. One would think it's against the law to speak on a public train. They all sit in stunned silence with blank faces as the train creaks and rolls southbound.

The journey to Union Square station is fifteen minutes of sheer uneasiness as I anxiously stand near the exit of the carriage, attaché case in one hand, and a sweaty grip on the handrail with the other. As characters of all shapes and sizes wander in and out at each stop, I study their features to maybe detect some hint of evil or criminal intent. They're all probably respectable citizens going about their own business, but my imagination is busy and it's causing my stomach to swirl. The further we travel away from the Upper East Side, the more suspicious they all appear.

Every time someone brushes past me, my hand tightens around the handle of the briefcase and I search for that green umbrella. My imagination tells me that the murderer could pull on the hooked wooden handle and unsheathe a razor sharp blade, to then plunge it deep down into my vital organs with one hand, while snatching the attaché with the other.

I exit at the Union Square platform and take up a defensive position with my back to the wall, glancing left and right for a clue as to what comes next. I wonder why and when I should use the .38. Is it possible to get the gun out of my pocket, aim and fire, and for what purpose? To save me getting shot? Or to apprehend the person myself? I decide to try and relax and not go off half-cocked. Surely, my use of the handgun would spell the end for Casey and I should try to settle my nerves. I redial Scooty's number on my phone and strain to listen through the shrieking noise of the outgoing train.

'Scooty? Are you there Scooty?' I squawk into the small microphone attached to my earpiece.

'Joey! Can you read me? I'm over Union Square. Where are you?'

I have to ignore Scooty's question and I quickly rip the earpiece from my ear. The kidnapper's cell phone is ringing to tell me that there's another instruction coming my way. My thumb hits the answer button, and I lift the receiver to listen to the machine-filtered message.

'Congratulations if you've arrived at Union Square station. Your daughter is cheering you on. Take the 10.10 train from platform four to Jefferson Street Station in lower Queens and wait on the platform outside the second carriage. Make sure you travel in the second carriage.'

The message ends abruptly with a click and the communication is once again dead. I quickly check my watch and get Scooty back on the other line.

'Scooty! They've sent me eastbound to Jefferson Street Station. Should take me twenty five minutes at least.'

'All right Joe. I'll be there waiting. I've got heaps of fuel. Looks like about three-quarters full. I'll be there.'

I'm once again running and bounding for the train. My heart is pounding at fever rate and I wonder why they just don't get it over with and let me give them the briefcase. What kind of game are they playing at, with all this switching and changing? I make it to the platform with a couple of minutes to spare and I'm able to watch as the train grinds into the station.

Several people now invade the platform from every doorway and I'm once again searching for a hint of evil madness, to attack me with an umbrella blade or shoot me dead on the spot with a concealed weapon. I'm spared the reality of such horror, and hop into the second carriage as instructed. This time, I'm sure the chilling end is near. They know what they're doing. It's obvious that the whole thing's been cleverly planned. They've actually nominated a carriage, to come face to face with me and carry out my execution.

The train is similar to the first, only the graffiti is more explicit and the seats are crossed with more razor slashes. Weary from my dash from the other platform, I sit amongst the gaping cuts to gaze around at the carriage interior and await my fate. The line to Scooty's phone is once again an unintelligible hash, so I end the call to lessen my anxiety. I then sneak the Smith and Wesson out of my jacket, and position it under the attaché on my knees. It's well concealed there and I feel a lot better.

I'm sitting against the sidewall facing inwards as the train groans onwards and I notice that the further away from Manhattan we go, the more anxious I become about the other occupants of the carriage. The only improvement in the situation is that there are fewer of them. More people seem to be leaving the train than there are joining it. By the time I reach Lorimar Street Station, I'm sitting in solitude. That is, until the doors slide open.

The three laughing and hollering characters who come swinging in through the doors, look to me like they're from a bad Vaudeville show. Maybe twenty three to twenty five years old, they're obviously in a happy mood, or could it be that drugs have something to do with it? I wonder? I have no choice but to stare at them because they sit directly opposite like the Three Stooges and size me up and down. I can feel the million butterflies in my stomach taking flight and swarming in a frantic frenzy. I wonder if these twisted individuals have anything to do with the kidnapping.

The best looking of the three has crazed eyes, pimpled white skin, and he looks stoned beyond understanding. He sits on the left with sagging posture, wearing a ragged baseball cap with the peak to the rear. His face is oily and unshaven. He smiles at me insolently to reveal a mouth half-packed with decaying teeth and he then snorts like a bull and spits off to the side. He's elegantly attired in a torn and dirty flannel shirt, with dark sweat stains under both arms, and unbuttoned at the front to reveal his body tattoos. He wears urine stained baggy pants that end just below the knee. 'Crazy Eyes' completes the look with a pair of black hobnailed boots, grazed and battered on the toecaps, probably from kicking people to death.

The most sinister looking guy on the right has a similar pair of boots worn below cut off black jeans. His chest is bare except for the tattoos and scars, and each nipple enjoys the pleasure of a large silver diaper pin pierced through the skin in a horizontal position. A flea bitten bulky black woolen coat is wrapped around his strong muscled shoulders, and his apparel is complimented by a red bandana, tied to encompass a shaved stubble head. 'Diaper Pins' doesn't smile at me. He just stares me down with his hollow eyes and a blank unresponsive expression on his face. I sink a few inches on the seat and have no choice but to eventually look away.

The most interesting of the trio is the olive skin 'Dreadlocks' guy in the middle. He really wins the prize for looking stupid. There he sits in all his glory, metal chains hanging everywhere from his studded belts and pockets. I wonder how he has the strength to carry it around because he looks so weighed down with all that hardware. His translucent skin is waxy and acne scarred, and his cold brown eyes are set deep in their sockets. He sports a thin line beard around his jaw and each cheek is tattooed with a small black crucifix. Sticky dreadlocks hang down beneath a woolen beanie. The beanie looks like it's had a lifetime of use as a teapot warmer. He lets his lower lip hang down to reveal a silver bolt through his slimy tongue and his two front teeth are cracked and nicotine stained. Tightly muscled tattooed biceps are straining the short sleeves of his black mesh tee shirt and his black leather vest is soiled and studded. It's difficult to determine whether his black baggy pants are long shorts or short longs. The fashionable attire of this individual is finished with heavily laced black military boots and black leather palm gloves.

I can feel 'Dreadlocks' pouring his eyes over every inch of my body and I know he's wondering what's inside the attaché case, held firmly on my lap. I hope he doesn't have to find out what I'm grasping on my knees beneath it.

I wait on tender-hooks for the next station, hoping that the carriage will fill with decent law abiding citizens to even the equation. I'm denied any relief from the agony when the only new passengers are an old black man and his son, who tentatively stick their heads into the carriage and back away when they don't like what they see.

The train snakes off the station and weaves into the next tunnel as 'Dreadlocks' tries to stare at me and hold my gaze. I feel strangely hollowed out inside as I play his game. It only seems to irritate him and he decides to walk across and sit down next to me.

'Excuse me sir. Would you please be so kind as to please tell me what the time is sir?' he taunts.

His words are smart and quirky and I try to draw my gold timepiece further back into my jacket sleeve. I just know he's already had a glimpse of it and I wonder what the hell I was thinking, to wear a solid gold Rolex into the New York Subway. My left grip is iron clad around the attaché and my right hand firms its position on the pistol grip of the .38 laying beneath it. This is my worst nightmare coming true before my eyes. Without moving from my frozen position, I take a guess at the time and try to put on my deepest and bravest voice possible.

'It's ten twenty.'

The guy with the diaper pins through his breasts is just sitting slumped on the other side and staring straight through me while 'Crazy Eyes' decides to stand up. He starts swinging and swaying on the overhead rails making noises like a monkey. His antics come to an end when he swings off the rail and plants his feet right in front of me with a boisterous grunt. I realize that the Smith and Wesson is pointing directly at his testicles as he makes his defiant stance to speak for the first time.

'What'ch'ya think he's got in da metal case boys?' He tosses his head and sniffs.

'Dreadlocks' sitting next to me vibrates his whole body.

He laughs out loud. 'Maybe it's full of gold watches. Maybe he's a traveling watch salesman.'

I know that I have to avoid a conflict with these imbeciles at all costs. But it's too late for that. Now that I'm stuck with this situation, the only course of action is absolute aggressiveness. I have to spring into action with the element of surprise, fight with such released fierceness that I'll break their spirit and they'll flee discouraged.

I know what I have to do, but I'm unable. If there's ever a time when every ounce of strength is required to spring forth, it's a time such as this. Why then, is my body numb and tired? Why do I feel like I'm wearing a lead suit and my limbs are devoid of any energy? This is depressingly bad, my darkest fear. My blood pressure is going through the roof and the perspiration is dripping down my cheeks.

The hoodlums obviously sense how I'm feeling. They're like animal predators smelling my fear. There's no doubt in my mind of the gravity of this life-threatening situation. These three men aim to rob me and possibly leave me stabbed and dying in this carriage. They're obviously not connected with the kidnapping, but ironically, they may now become the cause of not only my death, but Casey's as well. The situation that's unfolding right here in this train carriage may spoil the ransom delivery and any chance of Casey making it home alive.

I frantically try to weigh up my options here and now. I could come out blasting with the .38 and shoot the three of them in quick succession. Problem solved? I don't think so. Although I would surely inflict severe damage, I have my doubts whether I could get them all before being overpowered myself and probably stabbed to death. Also, my drained overwhelming tiredness tells me that I may not be capable of such an extreme act anyway. We all like to think we're macho warriors if the need arises, but now that I'm right smack in the middle of a threatening situation, I seriously have my reservations.

If they take my Rolex and my wallet and they're happy with that, maybe they'll leave me alone with the attaché and I can still deliver the diamonds. Hah! I doubt it. They mean to take everything from me, and that probably includes my life. Guessing that my best chance is to take the initiative and deal my way out of this, I firm my posture and speak with an authoritative tone.

'Listen to me. You boys want to get the most out of this as you possibly can. I can help you get rich tonight without committing any crime. You'll have a lot more than some cash and a gold watch, and you'll be able to walk away free.' I'm thinking of the bag of cubic zirconia in my jacket pocket.

'Crazy Eyes' is still standing in front of me and with a microsecond flash of his hand, he produces a large flick knife, which he waves for emphasis and then points at my face. The sensation of butterflies swarming in my stomach now turns to extreme nausea, and I'm on the verge of retching.

'Spill your guts man or I'll spill them for you!' he threatens violently, and I feel so sick that I'm literally about to comply with his demand.

I sputter out the words. 'Listen. Here's the deal!'

I'm looking down the blade of his flick knife and my trigger finger is twitching on the .38 as I continue.

'I'm in the jewelry business and in my pocket I have a small bag of precious diamonds, about ten million dollars worth. You can take them from me because they're insured. You can also take my cash and this gold Rolex. It's insured as well. And, you can walk away free. The metal briefcase here contains only papers, papers that are important to me, and they're of no possible use to you. You take the valuables and leave me with the briefcase. Okay? You'll never see me or hear from me again. You'll get away rich and free. Understand? Do we have a deal?' My voice is once again as important sounding as I can make it.

'Yeah we have a deal!' 'Crazy Eyes' is glaring down at me, and he laughs wickedly. 'Here's our deal! We take what ever we want and you shut your fucking mouth. That's our deal!'

He suddenly snaps the flick knife closed and then open again, and rams the blade forcefully through my left shoulder. The sudden excruciating pain causes every muscle in my body to recoil in spasm and I instantly lift the attaché with my left hand. My finger automatically jerks backward on the trigger. The deafening noise of the resounding gunshot fills the carriage.

My eyes open wildly and I'm stunned at what I see. Where, just an instant before, his genitals had cradled comfortably in the front of his urine stained baggy pants, there is now a mash of human flesh and blood. It's total obliteration. The projectile had ripped open his lower abdomen, destroying everything in its path. He screams and crumples to the floor in a fit of shakes and convulsions.

In my peripheral vision, I'm aware of 'Diaper Pins' coming to his feet. At the same time, 'Dreadlocks', who is sitting next to me, pivots to a crouched position, grabs a hold of my right wrist with his left hand, and pulls a stiletto knife from his black pants. He hurls a stream of incoherent abuse as he swipes it towards me. My left hand, although still spasmodically jerking from the pain in my shoulder, releases from the briefcase and clasps around his lunging wrist to interrupt the attack. The attaché goes flying across the carriage and we fall down in a gripping death roll. As my right elbow hits the floor, the gun discharges a second time. A sheet of pain spreads across 'Dreadlocks' face and his eyes drift back in his head. He collapses in a heap with a hole blasted in his chest. Blood starts to pool around his body.

The fragile bones in my right hand are then suddenly smashed by the steel toecap of a black hobnailed boot as 'Diaper Pins' comes bearing down on me, his feet darting in and out like a Thai kick-boxer. The Smith and Wesson is flung from my grip and I feel two knees pushing my shoulder blades into the floor. My left shoulder stab wound is under his right knee and the pain radiates through my whole body almost causing me to lose consciousness.

I'm writhing and twisting in an attempt to extract myself from his heavy weight and, in the moment of panic, can only manage to raise my head and jut it forward. The effort almost cracks my neck, but I manage to lunge far enough to get my teeth around his left side diaper pin. I yank my head back again and tear the pin from within his breast. The flesh is ripped open to reveal the white pectoral muscle underneath and he shrieks in pain and shock.

It's not enough to discourage him though, and I'm still overpowered and pinned down by the force of his knees on my shoulders.

I spit out the diaper pin and simultaneously expel a death-defying scream into his face as I see him pull a knife and raise it into the air above my head. He reacts by grinning wickedly, opening his mouth and sticking out his wagging tongue to show me the silver stud as a demonstration of his conquering victory. I know now that my life is about to end. I'm ashamed that the last thing I'm to see of this earthly existence could be that repulsive silver bolt. My head is incredibly clear. I blink my eyes and a microsecond image of Sharyn's beautiful face instantly floods my heart and soul. Death is a heartbeat away. As the deadly blade comes swishing down towards my throat, the curved handle of a green umbrella hooks around his forearm and rips back to dislodge the knife from his hand. He whips his head to the side, in an attempt to fathom the distraction, and the pointed metal tip of the umbrella rams mercilessly into his face, gouging out one eyeball socket completely, and damaging the other. The small lump of substance that falls beside me no longer has the appearance of an eye, rather a lump of jelly.

'Diaper Pins', with the one damaged blood-red eye he has left, recoils in shock and his weight is lifted from me as he tries to escape. He's not fast enough. As he leaps to his feet, the green umbrella comes smashing down into his shoulder blade, pulverizing the bone. He shrieks in pain. Deserting his comrades in crime as they lay bleeding and moaning, he scrambles on hands and feet through the end door of the carriage.

As 'Diaper Pins' ugly features have now moved from my field of view, standing upright with the umbrella gripped horizontally in both hands is the triumphant warrior who had saved my life. When I see who he is, every emotion fills my senses. I'm surprised, confused, grateful, and afraid, all at the same time. He offers out his hand and helps me to my feet, and I sputter out my words of gratitude.

'Thank you. You saved my life. I was finished. Thank you.'

I think it's the first time I've seen Leslie Murchison wearing anything other than his doorman's uniform, and it makes him all the more difficult to recognize. His black trench coat and slouch hat identify him as the sinister person who has been following my every move, and I'm waiting for him now to snatch the attaché and complete his mission.

'Are you all right sir?' With these polite words, he exonerates himself from suspicion. I'm hungry to hear an account for his behavior, as the train pulls into the Morgan Avenue Station.

'Yes I'm all right, thanks to you.'

With my right hand partially incapacitated by the hobnailed boot, I use my left hand to pick up the revolver and shove it back into my pocket. I then retrieve the attaché case and slump exhausted onto the seat. Leslie sits down next to me and begins his explanation while the train pauses at the station. I'm relieved that nobody gets into the carriage. The bloodied and mortally wounded bodies are still writhing on the floor and I feel no sympathy or desire to help them in any way.

I discover that the pain in my shoulder subsides if I don't move my arm, and I look down to survey the injury. By peeling back my sweatshirt, I can see a one-inch puncture that is trickling a steady flow of blood down my ribs. I wince with pain as I press the palm of my shattered hand onto the hole to slow the bleeding and the train jerks off once again on its final sector towards Jefferson Street.

'What in blazes name are you doing following me around?' I ask shakily as the tears are welling in my eyes.

'Well sir, I became very aware that you were in trouble when those suspicious envelopes were turning up in your mailbox. Also, I noticed the state you were in when you arrived back to Egan Center. I've never known you to look like that. After realizing that your daughter was somehow in trouble, and seeing those detectives coming and going, I decided that I should watch your back. You know? Look out for you. I had some days off that were owed to me by Egan Enterprises, and after all sir, I am a part of the security staff. It's my job.'

I'm astounded at his story and I feel like hugging him.

'Look, my good man, I know about your past and what happened in your business. I know I was partly responsible. I thought you were my enemy.' I'm still trembling from the ordeal as I speak.

'Sir, that part of my life was almost supernatural. It was like a carnival fun ride that had to end. Look what happened on Wall Street? It was destined to finish anyway. Easy come and easy go. That's what I say. Now, I'm just happy to be in your service.'

'Well then, you've certainly done me a great service tonight. I'm very grateful. But listen, there's more involved here than you understand. You have to get out of here now and leave me alone. If you don't, my daughter may be killed because of it. There's no time to explain now. This train is about to pull into the next station and I have to get off, alone.'

'I understand sir. I'll stay on board when you get off. Isn't there some way I can help you?'

'Yes. Can I have your belt to strap up my shoulder and do you have a handkerchief?'

Without answering, Leslie pulls a handkerchief from his vest and slips the belt from his pants. I pad the wound and he helps me to secure the dressing by wrapping the belt a few times around my shoulder and under my armpit.

'How else can I be of service?

'Stay in the carriage for a few more stops and call the police from a pay phone. Tell them there's been a shooting and there are wounded people in the second carriage of this train. Don't tell them who you are or anything else about what happened. Do you understand? Just make the call and get clear yourself, and stay away from Egan Center for the rest of your time off. Understand?'

'I understand.' Leslie bites the side of his lower lip as he speaks. 'You just look after yourself and get back safely.'

The door of the carriage slides open at Jefferson Street Station. I take a firm grip on the attaché handle, grind my teeth with determination, and apprehensively step out onto the concrete platform. It's like jumping from the frying pan into the fire.

CHAPTER 16

Frank Berne's mind was a perplexity of disjointed and conflicting information, and he was struggling to make head or tail of it. He sat back in his creaky wooden revolving chair, closed his tired eyes, and ran his fingernails back through his gray crewcut. It was now much later than he would normally stay back at the station house, but Frank was becoming increasingly exasperated at the lack of headway with this case. He had wanted it to flow like clockwork to a perfect conclusion, and his typically pessimistic cop's mind was worried about it all coming apart at the seams. It was two o'clock in the morning, and already thirty-nine hours since the murder and abduction. He realized that he was making too little progress in too much time.

His desk was a muddle of loose papers, all to do with the Egan murder and the whereabouts of Casey Egan. Showing through a small clearing in the middle of it all, was an area of blotting pad with names and places scribbled in a variety of orientations and styles. Some had been crossed out and some had been highlighted with a heavier impression of ink. The lines and arrows he had drawn between them were an effort to link implicated suspects and locations, and thereby provide theories and solutions.

There in the center of the blotting pad was the name Audrey Egan. Lines jutted out from it in every direction, like the spokes of a wheel, towards subjects and locations. Some were printed and some were sketched within stick figures. Frank pondered for a while on the names of Mary-Lou the housemaid and Benedict the chauffeur. He then picked up a ballpoint pen and let his hand drift to an ugly sketched face with the name of 'Featherman' written below it. He placed two or three exclamation marks next to it.

Blue Featherman was still out there with Casey Egan, and Frank shuddered to think what frightening and despicable acts he could be performing. He thought about the last time he had Feathers in his grip and how close he had come to administering his own justice. By ending that misfit's life right there and then in the alley behind Pelma's bar, he would have done the community a huge service indeed. If he had drilled that bastard when he had the chance, an inefficient justice system would not have given him early parole. A criminal of the worst kind would not have been released back into society to defile the lives of decent law-abiding citizens.

Frank rubbed his eyes with his fists, blinked them a few times, and made himself a promise that, if the situation was to arise again and he was given the chance, Frank would do things his way. He had done things 'the Frank Berne way' before and the Captain had always turned a blind eye. He would do it again. The trigger would be squeezed and a bullet would send Blue Featherman straight to hell where he belonged.

Frank sat forward again to resume his relentless examination of the facts. He raised his eyebrows and once again scrutinized the scribbles before him. This had become a complex and frustrating murder, which never should have happened. He knew that Feathers was the perpetrator of that nastiness in the elevator yesterday, and he had left his trail everywhere. He was equally as sure that the other person behind it all had a lot more intelligence than old Feathers ever would.

When Frank considered the disguise, the ether, the stolen laundry van etc, he was aware that this cleverly implemented abduction had required the faculties of a very talented and crafty person. It was certainly beyond the thinking capabilities of Blue Featherman. This extremely calculating mastermind had controlled from a distance and executed with precision. He had orchestrated the plot and had then used Feathers to carry it out.

Frank recommenced his doodling as his hand wandered in the direction of Joseph Egan's name. He then put several question marks next to it. Frank was actually certain that Joe was not behind all of this. The way in which he had reacted to Frank's interview was convincing enough for anyone. Yes, Joe Egan was an innocent party to the murder and abduction, but at the same time, he seemed to be hiding something. When Frank had informed him that Audrey Egan was dead, how could Joe be so very much in control of his emotions? Frank thought that maybe Egan should receive an academy award for 'Best Actor'. That left the jigsaw puzzle with other huge gaps to fill.

There were many little bits and pieces that were yet to fit into place. If Casey Egan was kidnapped for a ransom, why then had Joe not been forthcoming about a received ransom letter or telephone call from the source? The only logical explanation could be that if the blackmail involved something other than money, Joe Egan wanted to keep tight lipped about it. Egan was playing his own game.

Frank screwed up his mouth and tossed the ballpoint down onto the desk in frustration. He kicked the wooden chair back on its coasters and sprang to his feet.

'Enough for one day,' he murmured to himself. He reached for his jacket from the coat stand in the corner, and headed for the door.

'What in God's name? It's 2.15 a.m.' He was stopped in his tracks by the ringing of his cell phone.

'Berne here.' he called into the phone with a gruff tone to his voice.

'Frank. It's Jimmy here. Did I wake you up?'

'Actually, no you didn't Jimmy, but you're on shift. What's so important that you have to call me this late?'

'Well, I thought you'd better know straight away. A double homicide was just called in from Queens. They brought us in on it because they think it could have originated from the Upper East Side.'

'Really Jimmy. How did they come to that conclusion?'

'Here's the rap. The boys there get an anonymous phone call about a shooting on an eastbound train, so they go to investigate. When they arrive at the train carriage, they find it's been the scene of a fight, a real war-zone. Two guys left there. One dead. One hanging on by a thread. Both had gun shot wounds from a .38 caliber. Also a blood trail out the end door and into the next carriage, like the attacker was wounded himself and fled the scene.'

'Well, that's nice Jimmy. Real interesting. Why don't you tell me about all the other homicides that have been called in around New York, just to keep me in the picture?' Frank was both cynical and skeptical.

'Sure Frank. Sure. There's more, so keep your shirt on. I told you it might have something to do with our precinct. The guy who was still alive has had his balls shot off and there's blood everywhere. Maybe he's heard something while he was lying there wounded. He's able to talk before he turns carcass, and he keeps mouthing the same thing all the time. Wait till you hear this. He keeps saying the same words over and over till he finally snuffs it. Wait till you hear.' Jimmy had saved the best till last and he blurted it out loudly.

'Egan Center, Egan Enterprises, Egan Center, Egan Enterprises.'

'What the fuck?' Frank scratched his head. 'That baffles me Jimmy. What the hell do you think Egan Enterprises has got to do with that sordid mess?'

'Damned if I can figure it out Frank. These two guys were the lowest creeps that our good society here can manufacture. Real low life scumbags. I told you Frank, there's more to Egan than meets the eye. He's a pompous two-faced son of a bitch. I still think he's arranged his own wife's murder, and he's fucked it up. I bet he didn't know Feathers was into kids, and now he's lost his daughter as well.'

'Jimmy. Firstly, she was his ex-wife and they'd been apart for three years. Secondly, why would he want to bring all that grief to his own daughter?'

'Because he's a condescending asshole who thinks he's invincible, that's why.' Jimmy was restless and angry.

'You're not making any sense Jimmy.' Frank was irritated.

'Listen Frank! He's pissed because she had custody and he has to pay for everything. He's a tough businessman, and he hates to lose. Well, he did lose that one and he's waited three years to get even. Hey! Remember that blasé divorce judge who went to answer his doorbell. There to greet him when he opened the door were both barrels of a twelve gauge to blast his guts out. Don't you see Frank? These divorced guys have long memories and they're all fucked up with vengeance.'

Frank listened intently to what Jimmy was saying, and although he thought young Jimmy was paranoid, he was definitely swayed by it. If he was right and Egan was covering something up, Frank would send him his academy award to be enjoyed behind bars. He would make sure that Joe Egan came clean about his activities if it was Frank's last accomplishment as a law enforcement officer. On the other hand, Frank had an uncanny ability to recognize the basic goodness in human beings and he still had doubts about Joe Egan's behavior. In the pit of his stomach, having spoken face to face with the man, he found it hard to believe that Joe Egan could be basically evil and capable of much wrongdoing.

Frank also knew that he was walking a tightrope when it came to Jimmy. The young detective was hypersensitive and he required some delicate handling to keep him balanced.

'All right Jimmy. You may be right and you may be wrong. Just make sure you're not looking at this case with tunnel vision. Look at all the possibilities in case we're barking up the wrong tree.'

'I don't think we're barking up any wrong tree Frank. Egan's conjured this up and we should clamp down on him a lot harder. He's a shady son of a bitch and I know he's bitter and twisted as hell. You know there are guys still doing time, rather than pay their alimony. They choose to rot in prison on a principle. Like I said, it infuriates them like hell and they get all fucked up.' Jimmy was becoming more agitated.

'All right Jimmy. Let me see if I can contact him at this crazy hour and establish his whereabouts during the evening. That will be a start. Then, I'll also look further into it tomorrow and find out what he knows about this train episode. You get as much as you can from the boys over in Queens. Get the background history of the dead guys and see if you can link them to the Egan family in any way.' He paused to think.

Frank still wasn't fully satisfied. 'Hey! Maybe you can link them to Blue Featherman. He seems more their type. And, tell them to conduct a thorough search everywhere in the vicinity for the murder weapon.'

Frank ended the call with a huge sigh and tossed his jacket back over onto the coat stand. He trudged across to the coffeepot and poured himself a mug of strong black syrup to heighten his senses. It was time to bury his head back into some investigative planning. There was some serious thinking still to do and much to accomplish. Frank realized that he wasn't going to get much sleep.

He downed the coffee and sat down again at his desk, more determined than ever to break Joe Egan down in the morning. For now, it was important to see if Joe had spent the evening at home. He then wanted to plan tomorrow's questions carefully in advance. He would then be able to outsmart the clever business tycoon face to face and see through his masquerade of deception.

Frank wanted Egan to come clean and confess everything once and for all. If he was involved in deceit and play-acting, Frank wanted to bring him down from his high pedestal and teach him a valuable lesson, a lesson he would never forget.

He checked his diary for the number he required and reached for his desk telephone. He hesitated, checked the time, and thought about what he was going to say. Now that he was satisfied that he should make the call at such an unwelcome hour, he dialed the number of Joe Egan's personal cell phone and braced himself for the conversation.

CHAPTER 17

The train doors slide shut behind me and I can feel Leslie's eyes peering at me in sympathy as I stand alone and motionless on the platform of Jefferson Street Station.

The train carriage that has been my private hell for the last ten minutes, weaves off into the distant night and I'm once again in a state of purgatory. I wonder how long it will last, until I'm flung into the fire and brimstone once again. It suddenly goes through my mind that the injured occupants of that fateful carriage could survive and be able to identify me at some later stage. I feel no guilt whatsoever for their plight and ashamedly hope that they bleed to death before help arrives. It wouldn't surprise me if Leslie would oblige me and finish them off, when I think about his relentless wielding of the green umbrella.

I try to clench my right fist and discover that I can barely wriggle my fingers through the swelling. The pain in my left shoulder has settled to a steady ache and it occurs to me that the blade was, more than likely, contaminated with the dried blood of other victims. I try not to think about the possible consequences, and look the station up and down to familiarize myself with the next potential battlefield.

As the whoosh of the train fades into the night, my pain throbs like the rhythmic pulsation of Scooty's helicopter far in the distance. A few departing passengers from other carriages disappear through the exits and before long the whole station is empty and I'm left alone in an eerie state of solitude and expectation.

There's no doubt that I'm suffering the shock of a near death experience because my pulse is still beating at twice its normal rate and my body is a lather of perspiration. My thought processes have slowed considerably and I don't seem capable of calculating my next move. Nature has determined that, due to the extreme stress, my brain should take some time out. For a moment, I just stand there staring into space trying to get a grip on my own faculties. I realize that I've just come through another gateway of destiny, as everything about the train carriage ordeal comes flooding back like a fast forward replay. I close my eyes and force the images to the back of my mind. My father's words of wisdom whisper softly in my ears, and I'm helped to refocus to a new perspective.

'One obstacle at a time Joe. Try to put it behind you now and move on.'

Scooty must be wondering what's happening and it occurs to me, that if left out of the picture for too long, he may take the initiative to call the cops. God, I hope he hasn't done it already. The end result of Frank Berne turning up here would surely be devastating.

I look around, and I'm unable to see anyone watching. I decide to chance it with a phone call and I try to grab my cell phone. With my fingers clasping the small handset, the pain in my right hand shoots up my arm as my thumb fumbles with the buttons. The answer is immediate.

'Is that you Joe?' Scooty sounds unsettled.

'Yes. It's me. I'm down below you on the platform and still waiting for something to happen. Hah!' I understand the irony of what I had said, but decide to leave those gruesome details to tell Scooty at another time and place.

'Where the hell have you been man? I was really starting to get concerned.' Scooty sounds more worried than angry.

'I'm all right Scooty. I'll fill you in on the details later. It's too risky speaking into this phone. They may spot me. I'm going to have to turn it off again and put it away. Stay overhead Scooty, and wait for me to call you. How much fuel have you got?'

'You let me worry about that Joe. I'll be here for you until I'm running on empty. Reckon I've got about seventy five minutes.'

I glance at the station clock and see that it's 10.50 p.m.

'Right then Scooty! See if you can get a little bit higher. Your noise could frighten them off and ruin the whole thing. Have you seen anything suspicious through the camera?'

'Just cars and people coming and going Joe. Nothing unusual.'

'Please give Sharyn a call and tell her we're still all right. I'll call you back Scooty, when I can.'

With those words, I end the call and put the cell phone away out of sight. I struggle to squeeze my hand into my gun pocket and test my swollen fingers around the grip. Although difficult, it's not impossible, and I feel more secure that I can still use the .38. Any thought of replenishing the empty chambers with fresh ammunition would be out of the question. I started with five rounds and fired two in the carriage, so I realize that there are only three shots left if needed.

I place the silver attaché down between my legs to relax my aching left shoulder and stand watching up the length of the station for something to happen. A train from the opposite direction comes hurtling into the station behind me, and just now, the kidnapper's phone makes its presence felt. Snatching it up, I'm once again enduring the pain to press the answer button and bring it to my ear. I try desperately to distinguish the monotone voice from the gushing and rattling confusion of the slowing train.

'Follow these instructions precisely. Do not fail. Lift the lid from the litterbin closest to you and place the metal case inside. Leave it there. Get onto the next train and keep going. If you succeed, your daughter will be returned to you unharmed.'

I hesitate to hear more, but the line goes dead. As the call finishes and the westward train recommences its journey, I can hear the trembling sound waves of the next approaching eastbound train. I swivel around to complete my task. The litterbin is right there as expected, and I hurry over to try the lid. I'm not surprised that the lock has been sheered off in advance and the lid rises with minimal effort.

Although frustrated that they seem to be getting away with the real diamonds rather than the cubics, I'm nevertheless relieved that the mission is coming to an end. There's no way I can substitute the precious diamonds with the fakes at this stage. If they found out they had been tricked, it would be Casey who would pay the ultimate price.

I drop the attaché onto the existing trash and replace the lid. With that very action I'm suddenly overcome with a falling sensation of failure and despair. It's as though I've relinquished my only bargaining position and I've been defeated. Not only have I thrown the diamonds into that trash can, I also feel as though I've thrown Casey's life away as well, and I'm now helpless to rescue her in any other way.

Overcome with grief and emotion, I swing around to face the oncoming train with its brakes screaming and groaning. It's like an iron horse from another Shakespearean play. Suddenly realizing that I can end the performance quickly and relieve myself of further suffering, I look down at the steel tracks. They seem to be pulling me over the platform edge. It's as though I'm drawn towards them like a magnet. My troubles can be voided in one instant, one last concluding gateway. Everything would be voided. It seems so easy, suddenly so tempting. My body begins to sway and then teeter forward. My trance is broken. It's too late and the first carriage lopes past.

What in hell had come over me like that? I stand dumbfounded as the interior of the second carriage comes rolling into view before me. My brain is at bursting point when I see the person standing inside it. There is one, and only one, occupant in the carriage.

She's standing in the middle section looking straight at me through the glass. As she slides to a stop, her features become a fixture in front of my face. Tears of anguish are pooling in the corners of her eyes and her expression is one of earnest appeal.

My body is suddenly numb and devoid of any pain. My mind however, goes into an instant state of heightened panic as I stare into her compassionate eyes. It's all happening in an instant and the significance of what I am witnessing invades each and every brain cell I possess.

The pale figure is draped in white and hangs in suspension. My mouth is trying to call her name but nothing comes out. Audrey's tangled blonde locks are now streaked with gray and the daisies of her tiara are dried and wilted. Her face, although recognizable, is now the face of a tormented withered lady, and her wrinkled mouth is repeating a silent message. I try to hear through the glass window but the noise of the train makes it impossible. All of a sudden the message she conveys comes crashing through my senses as I recall her appearance in my dream and the advice she had then offered.

'Joe, you must find Casey and help her. He intends to kill her no matter what you give him.'

A wave of adrenaline floods my body and I know that I must act quickly. I now realize that Audrey's spirit is waiting for this terrifying ordeal to be resolved, and only I can somehow bring it to an end, both for Audrey to move on, and for Casey to live on. Moving to the carriage doorway, I then stand there shaking as the train hums and beckons for me to get on board. Seconds are ticking away and I'm caught in a moment of indecision. Go, or not to go? My feet are frozen and I'm unable to step across. I'm aware that I would be crossing the threshold to failure, and ending the life of my own daughter in the process.

The train trembles and groans, giving me one last chance to board, but my confused mind won't permit my body to submit to the devil's temptation. As the doors slide closed, my panicked thoughts stream an impulse for me to react in an outrageous and radical manner.

I don't have time to rationalize what my mind is instructing my body to do. I just do it.

Without hesitating, I jump three paces to the left, leap into the space between the second and third carriages, and tumble onto the tracks below. I instinctively stretch out my arms to prevent my body from landing heavily, and scream because of the pain. My fractured right hand has collided with the metal rail, and my wounded left shoulder wallops harshly with a solid sleeper. Surrounding me are the mechanical sights and hissing sounds of heavy steel machinery. The train jolts forward and the huge grinding wheels begin to turn. I withdraw my hand, roll to the side, and tuck myself in as far as I'm able to, away from the crunching steel.

I lay waiting under the platform edge in a state of terrified paralysis as the sparks fly around my face and the whole length of the train passes screeching by. A pressurized blast of hot air dislodges the dirt from around the tracks and black dust is flying around my face, filling my eyes and nostrils. The back of my throat is burning and I squeeze my eyelids tightly shut to endure the torture. Everything feels surreal to me and my nervous system is overheating. Audrey's haunting appearance is making me doubt my own sanity, and I'm thinking that this has to be another dream. It seems that the spiking torment will never end and the increasing momentum of each carriage brings my terrified mind to shattering point.

The crescendo stops suddenly when the last carriage flashes past and then speeds away into the distance. Dazed and bewildered, I crawl on my hands and knees in the direction of the disappearing train. Once clear of the platform, I sit in the darkness next to the rails.

I struggle to gather my senses and contemplate on what has just taken place. It's unbelievable. From a distance, it would have appeared to any onlooker as though I had actually entered the train. I'm amazed that I've accomplished a feat of such great magnitude and gotten away with it. A sense of strength and ability fills my being and I feel as though I've suddenly been endowed with supernatural powers.

I spring onto my hands and feet in a spider-like fashion, and crawl quickly across to the other side of the tracks. There's a cavity-like shelter there for the use of rail employees and I huddle inside the relative security of its darkness. I adopt a squatting position and, from here, I'm able to wait in secrecy and also look back along the platform without being seen myself. As I focus my eyes, I'm satisfied that I now have a clear view of the litterbin containing the ransom of diamonds.

I crouch here impatiently, but have no idea what I'm going to do or where this is leading me. I can only hope and pray that it's taking me to Casey. I anxiously wait for the kidnapper to make an appearance and then, maybe, I'll get some kind of a clue to take me further down the path to my daughter. I may even get a good enough look at his face to be able to identify him to the police at a later stage.

After all that's occurred tonight, I have a temporary sense of confident security here in this dirty black shelter. Leaning back into the darkness to watch the litterbin, I'm able to contemplate my pathetic situation. In contrast to my normal appearance, patches of dried blood and sticky soot now befoul my torn clothes. My face is covered with black railway grime and my battered body is bruised and injured. In spite of all this, I feel a strong sense of significance and purpose in where I am and what I'm doing.

I mustn't lose sight of my objective. This drama is far beyond the imagination of William Shakespeare. There's a greater spiritual authority directing this scene and I've had no opportunity to rehearse. One thing seems certain. This play is nowhere near finished. I'm determined that I must not let the curtain fall until I've succeeded and completed my part.

As the rumbling vibration on the steel tracks tells me that another westbound train is approaching behind me, a lone person dressed in dark clothes and a baseball cap enters the platform from the stairway. The somber image walks slowly in the direction of the litterbin. My heart skips a beat because this is the closest I've been yet to the person responsible for all this misery and pain. I want to grab the .38 from my pocket and shoot him dead on the spot, but common sense prevails and I subdue my urges. I decide to wait until he comes closer whereby his identity may be revealed. I strain my eyes through the haze to focus on his features.

The noise of the looming train is building behind me as he tentatively looks in every direction but mine. He's surveying the platform to satisfy himself that he's not being watched and that he has a clear escape path. As he finally reaches the bin and lifts the lid, he slowly turns his head in my direction and I think that I'm about to get a good look at his face. Suddenly, the train surges into the way and denies me that opportunity by completely blocking my view.

I spring out of the shelter and stand, as the flow of carriages is decelerating before my eyes. By stretching up on my toes, I get glimpses of him through the train windows as they flick past, and I can see him withdraw the attaché case and walk away. The train finally comes to a halt. I jump across the tracks and around the end carriage, and can once again view the platform through the gap.

I can see a few disembarking passengers scattered along the area, and beyond them in the distance, the lone person with the silver attaché. He is entering the stairway exit, and I have the uncomfortable feeling that I've failed. I'm annoyed and frustrated that I've missed my chance. I curse out loud as I realize that all of my hopes and expectations may come to nothing. With a new burst of energy, I ignore my aches and pains to clamber back up onto the platform.

The people making their way to the exit are startled by my disheveled and blood soaked appearance. They duck and ward me off as I run frantically, pushing and shoving to clear my way. My eyes are scanning everywhere to catch a glint of the silver case, and I jump three or four steps at a time, trying to catch up.

I spill out onto the street and can see a few people walking away, but almost half of them are dressed in dark clothing and wearing baseball caps. My lungs are now heaving and my body is damp from the combination of blood and sweat. I stand looking around and waiting for some kind of a clue. Then in the distance I see a flash of silver light, and there it is.

I run to the next intersection and look fixedly at the attaché case, lying open and discarded in the curbside gutter. The case is empty. In frustration, I swear out loud once again, and furiously kick it as far as I can along the road. In a last ditch effort, I take the chance to run further up the side road to the next street. I then turn into an expansive industrial area of vacant land surrounded by high mesh wire fencing. Several vehicles have been parked in the unlit compound and I slow my pace to walk onto the unsealed road that forms the entrance.

Then, from the darkness within the mass of vehicles, the outline of a pickup truck bursts onto the roadway towards me. I'm confused that its headlights are off and I can't understand why. One thing's for sure. I'm directly in his path, and without his lights on, there's no way he'd be able to see me in this darkness. My God! He's heading straight towards me. I dive to the side, out of its way, and the truck goes speeding by.

It's obvious that this was no innocent citizen speeding home from a long day at the office. Maybe his lights are off so that nobody can read his license plates as he leaves the compound. If that's the case, it's certain that he's up to no good. Yes, it all makes sense. My last desperate hope is to remember some identifying feature of the vehicle. I roll over to follow the truck with my eyes. I focus my attention on the back of the vehicle as the first street lamp illuminates it.

Before it disappears around the corner, I get a full view of its rear end. It's a black, late model Chevrolet Silverado pickup, like so many others on the streets of America. There on the bumper, is a large red novelty sticker, and I strain my eyes to decipher what's depicted on it. It looks like a picture of a chrome flaming engine with something printed below it. I can't distinguish with complete certainty, but I think it says...Is it? The streetlight is dim and the distance is now too far, and I'm unable to be sure. I can only listen to the engine's deep distinctive gurgling exhaust note as it fades into the night.

Replacing the pickup's engine noise is the sound of a police siren in the distance. As the siren tends to be getting closer, I'm increasingly nervous about my vulnerability. If apprehended by the police with a handgun in my pocket, I would surely be implicated with the train carriage episode. In a sudden fit of panic, I decide that I must dispose of the weapon quickly.

I can see a metal drain next to the wire mesh fence and I clamber on all fours to inspect its suitability for what I have in mind. The concrete and steel drain is deep and dark. Without giving it further thought, I take the gun and the box of ammunition and drop them through the metal grate. I listen to them clatter downward about two or three feet to a final echo at the bottom and I feel more relieved.

As the police siren fades away, I look skyward and listen to the distant beating of the Twin Squirrel rotor blades. Fully realizing now that there's nothing more that I can do, the thought occurs to me that Scooty may be able to track the pickup with his imaging equipment. I reach to make the call.

'Yeah! Scooty here.' he answers on the first ring.

'Have you got the Chevy pickup? It just sped away from the industrial area here.'

'Wait. What? What industrial area?'

My heart sinks. 'Scooty. I'm now outside the train station and I've moved to an industrial car park just to the north. Can you see any pickup trucks speeding away Scooty?' I wait, hanging on his reply.

'No Joe. Maybe we'll see something on the tape later. I'll tell you one thing I can see. I can see my fuel gauge indicating that I better get the hell back to base.'

'Really Scooty? Get going. I'm fine. I'll get myself back somehow.' My voice reveals a trembling wave of dejection.

'Are you together man? What the fuck happened to you down there? Are you in one piece?'

'Yes. I'll be all right. I'll make it back to Egan Center. Call Sharyn and tell her to get things prepared for me. Tell her to get my doctor Troy Darby on his emergency number and have him at my penthouse waiting.'

'Are you hurt Joe?'

'I've been stabbed, but I'll make it back home. Don't worry.'

Scooty's phone contact is suddenly ended and the faint even pulses of the Squirrel's rotor blades are immediately interrupted. They quickly transform into a forceful beat throbbing down from the night sky and the changed growl of engine power is evident in the background. I look upwards, expecting to see the chopper heading away, but can see no such thing.

Here comes Scooty, in some kind of spiral dive maneuver, heading straight down towards me, headlights blazing and power full on. As he gets closer with every second, I rush back from the wire mesh fence and wave my right arm furiously in the direction of a cleared area and away from the vehicles.

Scooty's halogen spotlights are beaming back and forth as the helicopter descends at a dangerous rate, closer and closer. I'm beginning to think that it may be out of control and Scooty may be crashing to his death. When it seems that there's no time or altitude to arrest such momentum, my fears are allayed when the pounding suddenly changes tone. Good old Scooty knows exactly what he's doing. The chopper heaves down a cyclonic blast of compression as the most skillful of pilots pulls hard on the collective. The pitch of the giant rotor blades carve into the cool air. Just in the nick of time, the body of the helicopter changes attitude and the death dive is arrested to a stable hover. In one more smooth execution, the skids are placed positively but gently onto the ground and Scooty's door swings open.

The blades are slicing rhythmically, and Scooty jumps out onto the surface. He's waving me forward to the front of the helicopter. I get up from my crouched position and stumble toward him, with head lowered to avoid the swishing blades. We circle together to the other side of the helicopter and he helps me get on board. Without uttering a word, he speedily secures my seat belt and slams the door shut.

I manage to fit my headset about my ears, as he quickly runs around the front and hops in. With lightning speed, Scooty straps in and winds on the power. As quickly as the helicopter has arrived, it's now primed to takeoff. The engine turbines suck hungrily at the moist air, and the rotor blades spin to a constant obscure disk, as we lift up and away on our freedom flight from hell.

'How you doin' Joey? Hang in there buddy. We'll have you home in no time.'

'Scooty! I saw him. I saw the bastard. I didn't get a good look at him, but I saw his vehicle.'

'What did you see? Did you see enough for us to find him?'

'It was a black Chevy Silverado. Real nice custom job. Couldn't get the plates but it had a red bumper sticker.'

'Well, that's something Joe. What kind of bumper sticker?'

'Had a picture of a big chrome engine and some print. Not a hundred percent sure of what it was, but I think it was….. It looked as though it said,'

UNLEASHED FURY

CHAPTER 18

With a population of only forty-eight people, the little pocket of Tuxedo Junction had barely the need for a general store. The inhabitants were mostly scattered around in decaying old farms, living in run down old farmhouses. Most of them would manage to scratch out a living by keeping cows and chickens or selling produce from roadside stalls. Others would exist by doing whatever odd jobs they could get. Yes, for the residents of Tuxedo Junction, life was difficult. For a young widow struggling from day to day with an asthmatic six year old daughter, it was even more difficult.

Louise Shackleton had lived her short life in a state of dull drudgery and hardship. Raised in a rented cottage in the backwoods of Tuxedo Junction, she was the orphan stepchild of old Pa and Ma Shackleton.

Louise was always an ugly duckling as a child, but as each teenage year passed, her more unfortunate features seemed to change for the better. When Pa and Ma Shackleton finally passed away within three months of each other, the seventeen year old young lady was indeed a rare beauty.

Louise had been endowed with a shapely and slender body, caramel complexion, and larger than usual dark pond eyes. Her angelic face was surrounded by rich folds of long chocolate colored hair draping elegantly to rest against her full bosom. At the age of nine, an accidental collision with the house fence had left her with a missing front tooth. Strangely, this only served to enhance her striking beauty by giving her face a greater personality. Louise was certainly attractive, and after spending so much of her young life nursing the Shackletons through their old age, she was now free to show her attractiveness to the world. She could now go into the Junction, and greet the young male farmhands who would visit the general store and buy cigarettes.

Old cranky Tom, the storeowner, allowed Louise to hang around as much as she wished. He liked the young girl and thought that her presence would foster plenty of business. He'd never seen so many new young farmhands visit the store. They'd buy cigarettes and beer, and hang around on the store's front porch laughing and joking.

With her long dark hair and big brown eyes attracting every man in town, it wasn't long before Louise fell pregnant to the most competitive of those young men. A rushed and contrived marriage soon followed, and the newlyweds moved into the back of the barn at Mason's farm where the father to be had found work. They awaited the birth of their child. While heavily pregnant, Louise would rest in the hayloft while her young husband would toil in the fields each day from morning to night.

They say that for every baby that's born, there's another person going to his grave. That must have been the way it was on the day little Nancy was born. Louise's screams for help when the baby was pushing her tiny head into the world were smothered by the many noises around the farmyard. They were smothered by the sounds of clucking chickens, wailing cows, and the frantic barking of dogs. Louise's delivery screams were also drowned out by the racing engine noise of the tractor, as it rolled upside down, crushing the young farmhand into a mangle of flesh and bone.

When old Tom found out about it, he took pity on the distraught young mother and offered her a place to stay. He was getting too old to do the work and he was glad to find some free help. In exchange for food and an upstairs room in that ramshackle general store, Louise would do the chores and care for Tom. With the meager amount of money he would throw her way, she was able to clothe herself and her daughter in second hand rags, and also provide Nancy with the asthma medication she so needed.

Louise was also able to put down a deposit on a second-hand Toyota sedan, by the time little Nancy was ready for junior school. That light blue Toyota was her lifeline and only possession. She cherished it and longed for the day when it would finally be paid off. On that day, she wished, she would simply drive herself and Nancy away from Tuxedo Junction, away to a new world and a new life.

For the time being, Louise considered herself lucky to be employed and have a roof over her head. Although the owner of the general store was an irritable abusive tyrant, he was now an old man confined to his bed, and Louise was usually left alone to run the business. Her day was long and arduous, not because of the few daily customers who might walk through the door, but because of old bed-ridden Tom, who would pull on that string upstairs. Whenever he did so, a little bell would shake and tingle downstairs on the other end, and Louise would have to attend. She wiped the counter and looked across at the one saving grace in her life, Nancy.

'How's your drawing going honey? Hold it up and show mommy.'

Nancy, although six years old, was a small immature girl for her age and Louise always thought that it was due to her asthma. When the little girl eventually heard the story of her father's death, her asthma attacks became more frequent and extended. Louise hoped that she would one day be able to better provide for the person she loved so much.

Every school morning was almost identical. Louise would wake at about 5 a.m. to the sound of the roosters crowing outside. She would be ever so quiet, so as not to wake Nancy sleeping next to her. Dressed in her old tracksuit pants and top, she would sneak downstairs to start the daily routine of cooking breakfast and opening the store. It was one of her favorite times of the day because cranky old Tom was still sleeping, and the little brass bell would stay still. At 6.00 a.m. she would wake Nancy and guide her quietly downstairs to eat her corn flakes, bacon and eggs, and pack her school bag. If by seven o'clock, the brass bell still hadn't started to ring, Louise was having a good day.

The night had been a constant pounding of heavy rain on the iron roof, making it difficult to sleep. After a restless night of tossing and turning, old Tom needed to sleep past his usual breakfast time. For Louise, it seemed that today was one of those good days. At 7.00 a.m. Louise had fed Nancy a substantial breakfast, put on a load of washing, cleaned the counter, and was now watching her daughter as she sat at her play table. Apart from the scrambled eggs, which were warming on the stove, old Tom's breakfast tray was well prepared with the usual cereal, cold toast and juice. Poor Louise now waited for the menacing bell to start ringing.

It was two rainy days now since Feathers had come lurching through the doorway, leering at Louise and smiling at Nancy, and her memory of him was giving her the shivers. It was probably his haunting image that was the reason for her sleeplessness, his dyed hair, rotten teeth, and evil eyes. What was he doing in Tuxedo Junction, all dressed up in white and wearing cowboy boots? Louise had struggled for the two days since, with the idea of reporting him to the local law enforcement officer. The problem was that she really didn't have anything to report. She just thought he looked suspicious. That's all. The way he looked at Nancy just wasn't normal, and the way that he called her 'little girl' like he was attracted to her or something. It all just gave Louise the creeps. She decided to leave it for the time being. But, the moment she might hear of anything going missing, or any strange unexplained things going wrong, she would definitely give his description to the police.

Louise jumped with fright when the brass bell began to ring and she gave it a short sharp tug as she called across to Nancy.

'All right honey. Mommy's going upstairs now to give Tom his breakfast. Then I'll be back down to take you to school. You all right honey?'

'Mommy, do you want to see my drawing?'

'Yes honey. You keep drawing and I'll see it when I come back down.'

Louise quickly emptied the scrambled eggs onto the tray, and carried the lot upstairs. Old Tom was already sitting half upright in his bed, and he growled a 'thank you' to her as she positioned the tray.

Women's intuition is a strange thing and Louise had a weird knowledge that something was amiss. She didn't know exactly what it was but she sensed something had gone seriously wrong. She had felt it from the moment she had climbed out of bed, but now the feeling was getting stronger and stronger.

As she stepped back from Tom and watched the eggs drool from the corner of his mouth, she had recollections of dingy Feathers drooling over Nancy, and she was suddenly overcome with panic. Louise had heard of missing children, children who were abducted, never to be seen again. Never, ever again! She took a deep gasp of air into her lungs and ran from the room.

'Nancy! Nancy!' she called out as she bounded down the stairs.

She reached the lower level to see little Nancy drawing away at her play table in the corner.

'Look mommy. Do you want to see my picture now?'

Louise gave a sigh of relief. What had come over her? Everything seemed absolutely normal, but the sensation of dread and misfortune was still occupying her mind. Nancy was safe and ready for school. Yes. But, wait. No! Something was still terribly wrong. She just knew it. Louise didn't answer Nancy. She walked over and looked down at the drawing on the play table. It was an ugly male figure with rotten teeth, a striking resemblance to Feathers.

Louise took Nancy by the hand, picked up her car keys, and grabbed an old umbrella from the tub beside the entrance. She made sure that the cardboard sign was turned to indicate 'CLOSED' before pulling the door locked behind her. With Nancy at her side under the umbrella, Louise walked around the side of the store and came to an abrupt stop in the light rain.

Her blue Toyota was gone. Her most precious lifeline and prized possession simply wasn't there. She thought immediately of that strange customer dressed in white, and she stepped into the pay phone booth to call the police. To her surprise, the police informed her that they were already on the way and she guessed they meant that they would attend to her call immediately. What they really meant was that they WERE already on the way.

Poor Louise and Nancy waited hand in hand for the police car to arrive. They didn't have to wait long to surprisingly hear sirens screaming in the distance. They stood there expecting one police vehicle to slowly drive along the road and calmly pull up to the store. Before long, they watched in amazement as, not one, but three, squad cars came speeding towards them. Instead of slowing down, they drove straight up to the store and swung right along the muddy dirt track and into the pine forest, with their spinning roof lights blazing and sirens blaring. Confused Louise wiped the tears from her eyes and just stood there dumbfounded that the police had missed her location.

She couldn't believe that they could be mistaken about the one and only general store in Tuxedo Junction.

CHAPTER 19

There's something magical about helicopters. Whether it's a pond of quicksand in the Amazon jungle, an overturned fishing boat in the shark invested seas of Australia, or an ambush of massacred and wounded soldiers in the combat fields of Vietnam, a helicopter can change your survival prospects with one swooping retrieval.

No matter what kind of a hell-hole you may be stuck in, a helicopter can make your world a better place. My world is definitely a better place as Scooty sweeps me up and away from the industrial site north of Jefferson Street Station. I'm up and away from the kidnapper's threatening truck, up and away from the path of that speeding train, and up and away from the three miserable thieving individuals who wanted to snuff out my existence.

When we reach an altitude of two thousand feet, Scooty levels out the chopper and drops the nose to gain cruising speed. Without asking, he leans over to shove a stick of spearmint gum into my mouth, and then takes one for himself. I'm so hungry, that I chew vigorously on the sticky globule and almost swallow it.

The lights of Manhattan are clearly visible out in front and I'm relieved that in a few more minutes, I'll be safely home to recover in familiar surroundings. Scooty's made the call to Sharyn and he's talking to her through his boom microphone.

'Sharyn! We're on our way. We'll be there in about ten minutes.' He pauses to listen to her reply, and then continues.

'We're okay. Joe's been hurt, but he's not too bad. He'll be needing a doctor. He said to get hold of Troy something or other.'

'Troy DARBY!' I'm yelling over the noise and Scooty looks across at me.

'Yeah! He says Troy Darby. Get him on his way, and tell him that it's an emergency. Tell him that Joe said. And tell him to keep it quiet.' Scooty pauses again, and then goes on.

'He'll be fine Sharyn. Just a slight stab wound to the shoulder. We'll be there soon.' He finishes the call and peers at the fuel gauges.

I sit back and try to relax my facial muscles as the chopper approaches the East River. I've come through the most harrowing ordeal of my life, and whatever happens from this moment, the events of tonight will be etched in my memory forever. For now, I try to remove the frightening details from my mind and switch to thinking of more pleasant things.

I think of little Casey and our Disneyland experience. I have beautiful thoughts of Sharyn, and how we have a new and wonderful development in our relationship. While the sparkling lights of the Queensboro Bridge float past below, I think of how much I appreciate having Sharyn and Casey in my life. Yes, I hold them dearly in my heart and pray for the time when we can all be happy together.

I look across at Scooty's face and can see that he's getting worried.

'How's our fuel Scooty? We going to crash and burn?' I ask, trying to make a joke of it.

'Never know until we know.' He smartly replies.

'Are you a lunatic or something, swooping in like a prehistoric pterodactyl to get me out of there? It looked too extreme Scooty, too dangerous.'

'Well, safely dangerous.' He grins. 'Been called a few things, but never a pterodactyl.' He then goes back to the fuel readings.

'Well Scooty, I need you to be a hero, but not a dead hero.'

Scooty remains fixed on his instruments and replies from the side of his mouth.

'You're not a dead hero until you're dead, man.' He smiles and continues.

'Anyhow Joe, maybe one day you can write a book and tell everyone how Scooty saved the day.' He tries to laugh his inimitable laugh.

We've been up in this helicopter together so many times now and I've yet to see Scooty nervous or apprehensive about anything. Tonight things seem a little different. Although I can see that he's putting on a brave face, I'm beginning to realize that all's not as good as Scooty is making it out to be. Small beads of sweat are forming on his upper lip, and thin worry lines crease his brow when he studies the instruments.

'After all that I've been through tonight, I'm just pleased to be here,' I murmur quietly to myself.

There's nothing that could happen that could even compare to the nightmare experience of being pinned down, watching that life-threatening knife wielded above my head. Yes. I'm happy to be right where I am thank you. Put me in a helicopter with Scooty any day and I'll take my chances.

I relax into the leather upholstery and gaze at the wondrous sight before me. New York is a beautiful city by day, but even a greater spectacle at night. From an elevation of two thousand feet, the city of Manhattan looks like a fantastic scale model, with not the faintest hint of the muggings and murders occurring within its twinkling display of lights.

I wish Casey could be here with me now. She loves to ride in Scooty's helicopter at night and she always squeals in delight. It reminds her of our trip to Fantasyland and the Disney night parade.

I shiver when I think of Casey's situation right now, and I simply can't bear the prospect of losing her. There's nothing else I can do, short of calling Frank Berne and telling him everything. Maybe that's the correct course of action now that I've played my hand. The cops could now take control and gain some kind of an edge. Then again, maybe they'd ruin the whole thing and get in the way. They'd probably place me under arrest and charge me with the shooting of those train thugs. No. I'll stick to the plan and wait for the kidnappers to call me. God! I've followed their demands and paid the ransom. What more can they want? I have no choice but to wait it out, just wait and hope that they'll return my princess to me. I fumble with both cell phones to ensure that both are on, then sit back to the comfort of the chopper's plush interior.

I'm mesmerized by the tiny light trails of the downtown traffic as the helicopter passes across the Lower East Side towards Central Park. Scooty has commenced his steep descent by easing back on the power and lowering the collective. He keeps it steep to minimize the noise and avoid complaints. Scooty looks more relaxed, now that our flight is approaching Egan Center, and his usual cheerful demeanor has returned.

'Almost there Joey! There's the place you call home.'

I lean forward and fix my vision on the three structures of Egan Center and can just make out the landing area on top of the tallest tower. We're passing down through eighteen hundred feet, and Scooty keys his microphone to activate the pad lights. Far below, the tiny concrete square turns brilliant white as the floodlights turn on. From this altitude, it looks to be such a very small target, and I'm once again amazed at the versatility of the helicopter.

The exhaust belches forth a deep cough.

My body stiffens and I look across at Scooty. His limbs have already reacted to the abnormality and his features are strained. The chopper shudders slightly and one engine splutters and quits. There's a partial power loss and the immediate reaction of Scooty's hands and feet are synchronized to his verbal outburst.

'Goddamn fucking son of a bitch!' he yells through the intercom.

I brace myself in the seat and watch Scooty. He raises the nose to reduce speed as his left hand reselects the fuel control. What follows is not exactly what Scooty or I would prefer to see. The second engine surges then also runs down, as the last drop of fuel drains through the lines. With the speed of a lightning bolt, Scooty's left hand drops the collective to the fully down position, a vital and immediate response if we are to have any chance of survival. The giant blades twist completely around to the opposite pitch and the rotor takes on the roll of a parachute. The full weight of the machine dangles beneath the blades, and the whole apparatus is dropping at an alarming rate.

'Fuck! We're out of fuel!' he exclaims with a new urgent tone to his voice.

My own heart begins pumping like a strained engine being forced to its limit. I've never heard Scooty sound like this and I know it means we're in trouble. His finger presses on the microphone button to transmit a mayday distress call, but he hesitates. He spins his head in my direction and thinks again. The call isn't sent.

The helicopter seems stabilized in a steady fall and Scooty's left hand is turning off the non-essential electrical systems. We're dropping rapidly through one thousand feet and the buildings are looming around me. The illuminated heli-pad looks even smaller than before and I can now make out Sharyn's tiny figure standing behind the railing under the spotlights. Having seen the way he flies, she probably thinks that it's one of Scooty's normal approaches. I can imagine that she's happily gazing up at us.

There's an important difference to this arrival. Without the engines providing thrust, Scooty has no power to correct an error in judgment. He has one, and only one, go at it. Our rate of descent and angle of approach must be exactly on target. Scooty's hands and feet have to act in precisely the correct manner at precisely the correct moment to flare the helicopter and achieve a touchdown on the pad. The alternative, as unthinkable as it is, would be to tumble off the edge and smash in an explosive fireball onto the pavement below.

Images of that calamity flash through my mind like a horror movie, and I wonder if I'm entering a state of shock. The gasps of my heavy breathing are sounding through the intercom and reverberating in my own headset. I look at Scooty, hoping he will offer me some confident words of reassurance, but his teeth are grinding and his lips are pursed. The normal relaxed laissez-faire attitude has gone and the veins are protruding at his temples.

His eyes dart in every direction and sweat is visibly dripping from his jaws.

Panic is racing through my overstressed body. Realizing that this is going to end in a disaster, I want to scream abuse at Scooty for running out of fuel. I force myself not to. If there's the faintest glimmer of hope left, it's important that I say nothing to distract him. I prefer instead to whisper silently.

'Dear God! Help us through this. Please bring us through!…Plea…..?'

Before I can complete my prayer, the pad surface rushes into focus and the yellow painted 'H' dominates my whole field of vision. I can sense Scooty counting down as we drop closer and closer, at what seems like a breakneck speed. Sharyn's eyes are peeled wide open with shock and I can see that she's frozen in position. I want to shout at her and tell her to save herself, but the tension in my jaw won't let my mouth open.

Just as I'm sure we're going to actually penetrate the concrete and smash through to my penthouse below, Scooty smoothly but assertively pulls on the collective. The rotor blades moan in protest as they're forced to reverse pitch once again. With a loud swoosh, the energy of that terrifying descent is transformed into lift, and the helicopter pauses to sit momentarily on the massive air cushion that's been created. Scooty's hands and feet co-ordinate the controls in a smooth but determined action, and the chopper sinks slowly onto the surface. It's over, and I can't believe he's pulled it off. He reaches across and grabs my right fractured hand, and I'm not sure whether to thank him or punch him. Behind his bravado, his heart is pounding so hard I can feel the vibrations. He exhibits his wide grin, wipes his brow, and then laughs as loudly as I've ever heard him.

'There you are Joey! That's why all the women tell me that I'm the best at what I do. And, I'm not bad at flying helicopters either!'

CHAPTER 20

Doctor Troy Darby was sinking into the deeper levels of slumber, when he was suddenly brought to consciousness by the menacing ring of his emergency telephone. He was still half-asleep and groggy as he listened to the worried tone of Sharyn Cooper's voice on the line. He knew immediately that this was a very serious matter.

'Troy! It's Sharyn Cooper here. Joe Egan has suffered a stab wound and he's returning to Egan Center as we speak. I'm very worried about him.'

Troy rubbed his eyes and tried to collect himself.

'You have to get him to the emergency ward. It's the best way. They can attend to him better than I can.'

'No Troy. He specifically wants you. Please come as soon as you can. Joe has asked that you keep this to yourself. He doesn't want anyone to know.'

When he heard the words 'stab wound', uttered by Sharyn's distressed plea, he was both shocked and surprised. He had been Joe's personal physician for two years now, and this seemed so inconsistent with the lifestyle activities of the man he knew.

Troy dressed and prepared himself in record time and reached for his doctor's bag. Thirty minutes later he was pulling into the entrance gates of Egan Center. The doctor's arrival was expected by the security guard, and he was immediately ushered up to the penthouse level. Sharyn was already standing at the doors, anxiously waiting to greet him.

'Hello Sharyn. I'm so sorry to see you under these circumstances. Is Joe here now?' Troy was cool, calm and collected.

'Oh Troy! Thank God you're here. Joe's inside waiting for you. Please come through.' Sharyn was still distressed.

The young doctor looked up with great interest at the buffalo heads as he was escorted though the sunken lounge area to the rooms beyond. Troy Darby was always amazed at the style and expanse of Joe's penthouse, but this time when he was escorted into the massive kitchen area, he was even more amazed. He couldn't believe that the gaunt, tired man he was looking at, was Joseph Egan. Could this dejected, semi-naked and trembling specimen be the man he knew so well?

There, in the center of that impressive state of the art kitchen, on glistening white tiles, Joe was sitting slumped on a metal chair with his back to Troy. Troy's gaze fell to the tiles below and he noticed that they were splattered with a mixture of water and red blood. He then lifted his eyes to see Scooty Menzies standing next to the bench top. Scooty was fumbling with two cell phones, and ensuring they were correctly attached to their respective charger units.

'Just make sure they're charging correctly Scooty, and that they're on and receiving properly,' said Joe as he looked up at Scooty, and at the same time noticed Doctor Troy Darby's presence.

'Troy, thanks for coming at such short notice,' said Joe as he raised his paled features into the light and looked at the doctor.

Troy could see straight away that Joe had been through a terrifying ordeal, and he could also see that the man was still in a state of shock. The weakness of his complexion indicated that he had suffered a loss of blood.

'Heavens Joe! What has happened to you? Have you been mugged?'

At this stage Scooty thought it was his turn to say something. He decided to interject so as to fully explain the circumstances to Troy.

'Ah! Yes doc. Look, my name is Scooty Menzies, and I was out there with Joe tonight,.....and..'

Joe looked across at Scooty and cut off his words in mid sentence.

'Scooty, that's all right. Thank you. Please let me tell the doctor about it.'

Scooty went back to checking the phones, and Joe continued to speak.

'Troy, I'll tell you the finer details later. I can tell you this. The wound to my shoulder is a knife wound. I was stabbed. The blade was about three inches long. Quite frankly Troy, I thought it would bleed a lot more than it has.'

The young doctor placed his bag down on the bench top, unlatched it, and allowed it to unfold, revealing the many dressings, implements, and medicinal supplies within. He quickly pulled on some latex gloves, picked up some antiseptic swabs, and turned his attention back to Joe.

'Well Joe, that probably means that it didn't sever any major blood vessels. You were very lucky.'

Troy noticed Joe shake his head in disgust, and he then continued.

'Just make sure that if you start to feel woozy or you feel that you might faint, let me know straight away. We may have to put you on the bed.' Troy was injecting Joe's shoulder with local anesthetic as he spoke.

Sharyn had done the best she could, under the circumstances, to cleanse around the wound. She was also suffering some mild shock from seeing the man she loved pathetically stumbling across from Scooty's helicopter. She had helped him undress from most of his clothes, and then she had used a sharp pair of scissors to cut away the final layers of material from around his left shoulder. With some boiled and salted water, paper towels, and disinfectant, she had managed to swab most of the dry blood away from the area surrounding the puncture.

As Troy now swabbed away, cleaning the center of the puncture, he lent forward and whispered into Joe's ear.

'You know Joe, since this is a stab wound, we really should inform the police. In fact, by law I am obliged to do so.'

Joe suddenly stiffened from his slumped position, looked the doctor directly in the eyes, and said with a stern voice.

'In no possible way can we inform the police. This is of the utmost importance. I'm not asking for you to understand, and I am not asking for your sympathy. All I am asking is that you don't let this go any further than this room.' Joe was quite adamant.

'Well that's fine Joe, but you also have to understand that I have a professional duty to...'

Troy was interrupted as he tried to state his case.

'Your professional duty is to patch me up, and patch me up as best you can. I'm saying again, you must not inform the police. Now I can't tell you anymore, except that the life of my own daughter maybe at stake here. So I plead with you. Please?' Joe spoke emphatically and convincingly.

The doctor's attitude changed in a second when he heard the sincerity in Joe's earnest appeal.

'Okay. Enough said. I really don't want to hear anymore about what happened anyway. All I'm required to know, is that you had an accident at home and you fell on the point of a kitchen knife. So let's leave it at that. Let's just get you fixed up.'

'Yes, he must have fallen at some point.' Scooty made a joke, and then bit his lip when he realized its inappropriateness.

Without any further hesitation, the doctor intensified his attention to medical matters and continued.

'What's happened to your hand? It looks so swollen.'

Joe looked up at him and smiled.

'Must have happened when I fell on that kitchen knife, Troy.'

Troy painstakingly took great care to thoroughly cleanse and sterilize the stab wound as best he could before sealing the opening with a line of ten parallel stitches. He then applied a layer of gauze dressing under a firm stretch bandage. After examining Joe's right hand, Troy decided that there was little he could do until some x-rays were taken. He positioned thin aluminum strips to brace it, and he then applied a wide bandage to the whole hand.

Satisfied that he had done the best job that he could possibly do without the conveniences of an operating theater, Troy was now mostly concerned about subsequent infection. He completed his task by the use of three separate syringes. The first one was used to extract blood for testing in the hospital laboratory. The second syringe was a large tetanus shot administered to Joe's right buttock. And, the third contained a single massive dose of antibiotic serum.

The time was approaching 2.00 a.m. when Troy was finally confident enough to leave Joe in his delicate but stable condition. He insisted that Joe swallow a powerful sleeping tablet to ensure an adequate night's sleep. He repacked his doctor's bag and stood there momentarily bewildered and shaking his head. There was more to this affair than he wanted to know about. He looked at Sharyn and Scooty and noticed that the strain was beginning to show on their faces as well. He recommended a good sleep for them all, then turned away and started towards the living room.

Sharyn, Scooty and Joe all accompanied Doctor Darby to the front entrance of the penthouse where they received last minute instructions on how to monitor Joe's condition. They now stood in the long entrance hall staring at each other with tired eyes. Joe was feeling more comfortable now that his injuries had been treated and properly dressed. The sleeping pill was already taking effect, and he was happy to follow the doctor's orders and get some healing rest. He was determined however, that this would not be before he enjoyed an adequate crystal glass of pure malt scotch whisky.

'Thanks Sharyn, and thank you Scooty. You've both been a great help to me tonight, or should I say this morning?' Joe was looking unsteady on his feet as he spoke.

Scooty reached out and held onto his friend by clutching him under his one good shoulder.

'Come on Joe. Let's get you back into the living area where we can all sit down.'

They moved back into the lounge area to relax their tired bodies into the luxurious leather sofas. It was obvious that Sharyn and Scooty were keen to question Joe about what had happened. Although Sharyn wasn't a scotch drinker, she gladly accepted one when Joe poured three adequate levels of Glenfiddich whiskey into crystal glasses and offered one her way. Joe was the first to speak.

'Scooty, correct me if I'm wrong, but I'd say that you're marooned here for the time being. You take the guest quarters in the north west wing and get yourself as much sleep as you need.' He checked the screen on the kidnapper's cell phone as he spoke.

Scooty took a long hard sip from his scotch, and it had the immediate effect of making him drowsy.

'Thanks Joe. I'll do exactly that. The helicopter is stuck here on your pad until I can arrange for drums of fuel to be brought here. Anyway, don't worry about that now. Are you going to tell us what the hell happened in that train tonight?'

Sharyn, who was sitting next to Joe and taking tiny sips from her own glass, now added her own question.

'Yes. That must have been terrible for you. Won't you please tell us what happened?'

Joe, who was once again studying the screen of the kidnapper's cell phone, responded with difficulty.

'Look guys. I don't think I'm ready to recount all that happened last night. I am afraid you'll just have to wait until morning for the gory details. For now, suffice to say that I wasn't the only one injured.' Joe was slurring his words as he continued.

'And, our doorman Leslie Murchison is responsible for saving my life.'

Sharyn almost dropped her scotch glass as her position jolted next to Joe. 'Leslie Murchison? But Joe, I thought... I thought...,'

Joe, who was now fading quickly, interrupted her as she spoke.

'Yes Sharyn. I know we thought that he could be the person behind this whole criminal affair. But, no, we've seriously misjudged him.'

Scooty, who now felt as though he was learning with each moment and becoming more involved, questioned Joe.

'You say that other people were injured. Can you tell us who it was who stabbed you in the shoulder?'

'Listen you guys!' Joe exclaimed. 'You are both like family to me and I intend to tell you the whole story to-morrow, or should I say, after we've had some sleep. For now, I will tell you that I was attacked by three hood-lums, two of whom I shot with your gun Scooty. The third was just about to end my life with a four-inch blade when Leslie Murchison came to the rescue.'

'Leslie Murchison rescued you?' Sharyn was puzzled.

'Yes. I owe him my life.' Joe was showing great signs of emotion as his voice trembled.

'Yes, you've been through hell,' Sharyn interrupted. 'You can tell us all about it after we've had some sleep. You need some rest.'

Scooty swallowed down the last of his scotch, and started to his feet. He hesitated and slumped back down into the chair.

'Whoa! That whiskey sure has the right effect Joe. Just tell me something. Did you manage to successfully deliver the ransom?'

'Yes I did.' Joe drowsily responded. 'All we can do now is hope for Casey to be safely returned. Maybe this cell phone will ring, or a letter will be received telling us when and where we can pick her up.'

Sharyn comforted him. 'Yes that's right. We should soon have her back with us.'

Scooty fidgeted again and this time managed successfully to get to his feet.

'Just one more thing Joe. You'd better give me back my gun. If it was fired in that train last night, then I'd better make sure that it never gets into the hands of the police. It will have your prints all over it, as well as mine.'

Joe, who had by this time been helped to his feet by Sharyn, replied. 'There's no need. I've already disposed of the weapon. We can rest assured that the police won't find it.'

With the cell phones positioned under Casey's photograph on the side table, Sharyn helped Joe into the comfortable warmth of his huge bed and watched him as he drifted away into a deep sleep. Unwilling to leave his side, she sat there on the bed next to him and looked at his face. Watching, as the lines faded from his brow and the tension from the corners of his eyes, she listened to his breathing take on a steady pulse. She caressed his cheeks and ran her fingers across his forehead and decided that she must stay close to Joe for the remainder of the night.

Satisfied that Joe was asleep, Sharyn nervously unbuttoned her dress and let it fall to the floor and she then dimmed the bedside lamp. Ignoring her fine upbringing and basic sense of modesty, she then slipped under the covers next to her soulmate.

* * * * *

She must have fallen asleep at some point because her eyelids were heavy when she was startled. Just as she was comfortably nestling her head into the soft down pillow, Joe's cell phone began to ring. She tried to rouse him, but because of the combination of scotch whiskey and sedation, Joe merely stirred in his sleep and grumbled.

'Is that Casey? Is that my princess?' he murmured.

Sharyn, on the other hand, sprang out of bed and circled to the other side. She looked at Joe and could see that he was again sound asleep. She realized that it was Joe's cell phone, and not that of the kidnappers, and she quickly picked up to answer.

'Hello this is Joe Egan's phone. Can I help you?'

'Yes. It's detective Frank Berne. I want to speak to Joe Egan. Who is this please?'

'Thank God! You've found Casey. Where is she?' asked Sharyn hopefully.

'No, I'm sorry. Who is this?' Berne asked gruffly.

'Oh! Detective Berne. This is Sharyn Cooper. Joe is sound asleep. Is it about Casey? Is she all right? Have you heard anything at all?'

'No. It's not regarding Casey. I need to speak to Joe about another matter. Is he there?' insisted Berne.

Sharyn immediately thought of her dilemma. She looked at Joe and quickly decided that he was certainly in no fit condition to speak to the police. The poor man was badly injured, exhausted, sedated, and intoxicated. It would surely spell disaster for him. Sharyn quickly took the initiative and spoke back to Frank Berne.

'Oh, yes he is detective, but with the stress he's been through, he's not been feeling well and he's asleep. Can I help?'

'Well, Miss Cooper, I want you to wake him up. It's important and I need to talk to him.'

'I'll try, but he's really not well and he's had some sedatives to help him rest.'

She was actually sure that Joe would not wake up, so she held the phone and sat down on the bed.

'Joe! It's the phone for you. Wake up now.'

'Oh, Casey...Casey?' Joe mumbled in his sleep.

'No Joe. It's Detective Berne. He wants to talk to you about something else.'

'No. No. Tell him..er..tell...eh..I'll talk in the morning,' responded Joe incoherently.

'Detective, I'm sorry. Did you hear that? Look, I'll have to get you to call back tomorrow afternoon, unless it's something I can be of assistance with.'

'Well, I did hear him mumble something. You can answer for me then. Where has he been since 8.00 p.m. and now?'

Sharyn now knew that this was very serious and she thought quickly.

'He's been with me all night.'

'Are you sure about that? Can you personally vouch, that Joe Egan is asleep there at home?'

'Yes detective. I give you my personal guarantee. He's sound asleep in bed.' Sharyn blushed as she declared her obvious impropriety.

'And, Miss Cooper, have you been with him throughout the evening? We may have to receive this from you in a written statement. So, please be sure of your answer.'

'Yes. I can personally state that I have been with him all evening and he has been at home here at Egan Center. I'll be happy to put that in writing for you Detective Berne, and you can talk to Joe tomorrow if he's feeling better.'

Sharyn realized that she had no choice as she answered that question. Any other response would have led to further questioning.

'Let him know that I'll be up to see him at 2.00 p.m.'

'Yes, I will tell him.'

Sharyn ended the call and replaced the cell phone onto the side table. She let out a deep sigh, as she looked again at Joe's face. He was perspiring in his sleep and she tenderly rubbed her fingers across his eyebrows. She hoped in her heart that she had dealt with the phone call appropriately. Sharyn had covered for him, but was so worried about the possible consequences of what she had said. Yes. She had previously chosen to involve herself in Joe's personal life. But now, she was seriously implicated in any criminal aspects of what had occurred in the subway last night. She had given false information to the police.

Sharyn thought about it some more and came to a rational conclusion. Any good personal assistant would have handled the situation the same way. The last thing a personal assistant wants is for her boss to have problems. Her job as Joe's personal assistant was to keep everybody happy, to 'keep the wolves from the door', and to be the sweet impenetrable barrier between Joe and his adversaries.

Sharyn switched off the light, quietly walked again to the other side of the bed, and carefully climbed beneath the bed linen. Without the slightest touch, she was exhilarated by her physical closeness to Joe and she wanted to reach out and caress him. She resisted the desire she felt, and within minutes her fears and anxieties were forgotten as a peaceful sleep descended upon her.

* * * * *

Sweet fragrances of blooming jasmine and honeysuckle were floating through the air. Joe stretched out across the broad picnic blanket, and gazed up at a floating eagle. Far above, puffy white clouds were intermingled with areas of liquid-blue sky. He had been trying to shape them into images of sheep when he was distracted by the laughter of his daughter. He swiveled onto his side and propped himself up with one elbow.

The scene before him was serene and quite lovely. There was Casey, God bless her, sitting in the long grass under a spreading shade tree, and tossing breadcrumbs to the visiting birds. The radiant smile on her youthful face and the way that she was giggling out loud, was evidence enough of the wonderful time she was having.

From across the surface of a yellow daisy laden field, Sharyn was approaching with a wicker picnic basket in one hand and a bottle of red wine in the other. Joe's heart was filled with love as he watched the woman he adored, her lustrous auburn hair thrown back, and her summer frock flowing in the fresh breeze. Her face gleamed with happiness and vitality as she called out to him.

'Come on sleepy head. Sit up now. You must be starving.'

Joe's tired body shifted to remind him of the aches and pains in his joints. He was aware that the scent of blooming flowers was actually the delicate fragrance of Sharyn's morning perfume as she came closer to him.

'Come on sleepy. I have something nice for you to eat.' Her voice was velvety soft.

'Wake up now. Here's some breakfast for you.'

His eyesight was blurry. Joe tried to make the distinction. He blinked his eyes and focused his mind, and the dream was transformed to reality. He looked around to find himself lying in his king-size bed. There was Sharyn, rested and ready, standing in the light of the window with the breakfast tray she had prepared.

'Here you are Joe, fresh orange juice, cereal, bacon and eggs, and hash browns. And, steaming hot black coffee, just as you like it.'

Sharyn was obviously delighted to have brought Joe this wholesome breakfast in bed. It would help him recuperate. She heard the same familiar words in his remark, as were so often directed at her each morning in the office. This time however, she sensed a new genuine meaning behind them.

'Good morning Sharyn. Don't you look the beautiful lady this morning?' Joe smiled at her as he shuffled to a sitting position under the bed linen.

'Is Scooty up and about this morning?'

'Yes. He's already up on the concrete checking over his helicopter.'

Sharyn grinned and Joe pushed himself up higher, propping some pillows behind his head.

Sharyn placed the breakfast tray across his lap and Joe breathed back heavily, enjoying the smell of bacon and eggs and the rich aroma of the fresh black coffee.

'Thank you so much Sharyn. This is exactly what I need.'

Sharyn smiled and then her expression changed.

'Listen Joe, I want you to enjoy your breakfast and prepare yourself for the day. Detective Frank Berne will be here to see you at two o'clock. He called last night when you were asleep.'

Joe took a gulp of black coffee and looked up at Sharyn.

'What? He called last night?'

'Yes. You were completely unconscious. It was impossible to wake you so I spoke to him myself.' Sharyn was now getting concerned that Joe might not approve of her actions.

'So tell me Sharyn, what was it all about?'

'Well, I hope I've done the right thing. He was asking of your whereabouts last night. He was very insistent. I had to give him an alibi.'

'For God's sake Sharyn, what did you say?' Joe paused his eating, and his cutlery clanged down onto the tray.

'He wanted to know how you spent the evening and I told him we simply spent it at home here together. Is that all right?'

Joe relaxed his shoulders and smiled at Sharyn.

'Yes Sharyn. You've done well. Thank you for saying that.'

Joe reached across for both cell phones and checked the screens for messages or missed calls. There were none. He then looked again into Sharyn's liquid eyes.

'They have their ransom Sharyn. When are they going to return my princess to me? We've done our part. I've complied with their every wish. Why haven't they contacted us?' Sharyn looked pitifully back at Joe and she was speechless. She had no comforting words to offer. In her own opinion, she suspected that Joe would never see his daughter again. She knew however, that he desperately needed some encouragement, so she shook the expression of doubt from her face.

'There's always hope. We must not give up hope.' Sharyn turned and left the room without saying any more.

By the time Frank Berne was announcing his arrival to the security guard in the lobby of Egan Center, Joe had made himself well prepared. With great difficulty, he had used plastic cellophane to cover his dressings and he had been able to shower. He had then used an electric shaver to remove the gray stubble from his chin, and he was now dressed in his finest clothes.

As a precaution, he had removed the bandage and aluminum stripping from his painful right hand, and he was satisfied that the dressing to his left shoulder was adequately concealed by his silk shirt and tweed jacket. He stood in front of his dressing room mirror, and could see no visible evidence of the terrifying events of the previous night.

Joe decided that he would leave Sharyn and Scooty in the penthouse for the time being, because he wanted them to receive any message about Casey, should one arrive. He stepped into his private hydraulic elevator to descend to his business office below. Joe was now ready to receive Detective Frank Berne on equal terms.

Settling back into the comfortable folds of his leather chair, Joe scanned the several items that Andrew had distributed evenly across his wide semi-circular desk. To the side, he also noticed the compilation of ten names that Andrew had previously prepared, the names of clientele who had purchased apartments in Egan Center, and who were most likely to be disgruntled with the management for one reason or another. He picked up the list and with a strike of his pen, he eliminated the name of Leslie Murchison. Joe stared at the list and became more depressed. He wondered what he might do about investigating the activities of the remaining nine individuals. The two paracetamol tablets he had recently swallowed were now settling the pain in his shoulder and right hand.

Joe dropped the list back onto his desk and swiveled around to the hypnotic dream world of the tropical aquarium. The soothing simplicity of that world helped him think more vividly about the righteousness of what he was doing. Maximizing the probability of Casey's safe return was the most important consideration. Joe checked his Rolex and saw that the time was approaching 2.00

p.m. He swung back to his desk and called through to Andrew Barton who was busy at work in the main central office.

'Hello Andrew. Just letting you know that I'm now in my office.'

'Oh, good. Mr. Egan. Detective Lieutenant Frank Berne is waiting to see you.'

'Okay Andrew. Thank You. Would you please show him in?'

When the policeman marched into the office, Joe noticed immediately that his demeanor had now adopted a regenerated air of authority. The attitude of sympathy and compassion that was evident at their last interview had now disappeared. In one way, Joe was relieved. He now knew he would not have to offer his injured right hand as a greeting. Frank Berne marched directly across and sat down opposite Joe. Joe decided that he would take the assertive position and speak first.

'Detective Berne, tell me that you have some good news about my daughter. Tell me that you have information about Audrey's murder.'

Frank Berne grumbled, cleared his throat, and stood up from his chair. He began to pace the length of the floor as he replied.

'No. I can't give you positive news on either count. I can tell you, however, that the man I told you about, Blue Featherman, remains at large. We're making every endeavor to find out who is behind it all. And so, Mr. Egan, I'm here today to ask you a few more questions.' Frank turned to face Joe head on.

'Well detective, I've consented to this interview, but I must tell you that I've been advised by my lawyer not to answer any more questions unless he is in attendance,' said Joe defensively.

271

After the last disappointment, Joe was doubtful that Wyatt Prendergast would make himself available at short notice. He also knew that he should try to encourage Frank Berne to work diligently towards Casey's rescue, and so he began to regret what he had just said.

'Listen here Egan!' Frank Berne exclaimed in a slow and deliberate manner. 'If you have any chance of convincing me that you are an innocent victim in this whole affair, you seem to be going about it the wrong way. If you have nothing to hide, I suggest that you co-operate with me here and now. I want nothing less than the absolute truth.' Anger was welling in his eyes.

'Yes, very well detective. I see your point. Ask me what you want and I'll do my best to help.' Joe had decided to soothe the situation. It was not the time for confrontational posturing.

Frank Berne walked back over towards Joe, sat down in his chair once again, and extracted his pen and notebook.

'All right then, we can keep this short and sweet. I need to hear from your own lips, Mr. Egan. Where were you between the hours of 8.00 p.m. last night and 2.00 a.m. this morning?'

This was the moment Joe had been dreading. So far he had avoided directly telling lies. Now the time was ripe for jumping completely into the quicksand.

Joe looked at Frank squarely in the eyes and answered promptly.

'Lieutenant, I was here at home in Egan Center during those hours you've just mentioned. I was here throughout that whole period, at home in my penthouse.'

'All right Egan. I also want to know, do you have any knowledge at all about an incident that took place last night on the subway? I'm talking about a homicide.'

'Lieutenant. I have no idea whatsoever what the hell it is you're talking about. I told you I was here throughout the entire evening.'

Joe hated telling lies to the police. It went against everything he held true and steadfast in his beliefs. He knew he had no alternative. The police themselves, in the way they had treated Joe, had left him with no choice. And, Sharyn's statement, with good intentions, had left him with no choice.

Frank Berne continued. 'I see. Then, it may interest you to know that one of the victims of this crime was calling out the words 'Egan Enterprises and Egan Center' as he was attended to. Can you think of any reason why he would do that?'

Joe put on his best expression of bewilderment to give credence to his story, and then answered the question.

'No. I cannot, for the life of me, understand why he would do that. Have you established his identity? Have you been able yourself to find any previous connection?'

'No. We haven't as yet, but believe me when I tell you, that I intend to.'

Frank Berne could see that there wasn't the slightest weakness in Joe Egan's barrier. He knew that any further interrogation would be a waste of time. He snapped closed his notebook, stood up, and concluded the interview.

'Thank you for your time Mr. Egan. I hope for your sake, that you're telling me everything. We shall notify you as and when there are further developments in our investigation.'

He turned, walked across the room, and paused at the door. He swiveled around with one more thing to say.

'Just let me reiterate Egan. We're to know the minute you hear of anything. And, I mean anything at all.'

He held Joe's eyes with his stare for a moment. Then he made his own way out of the office, pulling the doors shut behind him.

That final leer in Frank Berne's eyes stayed with Joe for several seconds. Joe shook his head, and rotated his chair once again to gaze at the world of tropical marine splendor. He knew now, more than ever, of the hostility that existed towards him by the police. If they knew of his actions, they would crucify him. Joe was weaving a tangled web of deceit for the sake of his daughter, and he was thoroughly convinced that his decision to act alone was in Casey's best interest.

Unfortunately, he was also beginning to fearfully accept, for the first time since Audrey's murder, that he might never again see his daughter alive. His eyes filled with moisture and a tear trailed down his cheek to salt his quivering lips.

Joe returned to his personal elevator and ascended to the penthouse level. He thought that the remainder of the day would be long, difficult, and depressing. It was. The afternoon was an endurance test of anxious anticipation intercepted by intervals of despair. Scooty was occupied with the delivery of fuel containers to the helicopter, and Joe and Sharyn suffered in their helplessness to do anything more in a constructive way to help Casey. Joe would pace the rooms and hallways of his grand premises, continually checking the two cell phones and mumbling to himself. On more than one occasion, Sharyn overheard him praying for forgiveness and mercy. She was beginning to believe that the personal torment being experienced by the subject of her deepest love was sending him insane.

Deciding that she would stay by his side and help in any possible way, Sharyn continually spoilt him with gentle neck rubs, tender words of encouragement and copious mugs of his favorite Brazilian coffee.

By the time darkness fell, Joe was completely at his wit's end. He tried to rationalize that the delay was due to the diamond evaluation. After all, the message did say that the authenticity of the stones would be established prior to the release of his daughter. Although a valuable parcel of diamonds, they were all individually acceptable in size and quality. All, that is, except for the outstanding enormous pink diamond. Surely, this would take considerable time and be the reason why Casey had not yet been released. On the other hand, the seed of doubt that was now germinating in his mind was driving him to a state of confused despair.

Joe explained to Scooty and Sharyn that he needed to be alone. He wanted them to stay in the guest accommodation, so that he could retire alone to the master bedroom to partake in some personal prayer. It was 10.00 p.m. when Joe finally positioned the two cell phones in front of the portrait of Casey on the side table, and climbed into bed.

Joe's restless and very tense sleep was a sequence of waking up and drifting off. On each occasion, he would check the cell phone reception, and then fall back to sleep. It was during the fourth such interval of this repetitive torment, that Joe had the revelation. He had taken more of the tablets that Troy Darby had given him and he was delirious from the medication. Joe was hallucinating about the black Chevrolet Silverado looming towards him. He then thought of the mysterious driver and the nine remaining names on Andrew Barton's list of suspects. Why hadn't he perceived this connection earlier?

Joe forced himself to sit upright in bed and he flicked on the bedside light. He noticed that it was now 2.15 a.m.

He shook his head and blinked his dreary eyes open as he considered this new possibility. Although it was a long shot, it now occurred to Joe, that if the Chevrolet belonged to the kidnapper, and the kidnapper was a person on Andrew's list, then it made sense that the vehicle could belong to a resident of Egan Center.

'My God!' Joe said hazily, then, silently continued in thought. 'That vehicle could, at this very moment, be parked in the underground resident car park of Egan Center.' Joe shook his head in disbelief at his own conclusion. Surely the odds are a thousand to one. No. It's an impossible chance, barely worth the effort of investigation. He switched off the light and tried to re-establish his sleep.

As much as he tried, he was unable to dismiss the idea from his thoughts. Even if it was a vague hunch, it was impossible to ignore it. At this stage, he had nothing else to cling to. Unable to leave the idea alone, Joe turned on the light again, stumbled out of bed, and then almost collapsed. He was in a drugged sleepy stupor and his body wouldn't obey his mind. Joe willed his legs into action. He didn't care what the time was, or how remote was the chance. Joe decided there and then to descend to the basement to satisfy himself that the vehicle wasn't there. It would only take a few minutes and he could be back in bed, and then able to sleep.

In his dizzy state, he completely forgot the cell phones. He stumbled into the dressing area, grabbed the first items of clothing he came across, and put them on. They were the same cream silk shirt and black woolen pants he had been wearing throughout the day.

Maybe it was his basic instinct and sense of insecurity that made his hand move, or maybe it was a subconscious inspiration from Audrey's heavenly spirit. He wasn't sure which. But, without thinking, he intuitively reached for the small sack of cubic zirconia and the silver paper knife that he had previously left on the dresser. He shoved them into his trouser pocket, and felt instantly more comfortable that they were once again on his person.

He automatically fastened his gold Rolex, slipped into his patent leather shoes, and walked quietly to the entrance hall. As he waited for the elevator to arrive, his mind was in a daze. His good hand slid into his pocket to establish the position of the small sack of cubics and the paper-cutting knife. He massaged the tiny replicas through the exterior of the velvet pouch and then withdrew the paper knife for another inspection. With a press of his thumb, the narrow blade slid outwards and a flash of reflected light glistened from its razor sharp edge.

CHAPTER 21

As I make the short descent to the basement parking lot, I'm wondering to myself whether I've finally gone completely mad. It's now approaching three o'clock in the morning and I'm exhausted, confused, and desperately clutching at straws. I simply cannot ignore the possibility that a resident of Egan Center may own the black Chevy. I also know that it would be impossible for me to sleep if I was to leave this stone unturned. I'll check to see, and that will be that.

Anyway, what in blazes should I do, if I do discover the kidnapper's vehicle in the parking area? Having come this far independently, it's almost impossible for me to now summon the help of the police. They would be far more likely to apprehend me, rather than arrest the owner of the Chevrolet. Maybe the better course of action would be to follow the vehicle when it leaves, and just hope that it might lead me to my daughter.

I look at my own reflection in the mirrored wall of the elevator and realize that I've been talking to myself. I wonder at my unbalanced mental state. Here I am, following a blind hunch, a trivial speculation with such miniscule odds of it leading to anything.

It's an uninterrupted descent to the second car parking level, and the doors slide open to a sea of parked vehicles. My immediate conclusion is that a Chevrolet truck would be too common to be a member of this elegant lineup of prestige cars. There are Bentleys, Porsches and

Mercedes Benz with the occasional Rolls Royce. Almost every car is fitted with a sophisticated individual alarm system, quite evident by the hundreds of tiny red blinking dashboard lights.

The atmosphere in the garage is cool and dust free as the hundreds of expensive motor vehicles sparkle and shine under the fluorescent lights. At this time of night there's no one else in the area, and my every footstep can be heard as a dull plunk followed by a muffled echo. I walk around the concrete supporting pillars from car to car, inspecting one after the other. There's no sign of the black Chevy truck.

It's taken me about ten minutes to get around this level, and in the process, I quickly glance in at my own vehicles standing side by side behind their caged barrier. The maroon Bentley contrasts appropriately with the silver Porsche Twin Turbo I've recently had delivered. Maybe one day, I'll have an opportunity to give that Porsche a good thrashing. These are frivolous mind games when I consider my current situation. Although I love automobiles, they now seem quite meaningless when I think of Casey and her predicament.

I proceed down the ramp to the first level car park and tediously continue the search. After another five minutes or so, I'm almost ready to abandon my quest. It's unlikely that I will find a pickup truck amongst these magnificent vehicles. That opinion is changed in an instant when I swing my head around, and my heart skips a beat.

My eyes are suddenly transfixed to the far corner of the area where the shiny black Chevrolet Silverado stands in isolation. Its familiarity crystallizes in my view as I walk briskly towards it. I know that it's not Casey herself that I've discovered, but I'm certainly one step closer to finding her.

My pulse is racing so forcefully that I can literally count the beats. I walk up to the Chevy for a closer inspection. The model and color are really not uncommon, and I'm afraid that it may be a similar, but different Chevrolet. With my heart in my mouth, I step around to the back end and stand there, frozen in a cold sweat. The red bumper sticker depicts the familiar shiny chrome V8 engine, exuding lashes of crimson flame. I can now silently read the words beneath.

UNLEASHED FURY

My panic subsides and I'm thrilled at the prospect of now finding Casey. I peer through the driver's window, hoping to gain some information as to the identity of the owner. I'm very careful not to touch the vehicle's surface and thereby possibly set off the truck's alarm. There is nothing unusual to be seen on the inside. The beige leather seats are clean and bare and the keys are not in the ignition. I step back and look into the rear tray compartment. It's empty apart from some strands of nylon rope and a calico canvas tarpaulin.

The clanging sound of the elevator door chime startles me. I wait and soon hear the echo of footsteps. When I realize that the person is walking my way, I duck down to a squatting position behind the pickup. Is it possible that this could be the kidnapper heading towards me? My inner fears are confirmed when he uses his remote-locking device to deactivate the security system and unlatch the doors. If he sees me hanging around the pickup it could be catastrophic.

Although he's not yet come into view, I can hear his footsteps coming from the far side of the closest pillar and they're getting closer. With no other course of action other than to confront him face to face, I follow a gut reaction. I impulsively leap into the rear compartment and conceal myself, sprawled out under the calico tarpaulin.

My left shoulder impacts with the tray floor and I bite my lip to smother any outburst. The adrenalin is pounding through my veins and my thoughts are of the silver paper knife in my pocket. How could I be so foolish as to discard Scooty's gun? If only I had it with me now. I've actually thrown my best means of defense into a storm drain. My breathing is uneven as I listen to the driver's door open, and then close again.

The powerful engine roars into life and the pickup moves off with a jolt. I'm both terrified and excited at where the ride might take me, but my instinct tells me that the destination will determine my fate. The prospect of finding Casey fills my heart with exhilaration, pushing aside fear and apprehension. I'm now increasingly conscious that the unaware kidnapper might be actually carrying me to the kidnapped.

'Goddamn it! Where the hell is my phone?' I'm cursing under my breath.

I can feel the cubic zirconia and the paper knife in my pocket, but I can't believe that in my state of delirium, I've left those cell phones behind. No way of contacting anyone, and one little paper knife to defend myself with. I wrap myself low in the tarpaulin and go with the ride.

The truck goes up and out onto the avenue, and we're soon traveling along the streets of New York City. I'm a willing captive being driven to God knows where. I know I have to concentrate on the trip and pick up any clues, keep track of the minutes and the orientation, and make mental notes whenever I can. I'm aware of the diminishing benefits of paracetamol because, with the swaying and jerking of the vehicle, I'm once again feeling the pain of my injuries and a tendency to throw up.

My one good hand and both feet brace firmly against the sidewall wheel housing and I decide to look out from beneath my cover to determine the direction. The pickup seems to be traveling further away from New York with every precautionary glance I take from under the canvas. It's too difficult to remember the route, and I decide to remain concealed to endure the pains and discomfort of the rugged trip. I remain there, without one decent idea about what to do at the end of the drive, and I think of how ill equipped I am to deal with whatever the future has in store.

The stop and go nature of driving through city lights eventually changes to a more fluent journey, and the volume of traffic lessens with each passing mile. After a while, the road becomes grainy, and I can hear the tires slicing through a thin film of water. Then, the ride becomes harder and the terrain more undulating.

While the light rain turns into a heavy shower, whacking the tarpaulin with greater frequency, I huddle to stay dry and wait for the drive to end. I'm aware of the city becoming suburbia, and suburbia becoming country. It's been more than two hours of torture, now worsened when the ride becomes unbearably uncomfortable on this very rough road.

I peer out through the blinding rain as we swing around a bend and I get a fleeting glimpse of a signboard 'Tuxedo Junction General Store'. After so much physical suffering, I'm thinking that I can't stand another mile. I simply have to get out. Surely the journey will end soon. Please, let it end soon.

Off to the side, there's a broken split-rail fence that borders an old cow pasture, now densely covered with grass from the constant rain. We continue sliding and spinning up a muddy winding track and I guess that I'm in the middle of a vast pine forest. It's difficult to be sure because the last street lamp is some time back and everything is stark darkness and pouring rain.

I'm now aware that the vehicle has suddenly stopped on a steep decline. I figure the trip so far has taken about two hours twenty. I'm at my wit's end. I listen as the driver shifts into four-wheel drive before continuing across a bumpy creek bed. The pains of my injuries are now excruciating as the pickup truck leaps and bounces across the rocks. It finally jumps and skids up the other side, slides through the mud for a further short distance, and then jerks to a stop.

I'm terrified at what might happen now, and I once again think about the only weapon I possess, the small and almost ineffectual paper knife. It's possible, that at any moment, the tarpaulin could be flung from above me. My hand is trembling as I try to grasp my tiny paper knife. I can do nothing but hope and wait. The driver's door opens and closes and I can hear his footsteps swishing and splashing through the mud. After a couple of minutes, the splashing is gone. I gain the courage to cautiously slide out from beneath the canvas and peep over the edge.

I quickly survey the surroundings and stare intensely into the blackness. Everything is a dark void beyond the surrounding pine trees, and steady rain still falls in bucket loads. I throw the tarpaulin to one side and tumble over the lip of the compartment to the damp and slippery surface below. All around me is soggy, slimy and wet. The atmosphere is a steady drone of impacting raindrops, and I'm quickly saturated from head to foot. I braced myself on the outside of the vehicle to gain my equilibrium.

There's a small break in the cloud and the moon shines through, enhancing my ability to see. Through the glistening sheets of falling rain, I look across to a small shabby cabin not more than twenty yards away. When I look back towards the creek we had crossed, my knees go weak at the sight. Things are slowly making sense.

Tumbled onto its side in the creek bed, I can recognize the same laundry van that almost collided with my yellow taxi outside the Icelandic Hotel. Casey would have been inside that van, and if the driver was Blue Featherman, I realize that he's probably here now. My brain is grinding, and I figure that with two vehicles present, it's more than probable that there are at least two kidnappers here.

Through the faded and decaying window coverings of the cabin, and the gaps in the rotting wallboards, I can see the blinking light of kerosene lanterns inside. I hope in my heart that Casey is alive and inside that cabin. I feel a shudder run through my flesh and I begin to shake furiously. Every bone, sinew and muscle I possess, is straining with the will to drive my legs through the mud, burst through that cabin door, and rescue my daughter, whatever it takes. My discretion and common sense subdue my anger, and I decide to bide my time. By doing so, I might just be able to gain some kind of advantage, and therefore have a greater prospect of a successful result.

The cabin of the pickup truck is unlocked, and I pull the door open to look inside. It's too dark to see much at all, but when I feel that the keys are still in the ignition, I wonder if I should simply drive away and then contact the police. No. I realize that would be a foolish thing to do. I've come this far alone, and it's now up to me to see this through to the end.

I feel for the latch on the glove compartment and find that the compartment is locked. I'm thinking that there's a chance the criminal might have a gun in there. I pull the keys from the ignition and quickly turn the lock of the glove compartment. My fingers run over the contents within and they can find nothing resembling a weapon. Amongst the many unfamiliar feeling objects there, I come across one familiar wonderful discovery. My fingers massage through the velvety material of a small sack and I recognize the contents. I can't believe my luck. These precious diamonds are ten million dollars worth of luck.

I peer through the blinding rain towards the cabin. I can just distinguish the silhouette of my daughter as she passes a cracked opening in the barricaded window at the rear of the cabin. I gasp. It's a strange sensation I feel. My stomach drops and my heart leaps with joy at the same time. Although she's in danger, I now know that Casey is alive and close to me once again. I watch until my eyes ache, for her to appear again. She does so briefly, and then she moves out of sight.

Now that I've found her, I'm faced with an unexpected window of opportunity. I have to act on the moment. Without thinking further, I extract the pouch of precious diamonds and exchange it with the identical sack of cubic zirconia from my pocket. I snap the glove compartment closed, lock it, and replace the keys into the ignition.

What a turn of events! The valuable diamonds are back in my possession. I quietly close the door and stand back to plan my next move. I have to get Casey out of there and I have to do it now. I firm my resolve, grit my teeth, and start out towards the cabin.

CHAPTER 22

Believe it or not! When you're locked away, lonely and cold in a dingy back room, then rats can be a welcome sight. For Casey Egan, the two confident rodents that were keeping her company didn't pose any threat whatsoever.

As Casey shrank as far back as she could into her dingy corner, the scene of two rats feeding on stale baked beans was the only entertainment she had. They also provided her with inspiring hope.

She wanted those rats to come closer. She wanted to hug them. She wanted to learn from their example. Rats were cunning, resourceful and feral. They can survive on the most meager subsistence. They gave her a reason to keep going, a determination to hang on, and a will to live.

Casey trembled, more from the shock of her ordeal than from the bitter cold and damp. Running her tired eyes down along her scratched and bitten legs, she decided that she was no better or worse than one of those rats. They would do whatever it takes to survive, and so must she.

* * * * *

Her shredded nerves had spiked with terror when the ugly laundry man had squatted on top of her weary pathetic body. Completely devoid of any energy, she had then lost her will to fight. Her blurry eyes had studied the big man's boots trudging back up the slope, and she remained limp and submissive over his shoulder. Once inside the stale smelly cabin, the monster laundry man had simply thrown her into a claustrophobic back room.

Casey's delicate little limbs were no match for the thick beefy hands of Blue Featherman. Poor Casey had recoiled in terror when the evil man had locked the door, swung around towards her, and erupted with a hideous wicked cackle. The poor little girl had almost swallowed her tongue when she had looked at his red glazed eyes and seen the saliva drooling from his mouth. Was this the ogre she had heard about in so many fairy tales, the devil she had learnt about at Sunday school, the bogey-man of her worst most terrifying nightmare?

Her captor had pretended to be like a savage wolf when he crouched down on all fours, snarled viciously, and began to chase her around the room. It was a sick game he was playing, his own kind of twisted fun. Every now and again, he would catch her, bite into her delicate pink flesh, and then release her to be taunted and captured once again.

The monster's game continued. With each repetitive capture, it became a little more serious with greater ferocity. Casey screamed and screamed. Her quivering body was now badly bitten and small droplets of her blood were beginning to appear. The more she cried for help and tried to scramble from his grasp, the more the predator had enjoyed the game. With his nostrils flaring and his glazed eyes darting wildly in their sockets, he had used his decaying teeth to rip the little girl's underwear into shreds. He had then nibbled beyond.

Blue Featherman's desire was to inflict as much suffering and torment as possible, before executing his final brutal act of rape and slaughter. He was so annoyed that he was not permitted to complete his game. It would have to wait. The warning he had received from the dude was playing over and over in the back of his mind. He must not touch the girl. He was not to lay a hand on her. It could make the difference between two hundred grand, or nothing. A new life in Florida, or a return to that filthy rotten prison cell. He reluctantly decided to leave her, and get drunk instead.

* * * * *

Casey sat there watching her companions. She gazed at the two rats. They had made their appearance once the monster had left the area and bolted her in. Casey watched them feed, and at the same time, listened to the monster man drinking, swearing, and stumbling about in the other room. She heard another person enter the cabin with a different voice, a calmer more sensible voice. The two men were arguing and cursing in the room next to where she was. Were they talking about money? Were they talking about her? She heard them agree to disagree. Payment was to come later for the laundry man when he was picked up from the cabin. The girl was not to be touched, and she realized that she was the girl. Then there was more cursing and arguing and the calmer more sensible man left. She wondered how long it would be before the wolf would be at her door once again.

Casey went back to the distraction of the rats. After a short time they became jittery, scampered briefly away, and then returned to feed on the spilled beans. What was it that had frightened them? Casey was sure she had heard something, or someone, moving around below the floorboards. She imagined that there would be many animals of the forest sheltering under the cabin to escape the heavy rain. There was that shuffling sound again. She could hear it moving under the floor. Casey decided that it must be a large animal, probably a wolf with huge decaying fangs, maybe a wolf like the laundry man. The image frightened her. She closed her eyes and tried to think of nicer things.

She thought of her father. He was always at her side to protect her and help her through life. She remembered the good times with her dad, just the two of them together, laughing and giggling with pleasure and happiness. During their holiday at Disneyland, he had never left her side.

'Always have to protect my princess.' he had said.

Why had he not come to save her now? He had never let her down before. Where was he now when she needed him most of all? Casey began to sob softly.

'Oh! Please. Where's my daddy?' she cried then paused.

She stopped sobbing because she wanted to listen once again to the faint scuffling sound below the floorboards.

CHAPTER 23

I come to a standstill in the boggy mud and stare hard through the torrential downpour. In the back room of that old cabin, my little daughter is waiting to be saved. The time is now. I hesitate and step back. To just go charging into the cabin with my tiny paper knife drawn at the ready, would be the same as committing suicide. I have to wait for the right moment. It's imperative that I must organize and control my emotions. I have to think smart, think clearly, and develop a winning strategy.

It occurs to me that the villain kidnapper could appear at any moment through the cabin door, and discover me out in the open. I have to hide and develop my game plan. Aware of my vulnerability, I begin to slip and slide across the muddy ground towards the creek bed. The surface gives way continually at my feet, and on several occasions, I fall face down into the slimy mud. By the time I'm safely concealed behind the mossy bank, my clothes and body are brown with sticky muck. Unintentionally, I've applied to myself the perfect camouflage for the existing environment.

By grabbing hold of a protruding plant root and bracing myself against the creek bank, I'm now steady in a suitable position to observe the Chevrolet and the cabin beyond. With my forefinger, I wipe the grime from the face of my Rolex, and the small iridescent marks reveal the time to be almost 4.50 a.m. I lean back to consider my options.

My mind is in high gear and many thoughts begin to rush in. I can use my managerial experience and business acumen to help me arrange those thoughts into logical order. The first step is to clarify the problem in its enormity by analyzing the factors involved. I begin.

Most importantly, my daughter is inside, alive.

There might be one, two, or even more, enemy to contend with.

With my injuries, I have a limited ability to fight aggressively or even defend myself.

I already have the advantage of surprise because they're not aware of my presence.

I have only one small paper knife to protect myself with.

I know nothing of the possible arsenal of weapons they might have inside.

Time is now of the essence because it won't stay dark forever.

There's probably one hour at the very most before the first hint of daylight.

In the same manner as I've dealt with so many complicated business situations, I have at least clarified the factors of the life and death situation I now face. The next step is to evaluate every possible course of action in order to select the best solution.

Firstly, as the white van is turned over in the creek and stuck, it's completely unusable. I could therefore simply drive away in the Chevy and leave them stranded until the police arrive to rescue Casey and arrest the culprits. I decide that this is not a good plan. Once aware of the missing Chevy, they could panic, kill the only person who can recognize them, and escape on foot.

Another course of action could be an attempt to rescue Casey without their knowledge. I could sneak up to the rear of the cabin, break my way through the decaying wall, and simply snatch her away from beneath their noses. I may be discovered by the kidnappers and subsequently fail in my attempt. Casey herself might be terrified when she sees my muddy ruffled features, and even call out for help. I decide that this is also not a suitable option.

My third choice is to wait for the development of further opportunity. Maybe they will leave Casey locked up in there and drive away for supplies. Even if one person is left to guard my daughter, my chances of succeeding in a fight to the death are greatly increased. I would use the element of surprise. I would burst through the door and attack with my paper knife. My entry would be forceful and swift, and I would scream with the full capacity of my lungs. I would attack with my slicing left hand, using such magnitude, velocity, and intensity so as to render that person impotent. Am I capable of such an act of violence? Who am I kidding? Anyway, I could also be killed in the process.

The longer I sit here, the more convinced I am that there's no perfect solution. I do know, that whatever I decide to do, I had better act on it before daybreak and therefore during the next hour.

As I concentrate to formulate my strategy, I decide on a compromise. I think again of the time factor, and acknowledge to myself, that although still alive, Casey could be killed at any moment. I decide to give it another half an hour for an opportunity to present itself. If nothing has changed by then, I should carry out my doubtful assault with the hope that there's only one dangerous person to challenge.

I mentally review my decision, and I'm struggling to contend with the prospect of failure. At this stage, now that I've found her alive, is it worth putting Casey's life at further risk, by attempting her rescue single-handedly? I'm thinking once again that maybe I should now leave the Chevy, and travel on foot to get police help. The advantage would be that the kidnappers would not know of their discovery until the police actually arrive. The problem is that I don't know which way, and how far away, help can be found. I may even become lost in the forest, after heading off in the wrong direction.

I'm now convinced that I should wait as planned. My troubled thoughts are suddenly halted when I hear the cabin door slap open, and then closed. I can see the dark outline of a person trudging through the mud towards the Chevrolet. He's holding a piece of material above his head to protect himself from the heavy rain. I watch intrepidly as he climbs into the vehicle, and it's impossible to get a clear look at his face.

The Chevy jerks forward and moves slipping and sliding towards the stony creek crossing. I'm straining my eyes to read the license number but it's impossible in the darkness and rain. I silently reprimand myself for not taking it into my memory when I had the chance, and now it's too late.

It's too far away for me to see anything more than the vehicle's black shape and waving headlights as it weaves into the pine forest and into the pelting downpour. When it disappears completely from sight, at least I now know that there's one less person left to deal with.

I wait momentarily and anxiously watch the cabin. I decide in my frustration that it's now time to act. Preparing for the worst, I leave the pouch of diamonds tucked securely in the base of my muddy and slimy pants, and extract the paper knife from my pocket. With the blade still withdrawn, I grip it between my teeth. After hauling myself up and over the slippery creek bank, I begin to slide on my stomach in commando fashion towards the cabin. My right fist is throbbing wildly and the pain in my shoulder intensifies as I dig one elbow after the other into the boggy ground to move forward. Slowly but surely, I slither to within ten yards of the cabin exterior.

The kerosene lanterns are still blinking inside, and it's strangely quiet except for the pounding of the rain around me. My immediate impulse is to crash through the front entrance and gain the upper hand, but my sense of caution tells me to act in a more prudent manner. I admit to myself that it's not only a sense of caution. I'm incredibly afraid. I'm terrified. My nerves are shredded, my heart is throbbing, and my hands are shaking uncontrollably.

I decide that I should crawl underneath the cabin. From there I will be out of sight and out of the rain. If I'm able to see and hear something through the floor planks, I will be better able to formulate a tactical plan. I continue my crawl to the sidewall of the cabin and wriggle my way underneath the floor. The dull roar of the falling rain is left behind, and the boggy mud becomes a powdery dust. Several jittery rodents, gathered under the cabin to escape the weather, now scurry and scamper away from me as I invade their space.

I roll onto my back and squint up through the tiny cracks that exist between the old wooden plank boards. The spider's webs with their captured insects restrict my vision, but I can now hear my beautiful Casey sobbing faintly from the back room of the cabin. Although my heart is aching for her, the noise she is making is music to my ears. It verifies that it's her, and that she's alive. I tentatively push with my legs, and gradually move on my back to a position beneath her location. By peering through between the floorboards, I get a partial view of Casey and I'm shocked at what I see.

My daughter is curled up in the corner of the empty room, and she's completely naked apart from some tattered and ripped underwear. In the pale light of an overhead lamp, she trembles with cold and fright, and I desperately want to cover her. There are some half-opened cans of beans scattered around her coiled body and a bottle of water for her use. Two large rats are loitering around the opened cans and Casey is just staring at them. I squint with my eyes to better focus, and my own torso goes into a state of shocked spasm.

Her soiled and bruised little body is covered with infected bite marks. Maybe they're from the teeth of rats, and maybe they're from the teeth of Blue Featherman.

I have to swallow hard to withhold a scream and then grind my jaw to force back my flaring temper. I shuffle and kick myself to the forward end of the cabin and gaze up. There, I can see and hear a man mumbling to himself, swearing profanity, and slurping on a bottle of alcohol. I wait and watch, thinking about my next move.

After ten minutes of his heavy drinking, he stumbles to the area directly above me and looks down. His glazed red eyes are set way back in his skull and his scabby lips are frothing with saliva. I see glimpses of this horrible individual fumbling with the buttons of his filthy crumpled pants and I swallow a choke of disgust. I'm on my back, looking up at him and he begins to urinate downwards and onto me. I grimace as the liquid stench filters through onto my face. Determined that I should not reveal myself to him, I remain frozen in position to endure this sickening process. I hold tight until he finishes and he saunters back over to the other side of the room.

It takes me a few seconds to recover, and I'm aware of him collapsing in a drunken heap on the couch. Within a few minutes, the constant silence tells me that he's fallen asleep. The kerosene lantern flickers yellow light as I watch and wait. Through the background din of teaming rain, I hear him begin to snore.

My first intention is to sneak past the sleeping giant and snatch my daughter away, but the words of Frank Berne rush into my mind as I listen to the kidnapper's alcoholic gurgling. Surely, this filthy person is the child-molesting monster who should never have been released from prison. This is the evil Blue Featherman who murders mothers, and kidnaps little children. I wait for a few more minutes with anger boiling in my veins until I can't stand it any longer. The sound of Casey's soft crying together with Featherman's snoring, creates a force in my body that cannot be withheld.

I tighten my abdomen and flex every muscle in my body to a state of extreme tension. Any senses of rationale and orderly function are now absent from my mind. Ignoring the pain that emanates from my hand and shoulder, I roll back out into the quagmire. Adopting a crouched position, I then stealthily sneak up the steps onto the front porch. With my shoes rolling gently on the damp timber floor planks, I approach the entrance.

The door lock shifts with a soft click when I turn the handle and the door creaks slowly to a half open position. Taking the silver paper knife from my teeth, I use my thumb to slide open the metal blade, and I ridiculously hold it out as a threat. With my red eyes steaming through a mud-caked face and the slime dripping from my clothes, my appearance is that of a zombie creature emerging from the swamp.

The cluttered room is musty, damp, and lined with mildew. As I inch forward, there's a rank smell of cigarette smoke, urine, and stale rum. The pungent tobacco odor invades the back of my throat and nasal cavities. My eyes are rapidly blinking as I look through the dim flickering light, expecting to see Blue Featherman snoring on the old disintegrating fabric couch. He's not there!

Nausea trounces through me. Every inch of my body breaks into a cold sweat. Where has he gone in that short time? My sixth sense tells me he's waiting for me. It's a trap! I swallow hard as I feel my neck hairs spring on end, and a river of adrenaline surges through my system.

From the darkest corner, and without any warning, he's suddenly lunging at me with surprising momentum. He's in a state of drunken stupor and his eyes are wild with fear and confusion. I'm looking into them, and behind them, at the devil himself. His leg thrashes out in an attempt to kick me, and his hands are groping for my head and neck. I move in one coordinated reflex action.

I duck to the side to avoid his attack but he grabs my hair and yanks so hard that I think he's going to pull it out. With every ounce of strength I can muster, I ram him backward, full force, and pivot around. We tumble onto the couch and I'm on top of him forcing my weight down onto his chest. I'm staring straight into his face. Black grime fills his badly pitted cheeks and his gray hair is stringy and greasy. His scabby lip is curled into a snarl and I cringe at the sight of his brown nicotine stained teeth. The villain's sunken glazed eyes are full of hatred and disdain as they lock onto mine. I despise his existence. His one hand is gripped around my right wrist like a vice and his other is ripping at my ear. He raises his knee and it crunches into my groin. The spasm of agony causes my left hand to simultaneously tighten around the paper knife. What happens now is a reflex over which I have no control.

With my own unleashed fury, I slice the blade in a sideways motion, and slash open his throat from ear to ear.

The noiseless action is swift and precise, and for a second there is no blood. Suddenly it gushes forth from the wide gaping slit and then spurts out in pulses from his severed jugular vein. He tries to speak, but there are no words, only a pathetic sucking noise combined with a trickle of red liquid from the side of his mouth. His inquiring eyes widen with confused shock at what has happened and they silently ask me for verification. I hold him down on the couch with the full weight of my body as I inform him.

'Your throat is cut! You are going to hell!'

I'm surprised at the callousness of my own words. My entire body begins to shake uncontrollably as he stares blankly into my face and I watch the devil fade away from his features. As his life-blood slowly drains away into a slithery pool on the floor, I whisper to him.

'She's my daughter! She's my princess!'

One more heartbeat, and he's gone forever.

CHAPTER 24

By taking the life of another human being, Joe Egan had passed through another gateway in his own existence. This time, it wasn't to a land of greener pastures and peace of mind, for he was now overwhelmed with feelings of guilt and self-contempt. To Joe's amazement, he had actually enjoyed the experience of cutting Feathers' throat and then watching the mad man's life drain away. He had felt a thrilling sensation of excitement and satisfaction by sending the monster's mortality to oblivion.

Joe remained in a squatting position looking down at the man he had just killed. The pressure was eliminated. He knew in his heart that this evil person had no right to a further existence in this world. Although he knew that justice had been dealt, he also was aware that he had crossed a forbidden line. His own life was now changed forever, and from this time on, he would always have doubts about his own salvation.

Joe's rage had now subsided and was replaced by a sickness in the deepest pit of his abdomen. He wanted to vomit and his throat began to convulse, but his empty stomach could only evict a small portion of bile and acid. He fell sideways, away from the lifeless carcass, into the puddle of red sticky blood on the floor. As he lay there with the silver paper knife still gripped tightly in his hand, his mind was a whirlpool of thoughts, emotions and sensations. There were odors of rum, perspiration, blood and tears crowding his brain. The sound of Casey's gentle whimpering could be discerned beyond a constant hum of steady rain. And, there was the visual impact of death itself that now swallowed him up into a personal hell.

It was the sound of his daughter's distressed whimpers that finally forced Joe to face up to the reality of the situation. Her cries were ringing in his ears, and he couldn't understand why he hadn't already rushed to scoop her up. There was something holding him back. A divine force of some type was telling his brain to wait. He knew it was no coincidence that he had come this far and succeeded. Joe stood up and walked backwards three or four paces and stopped. In the quivering light of the kerosene lantern, the room he was looking at once again resembled that of a Shakespearean stage. It was the final act. It was the macabre scene of death.

Joe looked down at the paper knife in his hand and stared at the blood already congealing along the thin blade. He pulled back on his thumb to withdraw the razor edge, and he then put the apparatus away into his pocket.

In the same manner that he would manage any successful business strategy, Joe knew that he had to adapt and blend, maneuver with the unfolding circumstances of the dramatic deal. He realized that this scene was yet to be completely acted, and he reaffirmed his determination to see it through.

Still faced with a powerful temptation to rush through into the back room and sweep Casey up into his loving arms, he instead remained steadfast, forcing himself to ignore her cries. He had to listen to his inner self, see beyond his impulsiveness to a deeper meaning, and heed his own instincts.

The immediate overwhelming desire was to now rescue his daughter and carry her away from harm, to take her through the pine forest and summon for help. Joe now hesitated when he thought of the consequences of such impetuosity. He once again tried to evaluate the factors involved, list them in his mind to be clear and specific, and think them through slowly and deliberately.

His mission was almost complete.

Casey was alive and within his sights.

The precious diamonds were stowed securely in the base of his pocket.

Blue Featherman would no longer be a threat to anyone.

No one else was aware of his presence.

Joe had been extremely secretive and acted alone. As far as anybody else was concerned, he was still sleeping in his room at Egan Center. Without anyone knowing, he had now arrived at this time and place with the death of Blue Featherman behind him, and a lifetime with Sharyn and Casey to look forward to.

As though guided by Audrey's spirit, a miraculous twist of fate had occurred. He had decided to investigate the basement of Egan Center at exactly the correct time. He had come across the Chevy Silverado immediately prior to the kidnapper's arrival. Like clockwork, he had concealed himself in the rear compartment without being discovered. A turn of events had led him back to the diamonds. The timing of his actions in the pine forest had been precisely accurate to achieve success. Suddenly, Joe no longer felt the shame and guilt of his actions. He no longer felt alone in his quest. Joe knew that he was definitely a member of an orchestra, being controlled by a more capable force, a maestro conductor.

One course of action was to now rescue Casey and carry her away to get help at the nearest farm or homestead. The consequences of this would be enormous. His cover would be blown wide open. Not only would Casey's fragile condition make it unsafe for her in those inclement weather conditions, it would really make their escape doubtful. Joe's own future would be ruined. He would be held responsible for deceiving the police and for taking the law into his own hands. He would be charged with Blue Featherman's death, and he would also be linked to the criminal investigation regarding the three hoodlums at Jefferson Street Station. Although it was agonizing, he had to deny himself the temptation. The opening of this 'Pandora's box' would also implicate Sharyn and Scooty as his accomplices. Last, but not least, Joe would be unable to be with Casey throughout her sensitive period of recovery. He would be locked away from the people he most loved.

Joe now stood with his aching left shoulder slumped lower that his right, and his head drooped in concentration. In his mind, he gathered all of these considerations and weighed them against the new strategy he was creating in his thoughts. This was an alternative and interestingly different strategy that seemed to have some merit. Slightly risky, but also daring and radical, it could be the answer to every problem. He decided there and then that this was the better alternative.

Yes! By leaving his daughter securely locked in the back room and carefully retracing his steps, Joe determined that he could remain completely incognito. Rather than rescue Casey himself, Joe would allow the police to do it.

He looked down at his watch and knew that he was to act swiftly and methodically to achieve his purpose. He looked around to ensure that no incriminating evidence had been left which could later lead to his identification.

By carefully stepping rearward and using a sideways scraping motion with the soul of his shoe, Joe ensured that his footprints were eliminated as he paced backward. With his heart going out to Casey as she cried in the other room, Joe took one last long look around at the musty den of iniquity and closed the door behind him.

It went against all of his basic instincts to leave his daughter behind, and it was surely the most difficult thing he had ever consciously required of himself. With Featherman gone, Joe was certain she would be safe for the short period of time required. He continued the foot scraping action until he was off the porch and into the soft mud.

Joe surveyed the boundaries of the clearing, and identified the melting wheel tracks of the Chevrolet pickup. As he pushed his way towards the creek bed crossing, he was deliberately clenching his fractured right fist and his eyes were streaming with tears. He hated himself for leaving Casey there. He wanted to share in her suffering. He clenched his fist as hard as he could. He wanted to feel more pain.

After crossing the small creek, he struggled up a slippery hillside and he was then swallowed into the black night of the forest. At first it was hard going. He was running in total darkness and blinding rain. He would stumble clumsily across the stony terrain, and then slip on pinecones to cartwheel down the slopes. Eventually, he was relieved when the rain lessened to a light shower and the black night became gray. He knew it would be light soon enough.

The further he traveled, the more defined were the wheel tracks before his eyes and the more secure was the soft earth beneath his feet. After approximately forty minutes, his tired legs were wilting from their task, and his body was swaying from side to side.

The darkness lightened to a milky mixture of outlines as the light of day intensified. With the thought of his daughter left behind, and a building apprehension about finding a way forward, Joe was beginning to consider a change of mind. Should he now turn around and make his way all the way back? He was on the verge of doing just that.

Looking hopefully forward one last time, through the light rain he could see the outline of a building. He remembered the signboard as 'Tuxedo Junction General Store'. He felt exhilarated. The closer he came to the store, the more excited he became. There on the exterior sidewall, was a telephone booth and the perfect means of communication he needed.

At this stage, after coming along so far, Joe was certain that he wanted to remain secretive. He adopted an attitude of stealthy awareness, and he slowly crept to the rear of the store and around to the side. Everything was falling into place. He knew immediately that the orchestra was still being conducted. Not only was the phone booth there for his use, also, standing in all its glory beside it, was a small blue early model Toyota sedan.

Joe's heart was beating with the anxious anticipation of his daughter's rescue, as he grabbed the receiver and dialed 911. By screwing up his nose and uttering through the corner of his mouth, Joe was able to contrive a voice that sounded completely different to his own. He spoke slowly and confidently, and as clearly as he could.

'The kidnapped Egan girl can be found in a deserted cabin a few miles to the west of Tuxedo Junction General Store.'

When the female operator asked him to repeat himself, Joe said it one more time in a louder voice.

'The kidnapped Egan girl can be found in a deserted cabin a few miles to the west of Tuxedo Junction General Store.'

The minute he had completed his statement, Joe hung up the phone, wondering if the voice that had been taped would sound sufficiently different to his own. He stood back, and gathered his thoughts. He realized that it was essential to contact Sharyn or Scooty to inform them of his whereabouts. The time was now approaching 6.45 a.m. and Joe realized that it was only a matter of time before they would worry about his absence. They could panic and contact the police thinking he was in grave danger. It was also now only a matter of time before the police would be calling Egan Center with the breaking news of Casey's rescue, and Joe would not be there.

It would be a monumental exercise to attempt to explain the whole confusing situation to Sharyn and Scooty over the phone. Their unpredictable interpretation of the information might make it too difficult if they were confronted by the likes of Frank Berne. It was actually preferable to leave them out of this mess. The less they were told, the better chance there was of Joe remaining undetected. To tell them the facts, was simply not worth the risk. Yet, Joe knew the phone call had to be made.

Joe decided on a simple solution to allow Sharyn and Scooty to give honest and sincere answers to the police, if so asked. Without any further hesitation, Joe picked up the receiver and placed a second call. This time it was a collect call to the home phone number of his Egan Center penthouse. At first there was no answer, and then Sharyn finally picked up.

'This is the residence of Joseph Egan. Hello!'

'Good morning Sharyn. It's Joe here. I thought I'd better call to let you know that I'm safe and sound.'

307

'Oh Joe, I wasn't aware that you had gone out. I thought you were still in bed sleepy head. Where are you?' She had a smile in her words, and after what Joe had been through, it seemed inappropriate.

'Sharyn, I didn't want you to worry. I just couldn't sleep so I went out for an early morning walk to think things through. Would you believe that I've left my cell phones at home? Just not thinking straight. Have you received any calls at all?'

'No Joe. Scooty's up top, but as far as I'm aware, this is the first phone call. When are you coming home?'

'I needed to get out for a stroll. I needed to think. I'll be back by mid morning and I'll see you then. I'm fine. Don't worry about me.'

'Okay. How can we contact you if news comes in?'

'Try to hold tight there until I get back. Don't worry.'

With those words, Joe ended the call. He felt partially relieved and he turned his attention to the Toyota sedan. He was hopeful, that with Audrey's spiritual help, he would find the car unlocked with the keys in the ignition.

Joe walked up to the driver's window of the Toyota and looked inside through the wet glass pane. He tried the door handle, and to his satisfaction it was unlocked. Climbing quickly inside, he settled behind the wheel and fumbled for the keys, but there were none. No keys!

Joe had never tried to steal a motor vehicle so he knew little about the techniques involved. He familiarized himself with the gearshift and made sure it was in neutral. When he bent down and gazed up under the dash, he was thankful that this was an old vehicle with a simple and clearly visible system of ignition wires.

Joe withdrew the silver colored paper knife from his pants pocket and extended the blade. By cutting the wires away, and then experimenting with their connections, he was able to successfully activate the vehicle's electrical system. It was then a matter of momentarily joining the correct two wires together.

To his delight, the starter motor engaged and the engine attempted to respond. After a few whirring rotations and two pumps on the accelerator with his left fist, the vehicle finally started. Joe quickly placed the paper knife into the glove box and returned to his driver's position behind the wheel. He wasted no time in getting the small car moving. He reversed back and onto the muddy dirt road as he engaged the windscreen wipers. With the wipers now beating time, Joe made an instinctive left turn and headed away from Tuxedo Junction.

Joe was unwilling to travel too far without first having some confirmation of Casey's likely rescue. He only drove about a mile or so along the road, pulled off onto a siding and parked behind a row of small shrubs. With the engine still running and the wipers beating, Joe felt comfortable that he could watch the main portion of the road without being detected.

The physical struggle he had endured and his lack of sleep were now taking their toll. His head continued to drop and his eyes were heavy. Within ten minutes, all of Joe's expectations, hopes, and prayers were answered when three wailing police vehicles came speeding past from the opposite direction. He snapped awake and watched with his heart in his mouth.

Their spinning colored lights flashed past and then faded through the shower of rain towards the general store. Joe knew then that Casey would be rescued. He thought that there was nothing else he could now do to help the situation, so he started off again along the road. He continued driving, driving away from his own daughter.

After several intersections and approximately one hour of intuitive choices of direction, Joe came to the conclusion that he was not precisely certain where he was, however he knew that he was closer to New York. At first, he had fallen into a comfortable driving rhythm, but then he had endured long stretches of drifting off, hallucinating, and shaking himself back to reality. He was wilting fast.

Joe hated stealing some person's car and he vowed to return it once everything had returned to normality. It was stolen nevertheless. He knew that the vehicle's uncommon age and condition made it all too conspicuous and he was unwilling to drive it into the city. The logical course of action was to leave it well hidden.

The rain had now stopped falling, and glimmers of sunlight were breaking through the heavy sky. The road, although sealed and well surfaced, was lonely and devoid of traffic. With so much rain, the surrounding pastures were richly green and fertile. There were very few houses, just soggy fields divided by areas of dense forest and rocky outcrops.

Joe came upon an old community hall put together with splintered wooden cladding. The hall must have been at least seventy or eighty years old and was now abandoned. The windows and doors were boarded and the front decking had rotted, causing it to collapse. A little further down the road, Joe could see a country pay phone at the T-intersection, and he pulled the small sedan off onto the adjacent siding.

Leaving the engine running, he took care as he stepped out because the gravel was loose and unsteady. Joe could see that the road fell away to become a steep cliff face and he looked down at the rocky stream below as he walked back to the phone booth.

Joe's plan was to arrange Scooty's helicopter for a speedy retrieval to Egan Center. With this in mind, he made a collect call to Scooty's cell phone.

'Hello Scooty. It's Joe. Are you up and about?'

'Yes Joe. Where are you man? Sharyn says you're out walking?'

'Listen to me Scooty. There's more to it than that. I need you to dust me off with the Squirrel. Can you do it?'

'Well, she's fueled up and serviceable. The lines have to be drained and checked over before she can fly buddy, maybe ten minutes. What can I do?'

Joe glanced at his watch and confirmed the time at 8.45 a.m.

'Scooty, you're a godsend. I need you to come and pick me up from the country. I'm not sure of my position and I don't have a road map with me. There's an old disused community hall, and I'm calling from a public pay phone just near it. I can give you the location information from the notice board in front of me. Are you all right to copy it down?'

'Okay Joe. Read it out. I'll take it from there.'

'That's good. I'm guessing that I'm about eighty miles northwest, but I'm not sure. Are you able to come in this weather? There are a few showers about.'

'On my way. Stay put. A few showers won't stop me, but I need a clearing to put down.'

'There's open space here Scooty. Plenty of paddocks. I'll be waiting for you at the call box.'

Joe gave Scooty the location details, ended the call, and returned to the vehicle. He had to pinch himself to stay alert, because he still had to hide the car. Joe would return it later, but he didn't want the police crawling over it just yet. Let things blow over and settle down first. For now, give the cops as little evidence as possible.

Joe shoved the car into gear and moved the Toyota across the road, into a small clearing within a dense cluster of bushes. He untwisted the ignition wires to stop the engine and walked back to check that the car was well concealed from the road. The vehicle was well hidden from every angle, and he was satisfied it would remain undiscovered.

With his clothes caked with dry mud and his exhausted troubled mind finally at rest, he slumped back against the phone booth to wait for the last segment of his journey home. Not the intermittent images of Blue Featherman's eyes of death, or the painful memories of Casey's blemished and bitten body, could deny Joe the deep sleep which now devoured him.

CHAPTER 25

It's not more than forty minutes since I fell asleep. I'm stirred and then shaken to sensibility by the familiar vibrations of Scooty's helicopter making an approach. Just as always, it's a welcoming sight for my aching eyes, and I inwardly smile as I watch the giant bird gently cushion down onto the moist soft earth.

My tiredness has only been tantalized by a brief sleep that has really done me more harm than good. I now feel worse than before, bleary-eyed and numb. It's a battle to keep my eyelids from closing. Although I'm feeling burnt-out, the sense of urgency created by Scooty's machine forces me to shake my weary bones into action.

Having done it many times before, I know exactly what to do next. I quickly scramble to my feet and stumble across to the old wire fence, which edges the grassy field beyond. The fence is heavily barbed and I rip my pants down one leg as I manage with difficulty to climb through to the other side. Scooty is sitting in the pilot's position and waving me forward to the front of the helicopter. Although I can't hear a word he's saying, it's not difficult to read his lips.

'Come on Joey. Come on. Let's go! Come on Joe!'

In a half-stooped position, I drag my tired legs around to the front of the helicopter and awkwardly press on through the soggy field to the passenger side door. As soon as I'm inside and safely strapped in, Scooty is already winding on the power. The huge blades pick up speed and muddy spray radiates outwards in a circumference, forming a flat circle on the wet pasture below. The Twin Squirrel rips upwards into the air with astonishing momentum. For me, it's a freedom flight, a wonderful transition from the several hours of anguish, discomfort, and violence, back to the existence I'm better accustomed to.

I look across at Scooty's face as the helicopter picks up speed and skims across the rural scenery below. It's not difficult to see that he's excited. His familiar grin is spread across his face, and he's motioning for me to put on my headset. I grapple with it and manage to get it settled around my ears. Scooty eagerly switches on the intercom.

'Joey, my man! What in God's name have you been up to? You look like you've been through a military obstacle course. Are you all right?'

I manage to smirk back at Scooty and give him the kind of reply he usually enjoys.

'I'm fine. My early morning stroll was a little bit further than I had planned. Don't ask me how or why. It just happened to turn out that way. I just thought I needed the additional exercise. There's something I need now. If I don't eat something in the next five minutes, I'll be a corpse before we get to Egan Center.'

Scooty's left hand moves out and grabs my elbow, reminding me of the delicate state of my injured right hand. I can see by the expression on his face that he's bursting to tell me something.

'Now Joey, do you want the good news first, or the bad news?'

'Come on Scooty! Give me the bad news, but you better follow it up with something I want to hear.'

I can see the distant outline of the Manhattan sky-scrapers as I brace myself to hear what he has to say.

'Well, the bad news Joey, is that I don't have any-thing here in this helicopter for you to eat.' He then whoops with joy. 'But, the good news buddy is that, just before picking you up, I had a call from Sharyn. The cops have found Casey and she's safe.'

I close my eyes, sigh with relief, and enjoy the flood of emotion that rushes through my body. It's the best pos-sible result to emerge from a harrowing experience. My daughter is saved, the villain is dead, and the diamond ransom is securely in my pocket.

From the air, the outskirts of the city are stunningly beautiful, and the majestic shapes of the wonderful New York City skyline become more dominant in the distance. Although I can barely keep my eyes open, I settle back to enjoy the scenery. There'll be time enough for sleeping when my daughter's back at home and my mind is finally liberated from this tribulation.

Scooty forces me to talk most of the way back, just to keep me awake. Considering my fragile physical state and all that I've been through, I would have preferred a gentle, stable and comfortable approach to the Egan Cen-ter helipad. Not so! Good old Scooty just can't help him-self. We come tearing down over the East River Heliport, around the top of several buildings in a curved spiral, and then steeply around at a forty-five degree angle of bank to a short final approach. I just hang on, grin, and bare it, knowing that Scooty just has to do what he has to do. The exhilarating approach terminates as usual in an astonish-ingly timely flare, followed by a gentle touchdown.

I get out feeling bone-tired, stretch my arms and legs, and wait for Scooty. His tall frame comes ambling around the front of the helicopter, and his face is beaming from the exhilaration of his approach. I'm happy as well, but it's due to the sight of Sharyn. She's there to meet us on the steps and she's smiling sheepishly. Her eyes widen to twice their normal size when she looks at my dirty and disheveled appearance.

'My God Joe, where have you been? What's happened to you?'

'I've been across in Central Park playing with the ducks,' I joke.

Sharyn looks absolutely ravishing. My fatigued body is instantly revitalized as her natural, very attractive beauty comes shining through. I'm so pleased to see her, I simply want to grab her and smother her with love and affection. The only thing that stops me is the fact that I'm muddy, slimy, unshaven and filthy, with a mesh of cobwebs, squashed insects, and blood, not to mention that I'm extremely smelly. I manage a full smile as I make a wide circle to move around her to enter the penthouse.

'Don't you look the beautiful lady this morning Sharyn? Far too beautiful for this monster from the swamp,' I joke and roll my eyes.

She gives me a loving smile and steps willingly to the side, with her eyes casting down on my ripped pants.

'Has Scooty given you the good news Joe? Casey's all right. They've found her and she's going to be fine.'

'I know. It's wonderful. Just wonderful. Where is she now?'

'She's at the Lennox Hill Hospital children's ward. They tell me that she's doing well. She's healthy apart from some minor scratches and bruises. We can go to see her anytime.' Sharyn is ecstatic. She can't get her words out quickly enough, and I'm still longing to kiss her.

'That's marvelous! Thank God. Just wonderful!'

'Yes Joe. It is a wonderful outcome.' Sharyn's eyes are now getting teary.

I look down at my pants. 'All right you two. I'm going to clean up my act. But there's one other important thing I have to attend to, and I need your help.'

Both Sharyn and Scooty answer in unison, eager to help me. 'What's that Joe?'

I put on my best swamp monster impersonation. 'Food! Food! I must have food!'

With that I move through into the penthouse towards my master bedroom, and Sharyn and Scooty walk through to the kitchen to fix me something to eat.

* * * * *

Before long, I re-emerge, and they're looking at a new man. The little velvet pouch containing the valuable diamonds is stored securely in my penthouse wall-safe, and although I'm incredibly tired and in desperate need of some well overdue sleep, I feel happier now that I'm showered and clean-shaven. The remnants of clothing that I had stepped away from are now beyond saving. They go quickly into a plastic bag and straight down into the garbage. Their destination along with any evidence of dried blood is now certainly to be the incinerator.

As I gobble down the enormous sandwich that Sharyn has hastily prepared for me, I know the sleep I am longing for will simply have to wait. I have two important things on my mind. The first item and most important thing, is to get to the hospital to see my little girl. And secondly, along the way, to see if there's a black Chevy Silverado parked in the basement guest parking area.

The three of us decide to go to the hospital together. Sharyn has already prepared Casey's room and she's holding a small carry bag of fresh clothes as we all descend to ground level. I leave them in the lobby and go it alone to the basement car park. A quick check of the vacant guest parking position and a brisk walk around the remaining floor area, tell me that it was only wishful thinking on my part. I stop worrying about it and decide to check again each night. Now it's time to see my Casey.

* * * * *

I'm bursting at the seams with anticipation as Sharyn, Scooty, and I alight from the taxi outside the Lennox Hill Hospital on East 77th and Park Avenue. The entire journey has been a barrage of inquisitive questioning by Sharyn and Scooty. I'm not surprised that they want to know more about my early morning walk. In a way, I guess they're entitled to get the full story. But, for their own sakes, I decide to keep it to myself. What had happened in that old forest cabin only a few hours ago would be difficult for them to come to terms with. It's something that I will have to live with alone, and never forget for the rest of my life. Was it an act of personal vengeance, self-defense, or my way of balancing the business equation? I don't know which. What I do know, is that the conclusion is favorable and the only result that I could possibly accept.

The elevator doors slide open on the sixth floor and the three of us stride down the corridor towards the children's ward. The clinical starkness of the hospital environment quickly changes to a happier feel when we enter the children's section.

The décor is colorful, bright and happy and I'm delighted to see the rows of children's storybooks and the shelves of toys. The walls are covered with the many characters of children's nursery rhymes and fables. The lights are colored like a rainbow and the ceiling is painted as a cloudy sky. I quicken my step and I just can't wait to see my little princess.

Unfortunately, as we turn the last corner, the first person I'm to lay eyes on is Jimmy the sidekick. He's standing in the corridor with notebook out and pen in hand, talking to an elderly doctor. When he sees me, he excuses himself from the conversation and turns to face me.

'Ah! Egan. Just the man I want to see. We have a few things to discuss and some matters to resolve.'

With Sharyn standing on one side of me and Scooty on the other, I come to a standstill in front of him. My body is too weary and sore to provide the required physical strength for what I have in mind, and I can do nothing but stare into his eyes.

'Whatever you want to ask me will just have to wait until later. Now, where's my daughter?'

When the doctor hears these words, he approaches me to speak and eagerly breaks into the conversation.

'You must be Mr. Egan. I'm Doctor Bartholomew Howard. Your daughter has been asking for you.'

'Thank you doctor. Is she all right?'

'She's fine Mr. Egan.' He smiles and nods. 'She has some superficial abrasions which we've treated, and I'm confident she'll make a full recovery.'

'Thank you doctor. She's had a terrible experience.'

He continues. 'Although she's reluctant to talk of what happened, she's mentally alert. She's suffering some mild shock, and I'd suggest the best remedy is the love and attention that only a parent can give. Your daughter's a very strong little girl Mr. Egan.'

'I know she is doctor. She's a very special little girl. Can I please see her now?'

When I walk into her room with a broad grin on my face, my beautiful Casey looks like an angel. She's sitting up in bed and her face lights up with joy. She struggles with the linen to get free, and comes forward on her hands and knees across the bed to meet me. I run to catch her and sweep her up into my arms. The minute I feel her weight, the pain in my left shoulder and right hand is too much to endure. I shriek with the agony of it. Casey falls from my arms back onto the bed with a bewildered expression on her face.

'Oh, daddy! Daddy? What's wrong daddy?'

As I roll to the side, I notice that Jimmy the sidekick is standing in the doorway wondering what's going on. He screws his brow in puzzlement and suspicion. I resent him being here and decide to ignore him completely. I return my attention to Casey.

'It's all right my darling. I'm just so pleased to see you again. I've been so very worried about you.'

Casey comes back to me and smothers me with kisses and hugs. The physical pain I feel in my limbs is quelled by the feeling of love and joy in my heart. Casey looks at me with pleading eyes.

'When's mommy coming? Where's my mom?'

I look up to see Sharyn and she's holding back the tears. Scooty stands beside her and he's also beginning to wilt, with moisture welling in his eyes. I look back at the doctor for support, and he gives me a compassionate stare and shakes his head as he speaks.

'She's been asking for her mother Mr. Egan. All she would say was that she had a bad dream, a terrible nightmare. And now it's all ended and she's glad to be awake.'

I turn back to Casey and I'm visibly sobbing. Ignoring the pain, I wrap my arms around her and pull her in tight.

I nuzzle my face into her golden locks and move my mouth close to her ear.

'It wasn't a dream my little darling. It wasn't a nightmare my princess. You have to be strong now. Your mommy's gone to heaven.'

'Oh no daddy. It was a dream daddy. Please no daddy. It was a dream. It was all a dream!'

'No darling it's true. Your mommy's up in heaven. She's now an angel, Casey. She's an angel.'

'No! My mommy! I want my mommy. Please! No!'

Casey buries herself into my injured left shoulder and I welcome the pain. She cries uncontrollably and I hold her tight. I begin to rock her gently from side to side, as I did when she was a little baby.

'Your mommy's gone to heaven my darling. I'll look after you. I'll always look after you. You're my little girl, my princess.'

I'm crying through my words and my heart is pounding. Casey cries and cries. Her little heart is beating forcibly and her breathing is heavy. We spend several minutes locked together swaying from side to side. After a while, I look back up at the doctor. Jimmy has moved to the far corner and he stands watching with a blank look on his face. He's decided to stay quiet for the moment and I'm glad for it.

I lower Casey back onto the pillow and I hold her hand and stroke her hair. Sharyn walks across and sits beside me with tears streaking her make-up.

The doctor steps closer to me and places one hand on my good shoulder. 'Are you all right Mr. Egan?' he asks.

'Yes I'm all right. I just need some sleep. When do you think my daughter can come home?'

'Home is the best place for her Mr. Egan. Her physical condition is fine. Her problems are emotional. She needs your own loving support now. I'm happy to release her into your care.'

Jimmy decides to interject in his inimitable way to spoil things for me as usual.

'Yes Egan. And, we'll be asking her some questions as well. We want to hear her story about what she knows, what happened out there in that cabin.'

I motion for him to follow me into the corridor outside and then swing around to face him.

'You'll not harass my daughter like you try to harass me. You'll stay away from her. Do you hear me? You just leave my daughter alone. She's been through enough without having to answer your cruel questions.'

Jimmy comes back at me glaring wildly. 'Now you listen here Egan,....'

I cut him off in mid sentence. 'No. You listen to me! She's my daughter and she's in my charge. I'll tell you if and when you can talk to her, and it won't be before. She's lost her mother and she's been through hell. Have some consideration for her innocence and age. Let her recover.'

'I hear you Egan. But, it's not only your daughter who we want to interrogate. We'll be in contact tomorrow, so don't you go anywhere.'

I realize that this whole sordid affair will never come to an end until the police have put their last jigsaw piece into position. Although my own personal objectives have been met, the police investigation still has some way to go. They still have to account for Blue Featherman's death. For the moment, they'll just have to wait for their answers. I don't have the time or patience to deal with Jimmy now. I turn and re-enter Casey's room, leaving him standing there. Scooty already has Casey in his arms and he's doing a good job of comforting her. Sharyn's taken some fresh clothes from the small carry bag and Casey's now dressed and prepared for her departure from hospital. I beckon for Sharyn and Scooty to follow me and we all pass Jimmy and head for the elevator. This evening is a time for rest and recovery, peace and relaxation. In fact, Casey is soon asleep on Sharyn's lap as we make the drive back to the familiar surroundings of my Egan Center penthouse.

* * * * *

I am content that the people I love are now safe and secure, but I nevertheless have another disturbed night of nightmares, contending with the demons of my mind's dreams.

Although I had a restless sleep of tossing and turning, it's a long sleep. I feel reasonably refreshed and well rested when I awake. I spend minimum time getting myself ready for the day. By mid morning we've all had breakfast and we're able to relax, surrounded by the comforts of home.

I'm amazed at how rapidly children can rebound from adversity and adapt so readily to their changing circumstances. Casey seems to have made an extraordinary recovery in such a short time, and to my delight, she already seems to be attaching closer to Sharyn.

'Joey, there's been no mention of the ransom. Do you think the police will recover it?' asks Scooty as he sprawls across the leather sofa beneath the council of buffalo heads.

I've been in a daze watching Sharyn and Casey playing games in the far corner of the living area, and Scooty's question stirs me from my trance. I take a few seconds to think about my answer, and then respond.

'There won't be any mention of the ransom Scooty.' I hesitate. 'Remember that the police don't even know of its existence. They know nothing of the letters and phone calls, and I've already stated that I was here at home on the night the ransom was delivered. That's the way it is, and that's the way it must be. All we know is that Audrey was killed and Casey was abducted.'

Scooty concentrates on the significance of what I have said.

'Sure Joe, I understand. But, why? Why haven't you told the cops more about it, now that it's over with?'

'Because it's too late now. The cops would have gone in with guns drawn and blazing. Casey would be dead for sure. It was the only way to get her back.'

'Where's the ransom now Joe? Where's all that loot?'

'There's a mastermind behind all of this. He used Feathers to carry out his dirty work and he's staying clear himself. He's the driver of that black Chevy truck and he's the one who received the diamonds. The case won't be closed until this mastermind is apprehended.'

Scooty digs deep for some answers and I let him struggle with it. He doesn't know the whole story about Blue Featherman's death. In fact, nobody does. That will stay between Feathers and me forever.

'I see Joe. But, you know what? There's one saving grace for you in all of this.' Scooty looks pleased that he has some comfortable words of wisdom for me.

'And, what might that be Scooty?' I ask him inquisitively.

'Well, with Casey now safely at home, and this so called mastermind happily in possession of his diamonds, he should leave you alone now. He has no reason to bother you any further.'

The irony stings. When I hear what Scooty has to say, it sends a shiver down my spine. I think about the diamonds in my safe. It occurs to me that the person in question would now be extremely bitter and vindictive when he discovers that his velvet pouch contains nothing more than worthless fakes.

'Yes. That's right. The criminal behind all of this should now be able to live it up in style. He won't bother us now,' I lie through my teeth.

I snatch my cell phone up quickly when it rings, and it's Andrew on the line.

'Mr. Egan. Andrew. I've detective Frank Berne here again to speak with you in the office. What shall I tell him?'

'Thanks Andrew. Please tell him to wait. I'll be down shortly and I'll be happy to talk with him.'

* * * * *

While descending in my personal elevator connecting my penthouse to my Egan Enterprises office below, my mind is a mash of thoughts and emotions. Although I've done everything in my power to cover my tracks, I realize that there's any number of things that could have gone astray along the way. In the last few days, four human beings have died, and three were by my own hands. The police will have to account for each death.

I don't know what to expect from my talks with Frank Berne. I can only hope that the police apprehend or kill the other mastermind person involved as quickly as possible. If he is killed, then Featherman's death and the train shooting fiasco could be attributed to him and Audrey's death attributed to Feathers. Yes. The police would be happy because the pieces fit. This whole sordid affair could be brought to a conclusion.

* * * * *

I turn my attention from my favorite weightless yellow and orange rainbow fish, and swing the leather chair around to face Frank Berne as he strides into my office. Once again, I'm spared the pain and discomfort of ceremonial handshakes because without being invited, he plants himself into the chair in front of me and smirks.

'Well Mr. Egan, how is your daughter? Is she recovering from her abduction ordeal?'

'Yes, she's doing fine detective. It never ceases to amaze me how resilient children can be. It just seems that she's bounced back and blocked it all from her mind.' I smile at him, and it occurs to me that I should ask questions about Casey's rescue, as though I know nothing about the circumstances.

'Tell me Lieutenant, how did you find Casey? How did you know where she was?'

'We were tipped off by an anonymous phone call. The lab boys are working on the voice analysis and we think it may lead to something. Let's wait and see.'

'Where had they taken her?' I ask innocently.

'They had her locked in an old timber shack out at Tuxedo Junction. It's an out of town, nothing, nowhere kind of place.'

'Well, I want to thank you for bringing her back safe and sound.'

He stands up and begins to pace. 'It's good that she's no longer suffering. However, we still need to talk to her and find out what she saw out there. It's better for her as well if she talks it out. Emotional scars can surface later on. You know, she has to face up to it and come to terms with the fact that not everything or everyone is necessarily good.'

'I'm sure that she's now well aware of that Lieutenant.'

'So, when do you think I can question her?' he says as he turns to face me.

I stand up and circle to his side of the desk. 'You can't question her at all. I've already spoken to her for you. She's told me what she remembers. I've spent half the night with her. She now wants to put it behind her and get on with her life.'

He shrugs his broad shoulders and then looks at me suspiciously.

'And, what exactly did she remember?'

'She remembers being at the Icelandic Hotel and going with her mother into the elevator. She remembers the laundry man hitting her mother and then the smell of a chemical rag around her face. And she remembers being hunted and chased around that cabin by the same disgusting laundry man. I'd say she's talking about your Blue Featherman.'

Berne doesn't look convinced, and his eyes are shifting from side to side.

'It's hardly appropriate that you question her for us Egan. You yourself are still a prime suspect in this case,'

'Oh, for heavens sake Berne, can't you see further than that? There's a criminal who's plotted all of this, and that criminal is out there somewhere, probably planning his next abduction. Why don't you see past trying to pin it all on me, and go and catch him?' Berne looks interested with my performance as I put on my best play-acting. 'Go and find this Blue Featherman character and he can lead you to the mastermind.' I frown and shake my head.

He rubs his chin and answers wryly. 'Oh, haven't you been told? Featherman's dead!'

'Dead? Feathers is dead?' I look surprised.

'Yes. I'm telling you he's dead. He was in the cabin with your Casey. We believe he would have killed her. We also think he's responsible for the murder of your ex-wife and the abduction of your daughter. He won't be leading us to any mastermind. He won't be leading us anywhere.'

'How did he die? Did the police kill him? Did you kill him?' I ask with apparent interest.

'No. We found him in the other room of the cabin with his throat cut. Now, we want to find the person who did the slicing, probably his own accomplice. The law wants him for killing Feathers. I want him to pin a fuck-ing medal on his chest!'

'Now you watch it Berne! You're talking about the same calculating person who plotted a murder and abduction. The mastermind. He's no better than Featherman.'

'Is that right Egan? There are many people who would have me believe that I'm talking about the same person I'm sitting and talking to right now.'

I instantly fire up. 'When are you people going to get over it? She's my own daughter. I had nothing to do with it!' I begin to walk back to my chair.

Berne seems to settle. 'Nevertheless, I need you to substantiate your whereabouts during the night before last.'

'That's easy. Apart from an early morning walk yes-terday morning, I spent the entire time here at home.'

Frank Berne sighs dramatically and locks his eyes into mine. 'I want you to know Egan that this case won't be closed until we find the last person responsible. He's on our hot-list. This is not ended until we find him. He's clever, cunning and secretive. And from what we witnessed of Blue Featherman's bloody execution in that cabin, he's a dangerous cold-blooded killer.'

CHAPTER 26

Wyatt Prendergast thought that Frank Sinatra was the second best singer of all time, himself being the best. Wyatt especially enjoyed playing Sinatra songs when he was driving alone in his car, because with no one else to hear him, he could sing along with Frank at the top of his voice. He had listened to those songs so often now that he knew most of the lyrics by heart.

Today was one of those Frank Sinatra days, and Wyatt was driving along and singing with all the passion and volume his lungs could provide. He was actually creating his own Frank duet right there in the privacy of his vehicle, and he was elated.

Although Wyatt couldn't afford the very latest model Mercedes, he still considered his four year old Benz to be preferable to a new BMW. His prestigious image required the Mercedes Benz insignia. He remembered what a friend had once told him. BMW meant you were on the way to the top and Mercedes meant you were already there. If his legal practice was to continue attracting high profile clients, Wyatt needed those clients to think he was already highly successful. His clients must never learn of his failed investment in 'Silicon Resolutions' and his burdening debts. They were not to know that his Benz was leased and not owned. For the sake of his practice, Wyatt Prendergast was to exude the image of the wealthy flourishing Upper East Side Lawyer.

Today, it was important for Wyatt to create a good impression. He stopped bellowing the words of 'New York, New York' as his royal blue Mercedes Benz sedan entered through the gigantic baroque iron gates of Brooklyn's Green-Wood Cemetery. He checked his face in the mirror and adopted a more suitable somber appearance. Although funerals were not his choice of daily events, they were an occasional necessity where legal implications usually implied monetary reparation.

Wyatt slowed to a more appropriate speed and eased the Mercedes around the broad circular drive surrounded by century old elm trees and giant spreading oaks. The park-like cemetery was indeed beautiful on this warm spring day with manicured lawns encompassing glacial ponds where cormorants and egrets were resting. A gentle breeze carried with it the fragrances of red roses, azaleas and gardenias from the many garden beds, and sunlight glistened in tiny flashes from the thousand headstones of marble and granite.

Up and down the rows of monuments, several family groups with bouquets of flowers were visiting loved ones. It all had a sobering effect on Wyatt's sing-along mood, and he tried to refocus his mind to the funeral he was to attend. He thought momentarily of his own mortality and how life was passing him by much too quickly. He began to calculate how long it would take him to settle his liabilities, and he compared the figure to his own life expectancy. The result wasn't good. If his income stream remained constant and he stayed on schedule, he reckoned he would be debt free by his ninety-seventh birthday. He had needed a new recipe to kick-start a new source of funds and this funeral was that perfect recipe.

Wyatt pondered on what there was to gain from the occasion and the possible financial rewards that may ensue. Since the completion of Egan Center and the pla-teauing of Joe Egan's business activities, Wyatt's legal business had diminished considerably. It now followed that Joe would be requiring his legal services in order to settle Audrey Egan's vast estate and establish the custo-dian authority for Casey Egan. He was aware that this contract would be lucrative, and therefore enable him to further repay some of his long-standing debts. Wyatt pulled to a stop in the visitors parking area of the in-ground chapel, adjusted his tie and cufflinks, and stepped out into the sunshine.

There was already a small assemblage of guests in the entrance vestibule, and Wyatt decided to stand to the side and out of the way. For him, it was not an occasion for chatting and socializing. His main objective was to be noticed by Joe Egan. He simply wanted to enhance his business connection by having his presence acknowl-edged at the funeral, and he could then escape the cere-monials.

It wasn't a large gathering, and Wyatt watched with slight interest only, as close friends and relatives mingled together exchanging condolences. He could see Joe Egan amongst them, but he couldn't seem to capture his atten-tion. Soon, everyone slowly migrated inside, and Wyatt walked over to sign the register of attendance. He ran his finger down the list of names and recognized maybe half of them. Wyatt wrote his own name below that of Mr. Jacob and Mrs. Sophia Zinkow, before entering the chapel himself to take a seat at the rear.

The chapel interior was pale yellow-brown stucco with sandalwood beams overhead and stained glass win-dows on each side. Wyatt lifted his gaze to the wooden station of the cross depicting a bronze Jesus wearing the crucifixion crown of thorns. Below it and covered with beautiful floral pieces, was the graceful copper casket of Audrey Egan. The organ accompaniment of sacred arias gently faded for the words of remembrance to commence. Then, through the sobbing and moaning, Wyatt could distinguish Casey Egan's steady weeping sounding from the front row.

Wyatt thought that the service was so predictable; he could have done better himself. The usual 'We are gathered here today to…' and 'We as children of God find it difficult to understand how…' was followed by 'Grief is a natural and necessary journey that follows the death of a loved one…' etc. etc. He listened reluctantly, enduring the monotony, and staring down at the mirror reflections from the toecaps of his expensive black shoes.

Wyatt was startled when two more people joined the congregation and sat down along side him in the same row. He glanced to the side, and was immediately surprised at the inappropriate crumpled tweed jacket and well-worn shoes, but he was more intrigued at the reflection he now glimpsed from his own mirror toe shoes. Was it? Yes it was! The man sitting next to him was wearing a gun on his belt.

The pallbearers took their positions, and the procession exited the chapel in turn. Wyatt followed them for the internment knowing that his purpose would not be complete until he had attracted Joe Egan's attention.

The burial location that had been chosen was in the most beautiful and exclusive section of the cemetery. Shadowed by a resplendent spreading sycamore tree, and just far enough away from a tranquil pond of paisley lilies, the gravesite had been prepared with a backdrop arrangement of sensuous flowers. Now that the mourners were gathered around in a semicircle for the final graveside service, Wyatt could better recognize those in attendance.

Standing at the forefront was little Casey Egan with her head slightly bowed, and holding tightly to a small bunch of yellow daisies. Her eyes were glazed with disbelief, and her complexion was as white as a sheet.

Joe Egan stood behind Casey with his head lowered and his hands lightly on his daughter's shoulders. His tears were shared both for Audrey, and for the bereavement experienced by his brave little princess.

Wyatt also recognized Joe's prominent business employee, Andrew Barton whose stern unsullied countenance matched his impeccable linen suit and crimson bow tie. This man always resembled a steel machine rather than a mortal being, and Wyatt wondered if there was ever a chink to be found in his armor.

Positioned between Andrew and Joe, was the engaging Sharyn Cooper. Her face expressed a multitude of emotions. Although she had known Audrey well enough, she was never as emotionally close to the woman as she felt at this very moment. It was as though Audrey had left a breath of life behind, and it had now become an integral part of Sharyn's soul. Sharyn loved Casey and Joe just as Audrey had done, and she now felt an immense responsibility to follow decently in the woman's footsteps. She was resolved to love and nurture Casey in her mother's honor, and ideally become the transcendent companion for Joe.

Even though there were many unfamiliar faces present, Wyatt could distinguish the prominent Manhattan surgeon Troy Darby, and he speculated as to whether he was the doctor that attended to Audrey's terrible injuries on that fateful day.

Audrey's Filipino housemaid Mary-Lou was leaning on the arm of the staunch pudgy chauffeur named Benedict, and together they appeared as visiting sullen-faced agents of death, as they swayed from side to side in their black garments.

Then there was the lanky graying helicopter pilot and owner of the successful Vision Helicopters Company, Scooty Menzies. Wyatt had met him before on several occasions, and although he was solemn and unsmiling at the moment, this guy was usually jovial. He obviously enjoyed his lifestyle to the fullest, was personality plus, and was always consistently cheerful against all odds. Wyatt was somehow envious of Scooty's happy existence.

Standing alone was Leslie, the utterly boring Egan Center doorman. He was almost without a personality at all, and Wyatt thought he looked strangely similar to the chief executive officer of the failed company 'Silicon Resolutions' in which Wyatt himself had forfeited all and more of his money.

Wyatt studied each person in turn. If ever a name was to fit an appearance, it was now. Surely the large bearded and heavily Jewish individual and his petite wife were the Mr. and Mrs. Jacob Zinkow that Wyatt had noticed on the register of attendance. Jacob Zinkow's abundant frame within a flowing cape seemed to dominate the scene completely. He looked more religious in his black garb than the minister delivering the service.

There, standing in the background under the sycamore tree, Wyatt could also now see the gun carrying person in the crumpled tweed jacket. It was apparent that he was more than likely a cop, with close-cropped hair and a typical cop's grim pout on his face. He was standing with another likely cop who was dressed in black with a slick ponytail hairdo.

Together, the cops seemed more interested in the people in attendance than the service itself. They were studying each guest in turn, and muttering to each other. Wyatt thought that it wasn't unusual. It was expected for the police to be attending this particular burial ceremony. After all, the woman was murdered, and it's well known that quite often, the killer will be present at his own victim's funeral.

When he noticed the older cop looking directly at him, Wyatt felt particularly uneasy, and he quickly looked away. He shifted his eyes to catch the stare of Joseph Egan and his task was completed. When Joe nodded in acknowledgement, Wyatt knew that he would now be able to go home. He would soon be in his car once again singing 'My Way' along with Frank Sinatra. Wyatt wasn't made to wait much longer because the sad occasion was soon to come to an end.

Beneath the overhanging guardian arms of the prominent sycamore tree, and within a framed setting of perfumed red roses, Audrey Egan's body was finally and reverently laid to rest.

CHAPTER 27

'Joey! Dry those tears. Things aren't as bad as you think. I know it seems like such a difficult task. I know you think you can't cope with it because the mountain before you is so very steep and high. But Joey, I want you to try something for me. Instead of seeing the whole problem in its enormity, I want you to break it down into little pieces. Try to negotiate your task in bits and pieces. One step at a time, Joey. Work it into tiny stages, and concentrate on jumping only one little hurdle. Once you've done that, put it behind you and only think of the next little hurdle. One obstacle at a time. Don't try to jump them all at once.'

My father's words of wisdom are playing once again in my mind as I'm now sitting in the waiting area of Zinkow Diamond Merchants on 47th Street. I've experienced for the second time, the process of iron bar doors and security cameras to gain entry, and Jacob's secretary Desdemona, tells me that I only need to wait for a few minutes. She's sitting at her workstation wearing a headset and typing furiously into a word processor. Every now and then she pauses, looks across, and smiles. I don't mind being forced to wait for a while. It's actually rather therapeutic, having nothing to do but to sit and think, think about the incredible gut wrenching moments of the last few days.

It seems that this whole dreadful saga of events has been a series of frustrating hurdles. I feel as though I'm now getting close to the finish line, and today's little hurdle is one of the last. I'll return these diamonds to Jacob, get that little blue Toyota back to its rightful owner, and keep a lookout for that black Silverado and its scoundrel owner.

It's the day following Audrey's funeral and it's a day not to be wasted. It's one more step in tidying up the loose ends and completing the dealings of a lifetime, Casey's lifetime! Although I've achieved greatness in rescuing my daughter, and ending the life of the murdering kidnapper, I'm also well aware that there's been some divine guidance through it all by Audrey's lingering spirit. I have the sensation that she's even here with me now, standing by me and giving me her blessing for my new and wonderful feelings towards Sharyn.

It's not co-incidental that amongst these beautiful precious diamonds there is one special pink diamond to light up the eyes of the woman I love. It's already quite apparent to me that this diamond has one destiny, one rightful home. It belongs on the slender finger of Sharyn Cooper. While I'm sitting here now, the idea is prefixed in my mind and the diamond's fate is preordained. This is one diamond I won't be returning for a refund.

It's only been a few days since I was last in this office, and I'm once again intrigued by the building's Victorian classical beauty. It's as though nothing has changed in this office for a hundred years and the atmosphere is stately, warm and ample. On the subject of stately, warm and ample, Jacob's office door swings open and the familiar loud boisterous voice bellows forth. Jacob is blackness. His hair is black, his yarmulka is black, his beard is black, and he's always dressed in black. Shining through the blackness is his face, so bright and cheerful with a broad smile.

340

'Joseph! Joseph! It's good to see you so soon. And, what a beautiful funeral you provided for dear Audrey, such a proper and graceful way to memorialize a remarkable lady.'

Jacob's large hands are gripping my upper arms and he's looking down at my face. I wince through my smile and try to respond.

'Hello Jacob....How are...'

He interrupts me. 'Joseph, it's a new time for you. It's so wonderful that Casey is back with you, and she's unharmed? Is she all right?' Jacob releases his grip at last.

'Casey is doing fine Jacob. She's at......'

'That's wonderful. Yes. Wonderful! And, where is Miss Sharyn Cooper today Joseph? She is not with you? Why am I surprised that she is not with you?'

'Well Jacob, Sharyn's getting to know Casey. I'm so glad that they get on so well together.'

'I see! I see! You have no need to explain. I suspect that it is meant to be. However, it is your business. Come in my cousin. Come in. Come into my office and we'll talk. Desdemona will bring us some coffee, and we'll talk. Come in. Come in.'

He walks before me and leads me through to his office. As I enter, I re-familiarize myself with the interior. The gray roosting pigeons still mingle outside the heavily barred window, and the poster cat-woman continues to prowl the Parisian rooftops as before.

'Come Joseph. Be seated and feel comfortable. Are you all right my friend?'

I sit down on the fabric wing-backed seat in front of his aged oak desk while Jacob circles to the other side and crashes down into his red leather chair.

'Yes. I'm all right. I won't say things are perfect, but they seem to be improving day by day.'

Jacob relaxes back into his chair, looks at me squarely, and his voice becomes even deeper. 'Now Joseph, I don't want to pry into your personal affairs, but my friend, what has been going on in your life? First the terrible murder of dear Audrey, and then the abduction of your daughter. Tell me. Is it now at an end? Can you rest from your troubles and trauma? Can you leave it behind and go on with your life?'

I glare into his stern expression. 'Well, things are slowly returning to normality. There are a few matters to resolve, but piece by piece I am completing the puzzle. Yes. When it is complete, I'm looking forward to a holiday and a new start with Casey.'

'Tell me, have the police found the people responsible for your difficulties?' His voice lowers another octave as he asks.

'The person who murdered Audrey and abducted Casey is now dead,' I murmur grimly. 'He was a known criminal and he is now no longer a threat to us. Unfortunately, he wasn't the only person involved. There was a kingpin or mastermind who controlled these happenings, and he is still at large.'

'I see. Mmm. Do you have any idea as to the identity of this person? Are the police hopeful that they will soon apprehend him before he can cause you more harm?'

I pause momentarily and answer solemnly. 'No. No. I'm afraid they are getting nowhere at all. They're becoming more and more frustrated. It's a great worry for me. This person may be vindictive because his plot has failed. The fact that he has gained nothing may make his sickness more malignant.'

'This is an insidious situation for you Joseph. You must be vigilant of security matters. It must be of the highest priority in your life until the villain is behind bars.'

'Thank you for your concern. I'm tightening all of the security around my family. I'll take care Jacob. You can be sure.'

'That's good! Now what is it that I can do for you today my good man? Have you come to purchase another ten million dollars worth of diamonds?' He roars with laughter, changing the tone of the meeting altogether.

I lean back in the seat, reach into my pocket, and withdraw the small velvet pouch of ransom diamonds and place them onto Jacob's desk pad.

'No. Not exactly to purchase diamonds. I'm here today to return diamonds. As you recall, our arrangement was that I could return them if they were not required.'

'It is no problem. No problem. It is no problem at all. All is reversible. Do you remember Joseph? You have the diamonds and I have the cash. I shall have the diamonds and you shall have the cash. This is the diamond business my cousin.'

'That's good. Thank you. You should first of all check them to satisfy yourself.'

'It is not necessary at this stage. You have my trust completely.'

'Better that you check the stones. I cannot guarantee that they're the same. They were out of my possession for a period of time. I would be happier if you would ensure that they're authentic and complete.'

'Oh! I see. I see. This will take several hours to do. It should be done. It shall be done.'

While we are talking, Desdemona overhears our conversation as she enters the office carrying an ornate silver tray. Neatly arranged are two small white cups of thick black coffee and two generous portions of rich dark fruitcake. She places it down on the side of Jacob's desk and stands back smiling pleasantly.

'Ah! Thank you Desdemona. Please don't go away. I may need you to help me with Joseph's account.' He pushes back on his chair and points towards the tray. 'You see Joseph? Sophia has baked her famous fruitcake, and you must have some. I shall tell her that you enjoyed it?' He laughs raucously.

I pick up the coffee after placing a piece of cake on the side of the saucer. 'I shall enjoy it then.'

He looks at Desdemona. 'You can get Isaac to check these stones for me. You understand the situation?'

'I understand. Yes.' Desdemona waits patiently for Jacob to continue.

Jacob spreads a sheet of white paper and spills the glittering contents of the velvet pouch across it. The readily distinguishable pink stone is outstanding as it outshines its companions with amazing color and brilliance.

'Jacob. See the pink diamond. Can you separate it from the others for me? I want to look closer at this one.' My eyes are bulging in my head as I stare at the glistening rock.

'Oh yes, yes my cousin. I remember this stone. How could I not remember such a beautiful stone? Here it is Joseph, so striking. Look how well it shows.' Jacob extracts the pink diamond with a long pair of tweezers and gazes at it through his eyepiece as he speaks.

'Yes my friend. It is exquisite and internally flawless, five carats of nature's finest creation. This one is indeed exceptional.' He turns it from one side to the other peering into each facet in turn.

'I want to keep this diamond Jacob. Is it possible to return all of the diamonds except this one? The value as I recall was one million, one hundred thousand dollars.'

'Yes that is the value. Of course! It is no problem. Should I ask for what purpose you wish to retain this stone? No. It is your own business. Could it have something to do with the beautiful Miss Sharyn Cooper? No. Of course it's not my place to ask such a question. Oh! My friend! I am pleased to provide you with this very unique diamond.'

'Thank you.' I sigh.

Jacob places the pink flawless jewel to one side and now uses the side of his tweezers to slide the remaining diamonds onto a small silver scoop. He pencils some instructions onto a small white envelope, funnels the diamonds inside, and seals it.

'Take this parcel Desdemona. You know what to do. Tell Isaac to give this priority.'

'Yes I shall. I know exactly what to do.' She takes the envelope and smiles at me as she leaves the office.

I eat the last morsel of delicious fruitcake and gulp down the last drop of coffee as Jacob goes on speaking.

'Now Joseph, the pink diamond? Should I guess at the purpose?'

'Yes, you may. I want the diamond set as a ring. It should be a simple solitaire white gold claw setting to maximize the presentation of the stone.'

I can see that Jacob is already becoming excited at the prospect of the completed ring, and his eyes widen with child-like glee. He bares his teeth in a broad smile through the furrows of his beard as he waves his hands in the air.

'Joseph! Joseph! This will be the most incredible possession.' Jacob trumpets loudly. 'Rest assured. I shall personally supervise the manufacture. The diamond shall be set as a tiffany style solitaire and the ring shall be delivered to you. This will be the most beautiful piece. A special ring for a special lady. It shall be so Joseph. It shall be so.'

CHAPTER 28

Joe Egan had watched his whole world tumble upside down and turn inside out in the space of a few days. It was now a time for rest and gratification, a time for simple things and nothing too complicated, a time to sit and think about everything that had happened since the Icelandic Hotel, and then a time to put it to bed and move on with life. Yes, this was now his time for Sharyn and Casey.

Joe stood on the manicured lawns of Mayfair Lodge with one arm around Sharyn, and Casey nestled against his leg. They waved as Scooty lifted the royal blue helicopter from the green velvet grass. It retreated rearwards and upwards and then away into the hazy distance.

For Joe, returning to Mayfair Lodge was like returning to a little bit of heaven on earth. Situated on thirty two manicured acres with extensive gardens, woods, and scenic ponds, Mayfair Lodge provided a myriad of atmospheres designed to delight the senses. It was the perfect sanctuary to escape the hectic stressful lifestyle of New York business life.

After watching the helicopter vanish into the blue, Sharyn, Casey, and Joe turned to walk up to the main lodge.

'Look around you Sharyn. See how the estate is so wonderfully kept. Old Angus does such a great job here, looking after it for me.'

'Yes Joe, it's excellent to be here. It's like a picture postcard with the cream rail fences and rolling green pastures. Surely one man doesn't care for all of this by himself?' Sharyn questioned.

'No he doesn't. Angus is an old man now, but he's an institution here and he manages Mayfair Lodge as if it were his own. He's been here for more than twenty five years and he'll be here till the end. There's old Miss Bee who comes from Flaxbridge to clean the house twice weekly, and a young farm hand named Josh who does the heavy work. Josh, the poor soul, lives in the gatehouse cottage and keeps to himself since his wife died of cancer two years ago.'

'That's sad.' Sharyn sighed. 'Will we meet them all?'

'Well, you'll probably only meet Angus on this occasion. He lives in the main lodge, and I get the feeling he rather looks forward to old Miss Bee's housecleaning visits, if you get my drift? I would say that Angus's two great loves are gardening and old Miss Bee.' Joe laughed freely.

Sharyn joined in and Casey laughed with them without knowing what the joke was.

Crab-apple trees decorated both sides of the cobblestone drive that led from the broad stone wall gates up the slight incline to the house. As they crossed the rock walled bridge over the entrance lagoon, the threesome paused to admire the scenery. Casey giggled as a frightened gathering of wild ducks splashed across the water to take flight. Joe was so pleased to hear her laughter, and the comfortable warmth he felt deep inside made the seventy-minute flight from Manhattan well worthwhile.

The threesome entered through the final hedge line and strolled in the ambience of an enchanting flower garden towards the front entrance of the homestead. There to meet them in the open doorway was the old gentleman who had meticulously cared for the property since long before Joe had assumed ownership.

'Hello Angus.' Joe said warmly. 'It's good to see you again.'

'Ah! It's good to see you too Mr. Egan, and welcome to you Miss Sharyn. And, how's little Casey? Still her daddy's princess I see. You're looking as lovely as ever Casey.'

Angus was looking lively for a gentleman of seventy seven years. It was obvious that life in the isolated confines of Mayfair Lodge precluded Angus from knowing of Casey's recent abduction. As always, Casey warmed immediately to the affection. Joe and Sharyn watched adoringly as the old man and the young girl walked hand in hand back into the garden, in the direction of the pondside gazebo. Joe knew that for Casey to be holding any man's hand after her ordeal, was miraculous and healing. His heart was lifted.

'Oh Joe, it's so lovely here.' Sharyn murmured. 'Such a change to what we're used to.' She hugged Joe's arm as the two of them entered the lodge.

'Yes Sharyn. I'll always keep this place. It nourishes my soul and recharges my batteries. It rarely gets much better than this.'

Joe sensed a real attachment to Mayfair Lodge. The grounds were large enough to ensure security and privacy, yet sufficiently quaint and small to provide a truly romantic setting. They were wonderful gardens and the accommodation was outstanding. The surrounding terrain ranged from mountains and lakes to undulating hills, with a climate that embraced everything from heavy snow to brilliant sunshine. All year round, Joe could enjoy his personal paradise whether it was settling down beside the warm stone fireplace protected from the winter snow out-side, or the gentle exercise of a woodland nature-walk that Joe craved in summertime. He could enjoy it all at Mayfair Lodge.

While staying there, Joe seldom had a need to venture outside the property boundaries. He would however, en-joy an occasional drive in the lush colonial countryside to the nearby old 'Flaxbridge Village' with its fascinating and historical grain mill.

Joe and Sharyn walked quietly hand in hand past the huge stone fireplace in the living room towards the stair-case. The furnishings were cozily tasteful with period an-tiques and the personal warmth of country chattel. May-fair Lodge was actually a restored colonial mansion and Angus had prepared the old building to perfection. Over-all, it was the epitome of country home comfort.

In the master bedroom, Sharyn was impressed with the luxury. There was a wet bar with refrigerator, and in a side alcove, a double Jacuzzi tub. Beamed cathedral ceil-ings complimented the king sized canopied four poster oak bed, end tables, writing desk and armoire. A floor to ceiling stone fireplace was anchored into the corner. On the opposite wall, french doors led out to a private bal-cony offering spectacular panoramic views of the western mountains. It was, indeed, a room designed to welcome and envelop with luxury those who entered.

When Joe and Sharyn had freshened up, they de-scended once again to the living area to find that Angus and Casey had already returned from their walk around the garden. Casey's mood had certainly changed for the better. Her previously sorrowful face was now glowing with renewed vitality, and she was brandishing a full smile as she held tightly to Angus's old wrinkled hand.

'Oh daddy, the garden is so beautiful. The flowers are all in bloom and they smell so good. Daddy, we saw birds and butterflies.'

Joe smiled at Casey and he felt his heart soaring to a new level. He grinned at Angus and the old man nodded in return.

'Yes Mr. Egan.' He crackled. 'This really is the best time of year. The gardens do so well. They're a miracle at the moment.'

'Yes. You've done a fine job of it Angus. Are we ready for tonight?' hinted Joe.

Angus smiled and winked back at Joe. 'Yes Mr. Egan. Everything is prepared.'

'That's good. Thank you.' Joe replied. 'You've done well with the lodge. It looks beautiful. I'm sure Casey will help you with the dinner table while Sharyn and I take a walk outside to appreciate your gardening skills while there's still sufficient light.'

Angus beamed a smile as Sharyn and Joe walked out through to the garden, closing the entrance door behind them. They strolled together through the surrounding gardens of the lodge and they could glimpse the colorful world of butterflies and flowers in their own sanctuary. As they passed, they could smell and almost taste the aromatic herbs of the kitchen garden. Their senses were enriched with the miracle of sensuous flowers and sumptuous vegetables in abundant growth.

They wandered across the small arched wooden bridge, which spanned a flourishing lilac lily pond, and into a white-laced gazebo. Angus had somehow anticipated their actions by cleverly positioning on the center table, an Irish linen tablecloth and a chilled bottle of French champagne with two crystal goblets.

Sharyn and Joe sat for almost an hour, sipping the sweet champagne and enjoying each other's presence. As though subconsciously understanding the other's thoughts, they simultaneously lifted their heads and kissed for a long interval. The two were lost in a wave of passion, and it seemed that in their dizziness nothing else mattered but the togetherness of the moment.

Joe embraced Sharyn as though he would never let her go and he could feel the overwhelming desire in his body. Suddenly everything made sense. The puzzle was clear and all the pieces seemed to fit. Sharyn and Casey would now make his life complete and Joe realized that from all of the wickedness, something wonderful was to unfold, a new happiness with the people he loved, a fairy-tale ending.

Light-headed with the mixed emotions of love, sadness, and confusion, Joe wanted to let everything go, confess his overpowering love and incredible longing. Although he was having trouble thinking in a straight line, he recognized his feelings as appropriate and sane, and he wanted to propose marriage to the woman he loved. As he gazed dreamily into Sharyn's hazel eyes, he knew now that he had fallen deeply in love. She had swooned after the sensuous kiss and had run her fingers back through his hair.

Joe knew that Sharyn was everything he wanted. She was familiar, serene and beautifully intelligent. The proposal of marriage was teetering on his lips, and he was having difficulty catching his breath. It was as though his brain had caught on fire, and he felt a deep craving for the most exquisite woman of his life.

Sharyn's auburn hair cascaded down to her shoulders and she was quietly staring back into his eyes. She politely nodded her approval as though she could read his thoughts. She then smiled graciously, even seductively, breathless and light-headed with lust.

They embraced once again and dreamily whispered their confessions of love. Although the crimson sunset over the backdrop of the Adirondack Mountains made the setting perfect, Joe knew that now was not the time. Today would be Casey's day, and tonight they would exclusively and retrospectively celebrate her ninth birthday in style.

Together, Joe and Sharyn wandered in the twilight, back through the sweet smells of magnolia and honeysuckle, between the flowering cherry and holly grape, amongst the chrysanthemums and roses of the perennial gardens, and back to the old world ambience and elegance of Mayfair Lodge.

The dinner that Angus served up that evening was certainly befitting the occasion of Casey's birthday. On one end of the old oak dining table, four places had been set with silver cutlery, delicate bone china, and a handsome bottle of fine rich cabernet wine.

Beneath the huge rustic timber beams of the vaulted ceiling, Casey, Sharyn, Angus and Joe enjoyed a candle-lit country meal of tender rack of lamb, mint jelly, and baked vegetables. They chuckled and told stories together, and Joe noticed Casey's new enriched spirit emerging from her sadness. He was happy that her rehabilitation process was well underway.

Angus momentarily excused himself from the dinner table and re-appeared with a sponge birthday cake, complete with tangy orange and mint icing. Nine tiny flaming candles were arranged in a heart shape pattern, and the cake was placed before Casey's glowing face. She giggled uncontrollably with the surprise of the occasion.

'Come on Casey.' Sharyn jested. 'You won't be able to blow out nine candles in one breath if you're giggling like that.'

Casey regained her composure, drew in her breath, and puffed on the candles, extinguishing them one by one. Everyone burst into laughter followed by a birthday song, and Casey's ninth birthday was engraved in her young mind forever.

'Now you have to close your eyes my princess and make a wish. Take your time now and wish for something good.'

When Casey closed her eyes and concentrated on her wish, Joe reached down into his pocket and produced the little velvet box containing her birthday present. He quickly positioned it on the table before his daughter, and then sat back to enjoy her reaction. Casey finally completed her wish and opened her eyes.

'Daddy? Is this a present for me?' she pretended.

Casey was beaming with pleasure as she flipped open the velvet box to discover the beautiful diamond earrings that Joe had been waiting for so long to present to her. Sharyn rose to her feet and stood at Casey's side.

'Let me help you put them on Casey. They're so beautiful, and they're real diamonds. You really are your daddy's princess.'

The fragrances of the flower garden were still lingering in their senses. The dinner had been nourishing and delectable. The birthday celebration was an outstanding success. The wine was rich and intoxicating. And, the romantic charm of Mayfair Lodge had cast its magical spell of love.

Weary from the excitement of the day, Casey retired upstairs to listen to one of Angus's famous bedtime stories. Sharyn and Joe settled down comfortably beside the fireplace to finish the last of their cabernet wine and listen to the sacred arias of Andrea Bocelli.

When the music ended and the lodge became quiet, the magic spell of love continued to have its way. Sharyn watched as Joe methodically tried to work the tactics out in his head. Finally his soft eyes returned briefly to her face. She stood up and quietly beckoned him to his feet. Moving slowly, they climbed the staircase and entered the master bedroom. It seemed so natural and so right for them to be together.

Sharyn sat on the edge of the bed as she had sat on the edge of Joe's office desk so many times before. She drew one shapely leg up and crossed it over the other in her natural pose. As Joe stretched himself out on the bed beside her, she let her body fall back beside him, her soft auburn hair spreading across the feather pillow. Without hesitating, Joe turned towards her and kissed her passionately on the lips.

'I love you Joseph Egan.' She whispered tenderly.

'I love you Sharyn Cooper.' He replied. 'Make love with me.'

The soft light of the bedside lamp illuminated his manly features as she looked at him, and he resembled an emperor issuing a royal command. His unconscious arrogance was simply too much for Sharyn to resist, and she found herself wanting more than anything to comply. Carefully and slowly she released completely to his charisma, and his folding arms wrapped around her and he enclosed her into his warmth.

She nuzzled her nose into his neck, sighed, and squeezed him tighter. The scent of his skin tranquilized her senses, and she drew breath to take more of him inside of her. Joe responded by gently running the palm of his hand around her back. Sharyn kissed the most sensitive part of Joe's neck before moving her lips to his ear.

'You feel so good to me Joe. I want you my darling.'

He responded by cradling her face in his hands and guiding her lips to his own. Their mouths touched smoothly as though it was their first kiss, and then hungrily, as though they couldn't get enough of each other. She murmured approvingly as their kisses became deeper and their hands became more knowing. They stayed together for several moments for what seemed like a sweet eternity before mutually sensing one thought. They removed the last of each other's clothing and slipped beneath the fresh cool linen.

Joe immediately pulled her mouth back onto his and she sighed with relief. She felt his breathing becoming deeper and more focused, and her body responded with pleasant surges to her heart and womb. She closed her eyes and enjoyed the sensation of his rocking motion until she heard him cry out faintly. She ran her hands through his chest hair as she felt a soft cry of ecstasy escape from her own throat. Sharyn opened her eyes to see a sweet look of joy on Joe's face, and she loved him for it.

'Sharyn.. Sharyn... That was...It was....' Joe was lost for words.

'I know Joe.' She said. 'I know. Hold me tight Joe.'

Joe squeezed her back into his arms, and whispered into her ear.

'I'm not going anywhere my darling. I'm not going anywhere.'

CHAPTER 29

Filtered morning rays of sunlight are streaming in through a tiny gap in the window drapery, and dancing across Sharyn's pastel skin. She's sleeping on her side and facing me as I study her beautiful face. Every now and again her eyelids twitch and her lips quiver slightly. As I gaze at her features, I'm trying to connect our minds through space and time, so as I may silently share her dreams.

It's the second morning I've watched her sleeping like this, and it's our last day at Mayfair Lodge. Our time here has been everything I could have hoped for, with peace, contentment, and the fulfillment of Sharyn's sublime love. Staying here has been so easy, peacefully kind, and therapeutic, but now there's more to do and it's time to move on. Just as I'm thinking of waking the sleeping beauty with a kiss, her eyelashes flutter open and she smiles as I look into her hazel eyes.

'Good morning my love,' I whisper tenderly. 'Were you dreaming?'

'Yes, I was dreaming of you, and my dream was here at Mayfair Lodge,' she murmurs sleepily. 'I wish we could stay here forever.'

'I know Sharyn,' I sigh. 'This place is so special for me as well, but I know where's there's an enchanted door to an even nicer place.'

Sharyn's smile widens and she lifts her head slightly off the white pillow. 'And, where might that be my prince? Where might that be?'

'Well, there's a door very precious I want you to find, where love is the key and our lives never part. There's a place that's so easy and peacefully kind, and that place is for you waiting deep in my heart.'

'Oh, Joe! You are so poetic. Did you just make that up?' Sharyn touches me beneath the sheets as she asks.

I smile at her. 'Well, maybe I did. It just seemed to come out like that.'

'Well, it's a love poem from you to me, and I want you to write it down for me to keep forever.' She hugs me tightly to her warm body.

* * * * *

Angus has set the oak dining table with great care and attention to detail to ensure a pampering breakfast. Casey is already at the table, happily eating her cornflakes and we sit down to join her. Sharyn is nicely dressed in a fawn pants suit with flat-heeled slip-ons, and I'm casually comfortable in blue jeans, black shirt and sneakers. Fine chinaware compliment the wholesome breakfast of fresh fruit, delicious eggs benedict, and aromatic coffee. It's a great way to start a fresh day and a fitting end to our stay at Mayfair Lodge.

I've spent many hours during the two restful days thinking over, and over again, the ordeal of the subway carriage and the circumstances of Tuxedo Junction. I've tried to rationalize and make sense of things that seem so senseless. Now that I'm so far removed from that chaos and terror in these civilized and peaceful surroundings, it all seems like the chronicle of a bizarre theatrical play, like something that never really happened. It's only my vague awareness of the indistinct pain that still remains in my shoulder and hand that verifies the reality.

Yes. I want to put it all to bed and move on with life, onto my new life with Sharyn and Casey, but there are still thorns in my side. The first and most painful thorn is the unresolved matter of that black Chevy Silverado pick-up. I can never feel safe until the owner is found. It's only a matter of time before he strikes again to feed his depravity, and to add to the derangement he's already inflicted. If I can find the owner, I can then somehow bring justice to bear on the heinous mastermind ultimately responsible for these vicious and cowardly acts of evil.

The second thorn is the blue Toyota. I have feelings of guilt, having stolen that little car. Everything is relative and I know that even though my own world places little value on that vehicle, there is someone who relies on it day in and day out, someone who values it as a prized possession. The car must now be returned to its true owner, and at least that wrong will be made right. To some extent, my conscience may then be eased.

As I take the last sips of my strong black coffee, I look at Sharyn and Casey, and can see that their minds are free of my troubles. Their faces are happy and content.

'Come on my lovely ladies. It's time to finish your breakfast and gather your things. In twenty minutes, Scooty will be arriving to take us back to Egan Center.'

* * * * *

Now that the three of us are standing outside the lodge, once again amazed at the sight of Scooty's helicopter touching down in front of us, it seems that the timing of our departure is perfect. The weather seems to be changing and the outline of the mountains to the west is no longer well defined. There's a hazy layer of stratus cloud hanging low overhead, and the sky in every direction looks dark and gloomy. Angus is standing at the door of the lodge watching us, and he doesn't seem perturbed at all about our leaving. Today is house-cleaning day, and Angus is expecting old Miss Bee to arrive at any moment.

I help Sharyn and Casey into the rear seat, and then help Scooty load the baggage compartment of the Twin Squirrel. As I take one last look around at the rolling green acres of Mayfair Lodge, there in the distance, I can see Josh riding the small red tractor as he slashes the weeds from the creek paddock. I now turn to wave my final farewell to Angus before jumping into the chopper next to Scooty.

Within minutes we're up and away, and after one low-level orbit of the property, Scooty sets course for the seventy-minute flight back to the busy hub of downtown Manhattan. After smiling a welcome over his shoulder to Sharyn and Casey, he nudges my elbow, sports his usual grin, and clicks on the intercom.

'You look like a new man Joe. This country style living seems to agree with you. I'd say the rest has done you the world of good. How was it?'

'It was simply heaven Scooty. No cell phones ringing and no New York detectives wanting annoying interviews.' I smile and keep the best of it between Sharyn and myself.

'That's excellent Joe. We'll have you guys back at Egan Center in no time at all,' says Scooty quirkily, using the plural sense about himself as he often does. 'We'll have to stay low at five hundred feet because of this cloud.'

I'm thinking hard as Scooty talks, and it suddenly occurs to me that this is the perfect opportunity to remove one of those thorns from my side. I can use this chance to return the small blue Toyota from where I had stolen it, from the general store at Tuxedo Junction. Within the space of a minute, the plan gels into place in my mind and I set about achieving my purpose. With a new sense of enthusiasm, I put the idea into action.

'Scooty, I want you to drop me off on the way at that old disused community hall, and then take Sharyn and Casey back to Manhattan. You know the one? There's that payphone at the country intersection where you picked me up the other day.'

Scooty looks at me perplexed. 'Why in hell Joe, would you want to be dropped off there again?'

'I can't tell you too much Scooty. I just have some unfinished business there and this is a good chance to attend to it. Do you think you can find the same location again?'

'Well, sure I can Joe, if that's what you want. How will you get back? Do you want me to pick you up again later?'

I pause and concentrate for the solution and answer to his question. I figure that if Scooty drops me off and leaves me at that same place, I can retrieve the Toyota from its hiding place and drive it back to Tuxedo Junction. However, it would be impractical for him to pick me up from there. Firstly, it would create too much attention, and secondly, it would be too dangerous with the surrounding pine forest and no suitable landing site for the helicopter. The optimum plan slowly crystallizes in my mind.

'Is it possible at this range to make a phone call to Egan Enterprises?'

361

'Sure it is Joe. Just stand by. I'll ring now and connect you through the intercom.'

By the time Andrew comes on the line and I'm able to speak with him, I have the instructions worked out in my thoughts.

'Andrew, I have something for you to do. I need you to drive out and pick me up from a country location northwest of New York. It's about fifty miles away and Scooty will give you the directions. You can leave as soon as possible.'

'Yes. That's no problem Mr. Egan. As soon as I receive the location details, I'll be on my way.'

'Thanks Andrew. I'll hand you over to Scooty and he will explain precisely where it is and how to get there.'

I allow Scooty to switch back the intercom, and I sit back to think about the logistic details of my proposal. It should work well. I'll get Scooty to drop me off at the intersection payphone, and he can then leave to take Sharyn and Casey back to Egan Center. I roughly calculate that if Andrew leaves within the next ten minutes, I shouldn't have to wait any longer than fifteen minutes after Scooty leaves me there, just enough time to retrieve the blue Toyota.

When he arrives, Andrew can follow me back to Tuxedo Junction, where ideally, I'll be able to anonymously return the Toyota to the same position where I had originally found it. I may also be able to identify the owner and organize some compensation to be paid at a later date. Andrew and I will then be able to drive back to Egan Center together and the task will be completed.

Scooty clicks off his telephone call to Andrew and gives me the thumbs up, indicating that the arrangements are in place. He then pulls out a map, orientates it, and changes course approximately twenty degrees to the right. He keeps the helicopter low so as to skim under the cloud, and before long we're circling over the old community hall. The helicopter puts gently down on the same field as before. I open the door to get out, and I have to yell at Sharyn and Casey above the noise.

'Scooty will take you back to Egan Center now and I should be there in a few hours.' I can see the worried look on Sharyn's face as she digests what I'm saying. 'Don't worry Sharyn. I'll be all right.'

I jump out, close the door, and walk out in front of the helicopter to watch them depart. They lift up and away again, soon to disappear into the murky haze.

Although the atmosphere is dull and the sky is sultry and overcast, the ground is now quite dry beneath my feet. I start making my way across the field in the direction of the wire fence and sealed road. After carefully negotiating the barbed wires and crossing the road, I walk the few hundred yards to where the car is hidden. I climb the small incline and walk between the shrubs to find the vehicle exactly where I had left it four days earlier. At first, it doesn't want to start when I connect the ignition wires, and I'm concerned that there may not be sufficient battery power to get it going. At last the engine coughs into action and begins to run evenly and I sit upright again in the driver's seat. After engaging reverse gear, I swing the car around. I then drive it forward, back onto the sealed road and the short hundred yards towards the community hall with its nearby payphone.

Pulling off onto the side gravel, I park the vehicle above the steep rocky slope next to the payphone, and yank on the handbrake. I check the fuel gauge and see that there's plenty of fuel so I leave the engine running on idle, just in case it doesn't restart. As I sit to wait for Andrew, I gaze down the steep embankment at the rocky creek bed below. After the wet weather of last week, it's still running freely with a steady flow of mountain water streaming about the granite rocks.

I look around at the surrounding area and a cold shiver tingles along my spine. There's a strange chill in the air and I suddenly feel eerie and anxious as though I'm in danger. The craggy old cladding hall looks ghostly and frightening, with cobwebs covering the boarded windows and doors. The ancient cow paddocks don't have any cows in them, and steam rises from the surface. The misty cloud layer hangs lower than before, and the atmosphere is now moist and filled with static electricity. I have a terrible perception that the forces of evil are in my midst. It's an unnatural sensation of dread that I now have, as though something bad is about to happen.

I glance into the Toyota's rear vision mirror and can barely distinguish the shadowy outline of a vehicle approaching along the stretch of bitumen behind me. The time is about right, and I guess that it must be Andrew arriving as planned. The shape of the vehicle looms closer and larger in the mirror, and the outline becomes clearer and more defined. I'm sensing the acid anxiety rising from the pit of my stomach. The realization doesn't punch me suddenly, but descends on me gradually. The vehicle is not only black in color, but it has the familiar shape of a Chevrolet Silverado.

The image of the same vehicle leaping out of the darkness of the Jefferson Street car compound flashes through my mind, and a river of adrenaline surges throughout my pelvis. I swing around to get a better view through the rear window and I'm in a state of panic. It looks like the same threatening black Silverado. It comes nearer and larger, closer and more imposing. I strain my eyes to see if I can identify the driver, but the windscreen reflections make it impossible. As the heavily chromed grill comes up behind me, my panic is boiling over.

The Chevy continues past me and pulls in on the gravel in front of the Toyota. I swivel around, following it with my stare as it passes, and now fix my gaze onto the rear of the vehicle as it grinds to a stop. My worst fear is confirmed. The red bumper sticker engine snorts smoke, and the inscription silently screams its threat of 'unleashed fury'.

I'm striving to comprehend what's going on. How can this be happening? Has he come to finish me off? How did he know I am here? Did he intercept the phone call from the helicopter? Surely he's here to kill me, to take his revenge for finding that the diamonds were actually fakes. For all I know, he could now leap out with a twelve-gauge shotgun and blast me to shreds.

I'm desperately struggling with my brain to give me some answers, how to deal with this, how to react. Do I drive away to be followed and then pushed over the edge of the steep crevice to crash and burn? Do I get out and run as fast as I can to be then shot in the back? Should I try to reason and buy him off? I've tried that before and know that anything can happen. It suddenly occurs to me that the only defense I have is the small silver paper knife that I had left in the glove compartment.

I'm looking through the windscreen, and the driver's door of the Silverado is swinging open. As my hand struggles with the clasp on the glove compartment, there's sweat dripping down my face. I can hear my heart pounding and my throat is dry. I'm wide eyed with fear. My hand freezes in position as I recognize the person who gets out of the Chevrolet. I'm completely stunned and perplexed by what I see. How can this be possible? My mind is striving to comprehend what's happening, for the driver of that Chevy is the last person I could have expected.

I realize that he's not upset in any way. His appearance is normal and his demeanor is calm. Andrew's black hair is slicked into place. He's wearing a cream suit with red suspenders, and floral bow tie under the collar of his white silk shirt. This is certainly not a man dressed in black. He doesn't fit the 'man in black' description of Audrey's spiritual warning.

But why is he driving that vehicle? That black vehicle! Could this be another interpretation of the 'man in black' words? Could Andrew be the evil mastermind? My temples are pounding furiously and the contents of my stomach are churning as I try to fathom some kind of sense of it. I open the Toyota door and leap out to come to terms with whatever awaits me.

Andrew looks at me slightly surprised when he sees I'm distressed.

'Mr. Egan. I had no trouble finding this place. Are you ready to go? Is it straight on back to Egan Center?'

I stare into Andrew's eyes searching for a sign, some hint of deception, but there's not a clue. His appearance is cool and collected as always. He's the same stern and serious office manager who has served me so well for so long.

'Andrew. What are you doing driving that pickup? Why are you driving that Chevrolet?'

Andrew is now standing about ten feet away from me, and his expression shifts from surprise to confusion and then to a state of concern.

'Why sir, this is the vehicle I've been driving. I've been using it for a while now.'

My body stiffens and I feel my hands trembling uncontrollably. I stare into his brown eyes that are bright and intelligent. His manner gives nothing away, whilst my own breathing is ragged and beads of perspiration shimmer on my forehead. There's no alternative but to bring this situation to a head. The time for altercation is now.

'Andrew. I know this vehicle. This is the Chevrolet that was driven by the person responsible for Audrey's murder and Casey's kidnapping. How can this be possible?'

Andrew's face turns a bright scarlet and he begins to stutter. 'Well, well, well,….' He has no explanation.

His stammering stops and he is suddenly quiet. His eyes roll back in their sockets and his attitude goes through a transformation. His thin lips form into a smirk and then they slowly change into an insolent sneer. His face contorts horribly and his dark eyes become small and much enraged.

'It is possible Mr. Egan Sir, because you're a self-centered pompous asshole who's been far too lucky for far too long,' he snarls viciously.

I can't believe what I'm hearing. This is the man I had trusted for so long, the man who I had thought was faithful beyond reproach. Now all is revealed, and I'm completely devastated at the metamorphosis.

'Andrew. I've always treated you so well. I've done no wrong by you. What reason could you have to hate me like this?'

Andrew tenses his body and his expression becomes even more violent. I can see the veins protruding from his temples, and his eyes are as cold as steel ball bearings.

'There are many fucking reasons, big boss man!' Andrew growls contemptuously. 'Who do you think put you up where you are? Who spent the many hours and hours, the long nights building your empire for you? Why should you have so much when I have nothing?'

We are face to face and eyeing each other as he rants irrationally. The sinews in his neck are straining and his fists open and close in a tense clenching action.

'Andrew. If you had financial difficulties, you could have told me. You must know I would have helped, but instead, you've chosen to harm me and my family.'

His eyes shift from side to side and his next remark stings the very inner core of my being. He flies into a rage and screams at the top of his voice.

'Fuck you Egan! Go to hell! Fuck you!'

He's mad beyond comprehension, and he lunges forward at me in a murderous rage. Andrew's body is fit and taut, and I'm surprised at the speed and agility with which he moves. He plants his left foot into the gravel and pivots to the side, lashing out with his right heel. It crushes into my pelvis and almost dislocates my hip. I'm forced backwards and my body slams into the front of the Chevy making me wince with pain. He comes at me again with both his hands thrashing in some kind of savage karate thrusts. They crunch one after the other into my chest and I collapse forward into his arms. His right knee thumps into my thigh as I go down in a heap. There's no doubt that Andrew is fit and strong, and I'm no match for the blows that his well-trained limbs are wielding.

I try to scramble from beneath his towering stance and manage to get to my feet as I scream, exhaling all the air in my lungs.

'Nooooooo!!!!'

Andrew's hands silence my scream as they wrap around my neck and squeeze tight. His face is a mere six inches away from my own and his thumbs are pressing into my windpipe, closing off my air supply and denying me of vital oxygen. Froth forms at the side of his mouth and his eyes are wild. He's no longer a man, but more like a ferocious animal.

My senses are fading as he strangles me, and seconds seem like an eternity. It's as though we're suspended in slow motion. My eyes are now drifting back in my head as he wrings the life from me. My body is devoid of any strength and there's nothing I can do to help myself. I'm waiting for Leslie's umbrella handle to hook around Andrew's neck and wrench him away, to save my life as he did in the train carriage. I know it won't happen. This time, I'll die a violent death, and all I've endured will be in vain.

Andrew's grip is iron tight and my body goes limp in complete submission. My brain is spinning with the images that only a dying man is familiar with, images of my childhood and my father and mother. Now, it's Sharyn's lovely face as she sleeps on the feather down pillow, and I'm strangely satisfied that my life has been somehow productive and worthwhile. Now there's an image of trembling little Casey, huddled in the corner of that deserted cabin. There's a flashing image of the bloody rail carriage carnage at Jefferson Street Station and the knife blade that penetrated my shoulder.

The next image is of poor Audrey's mutilated and dead body. Her face fills my mind completely, and now goes through a transformation of reversal. The facial injuries repair themselves and the blood disappears. Her eyes open and her features become serene and beautiful. She's looking at me and willing me to act.

I'm completely baffled as I sense an impulsive reaction building inside my diaphragm. It's Audrey creating the intensity. There's a spiritual energy intruding into my body, an incredible foreign force of great magnitude. It's a volcano of harnessed strength, previously unknown to me, and it now erupts limitlessly with incredible speed and power.

My hands clamp under his armpits, and I lift his entire body off the ground. I'm amazed at my own potency, and Andrew is completely taken by surprise. I whirl around and he falls backwards heavily, with me crashing down on top of him.

As his head hits the surface, I hear a sickening crunch of splintered bone. I'm looking into his eyes and they become gray and still. Blood stains the granite rock beneath his head and trickles onto the soil around his left ear. His loosened hands limply drop from my neck like jelly, and his face becomes lifeless. I roll him slightly to one side, and can see that the sharp edge of the granite rock has inflicted a severe deadly wound in the back of his skull, pulverizing the bone. His head falls back to where it was, and I simply stare at him in my state of shock and horror.

'Why you Andrew? Why does it have to be you?' I'm crying through my words at his dead face.

Feelings of confusion, sadness and trauma overcome me, as I raise my eyes to the clouds and cry out in despair.

'What kind of man am I? What have I become?'

Another person is dead by my own hand. Surely the nightmare is now ended. I can't take any more of this. I'm confused that I might be the doer of great evil, the mastermind of my own destruction. I shout to the heavens above.

'God! Why are you doing this to me? God! Give me peace. This must be the end. Let it now end.' My tears are flowing freely.

Several minutes of passion release before I realize that another car may come along the road at any moment. I have to get a hold of myself. I know that I must collect myself and act quickly. There's still a way out of this. If Andrew is the responsible person behind everything, then detective Frank Berne should come to the same conclusion.

I look up at the blue Toyota and realize that there's no time to waste. After scrambling to my feet, I move to behind Andrew's dead body. With my hands under his arms, I manage to lift and drag him to the Toyota. By pulling and pushing, I can eventually get his carcass into the driver's seat, where I allow it to slump forward onto the steering wheel with the door closed. My mind is on fire as the plot evolves.

I frantically check the car's interior to make sure that I've left nothing to link this to my own involvement, and then remember the small silver paper knife in the glove compartment. I grab it desperately and wipe my fingerprints from the handle as I recall that the dried blood of Blue Featherman remains congealed on the blade.

Remembering that Andrew is left-handed, I position the paper knife into his left hand and fold his fingers around it, pressing them firmly. I now carefully replace it back into the glove compartment, and I turn the steering wheel hard right. After winding the driver's window fully down, placing the gearshift into neutral, and releasing the park-brake, I use my handkerchief to ensure that the car's handles and knobs are free of my fingerprints.

I look down into the deep ravine to my left, and I have to tread carefully as I move to the rear of the Toyota. By turning around and pushing my back into the rear end of the vehicle, I can start it rolling. It creeps forward until the right front wheel drops over the edge of the embankment.

The car slips forward and the whole process suddenly accelerates. I gaze awestruck as the little blue car somersaults end over end with Andrew's lifeless body tumbling around inside. It crunches from one boulder to another, moaning and creaking, sounding like the death throws of a giant animal. It finally crashes to a mangled wreck on the creek bed below, and although there's a coil of dense black smoke from the oily engine, the vehicle doesn't catch on fire. I can distinguish Andrew's twisted torso hanging across the dashboard and I stand for two or three minutes, dumbfounded at the horrible spectacle. I'm sick with disappointment, sadness and disbelief that he could be dead. I take in a deep breath and recognize that there's no time to waste. This crisis must be seen through to the end one way or another.

I pick up the blood stained rock that gouged Andrew's skull, and toss it down after the Toyota. By using my shoe, I scrape the bloody soil away from the scuffle area and remove any footprints. After moving the Chevy onto the sealed portion of the road, I get out again and remove any tread marks from the gravel edge.

Now that I'm satisfied that my tracks are adequately covered, I leap into the Chevy Silverado and set off down the road. As I move the pickup into third gear, I realize that I've left just in time because another vehicle is approaching in the distance from the opposite direction. It passes by and I follow it in the rear vision mirror. There's still sufficient black smoke whirling up from the Toyota to capture the driver's attention, and I can just make out the car pulling over to the side for the driver to investigate. I know that it won't be long before the police are at the scene.

I settle into driving mode, and spend the whole journey back to New York pondering the consequences and significance of what has happened. My mind is a quagmire of thoughts, emotions and ideas. What to do now? How to brief Sharyn and Scooty?

It's now only a matter of time before the police will be contacting me about the discovery of Andrew's body. There's still the remaining uncertainty of what to do with the black Chevy? Where do I dispose of it? My mind struggles for the correct answer, and by the time I reach Manhattan, the one logical solution is obvious. I drive back under Egan Center and place the pickup in exactly the same position as it was parked when I came across it on that momentous sleepless night. I turn off the engine and leave the keys in the ignition. It remains where I had discovered it, in the far corner of level one car park.

Before proceeding to the elevator, I stand back, and take one long last look at the shiny black Chevy Silverado. In six days, this vehicle has strangely led me through the tangled web of evil to my daughter, to my realization of Andrew's connection, and now back again to the start. It no longer looks as sinister and threatening as before. If not for the shiny black paint and the red bumper sticker, it would look like so many others on the streets of America. I guess the police will impound it as part of their investigation.

As I contemplate the unfolding sequence of today's events, they now seem surreal and predestined. How can the circumstances be so complete? It simply cannot be coincidental that the jigsaw pieces should fall perfectly into place like this. Where did my amazing feat of strength originate?

Was this Audrey's helping hand once again? Was this her last earthly intervention? Can her spirit now finally free itself of worldly responsibility? I close my eyes in hope, and pray that it can.

CHAPTER 30

Joe was experiencing his own version of unleashed fury. His new silver inter-cooled twin-turbo Porsche accelerated through one hundred miles an hour when he shifted it into fourth gear and then slammed his foot on the gas. Joe held the car to an inside line as he powered through a long meandering S bend. The twenty-inch low profile tires gripped the smooth tar surface and squealed in delight, as though they were happily doing what they were designed to do.

The car entered a long stretch of road and Joe increased his foot pressure. The engine replied to Joe's request with a smooth purr, followed by a thick rumble as the twin compressors rammed the engine's throat with more air. He pushed through into fifth gear and was exhilarated as the Porsche shattered through one hundred and forty five miles an hour.

The car wanted to go faster, but that was enough for Joe. He backed off and recovered from the flood of adrenaline that had doused his senses. There was still one more gear to go, but he didn't know of a road in the state that was anywhere safe enough for speeds of over two hundred miles an hour.

Anyway, it wasn't the ultimate speed that thrilled his desire. It was the power. The demon inside of the man constantly needed to be fed as always. It seemed like it could never be satisfied. The more Joe gave it, the more it demanded. Joe always relished power. He thrived on the power of business, the power of money, and the power of love. Joe's demon was growling, and he had now nourished his demon with the growling power of the Porsche. He had served the beast with the incredible acceleration that had whipped his neck and tensed his shoulders as he had raced his car frenetically through the gears.

The tension now subsided as he settled into a more sedate style of driving and turned the Porsche back towards New York. The morning had been Joe's morning and the day was Joe's day. Since the discovery of Andrew's body, the offices of Egan Enterprises had been temporarily closed for three days now and Sharyn was spending the day in the penthouse bonding with Casey.

Although it seemed a little selfish for Joe to want to be alone, he felt he deserved a day of self-indulgence. He had some bonding to do himself, some Porsche bonding. It had been his first real hard drive of the new car and Joe was ecstatic. The vehicle was everything they had promised it to be. It was a masterpiece of handling, braking, and ample miraculous performance to satisfy any demon driver.

Joe paid the penance for his country driving pleasure by having to endure the stop and start frustrations of Manhattan traffic. By the time he turned the vehicle onto the down ramp of Egan Center, he was completely exasperated with Porsche driving. He longed for peace and quiet. He wanted to be back at Mayfair Lodge picking daisies.

Joe parked the car and headed straight for the elevator. His best and nearest refuge from the mayhem of weekend Manhattan was the peace and tranquility of his own personal office. There, he would be unhindered from interruption and free to do some soul-searching alone.

* * * * *

The minute Joe walked through the double doors into the expanse of his office, his attitude improved. An azure blue hue radiated from the velvet-covered walls and a subdued vanilla glow reflected from the pale washed timber floors. It all helped to soften his mood and put him at ease.

Joe slipped off his shoes to feel more comfortable. His feet felt instantly relieved as they spread inside his socks and slipped across the hard wooden floorboards. With the press of a button, a section of wall panel slid to the side to reveal a mirror behind a polished chrome cocktail bar. He reached for a crystal glass with a solid twenty-four carat gold rim, and poured a luxurious double measure of his favorite Glenfiddich pure malt scotch whiskey. One sip of the golden fluid had the required effect. He shuddered slightly as it went down, and a warm pleasurable wave occupied his body.

Joe took his drink with him and walked across to his hemi-spherical silver and black desk. He dropped back into the cushy stitched leather swivel chair, swung around to gaze into the splendid world of his tropical aquarium, and he felt his body unwind even more. Tropical corals and swaying weeds glowed under the neon lights. Striking fish of many colored species glorified the scene and hypnotized his mind. Joe's thoughts began to drift with the fish.

His life had at last returned to normality. In the space of ten days, Joe had been to the gates of hell and returned unscathed. He had faced almost certain death on four or five separate occasions, and he had survived them all. Now that it was ended, it seemed that his decision to go it alone independently had been correct. Although he had been punished with trepidation, the tangled web of deceit had gradually been re-spun, and now everything was in order.

Joe's favorite yellow and orange rainbow fish emerged from a hollow space between the coral to greet him. It stared directly at him, as though once again reading his thoughts. The fish had eyes that were blank and gray. Joe remembered the blank gray eyes of dead Andrew Barton. He recalled Andrew's lifeless carcass tumbling around inside the falling Toyota. He remembered how Frank Berne and Jimmy had told him of Andrew's death during their final interview. Joe had skillfully portrayed the picture of innocence and stupefaction. Joe replayed the scene again in his mind.

When the two detectives had come to see Joe, Frank Berne's attitude was friendly and polite. He spoke with an air of accomplishment, now having solved the crime.

'We were also surprised that it was Andrew,' Frank Berne explained. 'He was low on our list of suspects with no apparent motive for the murder.'

'Yes detective.' Joe replied with a grave look of dejection on his face. 'It was a great shock to us all when you informed us. Andrew was the last person in the world I would have expected to turn against me. It's very sad indeed that his mind was so troubled.'

Frank Berne raised one hand into the air. 'But, turn against you he did. It just goes to prove that you really don't know who your real friends are and who your enemies are.'

Although Jimmy eyed Joe warily during the interview, he had so far remained quiet. Now, he had decided to have one last comment, more as a face saving gesture than anything else, to retain his own credibility.

'I said we would crack this case. I always said the criminal was close to home. I knew it had something to do with this office, and in the end, I was right.'

Joe glared at Jimmy, but Frank interjected and answered for him.

'Yes Jimmy. You were right. You were half-right. Now, let's leave it at that.'

Frank spoke with an air of authority putting Jimmy in his place, and then returned his gaze to Joe.

'In the end Joe, everything came together and added up. The evidence was irrefutable. When he went off that cliff, Andrew Barton was driving the same vehicle stolen from near the scene of Featherman's homicide. The murder weapon was in his possession and his fingerprints were everywhere. We found them in the cabin where your daughter was held captive, and also on the same paper knife that cut Featherman's throat. There's no doubt he was behind it.'

Joe sat back and nodded in appreciation of the circumstances.

'Why would Andrew want to destroy me?'

'Well, your boy was living a double life, Joe. The man had a bad gambling problem and was in serious financial difficulty. I've seen it before, when fine upstanding people get mixed up with the characters of the underworld. He had heavy debts to pay and no way of settling. His plan was to blackmail you Joe.'

'Yes. I see Frank. Yet how could he turn against me like that after so long?'

Frank shook his head slowly. 'Intelligent people can resort to crazy irrational modes of behavior when they see their world of normality and security threatened. It's genius bordering on lunacy. Systematic guys like Andrew have a screw loose when disorder takes over, and they simply can't handle it. They take desperate measures when cornered.'

Joe thanked the detectives and sagaciously apologized for his initial lack of co-operation. He explained to them that he had been devastated by Audrey's death and that he was horrified that they had suspected him. Frank was unusually sympathetic and the interview had ended amicably. Joe was nevertheless pleased that it was ended and that he would have no further exchanges with shrewd Frank and the obnoxious Jimmy.

Joe sipped dreamily on some more whiskey and his thoughts drifted from the interview with Frank and Jimmy, to the state of his neglected business affairs. He was glad that he had a new administration manager, and that the offices of Egan Enterprises would not be closed for very long. The void left by Andrew's absence had needed to be filled by a new candidate, and the position required a person of many attributes. He needed to be a person with extremely high intelligence, unusual entrepreneurial skills, extraordinary business acumen, and also, proven uncompromising loyalty to Joe. Yes. He needed to be a person precisely like Leslie Murchison.

The rainbow fish opened and closed his mouth approvingly and then turned away. He swam quickly back into the hollows of coral and disappeared from sight. Joe swiveled around again and swung his shoeless feet up onto the edge of his desk. He cast his eyes across the room and through the wide tinted glass doors and across the terrace.

Joe sighed as the breathtaking Manhattan skyline shimmered in the afternoon light. It caused Joe to ponder where he now was in the space and time of the universe, what part he played in the whole scheme of things. He once again felt the power of his wealth and his premium position at the top of Egan Center.

After sampling some more whiskey, his mind drifted to Louise Shackleton and Nancy. Joe had commissioned Josh, the young farmhand at Mayfair Lodge, to travel to Tuxedo Junction, visit the general store, and anonymously report back with information about the owner of that little blue Toyota. He had felt terrible when he had learnt of the circumstances of the unusually beautiful woman with the missing front tooth, and of her asthmatic little daughter. Joe felt a warm sense of satisfaction that their world was now more comfortable and financially secure.

A lifetime annuity had been established to provide for Louise's financial affairs, Nancy's medical expenses, and her future education. In the place of the old blue Toyota sedan, Josh had now delivered a brand new Toyota Cressida registered in the name of Louise Shackleton. The new vehicle was the same blue color as her old one, but highlighted with dark-blue accents. It had luxurious leather seats and electric tinted windows. Joe was pleased that the Toyota would have a happy home and his conscience was relieved.

Joe was also pleased that Josh and Louise wanted to see each other again. It was instant attraction between them. Apparently, Josh was wearing a smile around Mayfair Lodge, not seen since before his wife's untimely passing. Joe somehow believed that the spark of romance could eventually blossom into a love meant to be, a love like Joe's with Sharyn. Maybe it was another example of something good resulting from something bad.

Joe smiled, took another long last sip of the last ounces of smooth blended amber fluid, and looked down at the little velvet box positioned at the center of his desk pad. He flipped the box open and smiled widely as his eyes feasted on the exquisite shimmering pink diamond ring. Yes. Today had been Joe's day, but tonight was going to be different. It would be a wondrous turning point in his life. Tonight was especially reserved for Miss Sharyn Cooper.

CHAPTER 31

It's not easy to toss the keys of a six hundred thousand dollar vehicle to a valet parking attendant, so I try not to think about it as I watch my graceful maroon Bentley glide around the corner out of sight. Sharyn and I are left standing on the red-carpeted entrance to 'Chateau Fleur de Lis' restaurant on Seventh Avenue.

Sharyn looks ravishing in a figure hugging cocktail evening dress of pale yellow satin. She wears gold strap-heeled shoes that peep from below the hemline. The dress drapes low to her waist at the rear, revealing the small of her back and accentuating the line of her shapely shoulder blades.

Her rich auburn hair is worn up with tangled strands framing her lovely face, and her elegant jewelry is not overbearing. She's so beautiful, even to the extent that she seems mysteriously forbidden. I'm dressed for the special occasion with a gold and black line wool twist jacket by 'Pour L'homme' of Paris, simple white cotton shirt, jet-black slacks and Gianni shoes. Tonight, Sharyn and I look rather good together and tonight, we feel very good together.

'This restaurant looks lovely Joe,' says Sharyn happily as we turn to enter.

We proceed up one wide flight of red-carpeted stairs to the dining room to meet the maitre-de', Pierre. The room is artistically decorated for fine dining, and the mood is soft and peaceful. Beautiful draperies adorn the red velour walls, and several Napoleonic portraits in gilded frames fill the panels. At one side, a Parisian porcelain fireplace blazes with a gentle radiance, and the background music is romantically French. Overhead, the ceiling is heavily ornate with white decorative cornices, and four stately chandeliers provide a mellow glow to illuminate the dining tables.

'Thank you Pierre.' I remark as he hands me the wine list.

We're seated at the most romantic table close to the fireplace and Sharyn is beaming with happiness. I take my time to choose prudently.

'Moet et Chandon, Brut, 'Cuvee Dom Perignon,' Epernay, 92'

'Very well monsieur, without delay.' Pierre acknowledges from beneath his thin black handlebar moustache and bows his head.

'Oh Joe,' Sharyn smiles. 'This is so enchanting, so romantic. I'm in seventh heaven.'

'Yes, they do it well don't they?' I return her smile. 'Pierre entered the fine dining business when he was nineteen years old and this is his fourth restaurant. He's been here now for more than two decades. I guess he's managed to perfect the art, after all that practice.'

I am glad we are at Chateau Fleur de Lis. There's no better venue for what I have in mind. It was a good choice. Sharyn's lively eyes sparkle as Pierre loops the serviette about his forearm and fills the tall stem glasses with the effervescent nectar.

'Merci Pierre.' I thank him and smile.

'Tres bien monsieur.'

The small round table has a crisp white cloth, and is graced with the quivering flame of pencil thin candelabrum. Delicate petals of a single red rose are glistening with moisture. After Pierre leaves, Sharyn and I raise our glasses and laugh. Her teeth are shiny white and her hazel eyes are lucid and intelligent. She reaches across and puts her hand lightly on top of mine as her tongue wets her upper lip, teasingly, seductively. We sample the champagne and she giggles briefly and squeezes my hand.

'This is so special for me Joe. I'm so happy.'

She swoons, leans in, and kisses me on the cheek. Her lips move briefly to mine and she lingers momentarily before regaining her balance. We're both trembling visibly with passion as Pierre reappears for a critique of the menu selection.

The dining experience is romantic and sophisticated. Our glasses are replenished, yet we're left in privacy and serenity. The champagne arouses our perceptiveness of each other and heightens my awareness of Sharyn's desirable qualities. Her beauty is enchanting, her conversation is lively and intelligent, and her Chanel No. 5 fragrance is alluring. There's no doubt in my mind that Sharyn and I are meant to be together. It's surely a match made in heaven and I realize that I no longer have any say in the matter. The attraction between us is irresistible, and that's that!

The cuisine is unforgettable. Our perfect meal consists of Lobster Bisque with snipped chives and claw meat, Chateaubriand with a béarnaise sauce, and Crème Brulee with fresh berries. We loiter over our coffee and she studies me over the lip of her cup. The music is tranquilizing and the time is ripe. I hand her a folded card in a dawn-tinted envelope.

'I have a surprise for you Sharyn. It's something you asked me to do. I just added a few more verses.'

'Joe! Whatever can this be? You seem to be full of surprises.'

Sharyn slowly opens the envelope and unfolds the card. She lets out a faint sigh, and her lips form into a little smile. I just sit and watch, taking in the scene and relishing in her pleasure. Never have I wanted to please someone so much as now.

'Joe! This is so romantic.'

She goes quiet and becomes teary eyed as she reads.

'A Place for Sharyn'

I know a place where you've never once dared,
We follow each ripple on a clear mountain lake.
There's a bed where dreams are silently shared,
And our touch is as gentle as a winter snow flake.
It's a land of rare beauty so special and true,
Our minds are connected through space and time.
We explore sweet pleasures with so much to do,
With peace and contentment and love so sublime.
Ocean waves crash, white clouds way up high,
We're gazing at seagulls as they hover in flight.
Still sun shower mornings and a full rainbow sky,
A walk in the sand, salty tasting delight.
There's a door very precious I want you to find,
Where love is the key and our souls never part.
It's a place so easy and peacefully kind,
This place is for you, waiting deep in my heart.

While she's reading, I secretly take the velvet box from my jacket pocket, flip open the lid and place it, facing her, on the table. Sharyn's cheeks are moist as she finishes my poem. She now raises her eyes to once again feast upon the exquisite jewel. She's silent and wide-eyed, too dazed to speak.

The huge five carat pink diamond ring flashes reflections of brilliance in every direction, ruling over everything around, and commanding our attention completely. Sharyn is finally able to speak.

'Joe. This is the special pink diamond that stood out so distinctly from all the others. I simply can't believe this is happening.'

I carefully take the ring and Sharyn instinctively offers her hand. I slide it snugly into place on her left ring finger and the fit is perfect. My heart is pumping fast and my head is spinning.

'Sharyn, will you marry me?'

She rolls her hazel eyes and smiles graciously.

'Yes Joe, I will marry you.'

Her acceptance is sweet, simple, not too complicated. We stare into each other's eyes and savor the exquisite moment, locking it into our memories forever. I reach into my inside coat pocket and withdraw the three airline tickets for Sharyn to see.

'Look! I've even chosen the supreme wedding location, and the perfect bridesmaid for you,' I boast proudly.

I splay the tickets out on the table and Sharyn stares at them as I speak.

'Sharyn, Casey, and Joe. Three first class tickets to one of the most spectacular places in the world, the magical island of Santorini in the Greek Cyclades. We leave tomorrow.'

'Oh Joe! This is so wonderful. I'm in dreamland.'

I lean forward and seal the happy occasion with a lingering kiss to the tender lips of my beautiful wife to be. In the corner of my eye, I can glimpse Pierre standing at the side of the room. His usually conservative face is bright red, and he brandishes a full glistening smile beneath his wide twisted handlebar moustache.

CHAPTER 32

It was a great day for flying. The morning was crisp and cool, and the sky was clear and bright as Sharyn, Casey and Joe traveled in the white limousine to New York's JFK international airport. The three of them already felt comfortable together as a family unit.

The atmosphere at the airport was normally chaotic and today was no exception.

Negotiating the frustration of check-in and security procedures was always a trial, but this time Joe thought it was a trial well worth the effort.

They had already checked in their baggage and received their boarding passes. All that was left was the short queue at passport control before they could proceed through into the first class lounge. Joe had all three passports and passes in his hand as he stepped smiling up to the emigration counter.

Joe's mind was at last completely free of anxiety and uncertainty. He was experiencing a great feeling of inner peace and contentment. His spirits were high and it showed that he was looking forward to the trip. Casey's tummy was tingling with butterflies. She'd never been on an overseas flight and the last time she had enjoyed a holiday with her father was the Disneyland experience. She stood behind Joe holding Sharyn's hand and she couldn't stop smiling. Sharyn felt warm and loving towards both Casey and Joe. She was waiting, hoping, and mesmerized by thoughts of her wedding on Santorini, the island in the sun. She was staring brightly into space, dreamily content to be entering a new life. She had never been to the Greek Isles, and she'd never been married to Joe Egan.

Joe glanced at his Rolex as he waited for the passport control officer to do his checks. Although time was ticking away, Joe estimated that they had a margin of about thirty minutes, maybe sufficient time for him to enjoy a Glenfiddich scotch in the first class lounge before boarding.

The officer spread the three passports onto his counter and began tapping into the computer. He paused in short intervals and flashed his eyes from the screen to Joe's face and back again. He fidgeted and shifted his eyes back to Joe with a look of consternation on his face. Joe picked up on it straight away.

'Is there a problem? Is there a problem with our passports?' he tentatively asked the uniformed official.

'No sir. Your passports seem to be in order. Would you mind waiting for one minute please?'

The officer stepped back from the counter, turned and beckoned to a nearby security guard standing in the background. Sharyn nudged Joe's shoulder and asked.

'Is everything all right Joe? Are our passports all right?'

'Yes I think so Sharyn. They're working on it now. Shouldn't be too much longer.'

They watched as the security guard came forward and began to inspect the passports himself. Joe became more and more concerned that there was a problem, and he began to sweat. The passport officer handed Joe the passports, and then strangely shook his head.

'The passports are in order sir. Please pass through the channel and speak to the security officer.'

Another security guard joined the first, and they intercepted the threesome on the other side of the counter.

'Mr. Egan, I'm afraid I have to ask you people to come with me. Please come this way,' said the guard with a serious edge to his voice.

Joe reeled back in surprised. 'Is there a problem? What is the problem? We have a flight to catch.'

'Yes. We're aware of that sir. Hopefully we can clear this up quickly. Please come this way.'

'What's wrong daddy?' asked Casey. 'When are we getting on the plane? Why do we have to go with these policemen?' Casey started to panic.

'Don't worry princess. Everything's all right. They just want to check our passports. That's all.'

Sharyn, holding Casey's hand in hers, now came to Joe's side and asked. 'What do you think Joe? Do you think we will be able to catch the flight?'

'I have no idea what's going on Sharyn. There seems to be a problem. I'll get it cleared up quickly and we'll be on our way. Don't worry.'

Joe was feeling the tension building. A slow veil of uneasiness was descending around him. He began to fear that it had something to do with his recent activities at Tuxedo Junction or Jefferson Street Station. He was now dreading that after all he had been through, this could be the beginning of the end. His eyes began to blink furiously, and he felt the pressure rising in his veins.

The guards led them through the departure lounge and past the gate for their flight. Passengers were already milling around in anticipation, and Joe felt indignant for being led in the opposite direction, for not being able to join them. They rounded a corner towards the administration area and Joe's fears were confirmed. His jaw dropped in shock and utter amazement. There standing in front of him was a familiar face, and the last person that Joe wanted to see. The man had close-cropped hair, crumpled tweed jacket, and a loosened tie beneath a dog-eared shirt collar.

'What's wrong daddy? Why aren't we getting on the plane? Are we going to jail?' Casey piped up.

Sharyn immediately stooped to quell Casey's questions. As Joe approached Frank Berne, he took the initiative to speak first.

'Detective Berne! You're the last person I expected to see. Do you realize that we have a flight to catch? We are in a hurry.'

'Yes. I do realize that Egan. However, it's doubtful you'll be doing any flying today. Miss Cooper and Casey can wait in this adjoining room where security will ensure they're quite comfortable. Joe, will you please step into this interview room where I can speak to you privately.'

Joe nodded approvingly to Sharyn and watched as they entered the small glass paneled room. Joe felt completely deflated as he stepped past Frank Berne into the other interview room alone. His mind was a confusion of disappointment, anxiety, and indignation. He wanted to lash out, protest, and escape from the situation. He wanted to catch the flight to freedom and disappear into the wide blue yonder, away from the stresses of New York, and away from Frank Berne. He knew he was unable. His face turned sallow, and his proud countenance sank and wilted.

Frank Berne motioned for Joe to sit down in the chair, whilst he himself circled to the other side of the desk. He planted himself down and frowned gravely. Joe looked with bewilderment and horror at Frank's stern face. He wondered if this was the end of his charade, the final judgement, the eventual disintegration of his power, his empire? He was beginning to feel nauseated when Frank began to speak.

'Well Egan, since our last meeting some new information has surfaced, new evidence that requires some new answers. There are serious inconsistencies requiring an explanation, and this case won't be closed until you come clean.'

'Come clean? What the hell are you getting at?' asked Joe with an expression of surprise.

Joe decided to make one last desperate attempt to extract himself from the sticky situation and the gnarling fangs of Frank's insinuation. He could now hear his flight being called in the departure lounge outside, and he decided to put on an aggressive posture.

'Detective! We have a flight to catch and they're calling for us to board. Why am I sitting here listening to this? If you have something to say, spit it out and let my family and I get on with our travels. Now, what in blazes are you talking about?'

Frank Berne sneered slightly and leant back in his chair.

'I'm very aware that your flight is leaving, but you listen to me. I have sufficient evidence to throw you behind bars for the rest of your life. It's time to come clean with me right here and now. Tell me the goddamn truth and admit that you've been lying. The game is up. It's time for you to come clean. I won't settle for less.'

Joe leant forward and removed his jacket. His body was hot and sweaty and the armpits of his shirt were wet and sticky. His blood pressure was elevated and his temperature was rising. He glanced at his Rolex to see that he had a mere ten minutes before departure time, and he imagined the last passengers filtering through to the aircraft.

'What do you mean? I've told you what I know. What are you getting at? What have you got?'

'This is what I'm getting at Egan. It's time for you to come down from your high horse. You think you're infallible, but you're not. I know you've been through a lot, but I also know that you haven't been straight up. You listen, and I'll tell you what I've got.'

Frank gave Joe a steely stare and continued.

'I've got a .38 caliber Smith and Wesson with your prints all over it. It's registered in the name of Scooty Menzies and was found near Jefferson Street Station. It's the same weapon used to shoot two members of a gang of three individuals recently on the subway.'

Joe's heart sank to new depths as the words came through. Frank continued.

'Secondly, I've got a third member of that gang who survived the massacre. Although he's totally blind from the attack, he can give an accurate description of the person involved and he's able to give a positive voice identification.' Frank spoke harshly as he went on.

'Thirdly, I've got a tape recording of a 911 call made from a payphone at Tuxedo Junction after Blue Featherman was killed. The extracted call-log printout from that payphone indicates that another call was subsequently made to the offices of Egan Enterprises shortly thereafter. Very strange indeed! Wouldn't you say?'

Joe shrank lower in his chair without answering and closed his eyes. Frank continued with the barrage.

'I've also got the anomaly of a little blue Toyota with the transmission in neutral. Now, I don't know about you, but I would imagine that it's unusual for a vehicle to drive off the road with the gear-shift in neutral and the driver's window wound down. Don't you think Joe?' Joe didn't answer. He just listened.

'Therefore, this is what I'm telling you in no uncertain terms. There's now sufficient evidence, to convict you for multiple homicide, have Scooty Menzies thrown in jail for being an accessory to murder, and have Sharyn Cooper locked up for obstructing the course of justice. That's what I've got Joe. Now what have you got? I'm telling you to bare your soul and give me the story. Tell me what happened.'

Frank Berne's words came crashing in through Joe's senses like a raging bull charging through a fabric barrier. He knew it was time to let go completely. His was a lost cause. Frank Berne was right. The game was up. It was time to come clean, time to pay his dues, and time to go to prison. He hoped that if he gave Frank the whole truth, he could plead for leniency for Scooty and Sharyn. After all, it was really Joe's doing.

'Frank. I did what any father would have done. Don't you see? The situation gave me no choice but to act alone. You yourself made it very clear I was a prime suspect, and your partner was intent on pinning it on me. He wanted to load the whole damn thing on me.'

Frank nodded. 'I'm listening. Go on.'

'Well, when it became apparent to me that the police weren't going to give me the kind of support I needed, I decided to act myself. I received a ransom demand for ten million dollars for the return of my daughter. The incident in the train carriage was purely self-defense. I was in the process of delivering the ransom when those three thugs tried to kill me. I had no choice but to fight. It was to save my own life.'

'Go on! Tell me about Feathers,' said Frank sternly.

'Yes. I was at Tuxedo Junction. I was alone and attempting to rescue my daughter. I had tracked her to that cabin and I tried to save her. Feathers got in my way and I ended up in a struggle to save my own life.'

'That leaves Andrew Barton. What happened there?' questioned Frank.

'When I suspected it was Andrew Barton, I decided to confront him. He went completely crazy and tried to kill me. I promise you Frank, his death was an accident. During our struggle, he hit his head on a rock and that's what killed him.' Joe let go completely and hung his head.

'I know that I've done wrong. It's not right to take the law into my own hands, but I did what I had to do. I wasn't prepared to sit back and let my daughter be sacrificed in the name of proper legal procedure. She's my own flesh and blood. I'm prepared to pay the price and go to prison. But, you have to believe me when I tell you that Scooty Menzies and Sharyn Cooper had no part to play in this, no part at all. I acted alone and there's only me to blame.'

Frank Berne leant back once again and scratched his head with both hands. He then sighed and rubbed his eyes. The final boarding call for the flight was sounding through the departure lounge when Frank spoke seriously, evenly, choosing his words carefully.

'Listen Egan, you seem to have this impression that the police are incompetent fools.

You think that they don't deserve recognition for their compelling dedication to duty. I'm here to tell you now that you're wrong. You're wrong about many things, and you're also wrong about me. I understand why you acted the way that you did. I'm not a father myself, but I can still appreciate what forces came into play, and what thoughts ran through your mind. What I didn't like, was the fact that I was being lied to.'

Frank's attitude softened and he spoke more slowly and deliberately.

'Although you may find it hard to believe, I fully understand why you acted in the way that you did. To be honest with you, if I was in your shoes, I probably would have done exactly the same thing. However, I don't approve of the way you tried to conceal the truth and lead me astray. You see, I'm not as stupid as you may think. And, I'm not as hard and unfeeling as you may think. I'm human also. I have understanding. I have compassion.' He locked his gaze into Joe's eyes and continued.

'Joe, the matters we've discussed within these walls go no further. I'm fully in charge of this investigation, and this investigation is now closed. I'm satisfied that justice has been done. The case is closed. Go and catch your flight.'

Joe couldn't believe his ears. He felt like throwing his arms around Frank Berne and hugging him. Instead, he expressed his gratitude with a wide smile. He rushed through the doorway to meet Sharyn and Casey.

They ran into his arms and it felt so good, such sweet simple pleasure. Joe Egan's name was being called through the public address system as they ran to the departure gate. They handed over their boarding passes and ran through to the boarding ramp. Joe was ecstatic with relief, Sharyn was laughing with elation, and little Casey was giggling with anticipation.

Frank walked slowly behind to watch them leave from the lounge. It was uncanny that he almost felt like waving them good-bye.

* * * * *

That evening, Frank Berne had decided to finish early. It had been a long and strenuous day's work and the end of his most difficult case yet. Yes. The whole Egan file was closed.

The case was dead, embalmed, and laid to rest once and for all.

Frank sat at home in his corduroy armchair and sipped on a cold can of Irish beer. He thought that he deserved it after the events of the last ten days. In fact, he was going to treat himself to a pizza and a few more of those icy cold beers. And, why should he not?

He decided there and then that he would go on down to his favorite bar. Yes. It was his turn to treat himself to a little indulgence. He swilled down the last dregs of beer, snatched up his car keys, and ambled out to the garage.

Before long, Frank was comfortably positioned on a barstool with another beer in his hand. He methodically lit up a self-rolled cigarette, sucked back heavily, and exhaled the brown smoke with a sigh of pleasure. What could hardly be called music, vibrated through some shaky ceiling speakers in a dull base beat, relentless in its pulsating monotony.

Frank wondered if he should later wander down to the gaming room to play a few hands of poker. He'd stayed away from his cards since the night of his huge win, the night young Andrew Barton had lost his shirt as well as his soul.

The atmosphere was rank and stale, and it felt strangely satisfying for Frank to be sitting in the very darkest corner of Pelma's Bar and Grill, slurping on a beer and sucking on a cigarette. He thought about old Feathers with the little children, and then about Andrew who wouldn't pay his gambling debts. Although Audrey's murder was an unfortunate sacrifice in Frank's perception of justice, he was pleased that once again two scumbags had been pitted against each other and eliminated from society. Blue Featherman was in hell, Andrew Barton was dead, and Joe Egan, one of New York's most powerful men, was forever in Frank's debt.

Yes! Frank's methods were frowned upon by his superiors, but once again, he knew they would all turn a blind eye. The results spoke for themselves. Oh yes! So very effective were the methods of Frank Berne.

Frank wondered if his vehicle was safely parked outside. Maybe it was too conspicuous in this area of the Bronx. He decided that it was safe enough. If not for the shiny black paint and red bumper sticker, the Chevy Silverado pickup would look like so many others on the streets of America.